Gemini's Blood

Michael Burns

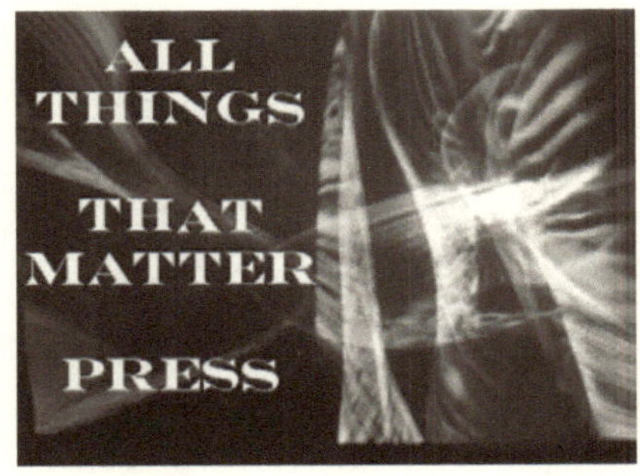

GEMINI'S BLOOD

ISBN 13: 978-0-9840984-3-9
ISBN: 0-9840984-3-7
Library of Congress Control Number: 2009907616

Cover design by All Things That Matter Press
Published in 2009 by All Things That Matter Press

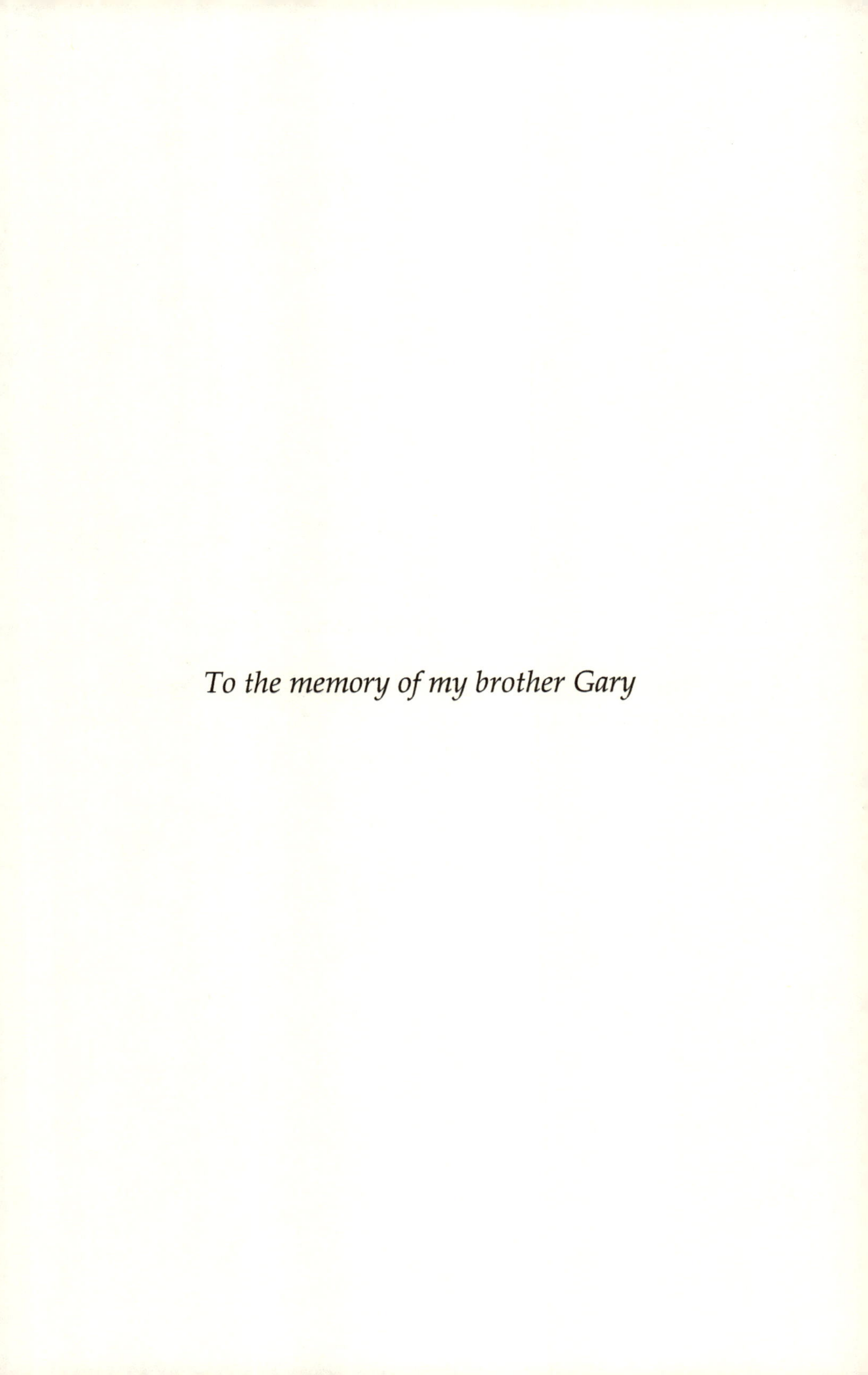

To the memory of my brother Gary

Acknowledgement

Again, my deep appreciation to Sandy Smoller for the many hours he spent on this manuscript, and for his keen eye and wise counsel.

I have journeyed back in thought—with thought hopelessly tapering off as I went—to remote regions where I groped for some secret outlet only to discover that the prison of time is spherical and without exits.

-Vladimir Nabokov *Speak, Memory*

One

Would Jack Scanlon forever associate the approach of death with the smell of ripe pineapple? There was no evidence of pineapple, ripe or otherwise, in Keith's apartment. When he found the nerve, he asked Keith if he smelled it. Lying in a morphine slumber on the adjustable bed provided by hospice, all Keith could do was smile and look at his half-brother as if he were daft. That was thirteen years ago, in the spring of 1986, the year the Celtics won their last NBA championship. Keith had told Jack he would give anything if he could get to a playoff game in the Garden and watch his Celts give the Rockets a lesson in basketball. Two months earlier he had talked obliquely of death, and now when he said he would give anything to get to a playoff game in the Boston Garden, it meant something. Talk of Keith's dying brought Scanlon to the edge of panic.

They were in Portsmouth, at a restaurant on the harbor that used to be a warehouse for boat parts. The fashion at the time was to take old abandoned mills or warehouses and convert them into upscale apartments for young professionals, or into chi-chi restaurants. Keith had just been through a tough round of chemotherapy at New England Deaconess, and the procedure seemed to have shrunk him; he looked to Scanlon like the kid in his biology textbook, a victim of progeria. The ball cap he wore to cover up his hair loss was a size too big for him, and he had taken to wearing sweat suits, also too big for him. He had on one of these sweat suits that night at the warehouse restaurant. He was in a lot of pain, even with a tablet of morphine in his system.

As if anybody with eyes couldn't see for himself, Keith had to tell the waitress that he had cancer and that it was really uncomfortable for him to sit down because the tumor that had started it all was still in his lower back. A tumor that had grown to the size of a softball before he bothered to have it looked at, the tumor that had been immediately diagnosed for what it was and surgically removed five years earlier. Except they had not got all of the cells. Enough remained behind to metastasize to his lungs and liver. The waitress was sympathetic and asked Keith if he would like a cushion to sit on. It wouldn't help, Keith told her, and Jack saw her eyes dodge around the cavernous room. Bring us a couple of strong drinks, Scanlon told her. That would be better than a cushion. If morphine couldn't deaden his pain a gin and tonic wasn't likely to touch it. But it got the waitress away from their table for a while.

"Why do you have to tell strangers about your condition?"

"Because it hurts and I feel sorry for myself."

"Nobody wants to hear. It reminds them of what might be in store for them."

"Maybe that's why I do it."

Scanlon couldn't remember what they had ordered to eat; he believed they had three drinks each. As the restaurant filled with people, and Keith finished his third gin and tonic, he seemed to be less uncomfortable in the sitting position, and Scanlon was ashamed at the relief he felt when his brother didn't engage the people sitting at tables near them with talk of his medical condition. They were both pretty tipsy when they left the restaurant. It was on the drive back to Garrison that he said it out loud.

"Jack, I'm really scared of dying."

Scanlon was disarmed, speechless, the way he had felt earlier that month when Keith's doctor unceremoniously informed Jack and his mother in the busy corridor of the hospital that Keith was going to succumb to this disease, and that it would happen soon. Having said that, he looked at his watch, and excused himself to attend to another chore, leaving Scanlon and his mother to look at each other in shock. His mother had a goofy half-smile on her face. Scanlon drove her home and then went home himself, still benumbed from the news. It was only later that evening, at his wife's urging, and after several bourbons, that Scanlon called the doctor to ask if he'd heard him correctly that morning. He was more sympathetic over the phone, but the message was the same. There was no known treatment for a case as advanced as Keith's—it was, after all, in the liver. If Keith had been more attentive in the early stages... It should have been obvious to all of them that this would be the only logical prognosis, he seemed to imply. All anyone could do now was to try to make him as comfortable as possible, which was to say keep him on heavy doses of morphine.

This was what Scanlon was up to that night at that ridiculous restaurant. He was trying to give his half-brother some comfort, trying to give him a little pleasure in the remaining days of his life even if he didn't believe in his heart of hearts that it was true that Keith was really going to die. Even as he confessed to Scanlon his fear of dying, Jack doubted that he believed it himself at the time.

"You know what I'd like to do, Jack?" he'd said. "I'd like to go to Atlantic City and gamble. Gamble until I either went bust or dropped dead."

"What about the playoffs? Wouldn't you like to see a game?"

"I'd like to hit the lottery. I buy eight tickets a week. I'd love to hit it for a million. I'd take it to Atlantic City and piss it away at the tables, every nickel of it. That's what I really want to do."

"What if you won in Atlantic City?"

"Then I'd find some way to spend it foolishly. I'd leave some for the kids, of course."

It was obvious that Scanlon couldn't get him a winning lottery ticket, but he thought he might be able to get some tickets for good seats at the Boston Garden for game five or six of the Celtics-Rockets series. That much he was pretty sure he could do, working at such a place as he did, teaching kids whose parents held positions in high places. The particular parent he had in mind was also a trustee of the School, and an alumnus. He'd sent five of his kids through the School, all of them first-rate athletes, and third-rate scholars. Dad was no intellectual giant himself, but he had been born to the manor and was rich enough to own season tickets in the Garden's expensive seats. He was also a nice guy, a genuinely nice rich guy. Scanlon didn't usually have a high opinion of rich people. It had always been a problem for him. When he told this rich parent, whose kids Scanlon had taught and coached, about his brother, he didn't hesitate. He had two tickets to game five just like that. They could pick them up at the Garden—they wouldn't even have to hassle at the ticket window. Just take the elevator up to the lounge. Tell them you're a friend of Bobby Childs.

Keith couldn't believe that Scanlon had actually scored tickets to a Celtics playoff game. Did he realize how hard to get they were at the last minute? Even if they hadn't seen each other five times in the last twelve years Keith knew what kind of a place his half-brother taught at, and what kind of people were associated with that school. He should not have been that surprised.

Two

Nine years later. October. This time it was his mother. Her tumor was compared to a grapefruit (not a softball) in size. It was in her lung. They were sitting across the desk from the doctor: Scanlon, his mother, and his other half-brother Billy. The doctor was a dour young man with thick lips, who gave them the biopsy report and the bad prognosis. Chemotherapy wouldn't help; radiation therapy would be a bad idea. What about surgery? Scanlon had asked. The dour young doctor was skeptical. The tumor was so large, and his mother was no spring chicken. Scanlon noticed the same goofy expression on his mother's face that she had had when that doctor informed them about Keith's terminal condition a decade before. What was it with the medical profession these days? They didn't seem to realize that this was the kind of news that scares people. Or maybe it was just that they had been unlucky enough to get unfeeling doctors. What about another opinion? They left with the name of a local specialist and got an appointment with the man for the following week. This guy wanted more tests and X-rays to see if the stuff had invaded other soft tissues. They waited for a week and a half for the results, all of them right on the edge.

Three

Three years later. The present. Now it was Scanlon's turn, or so he thought as he lay in a reclining chair in Day Surgery at the hospital. He was rigged up to an IV, and was receiving his first unit of blood. All told, he would require three units.

"You're getting some of your color back," the nurse, one of three who would attend him during the more than seven hours of transfusion, told him. "You looked like death warmed over when you checked in."

Death warmed over. That had been one of his grandmother's expressions. His mother had picked it up, too. Maybe Sylvia Sheehan had put it more politely a week ago in the cafeteria when she told him, her face in a frown of concern, that he looked "just awful." She suggested that the sooner he see a doctor the better. He was not particularly friendly with his Spanish teacher colleague, so he took her bald observation to heart. Scanlon's wife, Judith, was in California dealing with her recently deceased father's estate, and babysitting her neurotic mother, sister, and brother. Judith never would have allowed her husband to get to the point where people would take it upon themselves to describe him as looking like warmed over death.

Scanlon had just about convinced himself that he had colon cancer. The colonoscopy Dr. Dunham had scheduled for next week would confirm it as fact. He had been passing black stools all spring. He had also grown weaker by the day; he could not walk a hundred feet or climb a short flight of stairs without gulping for air, his muscles on fire. In less than a month Jack Scanlon would turn sixty. He was reasonably certain he would live at least that long. If his doctor was to be believed, he might not have made it to his birthday if he had not acted immediately on his suggestion that he check into the outpatient clinic for a transfusion. The doctor's voice had been calm on Scanlon's answering machine, calm to the point of indifference. "If you don't check in today, I'll probably have to order you to be hospitalized." Scanlon tried to match his doctor's emotional detachment when he called his wife in Los Angeles. She had sounded concerned, of course, but relieved to hear the news; it gave her an excuse to flee the emotional black hole of her bereaved and quarrelsome family.

Scanlon, bored, leaned back in the recliner and closed his eyes. The nurses whispered at his shoulder, worried that blood was starting to coagulate in the tube leading from the bag. He heard the word "heparinized." One of them went to call hematology. Scanlon remained calm; no worries about his mortality disturbed his boredom. His back was to the nurse's station; he could hear the voices of the nurses and staffers but could not observe their movements. Thirty years ago he had kept a journal briefly as he struggled to discover what it was he was all about. He considered asking the nurse for a notepad and something to write with. The nurse returned with a woman from hematology. They consulted in low voices about the accumulation of encrusted blood at the junction between the bag and the first few centimeters of tubing. The nurse left and came back with a fresh replacement bag. No one saw fit to explain to Scanlon what was going on, and Scanlon was too bored to ask.

Four

Back in 1995, tests revealed no evidence that cancer had invaded his mother's other soft tissues. She was given the green light for surgery. The malignant tumor was removed, along with her right lung. She had looked so tiny, so frail, as they wheeled her in on the gurney into the recovery room. Scanlon was struck by how much she resembled his grandfather, her own father. Keith, on his deathbed ten years earlier, had shown a similar resemblance to the old man.

She had been slow to recover from the operation. Two years before, she had suffered from several cerebral infarcts that had left her speech slurred, her thinking out of synch with her verbalizations; she would say yes when she meant no, and vice versa. She worried that she was exhibiting symptoms of Alzheimer's.

She could no longer maintain her own apartment, could not be left alone all day and all night. Scanlon feared he would be forced to take his mother in. To his relief, his half-brother Billy volunteered to do it. Billy needed desperately to earn his mother's love and approval for which he had, all his life, felt deprived. Scanlon had been ambivalent all his life where his mother figured in it. He did not object to Billy taking on the care of their mother. He was quick to offer whatever financial assistance he could for his mother's care, as if mere money could absolve him of what he knew was his moral obligation.

If her lung cancer had not spread to the other soft tissues in the fall of 1995 when she had the operation, it was not the case in the fall of 1996. In November she had been diagnosed with a malignant brain tumor. She had lost the ability to walk, or to take care of her most fundamental needs. The Visiting Nurses Association sent someone to look after her during the day, Monday through Friday, but it fell to Billy to look after her every night of the week, and all day on weekends. She had become incontinent and experienced several bleeding episodes that drove Billy into a state of depression. By December, he could not take any more of it, and filled with regret, and sorrow, and guilt, he had his mother admitted to the county nursing home. She died there in February.

Scanlon had visited the nursing home only once. He had been shocked at the appalling conditions in the place. The corridors were filled with the terminally ill, the terminally neglected elderly, cruising about in wheelchairs, or sitting in straight-back chairs against the wall in a glaze-eyed stupor. His mother, incapable now of talking, regarded her eldest son with vacant eyes in which Scanlon, nevertheless, saw rebuke. Once proud and fiercely independent, she was now as physically dependent as an infant. She seemed unaware of his presence. She flipped through the pages of a mail order catalog without looking at them. Scanlon slipped away, as if fleeing the abomination, the smell of ripe pineapple in his nostrils. It was the last time he saw his mother alive.

Five

"Would you like something to read, dear?" The nurse's nametag identified her as Linda.

"How about *War and Peace*?"

"Cheer up. Karla's going to stay late so we can get it done today. That way you won't have to come back tomorrow. You should be finished by eight o'clock at the latest, if everything goes smooth."

"Tell Karla thanks. I appreciate it."

"How about a magazine? You like *Sports Illustrated*?"

"I'm all right, thanks." Scanlon closed his eyes, tried to put away all thoughts. He had never had a talent, however, for shutting down his mind, of suppressing his memory.

December 1944:

Uncle Ira holds Johnny upside down by the ankles so he won't choke to death on cigarette smoke. Grammy yells at Johnny's mother for letting him drag on her cigarette. Dorothy Labalm ignores her mother, and concentrates on her crossword puzzle at the kitchen table. She is home for the holidays. She waitresses at a fancy hotel someplace in Florida—Tampa, Miami—someplace, Johnny isn't sure where. It is around Christmas time, early in the morning, still dark outside. Besides Johnny, Ira, Grammy, and Johnny's mother, present are Grampa and Uncle Mitch. Mitch and Ira are home on furlough. It is the first time they have been home together since they went off to join the Navy.

Grampa has been up all night with his sons drinking Pickwick ale. Grammy is as mad as a "wet hen." The old man is paralyzed on his right side from his second stroke in eight months, but it doesn't stop him from having his "liquor" as Grammy refers to all alcohol whether it is hard liquor or not. Grammy has to shave him, bathe him, supervise him on the toilet, and put him to bed like a baby. But he doesn't need help pouring his Pickwick, or raising the glass to his lips with a quavering left hand. Since he has been home, Mitch has taken over shaving Grampa. When he returns to duty it will fall back to Grammy again; her return to duty. In less than a year he will suffer his final stroke. In the meantime, his life will be one of increasing helplessness, incontinence and dementia. In fourteen years, Grammy will be dead from a stroke of her own. Her last few years will be spent in dottiness and poor health.

Johnny recovers from his fit of coughing. Mitch stands at the stove thawing out a quart bottle of ale in a pan of water. Grammy had deliberately hid the bottle in the shed, knowing that it would freeze up. This she had done to punish the old man. Mitch is laughing at Johnny. Johnny's eyes are filled with tears from choking on cigarette smoke, and there is spit all over his chin.

Five years earlier, in the front room of this same house, at four-thirty on a rainy Friday morning in June, Johnny Labalm had been born. It is a big, brick, two-family house, the Labalms on the right, the Soucys on the left as you face the front. Between the kitchen and the front bedroom, where Johnny was born, is the living room with the Philco radio, the wooden-armed sofa, one armchair and a rocker, and a hand-cranked Victrola. The bathroom is off the living room.

In the kitchen, two stoves face each other across the room, one that burns kerosene, the other wood. In the corner, by the window that faces the Lion's Club playground and the Groveton Trade and Elementary School, is the wood-box from where Johnny reportedly took his first solo steps on his very first birthday. There is a walk-in pantry; on the lintel of the entrance Johnny's Uncle Mitch has nailed a wastebasket with the bottom knocked out of it. Mitch has taught Johnny the two-handed set shot; Mitch tells him he must practice it every day until he can sink six out of ten shots consistently. At five years old, Johnny is well coordinated. Grammy worries that something in the pantry will get broken when Johnny throws the ball short, but since it was Mitch's idea to put up the basket she doesn't make too much of a fuss. Mitch may be her favorite son, but the sun rises and sets on her Johnny.

Ira is two years older than Mitch. He props an elbow against the shelf of the wood stove. He has on U. S. Navy issue dungarees and a T-shirt. He invites Johnny to punch him in the belly with all his might. Ira's stomach is as hard as a bag of cement. He once had been the welterweight boxing champion of his carrier division. For the short time he will be home, he has promised to teach Johnny the manly art of self-defense, as he calls it. Ira will re-enlist after the war, stay in the Navy long enough to make Chief Aviation Machinist Mate, and muster out after eight years because of a bad kidney.

If Grammy prefers Mitch to Ira, Johnny's mother is partial to Ira. They have more in common. Johnny's mother thinks Mitch is a snob, too big for his breeches. Ira would never say anything like that about Mitch, or anybody else.

After the war, Mitch plans to finish college. He also wants to start up a basketball team in Groveton, if the American Legion will sponsor it. He has not given any thought to what he might want to do after college.

There are hard feelings between Grammy and Johnny's mother. The smoking incident makes matters worse. Grammy accuses her of teaching the boy bad habits. Johnny's mother argues that by letting him try cigarettes now it will cure him of wanting to smoke them later. This theory will later prove false for both cigarettes and alcohol, as Johnny Labalm will start to smoke habitually in nine years, and to drink in ten. At present, Grammy and Grampa who look after his needs—Grammy obviously more than Grampa since his strokes—circumscribe his world. Johnny's Aunt Lily also lives in the house. When she isn't chattering like a magpie on the phone to her high school girlfriends about boys, and makeup, and people like Vaughn Monroe, and Frank Sinatra, she spends some time with Johnny. She walks around the house a lot with books balanced on her head to improve her posture, and she plays records on the Victrola and teaches Johnny the lyrics to songs like "The Old Lamplighter," "One Meatball" (with which you get no bread), and "Open the Door, Richard."

Grampa, comically tight, is grinning in anticipation of the quart Mitch is thawing out. There are three brown teeth left in the old man's head, but his pale blue eyes are bright and alive. Grammy shifts her anger from Johnny's mother to her husband. She is so upset she nearly loses her teeth. She is bandy-legged, scarcely four-feet-eight-inches tall, and built like a little turnip. She wears wire-rimmed glasses and an apron embroidered with buttercups over her gray dress. She has on heavy lisle hose and black high-top shoes that lace.

Mitch pokes fun at Grammy's anger at her husband. He likes to tell a story about the time, in the winter of '36, when Grampa brought home one his beer parlor cronies after an afternoon and evening of beer drinking. They sat at the kitchen table swapping shots of Four Roses and telling lies until Grampa passed out. Then his pal stumbled upstairs and crawled in bed, clothes and all, with Grammy. Grammy's screams were loud enough to wake up the Soucys next door, and the McGinnises across the road. She chased Grampa's buddy downstairs and drove both of them, Grampa and his friend, out into the cold winter pre-dawn with her broom. Grampa she wouldn't allow back in the house for three days.

After that Grampa had to resort to sneaky tactics to get at his drink. He'd hide his beer and his whiskey around the house, and wait until Grammy went to bed before he'd have his taste.

Once in awhile Grampa would take Johnny to the beer parlor with him (on the pretext of going to the store for the paper or tobacco for his pipe). He'd let Johnny have a sip from his beer glass. Johnny would be enthralled with beer parlor culture.

After Grampa's death, Johnny's mother will denounce Grammy for hectoring the poor old man to his grave. He will be seventy years old when he suffers his fatal stroke.

As Mitch retells the story of Grampa and his drunken friend (and Mitch is the only one who can get away with telling stories on her), Grammy gets embarrassed and flustered. Her false teeth drop out of her mouth onto the kitchen table. She swats Mitch across the head, but it is a good-natured swat.

Johnny wants some Pickwick ale. Ira obliges him, over Grammy's objections. First cigarettes, now liquor, she laments. Johnny's mother doesn't try to hold back her exasperation with Grammy, sighing loudly over her crossword puzzle. Mitch asks Johnny if he'd like to see more pictures and war souvenirs. These objects he has in abundance upstairs in his duffel bag. Mitch and Ira take Johnny up to the room they share on the third floor. In the hall, Ira allows Johnny a sip of his ale, but Johnny has to promise not to ask for any in Grammy's presence. Ira doesn't want Grammy upset.

Mitch's bomber had been shot down over the Philippines. Filipino guerrillas rescued him before the Japs could capture him and the rest of the crew's survivors. He was wounded pretty badly, and was laid up for three weeks in a thatched hut supported by bamboo stilts in the jungle before he was well enough to be evacuated to an Allied hospital in Luzon.

Mitch has pictures of the guerrillas, the hut, and several of himself in an Army hospital with Filipina nurses, one on each knee. Grammy, when she first saw the picture, said that he looked like death warmed over. The nurses put Johnny in mind of monkeys. Mitch and Ira get a big laugh out of this. They throw their arms across each other's shoulders and sing a song they call "The Monkeys Have No Tails in Zamboanga."

Mitch lets Johnny unsheathe a gilt-handled dagger that he got off the corpse of a Jap aviator. He has Jap cigarettes in a plain brown package with Jap writing on it. One of the pictures Mitch shows him is of an American airman, a bombardier like Mitch, named Hank Buchanan. Hank Buchanan is smiling, a cigarette in the corner of his mouth, his booted right foot on the naked body of a dead Jap soldier. The Jap's dead pecker stands erect. Over Buchanan's left shoulder is the fuselage of a B-17 bomber with a mermaid painted on it.

Ira observes that if the poor bastard couldn't die with his boots on, a hard-on was the next best thing. Afterwards, Mitch and Ira roughhouse with Johnny, put him through some acrobatics, have a three-way pillow fight.

The next time Johnny will see them together it will be fall, and they will take him out on the big front lawn and let him get a running start before they bring him down from behind with accurately thrown pillows. Hank Buchanan will be with them. It will be among many of the truly happy times Johnny will remember of his childhood.

"Get me the piss pot, Fanny," Johnny hears Mitch say to Grammy. "It's time for the old boy's haircut." Grammy leaves Mitch and Ira in the kitchen with Grampa and follows Johnny's mother into the living room. Johnny goes upstairs to the second floor where he can listen and watch what is going on in every room on the first floor through the radiator grates. Above the living room he hears his mother's voice rise in anger. They are discussing him. He feels his heart speed up; his hands get clammy. They both sound very angry. He clamps his hands over his ears, and retreats to the room over the kitchen, feeling as though he might have to cry.

Mitch talks to Grampa the way he might talk to a child. Johnny can see Ira pouring Pickwick ale into three glasses. Mitch and Ira talk to each other as if Grampa were not even there in the room with them. Their talk, though he can hear only snatches of their words, and doesn't understand half of what he hears, frightens him. He runs to his secret place in the attic where he can be afraid by himself, where he can think about things that are not so scary.

What had they said that upset him so? It had to have had something to do with his grandfather's failing health, his small pension. How would Grammy make ends meet on his meager income? It had to have been about those subjects. Or maybe Johnny's mother was the topic of conversation. Her presence in the house may have had something to do with all the tension Johnny felt. How long had she been away? How did Johnny feel about her coming home, right out of the blue? There was no father in this scene. Perhaps that is what he heard through that floor radiator; perhaps that was his first inkling that there was something amiss, that he was not quite like other kids.

Christmas day. Johnny is trying out his new skates, his very first (and only) pair, on the Lions Club rink across the road from the house. From the rink he can see Ira, Mitch, Grammy, and his mother watching him from the kitchen windows. Why isn't there someone out there with him? He spends more time on his rear end than on his feet. When he is able to stand at all, his ankles are practically flat against the ice, the blades sideways. When he comes home, everybody is laughing. They are laughing at him. He doesn't really mind being laughed at. To tell the truth, it makes him feel as though he belongs, as though he is the center of attention.

Not long after Christmas, Ira and Mitch have to report back to duty. Grammy is relieved that there is no more combat facing either of them. Johnny's mother has to get back to her job at the hotel someplace in Florida. The busy season for restaurants is yet to come. She promises to bring back something special for him the next time. That will be in about a year.

She doesn't touch him. There isn't even a kiss or a hug. She keeps her distance from her son. She will never be affectionate with Johnny in the years he will live with her, so why should she have been any different during the time she had abandoned him?

Six

"Your wife called, Mr. Scanlon. She'll be arriving tomorrow afternoon in Manchester at 5:49 on US Air, flight 241."

"I'll be able to drive?"

"You'll be fine. Doctor Dunham wants you to rest for a few days, but you should be all right to drive that short a distance."

"Thank you."

"Sure you don't want something to read?"

"Yes, I'm sure."

"Try to relax. I know it's been a long while, but it's necessary."

"I understand."

Scanlon hadn't always understood medical necessity. In fact, it had been only three years now that he'd had to deal with the world of doctors and nurses and medication and blood tests, EKGs, CAT scans, ultrasounds, and the like. His luck had run out in August 1996:

He had awakened at four-thirty on Thursday morning, August 30th. He sensed immediately that something was wrong. His left hand touched something foreign, something that felt like a disembodied appendage. When he discovered that it was his own right arm, and not disembodied at all, he tried to scream out, but could make no sound. He got out of bed and hurried to the bathroom, holding his dead right arm in his left hand. He'd had quite a lot to drink the night before. The first thing that came to mind was that he was experiencing some bizarre effect of alcohol poisoning; all the years of abusing the stuff was now coming back to exact a price. Judith had expressed concern when they went to bed at how red his face had gotten. "Hey," he had joked, "maybe a stroke's coming on."

In the bathroom mirror, Scanlon's reflection looked back in panic at him. He heard his wife call from the bedroom. He tried to answer. He could make no sound. He went back into the bedroom, holding on to his limp right arm in which he felt no sensation.

"What's wrong, Jack?" He read fear and concern in her face and in her voice. She was out of bed and heading for the phone on the bureau. "I'm calling 911."

No, no, no, he tried to say. His lips opened and closed soundlessly. He shook his head in the negative, as his wife looked at him, her eyes wide with fear. He sat down on the foot of the bed, holding his arm in his hand. He was desperate to explain to her that this had to be a temporary condition, that she shouldn't panic, shouldn't get outsiders involved.

"Hello," Judith said, "I think my husband has suffered a stroke." She gave the 911 operator the details of his condition, was instructed to keep him warm and to stay on the line until the EMT arrived and actually entered the premises. They would hold until she went downstairs and turned on all the outside lights so that they knew they were in the right place.

Judith put a blanket over his legs, tried to get him to lie down. He tried futilely to verbalize. When he attempted to lie back on the bed, he rolled off onto the floor where he remained until the EMT arrived, a few minutes later.

"How you doing, sir?" a young man in a blue uniform with a stethoscope around his neck, asked Scanlon.

"He's lost his speech," Judith explained. "He can't make a sound."

"You're going to be okay, sir," the young man said, joined now by a young woman, also dressed in blue uniform, who tried to insert an oxygen delivery tube in his nostrils. He pushed it away, shaking his head no. I can breathe fine, he would have said if he had been able to. Just leave me alone; this will pass.

"You having any trouble breathing? Any chest pain? Just shake your head yes or no," the young medic told him. Scanlon shook his head in the negative. He heard the young woman say something to his wife, something that sounded to him like T-R-A. Meanwhile, two more of the EMT arrived with a stretcher and Scanlon was lifted onto the rig and taken down the stairs and out the door to the awaiting emergency vehicle, which these days looked more like a paddywagon than the ambulance that Scanlon was familiar with as a boy.

On the trip to the hospital they monitored his blood pressure and pulse, and radioed to the emergency room staff. By the time they arrived at the entrance to the emergency room Scanlon began to feel a tingling sensation in the fingertips of his right hand. He tried to speak. Sound finally issued from his mouth, but the words he tried to form were unintelligible, even to him.

So this was it, he had thought on the ride to the hospital. It was only a matter of time; he'd been on a free ride for fifty-seven years. Now it was time to settle up. Paralysis and life as a mute seemed like a harsh sentence, even for Scanlon's sins. He would have preferred death; a fatal heart attack would have been better than this. Four months earlier, one of his colleagues had suffered a similar fate in the dog hour of an April morning. He had nearly lost his life, but had hung on to survive. The entire left side of his body was paralyzed, and he spoke only haltingly. Rehabilitation had restored some use of his left arm and leg, enough so that he could get around with the help of a cane. His car had to be rigged with special devices for the handicapped. Scanlon did not relish a future like that for himself.

He was wheeled into the emergency room and hooked up to an automatic blood pressure monitor that recorded data every five minutes. A neurologist was summoned. His first blood pressure reading was 190/100 and sent him into a mild panic.

The neurologist, a stout youngish woman of Indian or Pakistani descent, put him through the neurological checklist. By the time she had finished, he had feeling back in his right arm, and he could utter a few mushy words. She gave him a nonsense phrase to repeat until he could enunciate each word a little better with each try. They would keep him in the hospital overnight; see how he fared in the morning.

Scanlon was released from the hospital at ten-thirty the next morning, his speech and the use of his right arm fully restored. He was told that he had suffered a transient ischemic accident, a TIA, not a TRA as he thought he had heard. He should take aspirin and folic acid, and he was to cut down significantly on his alcohol intake. Scanlon appreciated the fact that he had dodged a bullet, but to be asked to cut down his alcohol intake didn't sit well with him.

That evening, seated across the dinner table from his wife, Scanlon saw a flash of peripheral light, and his right arm shot out from his body involuntarily. This time the TIA happened while he was awake.

The EMT carried him outside to the stretcher in the chair he sat in, mute again for the second time in as many days. On the ambulance trip to the emergency room he regained his speech, and the numbness in his right arm disappeared by the time they reached the hospital.

On this trip, the stethoscope revealed atrial fibrillation, and an EKG confirmed it. Scanlon was made to remain in the hospital for eight days. He was given blood thinners and subjected to CAT scans, more EKGs, and an ultrasound to plumb the condition of his heart chambers, and to detect clogged arteries. Judith told him that, when the EMT was hauling him out of the house for the second time, she had prepared herself for the possibility that she would never see him again alive.

For nearly three years now Scanlon had been a member of the Coumadin club. He also took medication to regulate his heart rhythm, drugs to lower his blood pressure, pills that kept his cholesterol under control. Jack Scanlon had become part of the drug culture, a fact that appealed to his sense of irony, if nothing else. He even made a stab at cutting down on his drinking, establishing a rule for himself: no more drinks after the evening meal.

Seven

"How we doing, Mr. Scanlon?" Grace had replaced Linda. Scanlon wondered idly who this Karla was who had volunteered to work overtime so that he could receive his complete transfusion in one sitting.

"Fine. I'm doing just fine." Please don't ask me if I want anything to read, Scanlon said to himself.

"That's good. Can I get you something to read? A magazine?"

"Yeah. Find me a copy of *Hustler.*"

Grace actually blushed. "I don't believe we have that in our library."

"Too bad. I was really in the mood for frontal nudity."

"Mister Scanlon!"

"I'm joking."

"You are very naughty."

"I know."

Grace was fiftyish and plump. If he had to be imprisoned in this chair for over seven hours it seemed that the least the staff could do would be to give him a pretty nurse or two to look at. Scanlon closed his eyes and wondered what Karla would look like.

* * *

"See the fat broad with the orange hair, in the corner with those two guys?"

"Yeah," Scanlon replied. Keith had on his oversized sweat suit and ball cap. His latest bout with radiation had left him without any hair on his head. They were drinking in a dark restaurant and bar in Garrison. Keith had put away three gins and tonic, and was happily drunk. Scanlon was feeling no pain either. It was April, still cold outside. Scanlon was planning to stay the night at Keith's apartment.

"She's the mother of Billy's bastard kid. She's the biggest slut in town, and Cory, Billy's love child, is up on a first-degree murder charge. He's only fourteen but they're thinking of trying him as an adult."

"Murder? You're joking."

"No, I'm not. Him and this other punk tried to roll a drunk in Hitchcock Park. The poor fucker woke up and tried to fight them off. They caved in his skull with a rock. Got about six bucks off the guy."

"And what does Billy think about this?"

"There ain't shit he can do about it, no matter what he thinks."

Scanlon had trouble getting his mind around the fact that Keith was thirty-nine years old and probably wouldn't live to see forty. For a time during the evening, while they were drinking and having some laughs, Scanlon believed that everything would turn out for the best with Keith, that the chemo and radiation therapy would bring the cancer to its knees, would send it packing into remission. The news about Billy's illegitimate son and the charge against him of this brutal murder, brought him back to reality, renewed his pessimism.

"Jesus, that's... I don't know what to say. And that's the kid's mother over there, being felt up by those two bikers?"

"Like I say, she's the biggest slut in town."

"Maybe we better make this the last one. I'd like to get us home in one piece."

"I'm having a good time, Jack. The best time I've had in a long while. I don't want it to be over."

Scanlon put his hand on his half-brother's back, gave it a few rubs. "I know, I know. Shit, I'll call a cab if I get too faced to drive. Drink up."

Keith lit a cigarette. He'd been off smokes for five years, but the cancer had metastasized to his lungs so he figured what more harm could a few cigarettes do him? Scanlon hadn't smoked a cigarette himself in fifteen years.

"You hear anything from Shelley?" Scanlon asked. Shelley was Keith's second wife, to whom he'd been married for less than five years. She had taken their two baby daughters and moved out when it became clear to her that Keith was a terminal case. She had been nineteen when he married her, Keith thirty-three. Nadine, his first wife, had custody of Keith's other two teen-aged daughters. She and her new husband, Tony, had been looking in on Keith during his ordeal, giving his mother relief from the caretaking of her youngest son.

"No. And she'd be smart to stay clear of me. If I get my hands on her I'll wring her fucking neck."

"It's her mother's doing. She never approved of your marriage. Even I could see that."

"I don't give a sweet shit whose doing it was. She had no right to leave me just when I needed her most. And she's got my kids. You, of all people, know how that feels. She knows I'll kill her, too."

Scanlon agreed. It seemed a particularly heartless move on her part. Of course, Scanlon knew little of what went on between Keith and his young wife. Only what he heard from Keith, and their mother, whose bias against the girl bordered on the irrational. He had stayed mostly out of the lives of his mother, stepfather, and half-brothers since he married Judith.

"You couldn't kill a fly. Everybody knows what a softie you are."

"That bitch I'd kill. What would I have to lose? What would they do to me, give me the chair?"

"I think in this state death is by hanging."

Scanlon regretted that he had allowed the conversation to take this turn. Keith had been having a good time, had for a short time put his fate out of his mind.

"Looks like the Celts all the way," Scanlon said. "What a year Larry's having."

"Parish drives me nuts. He's always giving up the ball in the low post. He's got no hands."

"You've got to admit, he can run the floor for a guy his size."

"Without Bird they're just another team."

Scanlon signaled for another round of drinks. The mother of Billy's "love child" was on her way out with her leather-jacketed biker friends. She waved and smiled at Keith when she passed by their table. Keith addressed her as Maureen.

"She ever go after Billy for child support?" Scanlon asked.

"Naw. She may be a slut but she's got a good heart. She never made a stink about it, but everybody in town knows it's Billy's kid. Why do you think Norma left him?"

The things Scanlon didn't know about his family could fill a book. He knew Norma, Nadine's older sister. Sisters marrying brothers. It had struck him as odd at the time. Neither marriage had worked out. Billy had a fifteen-year-old son by Norma, another son by Maureen; Keith and Nadine had produced two girls, a year apart in age.

The bartender announced last call. They drank one more round. With all he'd had to drink, Scanlon had no business driving an automobile. He got behind the wheel of his new Mazda anyway. Keith did not object.

Eight

"Mr. Scanlon, there's a Mr. Weber downstairs at the reception desk asking if it would be all right to visit you."

"I don't think I feel up to visitors."

"Of course. I'll call downstairs and tell them. Now try to relax. This *will* be over." Grace smiled and patted his arm.

Morris Weber was the head of his department, had taken over from Scanlon a year ago. Scanlon had told the headmaster that four years of coddling bloated egos was about all he could endure, and asked for permission to step down as head. Weber would consider it his obligation to visit a department member in the hospital to demonstrate to the administration that he "cared." He was new enough to the School to believe that good form counted for something. Scanlon bore no animosity toward the man. He simply did not want to see anyone, especially in his present condition, attached by tubes to a bag of some stranger's blood.

About his own blood, he still could not be certain. His mother had no idea what had become of the rapist Henry Bascomb, Scanlon's biological father. She thought he might have shipped out to Pearl Harbor after December 7, 1941. She wasn't even sure where he came from; possibly Providence, Rhode Island, possibly someplace else. Three years ago Scanlon had noticed a Henry Bascomb in the obituary section of a Laconia newspaper (the first place he turned to these days) who would have been of an age to have fathered Johnny Labalm. Scanlon went so far as to show up at the funeral home in hopes of catching a glimpse of the corpse, but it was a closed casket funeral. He didn't know how to begin to ask about the deceased without making the survivors think he was some kind of sick weirdo. The male half of his genome remained a mystery, as did much of his early life. He closed his eyes, tried to get back to 1944, 1945.

* * *

He can't be sure when Johnny's mother comes back to Groveton for good. He has it associated in his mind with Roosevelt's death. He can picture his mother sitting on the front steps of the brick house, smoking and watching Johnny play with the parachute his grandfather had made for him out of a handkerchief, string, and metal washers. He balls the works up and throws it up in the air as high as a six-year-old can. Sure enough, it shakes out and floats to the ground the way a parachute should.

His mother keeps her Christmas promise and brings him something from Florida: a red fire truck with hook-and-ladder. Not uniquely

Floridian but Johnny likes it nevertheless. Scanlon remembered a number of photographs from his mother's album of Johnny with that fire truck.

Grammy comes out of the front door and stands behind Johnny's mother. She wipes tears from her eyes with the hem of her apron. Johnny's mother drops her cigarette on the step and grinds it out with the toe of her shoe. She has on a pleated skirt, saddle shoes, and bobby socks. She is twenty-five years old. She wears her hair Joan Crawford style.

Roosevelt is a name spoken with reverence in the Labalm household, like Bing Crosby and Frank Sinatra, Aunt Lily's favorite singers, or Jack Benny, and The Shadow from the radio, or Lash Larue, Grammy's favorite cowboy, the man in black with the whip. For a few days it is quiet in the house as FDR is mourned.

The next thing he remembers, the war ends. The boys are coming home. Mitch and Ira will soon be home and Johnny is excited. Grammy has let Johnny's mother use the two rooms on the third floor until she can find a place of her own. Grammy and Johnny's mother don't get along. She is out of focus, Johnny's mother, Scanlon's mother. Does she try to act like a mother to Johnny? No, she is like a stranger to him.

King Reed's traveling carnival comes to Groveton. Johnny's mother has him by the hand as they walk among the booths, the tents with sideshows of sword swallowers, fat ladies, ladies with beards, men whose bodies are covered with tattoos, dancing girls with bare bellies and bracelets on their arms and legs, huge rings in their ears; men in leather jackets who ride motorcycles that defy gravity, around the inside of barrels. There are games where you can win prizes. Johnny is reticent with his mother. If Grammy had taken him he would have been hounding her to try every game, go on every ride. They stop at a booth where you have three chances to knock over a triangular tier of wooden milk bottles with soft, lumpy balls that are made to look like baseballs. The man running the booth is tall and thin; he has long sideburns, and his hair is slicked down and styled with a large pompadour. He seems to like Johnny's mother. While Johnny hurls balls at wooden bottles, the man in the pompadour and Johnny's mother talk and laugh and ignore him.

Pitching balls at wooden bottles wins Johnny a stuffed black lamb. His mother, in the meantime, has met Bill Scanlon who will change both of their lives in ways that Johnny Labalm (and his mother) could never dream possible.

The scene shifts to Grammy's living room. Grampa is helplessly bedridden in the front room. Grammy has to look after all his needs, now, and gets no help from Johnny's mother, which is the cause for bitter quarreling between them. And now she has the audacity to bring this creature from the carnival into her home.

Bill Scanlon sits on the couch, his arm around Johnny's mother.

Grammy refuses to look at them. She is furious with her daughter for bringing home this good-for-nothing, and angrily works her rocking chair back and forth, gripping the arms so tightly her knuckles turn white. Anyone with eyes can see that this man is worthless. It is later that Johnny hears his grandmother say this to his mother as he listens at the upstairs radiator.

"Johnny, come over here and shake hands with Mr. Scanlon," Johnny's mother tells him. Johnny looks to his grandmother for the countermand. Grammy can only fume in her rocker, mutter under her breath in French; her feet don't even reach the floor. Johnny approaches cautiously to shake hands with the carnival man. Bill Scanlon presses two coins in Johnny's palm when they shake hands. Johnny recognizes the smell of alcohol but the food odor Bill Scanlon gives off is unfamiliar to him. Something about the carnival man frightens him.

Bill Scanlon pats his lap. "Hey, chief, come sit on my lap."

Johnny declines out of shyness and this nameless fear of the man. He has no words at this time to describe what he sees and feels. Johnny retreats to his grandmother's side of the room and discovers two quarters in his sweaty hand. He likes money well enough. Money buys him soda pop and candy, gains him admission to the Saturday matinee at the Palace. He would like to have more things than he has. A BB gun, for example, a Red Ryder lever action BB gun. A bike would be nice, too, even if he doesn't know how to ride one. He has the sense that there is a serious lack of money with which to obtain these objects. No one has ever said anything out loud, but he senses it.

In two years Grammy will lose the house and they will have to depend for a while on Aunt Lily and her new husband who live in a small New Hampshire town twenty miles south of Groveton. Johnny and his grandmother will stay with them for five months, five months in which Johnny will pine for his beloved Groveton like a refugee. After they leave Aunt Lily's, they will go to live with an old friend of Grammy, a widow who lives with her unmarried sister. Johnny will be the only male in this house of women whose average age is sixty-five. In six months, Johnny will have changed schools three times.

When his mother refuses to stop seeing Bill Scanlon as Grammy has insisted she do, Grammy orders her out of the house. That is all right with Johnny's mother. She has been mistaken to think that she could come back to this house in the first place. Like everyone else in this little town, she tells her mother, Grammy has a small mind. On this day, Johnny gets an earful through the radiator. He is pleased in his heart to hear that his mother will be leaving the house. How long has she actually lived in the house with her parents before Grammy turns her out, if in fact she is turned out? In any case, Johnny Labalm's mother steps out of his life again for the time being.

* * *

Johnny's mother marries Bill Scanlon. Telephone gossip has it that Scanlon had been kicked out of the service for stealing. Where would this information have come from? Married or not, Grammy refuses to allow her daughter in her house as long as Bill Scanlon is with her. She comes to visit a few times by herself. Each time she ends up quarreling with Grammy. Despite it all, Johnny is happy. Why shouldn't he be? In the fall, he starts first grade, and as luck would have it, overcrowding forces half sessions and he has every afternoon to himself. He has many friends in Groveton, and virtually no restrictions on where he goes or with whom. In the summer he can stay out all night if he wants to. He earns enough money peddling newspapers to satisfy his appetite for candy, ice cream, soda pop, and movies. Some nights he shags balls for Groveton's semi-pro baseball team for which he is paid a dollar. A dollar buys a lot. So, he doesn't own a BB gun or a bike. He has absolute freedom.

In the meantime, his mother and her new husband take up residence in Groveton, but because Grammy is so adamant about keeping Bill Scanlon away from him, Johnny sees little of his mother. Mitch is discharged from the Navy and comes to the house to live until he decides what he wants to do with his life. He sleeps in the room across the hall from where Johnny sleeps with his grandmother. One night, Johnny hears a commotion in the hall and opens the door to find Mitch in his shorts, carrying a flashlight and talking incoherently. Johnny awakens his grandmother who gets up in time to keep Mitch from climbing out the second-story window. Mitch has many such sleepwalking episodes, all having to do with what happened to him in the war. When he shaves, he finds shrapnel in his face and will for years to come.

Mitch put away quite a lot of money while he was in the service, so he is in no hurry to find a job in the months before he will matriculate into teachers college. He hangs around the American Legion post and, as he promised he would when he was home for Christmas, organizes a basketball team from among the local vets. The post sponsors the team in a statewide American Legion league. Mitch also follows through on his promise to make Johnny team mascot. So now Johnny Labalm is the mascot of the Groveton Swish Kids of the American Legion League. What more happiness can he expect? He accompanies the team on road trips, and is allowed to stay up late with the men in the lounge of the local posts after games as they drink, sing, play cards, talk over the game just played, and their plans for the future.

Grampa dies. Grammy can no longer afford to keep up the house on what she receives from her husband's old-age pension.

Bill Scanlon and Johnny's mother let it get around that they are not pleased with the way his grandmother is rearing him. He has altogether too much freedom, and absolutely no discipline in his life. Who ever heard of an eight-year-old being allowed to stay out all hours of the night? Grammy is almost totally dependent on her children, or her friends, for support. Johnny's mother and new stepfather become more aggressive, more vocal in their criticism of the way Grammy is bringing up Johnny. They talk about legal action to get custody. Johnny is aware of what is happening with a keenness that frightens him. The thought of having to leave his grandmother to go live with his mother, her husband, and their two new children, fills him with fear and dread. One night, lying in bed with his grandmother, who weeps like a child next to him, Johnny formulates a scheme to run away with her to California where they will never be found. Grammy has a son and daughter living out there who will protect them from Johnny's mother.

Nine

Scanlon found Keith lying on his stomach on the sofa, watching TV. His mother sat in the armchair, doing needlepoint. Scanlon had arrived at four o'clock intending to drive to Boston early enough to get a bite to eat before the game. He had only to see the pain on Keith's face, and the look of gloom on his mother's, to know that there would be no trip to Boston Garden today.

"I can't make it, Jack. I'm sorry."

"We saw the doctor today," his mother said. Scanlon felt the blood drain from his head. He grew dizzy; he sat down on the sofa next to Keith.

Keith's face screwed up in pain again. "There's nothing more they can do. That's all the bastard could think of to say to me. 'Take your morphine and just wait for it to happen.'" Scanlon looked at his mother. She had what reminded him of a child's expression of grief on her face, as if she had just received news that her pet was going to be put to sleep. But it was her flesh and blood son who had been given the death sentence.

"Shouldn't we see another doctor, get another opinion?" Scanlon said without conviction, hearing in his head the words the doctor had for him last winter that Keith would succumb to this disease. Keith did not reply; his mother stabbed at her needlework. A second opinion, they both knew, would be no different than the one he'd heard today. It was no longer even a matter of opinion. Scanlon placed his hand on Keith's leg.

"You sure you don't want to try to make it to the game? They must have wheel chairs at the Garden they'd let you use. The tickets are there, waiting for us."

"I can't, Jack. It hurts too much." Keith rolled back and forth on his stomach. "You go ahead," he said through clenched teeth.

"No. I won't do that. We'll watch it on TV. They'll wrap it up tonight."

"Yeah."

"Can't you take some more morphine?"

"I just had a jolt."

"Can't they give you a stronger prescription?"

Keith forced a laugh. "It don't get no stronger."

Scanlon was at a loss for what to say, what to do. Here was his half-brother racked with pain, dealing with the reality of the news he had just received from some cold-blooded, unfeeling bastard of a medical man, and Scanlon could do nothing but sit there like a statue and stare at the television screen, uncomprehending.

"Are you hungry?" he asked Keith and his mother. "You want me to call for take out? Some Chinese?" Neither of them was in the mood to eat.

"Ma, why don't you go home and get some rest. Jack will stay with me," Keith said to his mother.

"All right." Their mother looked stricken, in a state of semi-shock. She picked up her needlework and put it in a canvas bag. Scanlon walked her to the door. In this low-rent project, her apartment was only three units away from Keith's. When they were out of earshot of Keith, Scanlon asked her how long Keith had to live.

"Two weeks, maybe more, maybe less. He's in so much pain, Jack." She began to cry.

"Where's Billy?"

"He can't stand to see Keith this way. He can't take it."

Neither could Scanlon, but he couldn't leave Keith alone. The morphine finally kicked in enough to at least take the raw edge off his pain, enough so that he could watch the game on TV, get a little fleeting pleasure at seeing the Boston Celtics finish off the Houston Rockets on the Garden's parquet floor, regretting that he had not been able to take Jack up on his invitation to witness it in person.

It would be Scanlon's responsibility to give Keith his morphine every two hours. It now had to be administered by injection. Keith showed Scanlon how to find the vein, how to insert the needle.

"Christ, what if I hurt you? I hate needles. I don't want to screw this up."

"Don't worry about it, Jack. You can't hurt me. It'll be all right. Just take it easy." Keith did his best to comfort Scanlon. He seemed all at once very calm, very much at peace. "Don't be afraid for me, Jack. I'm not afraid anymore."

Scanlon lay down on the sofa. He worried that he might fall asleep and miss Keith's medication. All night the smell of ripe pineapple filled the room.

Two days later, Scanlon got the call from his mother. Keith had died at 9:17 A.M. Scanlon got in his car and drove to Garrison, his mind a blank, his heart literally aching in his chest. By the time he arrived at Keith's apartment his body had been removed to Macauley's Funeral Home. Billy and his new girlfriend were there along with Scanlon's mother, Nadine and her husband Tony. Not present were Keith and Nadine's daughters.

Billy was drunk and his eyes were red-rimmed as if he had been crying. He sat on the sofa, his girlfriend beside him, rubbing his back, consoling him in a low voice.

"Hadn't we better get over to Macauley's and start making arrangements?" Scanlon said to Billy. He knew his mother was in no condition to deal with the matters of funeral and burial. By the looks of him, neither was Billy. Scanlon supposed he should handle it by himself.

"It ain't fair," Billy said. "It just ain't fucking fair."

"I know, I know," Scanlon replied. What did fairness have to do with it? Keith had sealed his own fate with his reckless habits, his refusal to deal with the tumor in its early stages. Billy would hear none of this, of course. He was in the mood to fulminate, to express his grief in the form of bluster. Scanlon's mother looked stricken and waif-like. Nadine comforted her while Tony looked on solemnly. Nadine was strong, a steadfastly loyal friend to her ex-husband as he slipped away from his life. Tony was like a saint the way he stood by his wife, the way he did Keith and his mother's bidding by running errands, and carting the girls back and forth to visit their dying father. He did all these tasks after twelve hours of backbreaking construction work. All Billy could manage to do was get drunk and rail against the unfairness of it all. It was just past eleven o'clock in the morning, but Scanlon wouldn't have said no to a drink himself.

"We'll be glad to help with the expenses, Jack," Nadine told him. "We've already collected nine hundred dollars from Keith's rugby teammates." Already nine hundred dollars before the kid had breathed his last, Scanlon thought. Impressive.

"That's very generous," Scanlon said, experiencing a twinge of guilt at the relief this news gave him. He had visions of having to foot the bill by himself.

Nadine had put on considerable weight, enough to put her in the obese category, in Scanlon's opinion. She had been heavy when Keith married her, and had gotten heavier after the birth of each of the girls. At one time, Scanlon believed that Nadine's weight was at the root of their breakup. That is, until Keith married Shelley, nineteen and herself on the plump side. Keith apparently liked his women with flesh on their bones. If obesity had a heritable component, both of Keith and Nadine's girls had inherited it from their mother. In his short life, Keith had always been slender and athletic.

"They're such good guys. They volunteered to be pallbearers. Anything Tony and I can do to help with the arrangements, just say the word."

Scanlon was moved by Nadine's words. In his present emotional state, it would take very little to start him in crying. "Thanks, you guys. I don't know how to thank you."

"Don't give it a thought. We all loved Keith."

Scanlon was feeling like a fraud and a hypocrite. He had been out of touch with his family for so long. The reasons were complicated by the directions their lives had taken since his return to Garrison after his tumultuous sojourn in Vermont. He had gone to graduate school where he met Judith, had taken a teaching position at a prestigious boarding school, had subsequently married Judith and settled into his new milieu of wealth and privilege the likes of which he had not believed really existed. Keith, Billy, his mother and her philandering husband whom she had finally put out of her life, but not out of the town, had tread water in the place where Keith and Billy had both grown up. Neither was educated beyond high school, and Scanlon's mother had not made it past eighth grade herself. They moved from one dead end job to another, abusing drugs, and abusing alcohol in ways that made Scanlon look abstemious by comparison.

Judith had tried to include Scanlon's family in their lives. She invited them for meals, entertained them and their friends with parties, welcomed them to her home even when they would appear, unannounced, at absurdly late hours of the night or early morning, in a party mood.

In time, they appeared less frequently for parties, ignored invitations to meals, and seemed to have no more interest in keeping up with their older half-brother and his lively new wife. For his part, Scanlon made little effort to make the one-hour journey to Garrison to visit them. In the years that followed, the only contact his family had with him was when a crisis was brewing, and a crisis in his family was always a financial one.

Now, here he was feeling guilty for being so long out of touch. Part of him missed his family, even if his life with them had been largely one of unhappiness, even misery. In the months he had been back in their lives, on what was for him a regular basis due to Keith's illness, it became obvious to all of them that as soon as it was over they would return to their estrangement. And so it was. Until nine years later when Scanlon's mother discovered the tumor in her lung.

Ten

Grace handed Scanlon a folded up piece of paper on which Morris Weber had scribbled a message in his sloppy hand exhorting Scanlon not to worry about meeting his classes or, for that matter, attending to any of his duties. He was to take it easy for as long as it took to recover. If he knew "Mo" Weber, the man was dying to know what it was that Scanlon would be recovering from. He had been deliberately cryptic with Weber earlier in the day when he stopped by his office to tell him that he would not be able to meet his after-lunch class, or attend seated meal that evening. When he told Weber that he needed a blood transfusion, Weber blanched, and looked like he could have used a pint of blood himself. Scanlon volunteered no more information. The truth was he had no information to impart; none that would have thrown light on his condition. He had only his suspicions, hunches that he was unwilling to share with Weber or anyone else, except Judith who was three thousand miles away dealing with problems of her own. Scanlon was relieved that she would be returning tomorrow. He needed to share his burden with someone he could trust. At the moment, Judith was the only person on the planet who fit that description.

He thought fleetingly of Bob Kennedy, his troubled counselor who had navigated Scanlon through his own troubled waters back in 1968, 1969. He had stepped out of Kennedy's life as adroitly as he had abandoned his family, and had no knowledge of what had become of the man. At a time like this he could use a man like Kennedy. In the past thirty years he'd thought about him often, yet had made no effort to contact him, and had no idea where he had gone after he left his welfare job in Groveton, Vermont. Kennedy had mentioned, in passing, a residency as part of a doctoral program at Harvard. He would not have been that hard to track down. Scanlon often wondered if Kennedy would be pleased at how he had got his life, if not his drinking, under control. Lately, even his drinking was in control after a fashion, though one could argue that the amount he imbibed day in, day out, was a long way from having it under control.

The young neurologist, in 1996, had been surprised his liver was still healthy after he revealed to her how much he put away each day, every day, which he estimated as on the order of four hundred and fifty milliliters of bourbon whiskey. She seemed to be as impressed with the fact that he reported the amount in metric as she was by the defense against this assault his liver had put up. That was when he went on his no-drinks-after-evening-meal regimen. It took him less than a year to fall from grace. What did it matter, now that he was doomed?

His back began to itch in a place he couldn't reach with his left hand. He couldn't bring himself to call on Grace to come and scratch it. Scanlon tried getting relief by rubbing against the back of the recliner's cushion, but that didn't help.

"Grace," Scanlon called, feeling self-indulgent, even silly. He listened for footsteps. Nothing. It was impossible for him to turn around for a look behind him the way he was tethered to the IV. "Grace," he called again, and again he heard no footsteps. He wondered if everyone had gone home and forgot about him. "Grace."

Scanlon fell asleep in spite of his itchy back. When he awoke, a nurse he had not seen before was hanging a new unit of blood on the IV stand. "You must be Karla."

"Hello, Mr. Scanlon. Did I wake you?"

"I thought you had all gone home and left me here to die."

"Come now, Mr. Scanlon. We wouldn't do a thing like that." Karla's affable condescension Scanlon found reassuring.

"How much longer?"

"This is your second unit. You can plan on going home in say five, five and a half hours."

Scanlon felt like telling Karla that she was very pretty, and even though his back no longer itched, he was tempted to ask her to scratch it anyway. She would probably think he was a pervert, a dirty old man.

"I think I'm beginning to feel better."

"That's very good, Mr. Scanlon. That's what we want to hear. Just give a yell if you need anything." And Karla disappeared in back of Scanlon's recliner; he heard the squeak of her crepe soles fade away down the corridor. He wondered what time it could be. He had been attached to the IV for an eternity. There was no window in his line of sight, and no clock. He looked straight ahead at the foot of a hospital bed in an empty room. The bed looked inviting at first, then it reminded him of Keith … and his mother.

Keith and his mother. Scanlon had never quite understood the bond between those two. Keith had always been the conspicuous favorite of his mother and stepfather. And when their mother finally summoned the courage to rid herself of Bill Scanlon, it was Keith who had aligned himself with her in that effort. He became her spy, her informant on the nefarious activities of her husband. Keith followed him, eavesdropped on him in bars, peered into the windows of the houses where his women entertained him. It had struck Scanlon as faintly perverse, as if Keith were his mother's lover. In a way, Keith and his mother's relationship was similar to the one between his grandmother and his Uncle Mitch when Scanlon was Johnny Labalm. Perhaps it was a truism that mothers had a preference for their youngest sons. Was there something to be made of the fact that their mother had outlived her youngest son? Mitch, on the other hand, was still alive and kicking, even if he had enough health problems to keep him busy every day keeping track of the forty or so medications he required just to keep on living. In the last couple of years he had undergone quadruple bypass surgery, been suspected of having colon, then prostate cancer (neither condition turned out to be positive) and if that weren't enough, he'd had two run-ins, literally, with moose. The first time, a bull moose had lost its footing on a ledge above the road Mitch and his wife were traveling on and had fallen on the roof of their car, flattening it. Mitch and his wife escaped, miraculously the state police said, with minor injuries. Less than a month later, while he was driving home alone from a high school basketball game (he had coached high school basketball for forty years) Mitch had his second moose encounter, this time colliding head on with the beast, killing the moose and rendering his new car a total wreck. Again, Mitch climbed out of his demolished vehicle unharmed. Mitch had wondered out loud what it would take to finally do him in. The Japs hadn't been able to do it in WWII, a bad heart and the threat of cancer had failed, and two attacks by Bullwinkle's relatives hadn't been able to subdue him. By contrast, a stroke had taken Scanlon's Uncle Ira down at age sixty. Ira's wife Alice had followed suit less than a year later, the cause of her death not a stroke, but the mere absence of her chief adversary and soul mate.

Scanlon's family was disappearing fast. His Aunt Lily and her husband Howard lived in Passaic, New Jersey. They'd had six children, two of whom had died young: Donald in a hit and run accident when he was fourteen; Anita had succumbed to leukemia at age nine. Scanlon had not met the other four kids in their brood, all of whom had long ago grown up, married, and gone their separate ways. He had not seen Aunt Lily or Howard since his mother's funeral two years ago. Howard had had his own bypass surgery, but otherwise seemed in good health; Lily seemed fit enough, though aging ungracefully. The only other surviving relative lived on the West Coast, in the San Fernando Valley. Jeanette was the eldest daughter in what was his grandparents' family of eight children. Aunt Jeanette had been too ill herself to travel east for his mother's funeral. Jeanette and Lily had figured large in his life when he was little Johnny Labalm ... more than his actual mother had. Jeanette, her moody husband Bernie, and their two infant children had struck out for California, the Promised Land, in the summer of 1952, and had settled in Pacoima where they lived to this day.

Karla returned with a magazine trolley. He would have to work to hide his annoyance at the staff's obsessive efforts to foist their bourgeois magazines on him.

"Honestly, Karla. I don't need to look at magazines. I've got enough going on in my febrile little brain to help me pass the time."

"If you ask me, you shouldn't let your little brain think too much. It only leads to needless worry. You're going to be all right, Mr. Scanlon."

"I know. I'm fine, believe me."

"Not even *Sports Illustrated*? I can find you the swimsuit issue." Karla's pretty eyes flashed mischief.

"I'd prefer to see you in a swimsuit, over those manikins."

"Mr. Scanlon!" Karla said with mock indignation (which Scanlon interpreted as condescension) as she wheeled off the magazine trolley. For the first time in his life Scanlon felt like an old man. Perhaps it was just as well that he check out early rather than endure the agony of steady deterioration, accompanied by the condescension of youth. Only he didn't want to suffer. He didn't want to suffer the way poor Keith had suffered, the way his mother had suffered right up to the end. He knew nothing of real suffering. He was content to keep it that way. Let the philosophers say what they wanted about the redemptive effects of suffering. Redemption from what?

His back itched again. He called out for the nurse. He listened, but heard no response. It was as if he were alone in the corridor. The itch grew worse. He writhed in the recliner, getting no relief from the smooth leatherette back.

"Karla!"

"What is it, Mr. Scanlon?" Karla appeared, as if from thin air.

"My back. It's on fire."

"Hold on, I'll get you a back-scratcher." Karla went off on her errand. She returned in a little while with a long wooden handle, the end of which was shaped like a monkey's little hand. Scanlon would have preferred Karla's fingers on his itchy hide, but he took the tool, and went to work on his back. Karla left him to his scratching; he thought he heard her giggle as she walked away.

Eleven

September 1945:

Aunt Lily giggles as the books she balances on her head (her home economics text, and The Holy Bible) slip off to one side and end up on the living room floor. "The Old Lamplighter" is playing on the Victrola. Johnny watches her from the armchair in front of the Philco radio. Grammy is in the hospital recovering from a goiter operation. Aunt Jeanette is in the kitchen making popcorn. Grampa's funeral was a week ago. Both of Johnny's aunts are quarantined to the house because of his scarlet fever. He may have scarlet fever, but he feels fine. He is enjoying the attention from his aunts, and he is allowed all the ginger ale and ice cream he wants.

The homemade ice cream, compliments of Stevie McIntyre who lives in the house next to the McGinneses with his widowed mother, appears on the back steps every evening. Stevie is sweet on Lily. That is why he leaves ice cream on the back steps every night. As soon as he has delivered the ice cream he calls the house to announce the fact, and to talk to Lily who calls him "Stevie darling." Johnny overhears Lily tell Aunt Jeanette that Stevie is "simple." Johnny takes this to mean that Stevie is simple in the head. Lily will be a senior in high school and is constantly on the telephone, giggling with her friends. Aunt Jeanette has a job in a munitions factory in Springfield, Massachusetts. She came home a week ago to attend Grampa's funeral. Johnny is diagnosed with scarlet fever before she can return to Springfield, and is told she will be quarantined for the time it takes him to recover. If Jeanette is annoyed or upset by the confinement she doesn't let on to Johnny. Johnny's mother is in Florida; she doesn't come home for her father's funeral.

"Guess what's on the radio tonight, Johnny. *The Shadow*," Aunt Lily says, giving up on book balancing. She has on flannel pajamas. Aunt Jeanette comes in the room bearing a large bowl of freshly popped corn. It is all right for Lily, a bobbysoxer, to wear her pajamas before bedtime, but Jeanette considers it unseemly for a twenty-seven-year-old woman to do so; she wears her daytime skirt and sweater.

"It's time for Gabriel Heater," Jeanette announces, setting the bowl of popcorn down on the coffee table in front of the sofa. "Why don't you turn off the Victrola now."

Lily wants to listen to Vaughn Monroe, but Jeanette will not be denied Gabriel Heater. Lily defers to her older sister.

Jeanette places the back of her hand on Johnny's forehead. "He's warm," she says to Lily. "He should be put to bed after *The Shadow*."

"Who knows what evil lurks in the hearts of men? The Shadow knows." Johnny's skin tingles at the sound of the announcer's sonorous voice. Aunt Lily tucks her legs underneath her and pulls Johnny to her side. Aunt Jeanette sits in the armchair and gets busy with some knitting Grammy had started before having to go to the hospital. Aunt Jeanette does not seem interested in *The Shadow*, and shows no sign of wanting the popcorn she has prepared; Aunt Lily holds the bowl in her lap. Johnny dips into it to fill his small hand. He is fond of popcorn, but he likes soda pop and ice cream better.

Too soon for his liking, *The Shadow* ends. He is not eager to go to bed in the front room where he was born, and where his grandfather died last week. On moonlit nights the oaks and maples on the front lawn cast monstrous shadows on the bedroom walls that play into Johnny's active imagination. How many times these shadow monsters have driven him to Grammy's bed he couldn't count.

To add to his worries, Johnny faces the prospect of starting school soon. He secretly hopes that his scarlet fever will last long enough to put off the day when he must begin first grade. The only good he can see coming of starting school is that he will be allowed to wear long pants like a grownup instead of having to go around in short pants like a little kid. He can't wait to be grown up like his uncles, like Hank Buchanan.

But his fever breaks, and the quarantine is lifted a day before he must report to the school for his small pox vaccination. He keeps himself awake all the night before, worrying about the needle. His worries are not unfounded as he waits in line with his howling future classmates while the big, white-clad nurse inflicts pain on them without changing her stern expression. Johnny keeps up a brave front, and the truth of it is that the needle pricks don't hurt that much.

At home, his bravery is rewarded with the last of Stevie's ice cream. Now that the quarantine is over there will be no more ice cream delivered to the back steps. Aunt Jeanette returns to her job at the munitions factory in Springfield; Lily begins her senior year in high school; Grammy returns from the hospital, and Johnny starts first grade.

Because of overcrowding, he will attend half-sessions for both first and second grade. Miss Bailey, a battleaxe with black high top shoes and lisle hose, her gray hair contained in a snood at the back of her neck, is his teacher. She is stern, and as unsmiling as the vaccinating nurse, but Johnny is not bothered because she teaches him to read, and suddenly a wonderful new world opens up for him. He is good at figuring too, but his penmanship is an "abomination" according to Miss Bailey. Try as she might, even the redoubtable Miss Bailey cannot cure Johnny of his tendency to allow his pencil to point out in front of him like a left-hander instead of over his right shoulder like a normal right- hander. He grows to hate the Palmer Penmanship Method, and lives only to read the books that occupy the shelves along the back of the classroom. The reward for finishing arithmetic exercises early, and correctly, is to be allowed to select a book of your choice from the shelves and read it for pleasure.

Johnny Labalm is an early admirer of biographies. In no time he finishes the biographies of Andrew Jackson (*Old Hickory*), Eli Whitney, inventor of the cotton gin, Clara Barton, Lou Gehrig, and Florence Nightingale. He has learned to tell time as well, something he had despaired of ever learning to do.

School turns out to be not as bad as he thought it would be. That is, until Margie McDermott arrives on the scene and turns Johnny's life upside down. Margie is the niece of Miss Leslie who will become Johnny's second grade teacher. Miss Leslie is not a battleaxe like Miss Bailey. She is dark haired, wears red lipstick, and smells good. She will not be as good a teacher as old battleaxe Bailey but all the boys, including Johnny, will have a crush on her. Margie smells good too. She wears soft cashmere sweaters and wool plaid skirts and patent leather shoes to school. Her short brown hair is cut pageboy style and is always shiny, in contrast to the dull hair of Clara Gilford or Loretta Sinclair.

Margie has transferred to his school because her family has moved from Portland Street to Summer Street, which puts her in Johnny's district. She homes in on Johnny at once. She is by far the cutest girl in the class, a fact she seems to know and to exploit. She is brazen in her pursuit of Johnny, accosting him right on the playground in front of his male classmates. He is embarrassed to the point of blushing, but he is helpless in her presence. In truth, the boys in his class are envious of the attention he gets from pretty Margie McDermott, and perhaps this is why they refrain from teasing him. It doesn't take long for news of Margie's overtures toward him to get back to his Aunt Lily, and his uncles, Mitch and Ira, who have no qualms about teasing him.

"Johnny's got a girlfriend," they taunt.

"Have not."

"Have too. What's her name, Johnny?" Lily sings.

"I hear her name's Gertrude," Uncle Mitch says, winking at Lily.

"It is not. Her name's Margie," Johnny says without thinking.

"Thought you didn't have a girlfriend," Mitch says.

"I don't."

"Who's Margie, then?"

"A girl at school ..."

"Johnny's got a girlfriend, and her name is Margie. Oh, Margie," Lily sings the popular song, "I'm always thinking of you, Margie." And so it goes until Johnny can't take any more of it, and runs outside and feeds corn to his two pet chickens. Now that Grampa is dead, the chickens' care falls to him. They are an Easter gift to him from his Uncle Ira, (a gift that will appear on the Thanksgiving table in November). He is upset and dismayed by what he considers his family's "betrayal" by serving his pets up for dinner, but he must eat the things he likes on the rare occasions they are served because the fare in the Labalm household, too often for his tastes, includes calf's liver and tripe. Except for peas, he has no use for vegetables. Johnny's parochial tastes in food persist for years. It is not until Jack Scanlon meets Judith that he dares throw caution to the wind and eat things like asparagus, broccoli, lima beans—and liverwurst.

Girls. Girls become the bane of Johnny Labalm's existence. Margie McDermott practically dominates his life all through first grade, and into the summer months between first and second grade as well. She invites him to her house for "tea" and silly games involving her dolls and making believe they are married with kids and pets and the like. She seems to be everywhere he is: at the library, every weekday morning on the back lawn in good weather for story readings. He wants to listen to the stories the librarian reads aloud; Margie wants to whisper in his ear and giggle; at the Lion's Club fair she is there with her mother and her Aunt Leslie who will be their second grade teacher. Johnny wins a two-dollar bill playing Beano and Margie wants him to spend his winnings on cotton candy, soda pop, and a hamburger. Then she suddenly disappears, just after school starts in the fall.

Johnny delights in his new-found freedom. He immerses himself in his biographies, unencumbered by Margie's constant attentions. The respite is short lived, however, as his Uncle Will and his family move back to Groveton from Boston, and Johnny's cousin Roddy joins his second grade class. Roddy has had the advantage of kindergarten and is therefore "advanced" compared to Johnny and his classmates. Johnny, who has become used to being considered the smartest kid in the class, is thrust into competition for that honor with the precocious Roddy. Johnny responds by going inside himself, by becoming sullen and uncommunicative.

One day, as Roddy and Johnny are walking from the school to Johnny's house across the graveled Lion's Club playground, Roddy says to Johnny,

"I thought you said you knew how to read."

"I do."

"Do not."

"Do too."

"Stephanie Daniels can read better than you."

Stephanie Daniels has dirty hair fixed in pigtails, and is the dullest girl in the class. She can hardly read at all, and she has bugs in her dirty hair, and smells of pee.

"Shut up, Roddy."

"I'm telling Grammy you can't read," Roddy sings.

Johnny, enraged, picks up a good-sized rock and hurls it at his cousin. It strikes him on the shoulder. His mouth drops open and his eyes open wide. He rubs his shoulder where the rock hit him; he looks on the verge of crying. Then he searches for a rock of his own on the ground, of which there are plenty right at his feet. Johnny turns his back on his cousin and walks away toward his house. A rock whizzes past his right ear. He turns around as Roddy prepares to launch another one. Johnny picks up a handful of rocks to answer fire.

Eddie LeClerc, who lives at the bottom of Barker Avenue, which runs between the playground and Johnny's house, rides by on his bike. He is eleven years old. He stops to watch Johnny and Roddy throw rocks at each other.

"Hey, knock that off," Eddie yells as Johnny takes a hit on his arm. "You wanna put somebody's eye out?"

"That's what I'm trying to do," Johnny says, heaving another rock the size of his fist at his cousin who ducks just before it can hit him in the face. Eddie drops his bike in the middle of the road and runs to Johnny and grabs his arm before he can get off another missile.

"I told you to cut it out."

Roddy has retaliated in the meantime, and his rock catches Eddie in the back of the neck.

"Ow! You little peckerhead."

"I wasn't aiming at you," Roddy shouts.

"Get over here before I kick your touchhole to kingdom come," Eddie yells at Roddy. Roddy obeys.

Eddie gets Johnny and Roddy in a headlock, one in each arm, and threatens to knock their heads together. "You gonna quit throwing fucking rocks or do I have to bang your heads together?"

"No!" they yell in unison.

"I think I'll knock your thick skulls together anyway." Eddie starts to pull their heads toward each other.

"No," Johnny yells.

"He started it," Roddy adds.

"I don't give a shit who started it," Eddie says, yanking at their heads again. "You gonna quit throwing rocks, or ain't you?"

"Okay, okay," Roddy says.

"You better or I swear I'll kick your touchholes to kingdom come." He releases his grip on the boys. "Now come on, I'll ride you home."

Eddie picks his bike up off the dusty road. Roddy climbs on the back fender; Johnny rides on the crossbar. Eddie pedals them to where Barker Avenue intersects with Western Avenue, and turns in the driveway of the big brick house on one side of which Johnny lives with his grandmother.

Twelve

"How's that back?" Karla asked Scanlon, breaking his reverie.

"What?"

"Did the monkey fist help?" Karla checked his IV. "Your wife called. You're to call her as soon as you get home."

"Why didn't you let me talk to her?"

"She didn't ask to talk to you. Besides, it would have been too much trouble to wheel you to the desk."

"You people don't have portable phones?"

"No."

Scanlon didn't believe her, but he was not in the mood to pursue the issue. He was annoyed that Judith hadn't insisted on talking to him. When Karla left he tried to get back to where he was when she interrupted him. It was no use. His mind was cluttered with the here and now, with what was at the bottom of his "condition," with what the future held for him. If he in fact had colon cancer (as he was convinced he did), what could he expect in the way of treatment—medical treatment, and treatment from the people he knew—his colleagues ... his wife? He remembered how Keith's wife, Shelley, had abandoned him, taking their two little girls, when she could no longer bear the reality of his terminal condition. Would Judith ditch him when the going got rough? He didn't really believe she would. She had put up with him for twenty-eight years; what would a year or two, more or less, matter? Besides, she was about to become a wealthy woman, as her father's estate would no doubt go largely to her given the irresponsibility bordering on profligacy of her mother and two younger siblings. Scanlon took little comfort in the fact that his own financial future would be secure with Judith's inheritance. On the contrary, he regarded it with a kind of bitter irony that he would have a pocketful after all these years only to take it to the grave in the pocket of his funeral tuxedo. As a youth Scanlon was always painfully conscious of the lack of money in his pocket. And when at the age of eight he went to work for it circumstances were always such that he could not keep for himself all that he earned. He could have as easily as not turned into a thief. This meditation on thievery brought him back to Groveton, Vermont, and Johnny Labalm's world:

September 1946:

Aunt Lily works after school at Moulton's Ice Cream Parlor. Johnny Labalm has been fond of ice cream for as long as he can remember; he is particularly fond of hot fudge sundaes with hot melted marshmallow and crushed nuts. Such an ice cream sundae costs twenty-five cents at Moulton's. Lily will fix him one for nothing when the boss is not around, but on days when the boss is on the scene, or when Lily is not working, Johnny has to come up with the quarter if he wants to satisfy his craving.

Johnny receives no regular allowance, and the money he earns peddling papers doesn't amount to much. Since Grampa was forced to retire from the foundry because of his strokes, money has been scarce; now that he is gone it is even scarcer. He picks up spare change from Uncle Mitch or whatever Grammy can give him from her small pension to pay for his addiction to sundaes.

There was a time when a wagonload of newspapers could get him admission to a Saturday matinee, but now that the war is over, he has to fork over twelve cents to get in the show. Twelve cents a week is one thing, his quarter a day ice cream sundae habit isn't so easy to satisfy.

At present, Tobias McClintock is Johnny's best friend. Toby is an only child like Johnny. Toby's mother and father are older, more like Johnny's Grammy and Grampa than regular parents. Toby himself seems older than his seven years. He is taller than Johnny, with square shoulders, a big head with matching big hands and feet. Johnny can read better than Toby (despite what cousin Roddy says) but Toby is better at figuring. Johnny can figure well enough, however, to total up the one dollar and nine cents in pennies, nickels, and dimes they have in their club treasury. The dollar nine represents club dues paid by the five members of the club Johnny Labalm founded, but which, as yet, has no name or particular mission save the goal of raising enough money to purchase, for the membership to share equally, a Red Ryder lever action BB gun.

They keep their dues in a rectangular metal box with a sliding top. Only Johnny and Toby know its hiding place; they have fashioned a hole in the ground outside Toby's garage that they camouflage with a mortar block. They hold their *ad hoc* meetings in Toby's garage.

Johnny finishes counting the coins in the treasury and slides the cover shut on the metal box.

"How much did you say the Red Ryder costs?" Johnny asks Toby who sits passively on a cable wheel while Johnny counts the money.

"I believe Pa said he saw one in the Sears and Roebuck catalog for eight dollars."

"Eight dollars! We'll never get that kind of money by the end of summer."

"Might," says the laconic Toby McClintock.

It doesn't occur to either of them that even if they are able to raise the price of the BB gun that the problem of how to share it among the five of them could prove insurmountable.

"It'll take forever to save eight dollars," Johnny says, despair in his voice. "Look how long it took just to get a dollar and nine cents!"

And it is this argument—the futility of raising eight dollars before the end of summer vacation—along with Johnny's growing dependence on hot fudge sundaes, that moves him to empty the club's coffers one

Sunday morning while Toby is at church with his parents. He leaves the empty metal box on the garage floor to give the impression that the thief left in a hurry after his act, thinking this will also steer suspicion away from himself, the only other soul besides Toby who knows of its hiding place. He doesn't feel good about what he has done, but he is helpless in the grip of his addiction.

* * *

Scanlon winced now at the recollection of Johnny Labalm's craven thievery. If that was the first time Johnny Labalm stole it was by no means the last. Scanlon tried to put these thoughts away, turning to the less unpleasant prospect, by comparison, of his mortality. He looked at the IV bag. It was still quite full and this was only the second unit. His rear end was numb, and his back began to itch again. For a moment he regretted not taking Karla up on her offer of a magazine.

Perhaps it was his training in the sciences that had got him in the habit of thinking chronologically, if indeed this way of thinking had anything to do with science. Even his excursions into his past had a way of arranging themselves in chronological order. Or maybe it was simply his anal retentive nature, as Judith had always jokingly asserted it was.

Thirteen

Summer 1947:

Johnny's back is to Eddie Leclerc as he sits sidesaddle, as it were, on the crossbar of Eddie's Schwinn. Even so, he can smell the tomato soup on Eddie's labored breath as he tacks up steep Barker Avenue. Johnny has tried to talk him into walking the bike up the hill from his house to where the road becomes level. Eddie has his pride.

"Well, then, let me walk. You can pedal up by yourself."

"And have to wait forever for you? Get on."

It is about two miles to the spot on Gilman's Farm where everyone who lives in that part of town prefers to swim, in the Manoosic River. There is a big oak tree on the riverbank with a rope tied to a low branch with which to swing out over the river and drop into its muddy depths. Only boys swim in the river on Gilman's Farm.

Eddie is twelve; Johnny celebrated his eighth birthday in June. Celebrate is probably too grand a word; there is no money in his grandmother's budget for celebrations or even birthday gifts. Uncle Mitch had given him fifty cents, which he spent the same day on two of Moulton's hot fudge sundaes.

Once they reach Western Avenue the rest of the way to Gilman's is all downhill. Eddie lets the bike coast down the steep hill, which, with the wind in their faces, feels to Johnny like a free-fall. They have their swimsuits on under their trousers. They haven't brought towels. Eddie prefers to let the sun dry them off.

Eddie turns off onto the dirt road on the Gilman Farm that runs along the river through a low pasture to the swimming place. It is about a quarter mile down the road. Cows graze placidly in the green pasture between the road and the river. The sun is hot and it is not yet noon.

"That water's going to feel good," Eddie says.

"Yeah." In the fall, on that part of the pasture that rises sharply from the road to the top of the hill where the Gilman house sits, Johnny has seen deer grazing among the cows, each oblivious of the other.

Eddie slows down a couple of hundred yards short of the big oak tree; Johnny feels his breath on his neck come quicker.

"Why are you slowing down?" he asks Eddie, sensing that something is wrong.

"You see someone up ahead?"

Johnny squints against the bright sunlight reflected off the emerald-green pasture. "I don't see anybody." Eddie stops the bike; they dismount.

"Look." Eddie points off in the direction of the oak. Johnny follows his finger. Finally, he spots several figures that could be human, not bovine.

"Probably kids swimming. So what?"

"I don't know," Eddie says, remounting his bike. "I got this feeling. Get on." He pedals slowly along the road in the direction of the figures. In a little while they make out five boys smoking cigarettes and throwing things, probably rocks, into the river. Eddie turns onto the pasture twenty-five yards from the swimming place and stops. The boys spot Eddie and Johnny and begin to walk toward them. Johnny senses Eddie's fear; it makes him afraid himself. As the five boys approach, Johnny recognizes the blond-headed Butch McKay. His fear dissolves.

"Hey, that's Butch McKay," he says to Eddie. I smoked cigarettes with him and Willie Mahoney up in the woods by his house." Johnny looks for Mahoney in the group, but he's not among them. None of the other boys is familiar to him.

"Get back on the bike," Eddie whispers. But it's too late. The boys, Butch McKay in the lead, are upon them.

"Whatta we got here?" Butch says.

"Looks like a fucking Frenchman to me," one of the boys answers.

"No, it's two fucking Frenchmen," Butch says. Johnny's neck hair bristles.

"What are two fucking frogs doing at our swimming hole?" one of the boys says, as they form a circle around Eddie and Johnny.

"Don't bother with the pollywog," Butch says. "You're lucky you're still a tadpole, Labalm," Butch says directly to Johnny before turning to Eddie to hit him flush on the mouth with his fist. Eddie is bigger than Butch, bigger than any of the other boys too, but the five of them are too much for him. They get him to the ground, and swarm over him, kicking him in the side, in the groin, in the face. They flick their lighted cigarettes at him when they're done kicking. Johnny watches, whimpering and sobbing.

"Don't let us catch you frogs down here again, understand? Next time you'll really get hurt. Understand?" Eddie is writhing on the ground, moaning, blood pouring from his nose and mouth; his hands are thrust between his legs. "Let's go," Butch McKay says to his companions. He stops and uses his heel to stomp on the spokes of the front wheel of Eddie's bike. The boys wander off, laughing.

Johnny, frightened by all the blood on Eddie's face, and by the sounds he is making, cries uncontrollably. He can't be sure how long they remain there, Eddie, crying and moaning with pain and humiliation, his red blood stark against the green pasture grass. Eventually a pickup truck stops on the road opposite where they are lying on the grass, and a young man in bibbed overalls and a billed cap gets out of the cab and walks quickly in their direction.

"What happened to you guys?" the young man says, squatting down beside Eddie, who has his back turned to him, and who continues to make those awful animal sounds. Between blubbering sobs, Johnny tries to explain to the man what happened. He knows he sounds incoherent. "Settle down," the man says in a calm, "settled down" voice. "I seen them kids swimming earlier when I came back from town. I'd recognize them if I saw them again. You want to report this to Chief Cristy?" At the mention of Groveton's police chief, Eddie rolls over to face the young man.

"I ain't no squealer."

"I guess that's your business." The young man notices Eddie's bike with the staved in spokes. "You're not going to be able to ride that." He picks the bike up off the ground. "Come on. Hop in the back of the truck. I'll take you home." He looks at Eddie's face. The bleeding has stopped; there is a crust of dried blood around his nostrils and on his chin. "You want me to take you down to the clinic to have that face looked at?"

"I'll be all right." Eddie gets to his feet. He touches his ribs with his fingertips and makes a face.

"Come on then." The man hoists Eddie's bike over his shoulder with one hand. "Watch your step. The place is mined with meadow muffins." He laughs, and Johnny laughs too, in spite of himself. Eddie does not laugh. They walk to the pickup truck, careful not to step in fresh cow droppings.

They sit in the bed of the pickup truck, which smells of manure, and is covered with loose hay, as it bumps along the road. Eddie is silent, somewhere inside himself. Johnny has a lot of questions he wants to ask him, but it is obvious to him that now is not the time to ask them. He doesn't understand why the boys—Butch McKay in particular, who he thought was a kind of friend of his—would want to beat up Eddie whom they didn't know except as a "Frenchman." How did they even know that? Did Frenchmen have a particular look about them that identified them right away to people who were not French? He knows, of course, that he is at least half French himself, but of his other "half" he has no knowledge. Butch knew, from his name, that Johnny was French, but had spared him because at eight years old he was considered a tadpole. From what he has seen of the way they hurt poor Eddie, he is grateful that he is a mere tadpole. But why should they be so hateful toward French people? He wants to ask Eddie, and wonders how long he will have to wait.

As the pickup approaches Royer's Village Store, Eddie turns toward the open back window and says something to the driver that Johnny can't hear. The pickup slows down and pulls to the curb in front of the store.

"Come on," Eddie says, picking his bike up and placing it on the sidewalk. "I'll treat you to a Fudgicle."

"You sure you guys are all right?" the young man says from the pickup.

"We'll be okay," Eddie says. "Thanks for the ride."

"Take it easy," he says and drives up Western Avenue in the direction of the Trade School.

"Watch the bike." Eddie walks up the steps to the store and in a little while returns with two Fudgicles. When Johnny can't afford the quarter for Moulton's hot fudge sundaes, he makes do with five-cent Fudgicles, the next best thing. Royer's has kids coming in every day in summer in hopes of discovering the word FREE burned on the wooden stick when they finish the one they purchased. Once Johnny landed back-to-back FREE sticks.

They sit on the curb to eat their Fudgicles, not wanting to leave the premises in case one or both of them should get lucky. It is by now after twelve o'clock; the sun is high overhead, and it is blazing hot on the pavement, with no shade.

"Does it still hurt?" Johnny asks his friend.

"Nah. Just a little here." Eddie points to his ribs. Eddie finishes his Fudgicle quickly. "Shit," he says, inspecting his blank stick. "Hurry up so we can get going. I got to get home and fix my wheel."

"Didn't it hurt your lip to eat the Fudgicle? What's your mother going to think when she sees you?"

"I'll tell her I fell off the bike on the street. She'll believe anything I tell her."

"Did you know any of those guys?"

"I seen 'em around, but I don't know their names or anything. We'll see how tough they are one at a time."

"What if they're always together?"

"Don't be stupid. They can't be together *all* the time. I ain't in no hurry. They're going to be sorry. Especially your pal Butch."

"He's not really my pal. I just smoked cigarettes with him once, him and Willie Mahoney up ..."

"I know, up in the woods by Butch's house."

"Willie had a .20 gauge shotgun. He shot this red squirrel out of a tree because it was bothering him with its chattering."

"Some pals you got."

Johnny carries the broken wheel, which Eddie removed from his bike; Eddie has the bike slung over his shoulder. They walk up Western Avenue, past the Trade School, and turn onto Barker Avenue where Eddie lives, at the bottom of the hill. Johnny can take a shortcut from Barker Avenue through the woods to the back of his house.

"He's not my pal," Johnny repeats.

"So what were you doing smoking with him?"

"Dan Bean brought me up to meet them—Butch and Willie. He's friends with them. They had cigarettes."

"You inhale?"

"I pretended to." Johnny remembered inhaling his mother's cigarette when he was a kid and choking like crazy. That memory was enough to cause him to refrain from inhaling the one Butch McKay gave him. "Are you going to beat them all up one at a time?"

"Goddamn right I am. I'm going to pound the living shit out of every last one of them." Johnny has no doubt that Eddie can do as he says. What he doubts is that he'll ever be able to take one of them on without the rest of them ganging up on him. Eddie sounds determined, so Johnny does not express his reservations. Just before they arrive at the path through the woods to Johnny's house, however, he hears himself blurt: "Why do they want to hurt French people?"

"I don't know. They got to hurt somebody, I guess. Might as well be a Frenchman. There ain't no niggers living around here."

Johnny has never laid eyes on a Negro except in the movies. "But why?"

"Don't ask stupid questions."

* * *

Johnny's mind is too active that night to allow him to fall asleep right away. He reenacts the scene on the Gilman Farm meadow that morning, except this time he comes to Eddie's assistance, tackling Butch McKay after he sucker punches Eddie. He pounds on Butch, while Eddie deals with the other four boys. They tussle for a long time; eventually Johnny and Eddie vanquish the boys, who run off crying and bloody. Johnny and Eddie are bloodied up pretty badly themselves, but instead of crying they laugh triumphantly, arms slung over each other's shoulders. The young man in the pickup truck witnesses the fight and expresses his admiration at the way the two of them handled the five bullies. Johnny puts himself to sleep with this version of the morning's events. Eddie makes him promise not to tell his grandmother what happened, and upon pain of having the shit kicked out of him, he is to keep his big mouth shut on the subject when he is around Eddie's parents. Eddie thinks Johnny runs off at the mouth too much. Johnny supposes Eddie is right, but sometimes his exuberance overwhelms him and the only way he can give it expression is with words.

"One of these days I'm going to stuff a dirty sock in that big mouth of yours," is one of Eddie's expressions. Eddie is his very best friend, and he prefers not to question why Eddie would want to hang around with him, an eight-year-old, instead of guys his own age. All that changes when Eddie enters high school a year from that fall.

It would possibly have crushed him even more to lose Eddie as his best friend had he not been preoccupied with a change in his life that was even more devastating than the loss of Eddie's friendship. It is the summer before the fall when Eddie enters high school that Johnny is forced to leave his grandmother's care and go to live with his mother and her husband, Bill Scanlon, and their two squalling children in their cramped third-floor apartment in the alley behind Main Street.

For reasons that don't need to be spoken of out loud, Eddie doesn't take Johnny swimming at Gilman Farm the next day as he had planned to do. Instead, they spend the day in the woods behind Eddie's house, on a steep hill, at a site where Eddie plans to build, with Johnny's help, a cabin—a secret cabin.

"You can help me clear the brush out. The cabin's going to fit right between those two birches," Eddie says, pointing to the thick undergrowth between the birches he refers to. "Nobody will be able to spot it no matter what direction they come from; the only way anybody could find it would be to stumble right into it." They sit on a piece of sloping ground among brambles, eating chokecherries, as Eddie explains his architectural scheme. Johnny nods his head at everything Eddie says even if he can scarcely picture what he is describing. Not that it matters; what matters is that Eddie has taken him into his confidence, even with Eddie's knowledge of what a blabbermouth he is.

Eddie seems not to have suffered any ill effects from the beating he received yesterday at the hands of Butch Mckay and his friends. Johnny feels a little guilty, not to mention stupid, for allowing himself to be carried away last night with his fantasies about yesterday morning. He would no more have gotten between Butch and his companions' fists and feet and Eddie's body than he would have walked in front of a moving car. The realization that he is a physical coward depresses him, and when he thinks about what his uncles went through in the war he feels even worse.

"What are you moping about? You weren't the one got the shit beat out of you," Eddie says, perhaps annoyed by Johnny's lack of responsiveness to his grand plan.

"I'm sorry."

"Don't go fucking bawling on me. It's not your fault. I'm kind of surprised they didn't pound on you too, come to think of it. They'll pay, just you wait and see if they don't."

"You should take them up here and beat them up. Nobody would ever know."

"Nobody comes here but you and me. Get that through your hard head. All right?"

"Okay. Did you fix your bike?"

"Took me all afternoon. Good as new."

"Want to go fish for suckers?"

"I thought we'd haul some two-by-fours up here while Pa's at work. He's got a bunch in the barn he'll never miss."

Johnny is not eager to do anything as strenuous as haul lumber up a steep hill through thorny underbrush. He would rather lounge on the bank by the river that runs below Barker Avenue, throw a line in the water and wait for suckers to bite. Eddie's father works in the foundry where Johnny's grandfather worked for over fifty years, and would have been working still if he hadn't been laid low by two strokes, and then the third, which was fatal. Johnny has a kind of dread of the foundry, though as close as he has ever gotten to the inside of it is just outside the dirty window where he used to deliver his grandfather's lunch pail. His grandmother prepared his lunch every day as close to noon as possible so that the poor man would have some hot soup in his stomach to get him through to five o'clock, quitting time. From what he could see of the inside through the window, opaque with what could be a century of grime, put him in mind of a dungeon. His dreams occasionally have this dungeon-like quality, and he sometimes experiences a dread of growing up and having to go to work there (the way his Uncle Ira will do when he gets out of the Navy).

"Come on. We'll do a little hauling, then have a piece of apple pie. My mother baked a couple fresh ones this morning." Johnny likes Mrs. Leclerc's cooking, especially her pies and cakes, but he would gladly sacrifice her apple pie if he could be spared the task of lugging heavy boards up the hill. He follows Eddie down the hill to his house.

"What did your mother say when she saw you yesterday?" Mrs. Leclerc is hanging out wash on the line beside the house when the boys arrive.

"I didn't give her a chance to say anything. I just told her we took a spill on Western Avenue. She was more worried about how you were than she was about me. Come to think of it, maybe we better not let her see you. I told her you scraped your arms and legs a little but weren't hurt too bad." Johnny has on short pants and a polo shirt. There are no signs of bruising on his arms or legs. "Why don't you head down to the river. I'll get my bike and a couple of poles, and some bait and pick you up. I don't want her to see you."

"Okay."

Eddie keeps a stockpile of night crawlers in a can of dirt in his shed. Johnny is relieved not to have to work hard and get all sweaty and dirty. He isn't that keen on fishing either, but it is better than heavy lifting. They catch half a dozen suckers and throw them back. Then, bored with hooking the passive creatures, Eddie, with Johnny on the crossbar, pedals a tacking path up steep Barker Avenue. Exhausted at the top of the hill, Eddie stops to rest. They are on the sidewalk in front of Johnny's house. The big front lawn is lined with elm trees on three sides. Next to the lawn is a deep gully separating Johnny's house from Barker Avenue.

Last fall Johnny and Gibby Gilbert, a sickly kid who lived in the mansion at the top of Western Avenue, hunkered down in the gulley at night and pelted cars traveling along Western Avenue with their pea shooters. One car they sprayed braked to a screeching stop and a man got out. Like frightened rabbits, Johnny and Gibby Gilbert scrambled down the hill to the bottom of the gulley among thick burdock. Gibby was so upset it brought on an asthma attack and Johnny, alarmed by his gasping companion, started to cry. Gibby, used to such attacks, recovered, but made it a point never to play with Johnny Labalm again. The Gilberts sold the mansion to the Elks that winter and moved away, presumably to a climate more suitable to their son's delicate health.

When Eddie gets his breath back he suggests they go to the Groveton Museum of Natural History and look at the new Japanese samurai collection. Johnny is put in mind of the souvenirs his Uncle Mitch brought back from the war: the sword taken from a dead Jap; Japanese cigarettes; a Jap aviator's goggles. Johnny likes to stop by the glass encased stuffed buffalo on the main floor; he likes to stare into its malevolent dead eye. He remembers the nature classes he attended at the museum after school last fall, and how confused he had been at the instructor's choice of words to describe the tongue of a dairy cow as consisting of microscopic "cunts" that were suited to its herbivorous diet. To Johnny the word "cunt" was associated with something naughty, a word used by boys like Alvin Farr. It may have been all in his imagination, but Johnny sensed that the instructor, a man with silky hair and very moist lips, delighted in using the word, and in fact used it many times. When Johnny got to school the next day, he tried to look up the word in the dictionary. It wasn't listed. After *cunning* came *cup*. No cunt. Johnny never went back to the nature classes at the museum.

As if seized by an irresistible impulse, Johnny takes two ripe tomatoes off the sidewalk display stand in front of Rouselle's Fruit and keeps walking. Eddie is a few feet ahead of him, pushing his bike on the sidewalk, and doesn't see Johnny steal the fruit.

"Johnny." Johnny turns at the sound of his name in the direction of the familiar voice. Uncle Mitch is getting out of the passenger side of a car parked in front of Rouselle's. Johnny had stuffed the tomatoes in his pants' pockets. "Did you pay Mr. Rouselle for the tomatoes you took?" Johnny is paralyzed. He can't speak. Tears well in his eyes as he shakes his head in the negative. Mitch reaches in his pocket and hands Johnny two quarters. "You must have forgot. By the way, I didn't know you liked tomatoes. You never eat the ones Grammy puts on the table. So, you like tomatoes?" Johnny nods again, this time in the affirmative. Johnny can see, peripherally, Eddie, in front of Goslin's Pharmacy, looking back at him and his uncle.

"I'll remember that," Mitch says. "I'll let Grammy know so she can be sure to get plenty of tomatoes for you from now on."

Johnny Labalm hates tomatoes, but he likes stealing things, whether it's tomatoes off Rouselle's Fruit stand, or useless trinkets from the Five-and-Ten Cent Store on Railroad Street. Eddie doesn't know about his penchant for shoplifting; somehow Johnny knows he would disapprove. He goes inside the store and hands Mr. Rouselle, who has apparently no knowledge of Johnny's attempted theft, a quarter for the two tomatoes he took. He gets back fifteen cents in change. Uncle Mitch is in the car again, and when Johnny comes out on the sidewalk it is backing out of its parking space. Johnny recognizes Sean Murphy behind the wheel. He is Mitch's old high school chum. Johnny finds himself forty cents richer, but he feels dreadful.

Eddie loves tomatoes; he bites into the one Johnny gives him the way one bites into an apple.

"You can have this one too, you want," he says to Eddie.

"What did you buy them for if you don't want them?"

"I don't know."

"You're such a dumb fuck sometimes." Eddie takes the other tomato and consumes it with a just a few sucking bites. "Ever try 'em with sugar?"

"No."

"You ought to; especially store bought ones. You don't need sugar on the ones Pa grows in the garden. They're sweet enough. Let's get going." The museum is a short distance away. Johnny has lost his enthusiasm for the new samurai collection. He can't conceal his misery from Eddie. "What the fuck's the matter with you now? I swear to God, you're moodier'n a goddamn girl."

"Sorry."

"Come on. I'm taking you home. Jesus H. baldheaded Christ!" Johnny does not object to being taken home, even though he is in dread of what faces him when Mitch tells Grammy that he caught her little saint stealing tomatoes like a common criminal. It follows that his secret life as a thief will be found out as well.

That is why he is surprised at Mitch's behavior toward him; he would have expected righteous outrage, a lecture on morality, a demand for penance. That is exactly what his mother would have predicted from her "self-righteous" younger brother. In the infrequent visits she has paid her mother and her son she has made no secret of her feelings about Mitch, whom she considers an uppity snob, who considers himself better than she is, better than Ira too. In Johnny's opinion there is nobody better than Ira, but he is also very fond of his Uncle Mitch. He has promised Johnny that he can be mascot of the American Legion basketball team he is starting up in the winter. Now he must worry about whether his tomato stealing will change Mitch's mind. Johnny goes into the bedroom, lies down on the bed he shares with his Grammy now that Grampa is gone, and frets.

That evening at supper Johnny discovers, to his surprise and horror, a plate of sliced tomatoes on the table along with the bowls of mashed potatoes and peas that accompany the hamburger patties. Hamburger is his favorite food (perhaps the only food that he truly relishes) and Grammy makes an effort to prepare it as often as possible. Mitch sits at the head of the table (the place Grampa used to occupy) watching Johnny, an amused expression on his face.

"I told your uncle you don't have no use for tomatoes, Johnny, but he tells me I'm wrong, as if I don't know my own Johnny."

"Just give him a couple of slices, Ma. Watch him eat them up as fast as he eats that hamburger. Just watch." And Mitch forks two thick slices of the vile fruit, as red as some bloody thing, onto Johnny's plate. Johnny feels as though he is going to be sick as he looks down at the two slabs of red pulp between his potatoes and his meat. Then he remembers what Eddie had said in front of the museum earlier that day.

"Please pass the sugar, please," he says to his Grammy. Mitch looks as much confused as amused as Johnny spoons sugar over the tomatoes before hazarding a bite. It is the first tomato to ever pass Johnny Labalm's lips. Until now, his aversion to them has been purely visual. The same cannot be said of tripe and calf's liver; his taste buds and olfactory gland have collaborated in that rebellion. Johnny discovers yet another reason for valuing Eddie Leclerc's friendship, and he has all he can do to refrain from expressing his delight at his uncle's sudden chagrin as he, Johnny, devours the two slices of tomato and asks for more. It occurs to his instincts, however, that he should not overdo it in case Mitch should decide that his little object lesson has backfired, and elects to tell Grammy all. He does no such thing, and over the years the incident becomes their shared inside joke.

Everything goes to pieces before the summer is over. Grammy is forced to give up the house on Western Avenue. She takes Johnny to New Hampshire to live with Aunt Lily and her husband. It happens so fast Johnny doesn't even have time to say goodbye to Eddie. A new town, a new school; he has to make new friends. Lily is pregnant with her first child (the first of seven); Grammy and Johnny are clearly a hardship for her and her husband Howard. The next thing he knows, they are back in Groveton, living in the house of an elderly widow, an old friend of Grammy. Johnny is delighted to be back in the town he loves even if he has to go to a different school than the one he attended last year. The first thing he does is call on Eddie at his house.

"Where did you disappear to? You been gone a long time."

"We went to live in New Hampshire for awhile. I didn't like it. Did you get to beat up Butch McKay and those guys?"

"I ain't seen any of 'em since that day."

Johnny assumes Eddie has not gone back to the swimming hole at Gilman's Farm.

"Funny how you never see hill kids in town. It's like they got their own little world up there." Johnny feels like he has said something smart, has made an astute observation about the kids who live in that part of Groveton above the foundry that everyone calls "the hill."

"Yeah. The hillbillies. I ain't in no hurry, but I ain't going to forget either." Eddie attends St. Ignatius, the French Catholic school, so he isn't likely to run into any of the "hill" boys there, they being mostly Irish and Scotch. Johnny has heard stories about the nuns of St. Ignatius that make the hair on the back of his neck stand up, stories about how they take a ruler to your knuckles if you speak out of turn. Last June, on the final day of school, Johnny watched from the sidewalk—separated from the St. Ignatius schoolyard by a chain link fence—the kids burning their textbooks in a fifty-gallon drum, the flames shooting up to the second story of the gray schoolhouse. The kids danced around the burning books like pagans. Johnny asked Eddie at the time why St. Ignatius kids burned their books. "Why not?" he had said. "We paid for 'em." Paid for or not, it seemed wrong to burn a book, in Johnny's opinion, although he wouldn't have known how to begin arguing against it with Eddie, or anybody else. For Johnny books have a magical quality, something sacred, like the things he is supposed to cherish about religion. Not being able to put into words what it is he feels about books, or why he thinks it amounts to a sacrilege to burn them, leaves him feeling frustrated. But who would know better about sin and sacrilege than the Catholic priests and nuns who run St. Ignatius School?

"You should come to St. Ignatius," Eddie says, as if he has been reading Johnny's mind.

"Sister Marie wants me to."

"You should. They teach you things, the nuns. Not like in public school."

Johnny wouldn't mind going to St. Ignatius if the nuns were like Sister Marie, his catechism teacher. But the things he's heard about St. Ignatius nuns frankly scare him. At least in public school there is no corporal punishment.

"What's Father Richard like," Johnny asks. At Sunday mass he seems remote, spiritually above the congregation, the kind of person Johnny associates with saints.

"He don't do no teaching. He's like your principal. If the nuns send you downstairs to his office in the basement, get ready to have your pants pulled down and a strap laid acrost your ass."

He can no more imagine Father Richard taking a strap to a kid than he could have pictured his Grampa doing it to his kids, Johnny's aunts and uncles. It's all moot, his going to St. Ignatius, because there is no money in his household for tuition. Johnny doesn't want to say this to Eddie. Eddie's family is by no means well off—far from it—but Johnny is ashamed of his circumstances, nevertheless.

"Being poor is nothing to be ashamed of," Grammy says over and over, as if she is trying to convince herself as much as her grandson of its truth. But saying it doesn't make it true. There *is* something about being poor that is shameful. Johnny will come to understand this more profoundly when he goes to live with his mother and Bill Scanlon a year hence.

"I've got a teacher named Mrs. Bowan this year," Johnny says, as if this is the reason he's giving to turn down the superior education offered by the nuns of St. Ignatius. "She's nice." Eddie grunts his contempt of "nice" teachers.

"St. Ignatius kids always do better at the Academy than public school kids," Eddie argues.

Johnny can't see how this could be possible given that St. Ignatius students have so little respect for knowledge that they show it by burning their books. Johnny doesn't dare say this to Eddie. Eddie has rigged a basket and a wooden backboard on one of the trees at the end of his driveway.

"Come on, I'll take you on in a game of HORSE." Eddie puts up a one-handed push shot that goes cleanly through the new twine without touching the rim. "I'll spot you H-O-R."

"Can I shoot two-handed?" Johnny hasn't the strength to carry the ball in the air the distance that Eddie made his shot. He comes up short.

"Give the boy an H." Eddie now lays a hook shot in off the backboard. It takes Eddie a mere five shots to beat Johnny, with his three letter spot.

"You finish the cabin?"

"Still ain't got a door on it. I got time before it snows, if I still feel like it." Eddie sinks three fifteen-footers in a row. He wants to make the Academy varsity squad by his sophomore year. Johnny should work on his own game. He starts his mascoting duties for Mitch's Legion team in the winter, and Mitch wants him to lead the team onto the floor and take the first shot of the pre-game warm-up.

"Can we go up and see it?"

Eddie shrugs his square shoulders. "I guess." He takes one final shot before leading Johnny up the path behind his house to the secret cabin, where Johnny had, earlier that summer, just after school ended, confessed to Eddie that he hadn't been able to screw Mary Alice McGinnis after all the trouble he and Alvin Farr had gone through (Alvin more than Eddie) to set it up for him. What he has not confessed to Eddie is what happened later on, after the Mary Alice McGinnis fiasco.

It was just before the grand opening of the new Lion's Club swimming pool. Johnny, who had "supervised" the construction from the ground up by making a nuisance of himself with the workers, took an almost proprietary interest in the pool, and was excited at the prospect of its actual opening. So absorbed was he in the sight of the finished product that he took no notice of the approach of the car behind him, or the appearance of the man beside him at the chain link fence.

"I didn't mean to startle you, son," the man said with a smile. He had a soft, friendly voice; he wore a brown suit and a gray broad-brimmed hat. What caught Johnny's attention, however, was the hand painted head of a collie dog on his necktie. "Bet you can't wait for the pool to open so you can go in for a swim." Johnny nodded his head. The truth was he didn't know how to swim (Mitch would give him his first lesson in a couple of weeks by throwing him in at the deep end of the pool). The man continued talking in his quiet voice. He asked Johnny questions about himself: did he like baseball? Did he have a lot of friends? Where did he live? What did he like to do on his summer vacation? Ever since Eddie had completed the frame of their secret cabin Johnny had been almost ready to explode with the desire to boast about it to somebody. The stranger with the painted necktie seemed perfect inasmuch as he was a grownup and would therefore have no territorial designs on the cabin, the way kids his own age would have if they found out about it, which was why Eddie had promised to pound the living shit out of him if he blabbed to anyone.

The man seemed very interested in the secret cabin, and before he knew it Johnny was leading him through the woods behind the swimming pool. When they got to the cabin with its four posts, a doorframe and floor in place, the man sat down in the doorway and, after admiring the workmanship (Johnny claimed to have had an equal hand in its construction) he pulled Johnny down on his lap, gently, not forcefully. But however gently the man handled him, Johnny's fear was instantaneous. Instinctively he squirmed off the man's lap and bolted for the path in back of the cabin that led to Eddie's house. He ran as fast as he was able (which was not, and never would be, very fast) not daring to look behind him for fear that the man would be in pursuit. He made it to the clearing by the shed behind Eddie's house, gasping for breath, sweating like he had never sweat before, his bare arms bleeding from running through thorns and brambles. He collapsed on the ground in front of the shed, not caring at that point whether the man with the collie necktie had followed him or not. Neither Eddie nor Mrs. Leclerc was in the yard or in the garden by the side of the house; Eddie's father would have been at work. Johnny, when he had regained his breath and become fearful again, turned around slowly and looked in the direction he'd come from. He could see no one. He breathed easier, becoming conscious at the same time of the painful scratches oozing blood on both arms.

"What the fuck happened to you?" Eddie had said when Johnny found him in the kitchen.

Johnny made up a story about taking the path from the swimming pool to the cabin, and thinking he heard someone following him, he ran off the path into the woods so he wouldn't lead whoever it was to the cabin.

"I think you're lying through your ass," Eddie had said. "You brought one of your fucking buddies to the cabin, didn't you, you little shit."

"I did not." Johnny began to cry. In a way it was the truth. The man with the painted necktie was certainly no friend of his. Eddie had been hard to convince, and Johnny was never really sure if he believed his story. Nothing could have persuaded him to tell Eddie what really happened.

By now there is a roof on the cabin, and four walls with spaces between the barn boards large enough to let in shafts of sunlight. There is the doorframe but no door.

"When are you going to put the door in?"

"Never, probably."

"Never? Why?"

"I got no more interest. It was a stupid idea in the first place, a 'secret' cabin," Eddie says, contempt in his voice. "Who would give a shit?"

"You don't think I showed anybody, you know that time?"

"Don't matter. I don't give a shit now." Eddie produces a pack of cigarettes from his back pocket. Eddie doesn't offer him one even though he knows that Johnny has smoked before. He has always preached against smoking cigarettes if you were ever serious about playing sports.

"I thought you wanted to make varsity at the Academy," Johnny says.

"What do you mean?" Eddie extinguishes the match between his thumb and forefinger.

"You're smoking."

"No shit, Sherlock. So what?"

"You told me not to smoke if I wanted to play ball."

"I did?"

"Yes."

"Well, now that you've seen the fucking cabin …"

"Can I have a cigarette?"

"No. You're too young."

"You didn't say I was too young when I told you I smoked cigarettes with Butch …" Johnny thinks it might be a mistake to mention Butch McKay's name to Eddie. Eddie gives him a look that tells him he is correct in thinking it's a mistake to mention Butch's name. "Sorry," Johnny says, his voice barely audible.

"You should be Here, you want to smoke so bad." Eddie shakes a cigarette out of his pack of Lucky Strikes. Johnny takes it and places it between his lips waiting for Eddie to light him up. "What?" Eddie says.

"You going to give me a light?"

"I gave you a cigarette. Find your own light."

Johnny hands the cigarette back to Eddie. He doesn't really feel like smoking anyway.

"After you nigger-lipped it? No thanks. Here." Eddie strikes a match on the rough doorframe and offers Johnny a light. Johnny puffs on the cigarette but doesn't dare inhale. He sees that Eddie does inhale. "Make sure that thing's out," he says, digging a hole in the dirt outside the cabin door and burying his lighted butt. "I don't want you burning down the fucking woods on me."

There is a long silence between them that has Johnny feeling uneasy, as if Eddie would rather be anywhere in the world at this moment than with him. If Eddie thinks he, Johnny, is too young to smoke maybe he realizes—even after all the time they have been friends—that he is also too young to hang out with. Eddie smokes another cigarette. The silence between them is palpable. Johnny pretends to inspect the inside of the cabin, as if there is anything about the floorboards and four walls that need inspection. Finally, Eddie grinds out his cigarette in the dirt with the heel of his shoe, gets up and brushes off the seat of his pants.

"Let's get going," he announces. Johnny follows him down the path feeling wretched in his wake, looking at Eddie's indifferent back, clad in denim shirt.

Back at the house, Eddie picks up his basketball and takes random shots at the basket. He doesn't offer to let Johnny take a shot, or challenge him to another game of HORSE.

"I should be going," Johnny says after awhile, his voice almost breaking. Eddie acts as though he doesn't hear him; he continues to throw up shots at the basket. Johnny walks away. Halfway up Barker Avenue he starts to cry. He cries all the way home.

* * *

The next time he saw Eddie Leclerc was a few years after he had moved away from Groveton, when he returned to visit his grandmother who was living, at the time, with his Uncle Ira and his wife Alice. Eddie was by then a senior at the Academy, and had grown to a height of six-feet two inches, and had been starting forward on the varsity basketball team since his sophomore year, cigarettes and all. Ironically, when Jack (as he was by that time calling himself) went to visit him, Eddie was shooting baskets at the end of the driveway. If he hadn't seen him in the familiar setting of the house on Barker Avenue, Jack doubted that he would have recognized him. He was a man now, with well-formed features, a muscular upper body, and a full head of dark brown hair. He had wondered if Eddie had ever taken his revenge on Butch McKay and his friends. Something prevented him from asking Eddie. Eddie was bound for Springfield Teachers College on a basketball scholarship after graduation.

* * *

Scanlon paid frequent visits to his hometown while he lived in Garrison, New Hampshire. Each time he was filled with nostalgia and regret that he had ever been forced to leave. Groveton held, and continued to hold, for him a special tender place in his soul, and when he left it for the second time in 1969 it was with a similar feeling of sorrow and regret, although for quite different reasons.

And now he was put in mind of his poor grandmother, who had succumbed to dementia late in her life, who little Johnny Labalm had clung to for dear life for the first nine years of his life.

Fourteen

Picture a warm evening in June 1948, the air softened by a late afternoon shower. Here come Johnny and his grandmother on their way to the Palace Theater to watch their last movie together, probably a western if Scanlon knows their taste in movies. Next door at the Arcadia, a romance starring Virginia Mayo is playing. Neither Johnny nor his grandmother can stomach that kind of movie.

Across the street, on the sidewalk in front of Sears and Roebuck, Wally is setting up his wagon for the movie crowd. Wally sells nickel bags of popcorn, and steamed dogs for a dime. He is a funny-looking little man with his straw hat, wire-rimmed glasses, and arm garters on his shirtsleeves. Grammy buys Johnny a bag of popcorn to take with him into the theater. The Palace management has given up trying to stop customers from bringing Wally's popcorn and dogs into the theater. They sell their own popcorn at the concession counter, but it is stale and they charge a dime. They sell enough of it in the winter when it is too cold for Wally to be on the street with his wagon.

Grammy holds his hand and cries through the whole movie. What little popcorn Johnny can eat lodges in the middle of his chest. He watches the movie but his mind couldn't have been on it.

Out on the sidewalk in front of the Palace after the movie: Neither of them knows how to say goodbye. Grammy starts to weep noisily, and as miserable as he feels himself, her crying like that in public embarrasses him to the point where he almost runs away from her. He tries to concentrate on Wally's popcorn wagon across the street so he won't have to deal with saying goodbye forever to his grandmother. It is not that he won't see her again, but it will never be the same. Freshly popped kernels of corn escape from the metal container like newborn animal creatures and fall to the bottom of the glass showcase. The smell of popcorn is all through the air.

Next door to the Palace is a barbershop with a big, lighted pole. The red and white spiraling pole holds Johnny in a trance-like state. The Italian Villa restaurant, owned by the Mancuso brothers, chums of Mitch from high school, is next door to the barbershop. Mitch has taken Johnny there for spaghetti a few times. It is a popular spot with people after the second show. There are the streetlights, the lights from the storefronts and from the movie theater marquees. The evening is warm and full of this artificial light and the pervasive odor of Wally's popcorn. Johnny feels hot, his skin alive, as if he has on a wool shirt. Grammy is making a public spectacle of herself with her crying. What a tableau they must have presented to the passerby, this silly little bird of an old woman and her spoiled nine-year-old grandson, standing on the sidewalk in front of a small-town movie house, she carrying on as though gypsies have snatched away her beloved grandson, he trying to act like he's never seen this crazy woman before.

Scanlon can't remember how they ever managed to part. The next image he has is of his grandmother walking away from the front of the Palace down the street in the direction of the railroad station, and Johnny walking up the steep avenue in the opposite direction. He stops once and turns for a last look at his grandmother, no doubt expecting to see her standing there on the sidewalk watching him go away from her. Instead, she is walking in her comical bow-legged way, down the street and out of his life. He wants very much to cry himself, but he would never allow himself, not even at nine years old, to do it in public.

His mother's apartment is on the third floor of a tenement building in the alley behind Main Street's stores. There are three identical such buildings; he will live with his new family in the middle one. The address is Freeman Court, but the address doesn't make it any less an alley, and on this moonless night, a very dark alley. Johnny turns in at the Western Avenue entrance and is at once swallowed up in darkness. There is only sound and smell: water dripping, a fan blowing kitchen smells out of a Main Street restaurant, something rattling the garbage cans that are numerous in the alley. Cats? Rats? Johnny hurries his step; it is treacherous underfoot, the pavement broken in places, and slippery. There are potholes that can turn an ankle if you aren't careful. Despite the warmth of the June evening, in the alley Johnny feels a chill.

A single low-watt bulb lights the front door of his mother's building. Inside, the light in the vestibule is out. It stinks in the hallway even if he can't identify the source of the stink. Dirt is what it smells like. Dirt, Grammy's catchall word for everything that is vile. There is no handrail; he has to reach out until he can touch the clammy wall and at first has to get both feet on a step before he dares to try for the next one. It takes him a long time to get up the three flights of stairs. Thin cracks of light emerge from the bottoms of the doors to the apartments on either side of the hall. There is only noise—blaring radios and wailing babies, people swearing. It could be a scene from a Palace Theater movie. He has visited his mother here two or three times before, but always in daylight. He is deeply ashamed to be a part of this world, and will lie constantly to his schoolmates about where he lives. He will manufacture elaborate excuses for never inviting any of his friends to his home.

He is exhausted by the time he reaches his mother's apartment off the third floor landing. He raps softy on the door. His mother's voice on the other side is cheerful as she invites him to come in.

She sits at the built-in kitchen table in a tiny alcove at the far end of the narrow room. There are benches, like restaurant booths, built in the walls around three sides of the table. She is smoking and working a crossword puzzle. Once he is inside, she doesn't seem particularly pleased to see him. She offers him a glass of cider, asks him if he wants to sit down. It is all so utterly unceremonious that he wonders why she has put up such a fuss about having him come to live with her. He sits at the kitchen table and drinks his cider. The climb up the stairs has made him thirsty. He has always been struck by what is not in this room more than what is. There is no refrigerator. Food has to be kept cold on the window ledge. What happens in the summer? The oil range has a single burner, no oven. The sink is tiny and has only a coldwater tap. In the bathroom there is no tub, only a small sink, and a toilet with an old-fashioned pull-chain flusher. There is no hot water in the bathroom either. There are two other rooms in the apartment, both bedrooms. His mother shares one with Bill Scanlon, and Johnny will share the other with his two half-brothers. Billy is a year and eight months old, Keith just seven months. Billy is a colicky baby and has problems sleeping.

His mother shows him the narrow bed he will sleep in, in the small room made to seem even smaller by the presence of two cribs. Sick at heart, Johnny undresses for bed, conscious of the breathing coming from the cribs. He has brought no clothes with him, no possessions at all. Scanlon wonders why. As he undresses, the clouds break and moonlight illuminates the room through a single window, a window that looks out on the adjoining tenement, which seems close enough to reach out and touch. He can see enough beyond the edge of the building to recognize the playground of St. Mary's School for Catholic Girls. There is a seesaw, and a swing set with three swings, one of which is broken.

He lies awake on his back for a long time. There is no sign of his stepfather in the apartment. Bill Scanlon's presence will be felt soon enough. He awakens his first morning in his new home to the sound of Billy sobbing in his crib.

* * *

Why these excursions back to his youth? Scanlon wondered, lying there in the uncomfortable recliner, attached by neoprene tubing to a plastic bag of an anonymous donor's blood. For all he knew it could be teeming with AIDS viruses. Could this going back be the psyche's reaction to the first sighting of the Angel of Death? He remembered reading somewhere that death had a talent for taking care of itself. And so did life, life as it played itself out in the consciousness of the individual. Scanlon believed this. He had seen it when Keith had battled death thirteen years ago. Toward the end, it became clear to him that Keith's dying was more an issue for the survivors than for Keith. For some reason, Scanlon took comfort in this notion.

Karla appeared to check on the progress of the transfusion.

"How are we doing?" she asked with the benign condescension of the "caregiver" as they were called these days.

"We're doing just fine. All of us."

"Fresh."

"What time is it?"

"Almost three."

"You're kidding. That's all it is? I feel like I've been hooked up here for ... I don't know how long. Do you people check this blood for AIDS and such?"

"You should have let me get you something to read. The time would pass faster. Your color's improving."

"It better be. So what about it? Could there be AIDS viruses doing the back stroke in that bag of blood, or what?"

"Don't be silly. Of course it's screened. This is 1999." Karla gave the neoprene a finger flick. "You lost a lot of blood, Mr. Scanlon." Scanlon thought he heard the mildest rebuke in Karla's remark. How could you have let it go so far? was her unasked rhetorical question.

"Yes. I didn't even realize it until ..."

"We'll have your tank on full in no time. You've got to be careful in the future, more alert."

"Yes, ma'am." Scanlon meant no sarcasm, only playfulness. And Karla swirled off to her other nursely duties.

The end of the corridor where he had been placed to receive his transfusion was quiet, like a dead-end street at three o'clock in the morning, instead of three in the afternoon, as the nurse had reported the time. He was uncomfortably disoriented, but at least his back had stopped itching. Scanlon closed his eyes, a willing subject for wherever memory and nostalgia chose to transport him.

Fifteen

June 1950

Johnny Labalm spoons cereal into his mouth. There is no fresh milk in the house. He has to settle for a mixture of canned evaporated milk and confectioner's sugar. Canned milk alone makes him gag.

He hears Charlotte Toney at the screen door before he sees her; hears the rustle of her skirt, the clang of her bracelets.

"Whatcha doin', Johnny Labalm? Can I come in?" She comes in without waiting for his permission. Johnny's face gets hot the way it does whenever Charlotte is around. "I take three baths a day, Johnny Labalm. I bet you don't take that many baths in a week."

"Do too." If he ended up in the tub three times in three months he'd be surprised.

"Where your daddy, Johnny Labalm? Your mama?"

"He's working and my mother's out for a walk with my brothers."

Charlotte comes into the kitchen, one hand on her hip. She traces her finger along the edge of the table until she is standing in front of Johnny. Then she places her fists on her hips and strikes one of her movie star poses. Charlotte is spoiled rotten, the way he was supposed to have been spoiled rotten by his grandmother. She is allowed to go to the movies anytime she feels like it, and she feels like it all the time. She can have all the candy she wants, all the clothes.

"I'm gorgeous, Johnny Labalm. Like chocolate fudge. Don't you think so?" She strokes her bare arm, wiggles her fingers all the way up the length of it. "Bet you'd like to have a taste of chocolate fudge, wouldn't you, Johnny Labalm?"

He picks up his bowl and spoon without answering, carries them to the sink. His scalp crawls, his neck is on fire.

"Tell the truth. You think I'm gorgeous." Charlotte sashays around the kitchen, jangling her bracelets, holding the hem of her orange and black taffeta skirt above the tops of her white socks and black patent leather shoes. Her hair is done in pigtails tied with pink ribbons. She smiles at him when their eyes meet, in this wild, scary way he's never seen anyone smile before. Charlotte is only the second Negro he's ever laid eyes on. Her dad, Satch, had been the first.

"Your daddy not working. He out on a bender is where he at."

Johnny's stepfather hasn't been heard from in over a week, which is just fine with Johnny. There is no money, and no food in the house to speak of, but Bill Scanlon is gone, and whenever he is gone Johnny feels better about his life. How Charlotte knows that he is on another bender is anybody's guess. She knows a great many things she has no business knowing. He is beginning to think that she is some kind of a witch. She is right about him thinking that she is gorgeous. She is one of the most beautiful girls he's ever seen, more beautiful than anyone he can think of in Groveton, even Margie McDermott. He is also scared of Charlotte. She confuses him, makes him feel every which way. When she isn't around he misses her. When she is around, he wishes she would go away, and when she does go away he wishes she were back. She knows everything about him, seems even to know what he is thinking.

"I want you and your mama to come to my birthday party on Sunday, you hear me, Johnny Labalm? We havin' chicken and mashed potatoes, and collard greens, and for dessert there's gonna be ice cream and birthday cake. I'm gonna be tin on Sunday."

And I'm going to be gold on Wednesday, he says to himself before he remembers that Charlotte can read minds.

"You better be there or my daddy won't let you watch no more stupit baseball on the television."

"I'll have to ask my mother."

"You all just better be there." Charlotte leaves, nose in the air, hands on her hips. She lets the screen door slam behind her.

Satch has invited him over to watch the Braves take on the Dodgers tonight. In fact, he hasn't missed watching a televised Braves' game with Satch in the two weeks he's been living here.

On the warm Sunday morning his mother and stepfather had been moving in what little furniture they owned, Satch had paid them a call. He was dressed for church in a brown pinstriped suit. As warm as it was, he had on a long brown overcoat and a big hat, the brim of which hung over his forehead accentuating his large watery eyes. He wore a pair of brown and white wing tips with perforations in the tops. He walked with a half strut, half shuffle, one shoulder lower than the other.

Satch had pulled Johnny aside in the kitchen, draped his long arm across Johnny's thin shoulders and whispered, "I can tell you a man who like baseball. Am I right?" All Johnny could do was nod, a little in awe, a little in fear of this strange brown man. "And I bet you a Braves fan too." Johnny nodded again even though he was partial to the Yankees. He could learn to like the Braves if it meant being Satch's friend. "How 'bout you come round my place tonight. We get the women out the house so we can have some QT. We watch the Braves scalp the Pirates. Whatch you say to that?"

He had gone to Satch's that night, and every night a game was televised after that. Bill Scanlon would say to his mother as Johnny was about to leave to go over to Satch's, "Johnny visiting the jigaboos again tonight?" He'd laugh in a way that made Johnny feel like punching him in the face. His stepfather didn't seem at all pleased to have a Negro for a landlord.

Johnny's mother and his two half-brothers, Keith, almost three, and Billy junior, four, come in from their walk. Johnny hasn't set foot out the front door since they've lived here. He won't admit to anyone, not even to his mother, that he is scared of the neighborhood kids, who ride their bikes up and down the street all day long and half the night. He's watched them from the curtainless living room window, has even learned some of their names, dangerous sounding names like Jima Frecarsi, Primo Donini, Paul Beady, and the Dagget brothers. When he goes over to Satch's to watch a game, he uses the back door.

Keith is crying. He has been denied candy, and all he ever seems to want is candy. There is no money for food, let alone candy, but of course he can't understand this. Billy junior, fed up with his brother's crying, pushes him down on the bare living room floor, which only makes him cry harder, and louder. Johnny's mother cuffs Billy behind the head and threatens to put him to bed. This gets Billy crying, too. She is always threatening to send one or more of them to bed, even Johnny, though he is almost eleven and grown up. He's her "little man" when her husband is on a bender.

It seems that it is always Billy who gets cuffed, spanked, banged around. Johnny has even smacked Billy once or twice himself. He feels awful afterwards. When he is sick and hungover, sometimes Bill Scanlon will hit Billy so hard Johnny is afraid he'll kill the poor kid. And this makes Johnny want to kill his stepfather even more. If Sister Marie knew what murderous thoughts fill his head, she would change her mind fast about her little saint.

"A man came by looking for him while you were out," Johnny tells his mother in the kitchen. She sighs, lights a cigarette, and prepares to begin another crossword puzzle. Whenever Bill Scanlon goes out on one of his benders she'll do crossword puzzles day and night.

"Who?" she asks, squinting through smoke.

"Who do you think? A guy from the restaurant. He said if he didn't show up for his shift tomorrow they'd have to let him go."

Bill Scanlon's current job is working the short-order grill at Howard Johnson's. His real ambition is to become a professional boxer, which is why they have moved closer to Boston.

"What did you tell him?"

"That he was in bed, sick."

"He should have some pay coming. You'll have to go down for it later."

"Shit, why do I always have to be the one?"

"Would you like Sister Marie to hear your mouth?"

"I just don't see why it always has to be me who has to go and beg for his pay. I hate it."

"Johnny, don't argue." His mother looks tired, worn out, pale and thin. Her hair is dull and hangs limply down the back of her neck. Johnny gets his tennis ball and goes outside. He forgets about the screen door. It slams behind him.

"And when was the last time you went to mass?" his mother shouts. "Sister Marie would be real proud of you, young man."

Johnny throws the tennis ball against the back steps with all his might. It sails over his head, way out into home run territory, and rolls into the tall marsh grass at the edge of the cove. He retrieves it and comes back to find Charlotte sitting on her back steps admiring herself in a plastic hand mirror. She is licking a Sugar Daddy.

"What kinda stupit game you playin', Johnny Labalm? I never see nothin' like it. All the time throwin' that stupit ball at them stupit steps."

"This is a good chance for you to mind your own stupid business," Johnny says, using one of his stepfather's favorite expressions. "Don't you have to take a bath or something?" With a runner on first, Johnny pitches from the stretch to Carl Furillo. He is Johnny Sain. He offers up a fastball. It bounces off the step in a high arc to deep centerfield. He chases it to the edge of the marsh and gathers it in with one hand.

"Ain't you somethin' special, Johnny Labalm. Good at catchin' tennis balls, but you won't never catch him goin' out in the street. No sir."

"Why don't you shut up?"

Charlotte laughs. "I know all about how you scared a them boys out there, Johnny Labalm. There ain't no use makin' believe you not. You scared a Jima Frecarsi, and Primo, and all them kids. You a big scaredy cat is what you is."

He is so mad he can barely think. "And you're a ..." He can't find the word that expresses his anger.

"Go ahead, Johnny Labalm, don't be bashful. Say it. Come on, Johnny Labalm," she taunts. "You can say it."

"You jigaboo!" He knows instantly that it is a terrible thing to say, if for no other reason than that Bill Scanlon uses the word to mean something hateful. But he's said it, and he can't get the words back now.

Charlotte laughs like a crazy person. "That the best you can do, Johnny Labalm? You tryin' to hurt my feelin's? You somethin'. You want a taste my Sugar Daddy?"

"I didn't mean to call you that, Charlotte," Johnny says, sitting down beside her on the steps.

"Hah." She offers him the Sugar Daddy, already glistening from where she's licked it. He reaches for it. She pulls it away. "Don't be grabbin'. I'll hold it You can have a lick, is all."

Awkwardly, he runs his tongue along the edge of the candy, barely able to get the taste of it before she pulls it away.

"That's enough, Johnny Labalm. You such a pig!" She smells perfumed; probably has just stepped out of one of her three baths a day. They sit and look out on the cove. Charlotte is quiet. Johnny is oddly uncomfortable, not used to a quiet Charlotte.

"I'm really sorry I called you that name, Charlotte. I didn't mean it."

On the horizon, they can see the big green drawbridge. In the morning it is sometimes cloaked in mist or fog, like something mysterious, right out of the movies.

"You know what's on the other side of that bridge, Johnny Labalm?"

"Yes." They'd had to cross the bridge in Curly's Buick from wherever his sister lived near the ocean. It had been exciting. They had to stop for a ship to pass under the bridge. The middle of the thing just lifted up. On the other side was a small village with nothing much to see: a little general store, post office, gas station, and a statue of a soldier of the Revolutionary War.

"You do not! Don't be lyin' to me, Johnny Labalm!"

"I'm telling you, I've been over there. So don't go calling me a liar."

Charlotte laughs again. "You not only a liar, Johnny Labalm, you an *amazin'* liar. Just amazin'." Johnny isn't eager to get into an argument with Charlotte.

"So why don't you tell me. What's on the other side?"

"Ha, wouldn't you like to know?"

"I don't care."

"Do too."

"No, I don't."

"Hollywood."

"What do you mean Hollywood? Where the movie stars live?"

"That's right. That's where I gonna go when I grow up. I gonna be a star, like Rhonda Fleming." For someone as smart as Charlotte, she can act pretty dumb when she wants to, Johnny thinks. He knows it would be a mistake to remind her that Hollywood is in California, clear across the United States, and not on the other side of the big green bridge. One of his aunts and her husband moved to California a few years ago. They wrote once that they had actually met Bing Crosby in a restaurant in Hollywood. Bill Scanlon laughed when he read the letter; Johnny's mother said something about how pathetic her brother-in-law was. But Johnny had wanted to believe that they had seen Bing Crosby; he couldn't wait for the day when he'd be old enough to travel out there for a visit. Sometimes he dreams of going out there to live. Permanently.

"Don't be lyin' to me no more, Johnny Labalm. You hear me?"

"I hear you." Charlotte's fat older sister, Beatrice, calls her inside to pick up her room. Johnny sits on the Toney's back steps alone, bouncing his ball between his feet on the step. He feels confused and desolate.

That evening, in Satch's living room, Johnny gets comfortable in the overstuffed chair he always sits in for games. The window shades are drawn. The room's only light comes from the round-screened television set. Satch is lying on the sofa, one of Mrs. Toney's run nylon stockings on his head, a glass of beer on the floor by his side. The National Anthem is coming to a close. Johnny's insides are fluttering with excitement.

"Hey!" Satch yells up the stairs, "We tryin' to watch a ballgame down here. Goddamn!"

Upstairs, Mrs. Toney is supposed to be showing Charlotte how to sew on their new electric machine. Johnny can hear Beatrice giggling. The sewing machine interferes with television reception.

Satch's television is the first Johnny has ever seen. For all he knows, in Vermont there is only radio. He could watch television all day, all night. As far as he is concerned it is almost as good as the movies. It makes him sick to think that he will never have one of his own.

Satch's living room is filled with furniture the way Johnny's living room is empty. Johnny feels comfortable here, right at home. The only bad part about coming over here is having to leave.

Satch rubs his hands together. "We gonna win big tonight, Johnny," he says, "Ooooeeee! I feels a big win coming on!" Erskine is on the mound for the Dodgers, Spahn for the Braves. The announcer predicts a pitcher's duel. Spahn mows the Dodgers down in order in the top of the first. In the Braves' half of the inning Sam Jethroe, the fastest man in baseball, beats out an infield grounder.

"Lookit that nigger run!" Satch shouts. Johnny holds his breath in surprise. Walker Cooper brings Jethroe home with a double to right field and it is looking good for the Boston Braves. They hold on to the one run lead until the eighth when Duke Snider belts a two-run homer. The Braves leave the bases loaded in the ninth and the Bums from Brooklyn trot off the field with the win.

Toward the final innings of the game, Charlotte comes downstairs in a white terrycloth bathrobe, her hair wrapped turban fashion in a white towel. She seems almost to glow in the semi-darkness. She makes Satch sit up and hold her in his lap. Johnny tries to concentrate on the game, but he finds it hard to ignore Charlotte whose fragrance fills the room. He may as well be invisible for all the attention she pays him. She puts her face in her father's chest while he rubs her back with one huge hand.

"Damn," Satch says, shaking his stockinged head, "What we gotta do to win a game? We keep playin' this kinda ball we never catch them Phillies."

Johnny feels empty and let down at the prospect of having to return home. He also worries that Charlotte will tell her father what he called her this afternoon. He never knows from one minute to the next what to expect from her.

"Johnny Labalm's daddy on a bender. You know that?" Charlotte says into her father's chest. Satch reaches over and turns on the lamp on the table beside the sofa. The sudden appearance of so much light makes Johnny squint.

Satch holds his daughter at arm's length and looks hard at her. "That any way to be talkin', little girl?" To Johnny he says, "This one got some kind of mouth on her. Now, you tell Johnny you sorry for your mouth."

Charlotte turns to Johnny and scowls at him from her father's lap.

"You better not be late for my birthday party on Sunday, Johnny Labalm. You hear me?" Satch slaps her on the rear end, but not hard.

Johnny thanks Satch for letting him watch the game, and starts for the back door

Satch says, "Don't forget, the Phillies in town tomorrow night."

"I mean it, Johnny Labalm," Charlotte adds, "You better be at my party, or else."

His mother angrily works a crossword puzzle at the kitchen table. He hears voices in the other room; his stepfather is back. Johnny suddenly feels sick to his stomach.

"When did he get back?"

"About an hour ago. He wants to see you." His mother doesn't look at him.

"What for?"

"How should I know? You'll have to go in and find out for yourself."

"Who else is in there?"

"His very good friends, Curly, and Mr. Peacock. Such refined gentlemen." His mother bears down hard with her pencil. She looks thinner, if that is possible, and more tired than she had this afternoon. She hasn't changed her dress in days.

"Is he mad at me, or what?"

"When have you ever known your father to be mad when he's drinking?" It burns him to hear his mother refer to Bill Scanlon as his father. Someday he might even have the guts to tell her so. It is true that his stepfather is a lot easier to get along with when he's drunk. Drunk, he can be generous with his loose change, laughs a lot, and when he gets just drunk enough he'll hold Keith and Billy, one on each knee, and croon, "You're Daddy's Little Boys," and Johnny will feel like throwing up. Sober, he is most always cross. Everything he says or does frightens Johnny, and Billy has even more reason to be afraid of him. For some reason, Scanlon doesn't get after Keith as much. Probably because he is the youngest, because his father favors him. Bill Scanlon has never laid a hand on Johnny except when they put on the gloves, and now it dawns on him why his stepfather wants to see him.

"I don't feel good. Can't I just go to bed? I think I have to throw up."

"Talk to him first, then you can go to bed." He doesn't know why she can't tell his stepfather herself that he is sick. She could do this one thing for her "little man," after everything he's done for her. Now that her "big man" is back everything will be different. It is always that way.

Bill Scanlon and his friends, Curly and Mr. Peacock, are in the living room, passing around a bottle of whiskey.

"Johnny boy," Bill Scanlon says, "come over here. Where you been?"

"Watching the game with Satch." Scanlon gathers Johnny to his chest, rakes his whiskered chin across his face. His stepfather smells of hair oil, whiskey, and sweat. It is a manly odor, not at all disagreeable. Johnny wants very badly to be a man himself, though not a man like Bill Scanlon.

"My boy's taken a shine to the shines," Scanlon says. This gets a laugh from his friends. His mother refers to Curly and Mr. Peacock as Bill Scanlon's "flunkies." Scanlon is their hero. They are his sparring partners. Because he's had a few bouts in carnivals and smokers for which he's been paid, Scanlon is a big shot in their eyes.

Curly has black hair, so heavily pomaded that all the curl has gone out of it. He is pale, with lots of angry looking boils on the back of his neck. Mr. Peacock is tall; he wears his hair in the fashionable pompadour, and has his sideburns long like his hero Bill Scanlon. He wears a thin mustache over his crooked mouth, and his long, slack jaw is Bill Scanlon's favorite target when they're in the ring together. Every so often, Scanlon will take it in his head to train. He'll arise early, for him, skip rope for five minutes, do ten minutes road work behind Curly's rusty Buick, put on the gloves with Mr. Peacock for two or three short rounds at the gym. But he has never been in good enough shape to last beyond the second round of a fight. The only time Johnny has ever seen him in the ring was at a carnival in Groveton, Vermont. The ring had collapsed on him twenty seconds into the first round. Scanlon, up to his knees in canvas, took three or four good punches to the head before the referee got around to stopping the fight. He hadn't been able to continue, and had to forfeit. The loss had been such a blow to his pride that he took off on a three-week bender.

Scanlon presses a half-dollar into Johnny's palm and whispers, "Go get the gloves, Johnny. The sixteen-ouncers." Johnny sighs and goes upstairs for the big gloves that smell of leather and sweat. Curly helps Johnny on with the gloves. They come all the way to his elbows.

"Tight enough?" Curly asks him, knotting the laces.

"Yeah."

"Listen. Do like I tell you. Keep the left in his face, and when you see an opening use the combination I showed you. Bam, bam, bam." Curly throws three punches at the air, left, right, left. Mr. Peacock acts as Scanlon's second. He makes a show of cautioning his man against Johnny's right hand. Johnny doesn't much enjoy being made fun of by some flunky. Scanlon drops to his knees, puts both gloves up in front of his face, and tucks his elbows in tight against his mid-section in mock defense. Angered, Johnny moves in quickly and swings a haymaker with the heavy glove at his stepfather's right ear. Scanlon takes the blow on his glove, goes through a few head feints before flicking a left jab that is so quick Johnny doesn't see it coming. The next thing he knows he's sitting on the floor, his eyes out of focus. He feels something warm in his nose. Pretty soon blood trickles over his lip into his mouth, splashes on his glove. He can see the shadowy outlines of Curly, Mr. Peacock, and Scanlon standing over him, laughing. Johnny gets to his feet and lunges at Scanlon, both heavy-gloved hands flailing. Scanlon catches him in his arms, wipes blood from his nose and mouth with the thumb of his glove.

"You okay, champ?" Scanlon laughs.

"That's enough," Johnny's mother says, coming into the room, a cigarette hanging from the corner of her mouth. "Let him go to bed. He's not feeling good."

"I'm all right," Johnny says. He isn't ready to stop now.

"Go to bed, Johnny."

"For crying out loud, I'm okay." But his mother is firm, and he goes upstairs to bed.

Johnny shares a bedroom with his half-brothers. Billy is a bed-wetter, Keith a mouth-breather. The room smells heavily of pee. One thin wall separates their room from his mother and Scanlon's. He wonders, with dread, if they'll go at it tonight the way they usually do when his stepfather comes home from his benders. He can only hope that he gets to sleep before they get going.

He lies in bed listening to Keith's rhythmic breathing. He can hear the muffled voices of the men downstairs, every now and then punctuated with outbursts of laughter. He feels an ache begin to grow in his ribcage; the room seems to close in on him; the walls begin to pulsate. He feels as though he is suffocating. He sits up in bed, breathing rapidly. Billy stirs, mutters something incoherent in his sleep. No light comes through the room's single window. Tonight, Johnny is afraid of the dark. There is only a ceiling light in the room. If he turns it on, it will awaken Keith and Billy; if he gets up there is nowhere to go but downstairs.

"Jesus," he says under his breath, and thinks about Sister Marie and the people he's left behind in Groveton. Thoughts of Groveton only make him feel worse.

Scanlon and his mother had practically kidnapped him. He'd been on an overnight camping trip on Crow Hill with his Boy Scout troop. Early next morning he came down the hill to find Scanlon and his mother waiting for him in Curly's Buick. The trunk was half open, tied down with clothesline rope, and contained all their belongings except for the few pieces of furniture they owned. Keith and Billy were in the back seat with his mother; Scanlon sat up front with Curly. Johnny was not given a chance to say goodbye to his friends. He rode in silence for what seemed many hours. They arrived at Curly's sister's place, somewhere near the ocean, in the middle of the night. A week or so later they moved into Satch's duplex.

Johnny awakes and listens. It is dawn, the light gray. All he can hear is Keith's breathing. Outside, the street is quiet. He can't remember falling asleep. Neither can he remember any of the usual sounds from the bedroom next door. He feels a little better in the light of day, but only a little. He remembers that he is expected to go after his stepfather's pay at Howard Johnson's. It makes no difference that Scanlon is back; Johnny will still have to go after it. He has no idea how to get to Howard Johnson's. He can be sure his mother will give him directions. The neighborhood kids will beat him up. He can't bring himself to tell his mother that he is afraid because she will only tell Scanlon, and Scanlon will accuse him of being "yellow."

Unable to lie in bed a moment longer, out of fear and restlessness, Johnny gets up, dresses quietly so as not to wake up Keith and Billy, and tip-toes downstairs.

Bill Scanlon is on the sofa, naked, on his side, both hands tucked between his knees, which are drawn up close to his chest. Johnny hurries into the kitchen to find his mother bent over another crossword puzzle, wearing the same dress she's had on all week. She has a cigarette in her mouth and has to squint and tilt her head to see through the smoke.

"You're up early," she says without more than a glance at Johnny.

"Who can sleep in that room?" His mother doesn't answer. He is never so totally ignored than when she is involved in her crossword puzzles. There are moments when he has a powerful urge to snatch it away, and tear it up right in front of her.

In the refrigerator there are three bottles of beer, an open package of American cheese, a quart-sized container of Bill Scanlon's spaghetti, which he seems always to bring back with him from benders, and a can of evaporated milk. Johnny slams the door shut.

"What's eating you?"

"What's eating me is that there's nothing to eat."

"There's a little cereal in the cupboard. Leave some for the kids."

"There's no milk."

"Didn't you see the can in the refrigerator?"

"I hate canned."

"Then you'll have to do without until we get your father's check." Who is his father? Only God, and this woman, know. And who is this woman he calls his mother? He's been living with her and her husband and their two children for over two years, and she is just as much a stranger now as she was when he first came to live with her. He wonders what his grandmother is doing at this very moment, whether she thinks about him, misses him. He is sure she does, just as much as he misses her. That is one thing in his crummy life of which he can be absolutely certain.

"I don't know where Howard Johnson's is. Why can't you go after his damn pay? Why can't he go himself?"

"He's going to see if they'll let him come back to work today, so you can stop worrying."

"Charlotte invited us to her birthday party on Sunday. Can we go?"

"All of us?"

"Well, she said you and me, but I guess she meant all of us. I can ask her."

"We'll have to see what your father says. You know how he feels about those people." The only thing Bill Scanlon seems to have against the Toneys is that they are colored. Yet he never puts up a real fuss whenever Johnny asks to go over to watch a game with Satch. The worst he will do is make some joke about him coming back a shade darker, rub his head and say, "Just checking for kinks." But there is no telling how he'll react just after returning from a bender. Johnny has the feeling he won't be sharing Charlotte Toney's birthday celebration. What Charlotte will have in store for him if he doesn't show up for her party is just one more thing to worry about.

"I'm going outside." Johnny gets his ball and starts for the back door.

"When are you going to make some friends in the neighborhood?" It would be nice if his mother looked at him once in awhile when she talks to him, he thinks.

"Satch is my friend."

"I mean people your own age. We've been living here for over two weeks and you haven't gone anywhere except the back yard. Are you planning to wait until school starts before you get acquainted with kids?"

If I have to, Johnny thinks. I'll be in the back yard." He leaves before his mother can ask any more questions.

Early morning fog is burning off; mist rises off the water and the little island in the cove where, in the late afternoon, he watches the neighborhood kids play stickball. The drawbridge is just visible through the fog. He can't get over how hardheaded Charlotte can be when she has her mind made up. It is probably her sister Beatrice who fills her head with this nonsense about Hollywood, probably because she is jealous of how pretty Charlotte is compared to ugly old Beatrice.

Johnny throws some warm-up pitches in preparation for a replay of last night's game. He will see to it that things turn out differently today. One thing about this game he's invented; he is in control of the outcome, even if it is a little like cheating at solitaire. Who is to know or care? He plays hard for about an hour. For all he knows, Charlotte could have been watching him from her back steps the whole time, so absorbed is he in the game. In any case, her presence startles him. Today she has on a white blouse, a full black skirt and white shoes. She makes believe he doesn't exist. He is all sweaty and dusty, and doesn't want to get too near her. Under the circumstances, he is not eager to get onto the subject of her birthday party either.

"Hello, Charlotte," he says with utmost caution. Charlotte doesn't answer. She studies the sky, which by now is cloudless and blue. Johnny bounces his ball against the steps a few times, showing a little indifference of his own, but his insides are jumping. He makes up his mind to go back inside when Charlotte says,

"I see your daddy back from his bender, Johnny Labalm. He can come to my birthday party too, he want. And your little brothers too. I don't care. *We* got plenty a food."

"I don't know if we can come."

"You all better come."

"Or else what?"

"You find out. Don't you worry." Johnny imagines that she will tell

Satch that he called her a jigaboo and that will be the end of watching ball games on television for him. He throws the ball hard at the steps. It goes wild against his screen door, and caroms off the side of the porch. Charlotte finds this amusing.

"You just amazin', Johnny Labalm. Come over here," she orders, patting the step beside her. "This minute!" Johnny obeys. "Whew! My God, Johnny Labalm, how you stink!" Johnny gets up to leave, feeling himself grow hot all over. "Where you think you goin'? I didn't say you could leave."

"I don't need you to tell me what I can do you ..." Nigger is in his mind and almost out of his mouth. He catches himself in time.

"What you gonna say, Johnny Labalm?" She has that awful smile for him. "What you want to say? I know what you want to say?"

"You do not."

"You too stupit for words, Johnny Labalm." He's never been called stupid so much. In school he was always the best in his class. Stupid is not a word he is used to hearing applied to himself. If she is so damned smart how come she hasn't figured out that Bill Scanlon isn't his father? "Why don't I get you a nice root beer Popsicle. That make you feel better, Johnny Labalm? I bet it do."

It drives him crazy her calling him Johnny *Labalm* all the time. She goes inside and comes back with two halves of a root beer Popsicle.

"You want it, you gonna have to come over here and get it." He doesn't like the way he allows himself to be ordered around by her, but here he is, back on the steps beside her, accepting her offer of a Popsicle. Something tells him there will be a price to pay. They suck on their Popsicles for a while without saying anything. Then Charlotte, without any warning, announces that she is a Gemini in a way that makes her sound superior to him.

"What's that?" Johnny asks.

"That's where I was born. Colored kids born in June all come from Gemini. Beatrice tell me that." Beatrice again, Johnny thinks. No end to the nonsense she can fill her sister's head with.

"So where is it?" Before Charlotte can reply, Beatrice is at the back door.

"Charlotte, mama wants you to go to the store for her."

"All right." Charlotte loves to go to the store. It gives her a chance to show off her clothes. And she isn't afraid of the neighborhood kids, no matter what kinds of names they call her. "Want to come to the store with me, Johnny Labalm?" she taunts. He is still smarting from being called stupid by her so much, and the idea of going out into the street makes him feel faint. But there is Charlotte, a root beer Popsicle in her hand and a smirk on her face.

"Sure. Why not?"

Charlotte frowns. "You sure, Johnny Labalm?"

"Yeah, I'm sure."

And just like that he finds himself out in the street for the first time since he's moved here. He is conscious of his heartbeat. It is midmorning, already hot and very humid. The street shimmers in the heat. There is no sign of any of the neighborhood kids, but he knows they are around. Charlotte tells him the grocery store is only a short walk. As they walk along the hot sidewalk, Johnny begins to feel better.

Three bikes lie on their sides in front of the store. He recognizes those bikes, and if it were not for Charlotte he would turn around and run home. In any case, it is too late for running. The boys come out of the store and spot Johnny and Charlotte. Johnny recognizes Jima Frecarsi, Primo Donini, and one of the Daggett brothers whose first name he doesn't know.

"Look at this," says Primo Donini, "a tar baby and a pecker head." The three of them stand in ranks, side by side, blocking the entrance to the store. Charlotte isn't fazed; she puts her fists on her hips and leans toward them.

"You just stand out the way so we can get in. You hear? You want me to get my daddy after you?"

"Who's this, Charlotte, your new boyfriend?" Jima Frecarsi says. He measures Johnny top to bottom with his eyes. Daggett breaks away from the others and walks slowly behind Johnny. Primo is looking at Johnny in a way that makes him feel cold despite the heat. He begins to tremble. Sweat breaks out on his upper lip and forehead, under his arms. Charlotte starts to say something. Frecarsi tells her to shut up.

"Who are you, kid?" Primo Donini wants to know. He is a big, beefy kid with a wide, red face and not much of a neck. His arms are thick and dirty, dimpled near the elbows. All three of them are a lot bigger than Johnny.

"My name's Jack Labalm. I just moved here a couple weeks ago."

"What's this Jack business?" Charlotte says. "You such a liar, Johnny Labalm."

"Who asked you, Aunt Jemima?" Primo Frecarsi says without taking his eyes off Johnny. Johnny is worried about Daggett. He has disappeared. Primo Frecarsi suddenly rushes him, tipping him over Daggett who is crouched down behind him. Johnny reaches out his hands to break his fall and scrapes his palms on the gravely sidewalk. The three of them are standing over him, laughing, the way Bill Scanlon, Curly, and Mr. Peacock had laughed at him last night. Charlotte is speechless, mouth agape. Johnny gets up slowly, brushing gravel off the seat of his pants. The heels of his hands are cut and bleeding, and smarting like hell. He is trembling, this time with rage. He goes for Frecarsi with a looping right, his small fist clenched as tight as he can make it. He catches the surprised Frecarsi flush on the mouth. His eyes open wide. His hand flies to his face. Johnny leaps on him, wrestles him to the ground, getting in two or three good punches to Primo's fat face before the others get around to pulling him off Frecarsi. They fling him to the sidewalk and start to kick at him when a man wearing a white apron comes out of the store and drives them off. But not before one them gets off a good one to Johnny's face. Charlotte has been screaming in her shrill voice. This is what no doubt brings the grocery man out of his store.

"We'll be seein' you later, fuck stick," Daggett says as they mount their bikes and ride off down the street, pumping furiously. Johnny's face throbs where he has been kicked. When he gets up he feels a sharp pain in his ribs.

"You all right, chief?" the store man asks.

"Yeah. I'm okay." Charlotte is by now jabbering out of control. "Take it easy, Charlotte," Johnny says, amazed at himself at how calm he sounds. "Everything's all right."

On the walk home, Charlotte seems not at all impressed with his performance, his display of physical courage, his bravery in the face of being outnumbered by kids bigger and older than he is.

"If you hadn't gone fightin' with that Primo Frecarsi and his friends we'd a been back by now. My mama gonna wonder why we took so long."

"So why don't you tell her what happened?"

"You nothin' but a trouble maker, Johnny Labalm. A stupit liar and a trouble maker," Charlotte says before stalking off ahead of him down the street, confounding him yet again.

Johnny puts a finger gingerly to his face. It is so tender he winces. He thinks his left eye is beginning to close. If Charlotte's behavior puzzles him, the things she says and does no longer surprise him. He would have liked a little show of gratitude if not admiration for what he has done. In any case, he will see her tonight when he goes over to watch the Phillies' game with Satch. Satch will be proud of him even if Charlotte isn't. So will his stepfather for that matter.

"What in the name of God happened to you?" Johnny's mother says when he comes into the house through the front door for the first time on his own.

"Just making friends in the neighborhood. Kids my own age." He had rehearsed that little speech on the walk home.

"I thought you had more sense," she says, shaking her head. Bill Scanlon is still asleep, bare-assed, on the couch. "Come up to the bathroom and let me put some Mercurochrome on that face." He doesn't resist, as much as he hates the sting of Mercurochrome.

"I couldn't help it. I was attacked, and there were three of them, and Charlotte was with me. What was I supposed to do?"

"The police are going to hear about this. Who are these boys? Do you know their names?"

"If you call the cops you might as well sign my death warrant." He'd heard that line in a James Cagney movie. And it could very well be true, he thinks, remembering Daggett's parting words for him.

"Anyway, I don't know who they are. I've never been in the neighborhood before. Remember?"

"And it'll be a long time before you go out in it again. Not until school starts if I have anything to say about it." An hour ago this news would have been music to his ears, but now the idea of being confined to the house and back yard for the rest of the summer has lost its appeal.

"I doubt if I'll have any more trouble with those kids. I got one of them pretty good." He hopes he sounds more confident than he feels. He has probably not seen the last of Primo Frecarsi, Jima Donini, and Daggett.

"Why don't you run a warm bath and soak for awhile," his mother says, and leaves the bathroom. What he really wants is for his stepfather to see him and ask what happened. He would like to describe to him the whole scene in careful detail. The sound of Bill Scanlon's braying snores fill the all but empty house.

Johnny lingers in the bath so long his fingers start to wrinkle. How Charlotte manages to take three baths every day and look so smooth is more than he can figure. And what a waste of time.

He can't help thinking about what happened to him today, and how much it was like what Butch Mckay and his friends had done to his friend Eddie Leclerc back in Groveton not so long ago.

His stepfather is no longer on the couch when Johnny comes downstairs. His mother tells him that Scanlon has gone to try and get his job back at Howard Johnson's, and if that doesn't work out to at least collect the money owed him. Without even brushing his teeth, Johnny thinks with disgust. The question neither Johnny nor his mother dare ask, for different reasons, is will he come back home if he has a pocketful, or take off on another bender?

A whole afternoon lies ahead of him before it will be time to go over to Satch's to watch the game. His ribs are so sore from where he's been kicked that it is hard even for him to breathe. Playing ball in the back yard is out of the question. The radio doesn't work, and there is no television. The only reading material around the house is his stepfather's *Police Gazette* magazine. He supposes he can go out and try to find the library. He isn't as much afraid of running into the neighborhood kids as he is of getting lost.

Scanlon hasn't come home by the time Johnny is ready to go next door. His mother is back in her crosswords.

"I'm going next door to watch the Phillies' game with Satch."

"With your face looking like that? You'll scare those people to death."

His face is one reason Johnny is eager to get to Satch's early. His left eye is by now a narrow slit, the skin around it a nice purple. In his condition he might even get a little sympathy from Charlotte.

He goes outside to a vivid sunset, all pinks and purples, and the air deliciously muggy; a perfect night for baseball. He lingers on his back steps for a while to savor the evening, feeling better than he has felt since moving away from his home and friends in Vermont. It is early but Satch won't mind.

Satch meets Johnny at the door as if he is expecting him early. He lays his big hand on Johnny's shoulder and steers him toward the steps. Johnny senses something is wrong just in the way Satch touches him.

"Come on out here a minute, Johnny. I want to talk at you a bit." Satch's eyes are forever bloodshot and watery. They sit down on the steps. Satch rubs his hands together. His lips move as if he is talking under his breath. No words come out of his mouth.

"What is it, Satch?" Johnny's voice is small in his throat, almost a squeak.

Satch turns to him so fast it startles him. "What you tryin' to do to my little girl? What kind of nasty things you been sayin' to her?"

"I told her I was sorry." He stares down at his feet, unable to look at Satch, unable to say anything more.

"You and your friends tryin' to make my little girl do those things. You should be ashamed of yourself, little boy." Satch says this as much to himself as to Johnny. He has turned slightly away from Johnny, and is looking off toward the island in the cove. Whatever story Charlotte has concocted to get back at him, Satch has believed it. And whatever Johnny says now won't matter. He wouldn't be able to say anything, either way. He feels as though he is strangling. Tears fill his eyes, and he is suddenly sobbing out of control.

"Ain't gonna do you no good to cry," Satch says, his voice sounding hard and unforgiving to Johnny. "I won't let no harm come to my baby. No white trash gonna make my child unhappy."

"I didn't do anything," Johnny says between sobs. Where did Satch think he'd got his swollen face, his black eye? From his *friends*?

"You best get on home now. And maybe it be best you not come by no more. Everything be better you stay on you own side the house." Satch gets up, brushes off the seat of his trousers and goes inside, leaving Johnny alone on the steps.

Johnny sits crying for a long time. When he finishes, he gets up and brushes off the seat of his pants as Satch had done, and walks down to the edge of the water. The sun has gone down, and over on the island the neighborhood kids are playing stickball in the dwindling light. He is no longer afraid of them; neither does he have a desire to join them. His chest is tight from all the crying he's done. He can't go home now because it is too early and his mother will only ask a lot of questions.

He goes out into the street for the second time that day, and retraces the route he had taken with Charlotte to the grocery store. As he walks along the sidewalk, people sitting on their front steps stop their conversations to stare at him. He must be quite a sight at that. There is no sign of the boys he'd tussled with this morning. They are probably still out on the island. They get back and forth by rowboat.

Johnny walks past the grocery store into unfamiliar territory. About a block from the store, the street forks. He stays left and walks another few blocks. Twilight is giving up to early darkness, bugs are coming out in greater numbers and people are going inside to watch their television programs or listen to the radio. It is still too early to go home, but he is beginning to feel the night close in around him. He hurries back the way he has come. The big trees along the sidewalk take on monstrous shapes. He breaks into a jog. He slows down as he approaches the grocery store where a street light is burning, making the trees less menacing.

He sees what looks like the glow of cigarettes in front of his house. He stops and strains his eyes; he can make out three separate lighted cigarettes and he knows whom they belong to. At this point he doesn't care. He goes on to meet them. One of the cigarettes arcs toward the street like a shooting star. By the time he reaches his house the boys are gone.

From the sidewalk he can look into the Toneys' living room. The whole family is gathered: Charlotte in her terrycloth bathrobe, her hair wrapped in a towel, sits in Satch's lap, head against his chest. Beatrice is at the ironing board, watching the television, running an iron over a piece of clothing. Mrs. Toney occupies the chair he usually sits in, and all he can see is the back of her head. On the television screen Uncle Milty, dressed to the neck in a gorilla costume, carrying the head of it football fashion, is moving his lips and sending the Toney family into fits of laughter. Johnny wonders why Satch isn't watching the game. He stands outside for a while and watches the Toney's enjoy the television.

He goes into his house through the front door to find Bill Scanlon asleep on the couch, snoring loudly enough to shake the house. He is fully clothed and stinks of whiskey. His mother is no doubt in the kitchen with her damned crossword puzzle. He goes upstairs without saying good night to his mother.

Billy is whimpering. Keith is awake too. They sleep in bunk beds, Billy on the bottom because of his bed-wetting.

"What's the matter with you?" Johnny asks Billy.

"He wet the bed," Keith says, "and daddy's going to give him a licking in the morning."

"You don't have to sound so happy about it," Johnny says. He sits down on the edge of Billy's bed and puts his hand on his half-brother's damp back.

"Stop crying. It's all right. We won't let him find out."

"How?" Billy sobs, "The bed's all wet."

"Come on. Get up." Billy gets out of his wet bed.

Johnny pulls off the mattress off and swaps it with the one on his bed. "You've got to try hard not to pee again tonight. Do you think you can do that?"

Billy nods. Johnny makes him go to the bathroom just in case. He makes Keith promise to keep his mouth shut.

Johnny spreads a blanket over the sodden mattress and lies down, enveloped in the smell of pee. He closes his eyes; the events of the day race past his eyelids. Thinking about Charlotte only makes him angry, so he tries to put her and her father out of his mind. From now on he will concentrate on getting back to Vermont, even if he has to run away and take Keith and Billy with him.

While he is still very wide-awake, the bedroom door opens. His mother appears in the doorway, framed by the light from the hall behind her. A cigarette hangs from her mouth. Johnny pretends to be asleep. She stays in the doorway for a long time, it seems to him. Then she closes it quietly without coming into the room.

***

Why Scanlon would dredge up the memory of that period in his life, almost 50 years past, interested him. It made him question the reliability of long-term memory. Had any of what appeared so vividly in his mind's eye actually happened? He lived in that place for such a short time. He remembered that at some point during the summer his family lived in Satch's duplex he had become friendly with the boys who had attacked him in front of the grocery store. How the transition from being the object of their bullying to becoming one of "them" was not clear in his mind. Charlotte he hadn't thought about a half dozen times since he'd moved away from the place. Could she have been so much the temptress at nine or ten years old? So manipulative? So vindictive? Did memory simply alter facts, or did it invent them from whole cloth? And why now?

In late September of that year, he was uprooted again. This time the destination was Garrison, New Hampshire, fifty-five miles to the north. It was here that he came of age, so to speak, and here was where his family took root after a fashion. It was here where Billy and Keith, his mother and stepfather, would remain.

Crime. As a youth Scanlon had gone through a period of fascination for the underworld, for all that was criminal and punishable by law. His favorite comic book, if it could be called that, was *Crime Does Not Pay*, yet in his heart of hearts he sided with the outlaw, and fervently yearned for crime to indeed pay. When he was in sixth grade Scanlon went on his own version of a crime spree with his newest best friend Terry Stickney:

Sixteen

Fall 1950:

In October, a month after Bill Scanlon moved his family to Garrison, New Hampshire, and in a rare moment of sobriety, he decided that it would be proper to legally adopt his wife's illegitimate son. Johnny had been using Scanlon's surname ever since he came to live with his mother and her husband, so now he could use it legally. He felt like he had given up something of himself that was important, but he couldn't figure out what. Since moving to Garrison, he had introduced himself to his new acquaintances as Jack, not Johnny. Jack Scanlon, he had to admit, had a more manly sound than Johnny Labalm.

Terry Stickney, a tallish, wiry boy with blond hair, ears that stuck out, and shoulders that sloped away from his thin neck, sat in the back row of Mrs. McConnell's sixth grade classroom ... by choice. He never paid much attention to what was going on in class, preferring to amuse himself by doing pencil sketches of the profiles of WWII fighter planes. He wanted to pilot one of those fighters when he became a man, but first he wanted his own car, and the waiting until he was old enough to go for his driver's license he sometimes found unbearable. He knew how to drive; his father, who drove Greyhound buses, had taught him when he was nine. Terry Stickney saw no sense in a law that made you wait until you were sixteen before you could legally operate a car. In the meantime, he kept his mind busy imagining the kind of car he would have.

If Terry Stickney couldn't be bothered to pay attention to Mrs. McConnell as she held forth in class, Jack Scanlon, the new kid, hung on to her every syllable. His hand would be the first one in the air whenever a question came out of her mouth. And his answers were *always* correct, which would inspire Mrs. McConnell to remark in a loud, admiring voice "what a smart young man" she had in her class—finally. Her words both thrilled and embarrassed him. He had never before had so much attention lavished on him by a teacher, not even by Miss Abbott in fourth grade. He became Mrs. McConnell's unwilling teacher's pet, and he paid for it on the playground at recess and after school. He was always the last one picked for basketball games. In time, however, when it became obvious that he could pass and dribble, shoot and head feint the way his Uncle Mitch had taught him to do, the other kids, who were less in Mrs. McConnell's favor, accepted him. It wasn't his fault he was smart, they seemed to conclude. If he was the smartest kid in Mrs. McConnell's sixth grade class, Terry Stickney, by virtue of his strength and speed, was the best basketball player.

When the after school scrimmage ended, and kids drifted away from the sloping asphalt basketball court, Jack lingered to play a game of

HORSE with Terry Stickney. Jack had stolen three cigarettes from his mother's pack of Pall Malls. He offered one to Stickney after they finished playing ball, and were headed home.

"You know how to inhale?" Stickney asked him.

"Sure. You?" Jack scratched a wooden kitchen match along the rusted metal railing of the Washington Street Bridge; the smelly Cocheco River flowed sluggishly below. He lighted up their cigarettes.

"Yeah." Stickney inhaled deeply in case Jack Scanlon was a skeptic. He exhaled smoke through his nostrils. "I like Camels better."

"Me too, but these are what my folks smoke. When I was a kid I used to smoke leaves rolled in notebook paper." Jack laughed. Stickney looked at him as if he didn't understand what was so funny.

"Why?"

"I don't know. I was just a kid. We didn't know how to get our hands on real cigarettes."

"So now you know?" Terry Stickney chuckled. Jack thought he was making fun of him.

A souped-up Chevy with dual exhaust pipes and a loud muffler came ripping down Washington Street. Terry Stickney watched it intently until it turned up Main Street and was out of sight.

"I'm going to have a rod like that," he announced.

"You know how to drive?"

"Of course."

Stickney's forthright use of "of course" made Jack feel uneasy, inferior because he couldn't drive. He didn't have any interest in cars the way Terry Stickney did. He was content to be a passenger. As a mere passenger he could give all his attention to what was going on outside as he was transported through space. He hastened to change the subject.

"You got any brothers or sisters?"

"Two brothers and a sister. Derrick's my older brother. He's going in the Army after Christmas. He wants to get over to Korea."

"If I was old enough to go I'd join the Navy."

"Navy don't do no fighting." Terry Stickney put his arms up on the bridge railing and spit into the Cocheco River.

"They do too." Jack informed his new friend that his uncles, Mitch and Ira, had seen combat in the Philippines and in the battle of Okinawa, respectively. Terry Stickney flipped his cigarette into the Cocheco, seeming not to have heard or not to have been impressed by Jack Scanlon's uncles' war experiences. "Did your father fight in World War II?"

"He was too old. What about your old man?"

"He was in the Navy, too." Jack did not elaborate further. He had no wish to reveal the fact that his stepfather had received an undesirable discharge from the Navy for stealing. Neither did he tell Stickney that Bill Scanlon was not his real father. It was a fiction he had already boxed himself into with his new acquaintances, and he saw no way out of it.

"Derrick can't wait to go. Let me have a drag of that." Stickney picked the cigarette from between Jack's fingers and put it in his mouth. Jack didn't object. There was something physically menacing about Stickney even if he was a beanpole. As far as Jack knew, however, he was no bully. He took one puff and handed the cigarette back to Jack. "Come on over to my house. I'll show you my .22."

"You got a .22?" Jack asked, trying to sound impressed. "You got ammo for it?"

"Of course. We can go up to the sand pit and shoot at beer bottles. Not today though."

Jack lied and told Stickney that he had owned a .22 when he lived in Vermont.

"What happened to it?"

"My folks made me get rid of it when we moved. They said guns weren't allowed where we were going."

"Where's that?"

"Massachusetts. That's where I lived before I moved here." Stickney looked at Jack as if he didn't believe him, but said nothing.

"Well, they're allowed here."

"Will you let me fire it?"

"Why not?"

Johnny Labalm had fired Eddie Leclerc's .22 in Vermont and discovered that he didn't have a very good aim. Later on, at boot camp in Bainbridge, Maryland, he would barely qualify on the rifle range. He regretted asking Terry Stickney if he could fire his rifle; he often spoke without thinking. When Stickney found out what a terrible marksman he was, that would probably be the end of their friendship. It wouldn't be enough that he was the best foul shooter in Franklin School.

Terry Stickney lived with his family in a tiny yellow house with peeling paint on a back lot off Locust Street, near the library and the high school. They entered the house through the back door into a small kitchen. Mrs. Stickney sat at the kitchen table with a white enamel top, her hands lying palms up in her lap. Jack was struck by the unblinking stare on the woman's thin face. She looked stricken, as if she had just received news of the death of a loved one. She continued to stare vacantly into space, seeming to take no notice of the boys entering her kitchen. Terry Stickney neither greeted his mother nor bothered to introduce Jack to her. He went straight to the icebox, opened the door, peered inside briefly, and slammed it shut.

"Let's go upstairs," he said.

There was not much room to maneuver in the small bedroom Terry shared with his two brothers; most of the space was occupied by bunk beds against one wall, a single bed at a right angle to the bunk beds against the adjacent wall, and two bureaus against the remaining two walls. There was no closet in the room, and the only illumination came from a naked incandescent bulb hanging by a cord from the ceiling.

Terry and his younger brother slept in the bunk beds, Terry on the top because he was a year older, his brother Larry on the bottom. Derrick had the single bed.

Terry reached under Derrick's bed and pulled out a long object wrapped in a thin blanket. He unfolded the blanket carefully to reveal the .22 caliber rifle.

Jack was surprised (and disappointed) that Terry Stickney should own a single shot bolt-action rifle and not a pump action automatic. In seemed out of character somehow; old-fashioned, like something his grandfather might own. Stickney acted like he sensed Scanlon's disappointment.

"It's got perfect sighting. I never miss with this bastard. Christ, my sister could hit a half-dollar with this thing at a hundred feet."

If that were so, Jack thought, maybe he wasn't such a bad shot after all. Maybe Eddie Leclerc's .22 just hadn't been properly "sighted."

"Can we take it to the sand pit and try it out?"

"Not today, I told you." Terry Stickney took aim at the small bedroom window, then lowered the rifle and wrapped it back up in the blanket as carefully as he had removed it. He offered no reason why they couldn't shoot today, and Jack knew better than to press him.

A baby carriage was pushed up against the wall at the bottom of the narrow stairs, in a short hallway that ended at the stairwell. Jack had assumed that Terry's younger sister was not an infant, not if she could nail a half-dollar at a hundred feet with his rifle, as Stickney claimed she could do.

"How old's your sister?"

"Ten." Stickney pushed through the front door. "Let's go to Green's and get some French fries. I'm hungry. There's nothing in the ice box."

"Green's?"

"Green's Fish Market. You never had their French fries?" Stickney asked, almost sounding incredulous.

"You forget, I just moved here."

Green's Fish Market wasn't much bigger than the Stickney's kitchen, and the showcase and counter occupied the full width of the room. Several grease stained brown paper bags were arranged on a tray on the top of the showcase. The limp, greasy fries sold for fifteen cents a bag, and customers were urged to use vinegar on them instead of ketchup. Jack was frankly surprised at how good they tasted with white vinegar and lots of salt. He'd never eaten a French fry except with ketchup.

They walked down Locust Street toward the high school, eating the limp French fries. Near the end of Locust Street Stickney ripped a side mirror off the passenger side of a gray Nash. Jack's eyes opened wide; he looked back down the street behind him instinctively.

"What are you doing?" he whispered, as if someone would hear him if he spoke out loud, even though the street appeared deserted.

"Collecting," Stickney turned into the alley behind the Lipson

Company, produce wholesalers. Jack followed, glancing once more over his shoulder.

"What for?" Jack asked in the alley, his stomach fluttering with nervousness.

"For my car." Stickney wiped the mirror with his elbow.

"What car?"

"The one I'm going to get as soon as I save the money. What are you doing tonight?"

"I don't know. Nothing, I guess. Why?"

"You can help me collect more stuff ... after it gets dark." Stickney turned the side mirror over in his hands, as if he were looking for defects.

Back at his house, Stickney tossed the stolen mirror in the baby carriage in the stairwell. Jack told him he had to get home.

"Meet me in front of Garrison Savings at seven o'clock," Stickney said to him on his way out.

"Maybe." Jack had made up his mind beforehand that he wanted no part of Stickney's "collection."

* * *

"Where are you going this time of night, Johnny?" his mother asked him, as he was getting ready to leave the apartment before he went crazy in the three tiny rooms with his noisy half-brothers. His mother smoked cigarettes and worked crossword puzzles at the kitchen table. And he was annoyed at her for persisting in calling him Johnny, knowing how he felt about being addressed by that name now that he was no longer a kid.

"To the library to do homework." That was actually his intention when he put on his jacket, but Terry Stickney's invitation to meet him at the bank found its way into his head.

"Be home by nine o'clock," his mother said without looking at him.

"All right."

It was not yet seven o'clock but dark as the middle of the night outside. Jack hurried down two flights of evil smelling stairs and out onto the sidewalk and fresh air, crisp autumn air with the smell of fallen leaves. He paused on the sidewalk to breathe deeply. Across the street in the Newman Building, a two-story terra cotta brick building that housed a meat market (with prices beyond the reach of his family), a barbershop, and Newman's Drugstore. Lights were on in the drugstore, but the windows in the market and the barbershop were dark. The bell in the Congregational church steeple on the corner of Center and Clark Streets started to ring the hour. Jack jogged across the street at the intersection, and broke into a steady trot on the other side. He was anxious, afraid that Terry Stickney would think he was not coming and would set off on his own, or if he did wait, would be angry at him for being late. It had to be at least a half-mile to the Garrison Savings Bank on the corner of Washington and Center Streets. He picked up his pace.

Soon he was running full tilt, breathing hard.

He spotted Terry Stickney leaning with his back to the bank, his elbows up on the big tarnished brass rail. A lighted cigarette hung from the corner of his mouth. He looked like a tough guy this evening, like one of the East Side Kids in the movies. There was not much traffic on the street. The sky was clear, full of stars and a bright half moon. Jack slowed down to a walk when he saw Stickney, not wanting to appear too eager. He waved at Stickney from across the lower square. If Stickney saw his wave he didn't acknowledge it. He continued to slouch against the bank's railing, looking tough and aloof.

"You took your time," Stickney said, flicking his cigarette into the gutter. "Did you bring any cigarettes?"

"No. I couldn't. My mother was home and ..."

"Let's go." Stickney thrust his hands in his jacket pockets and started across the intersection to the east side of Washington Street, on the corner of which was the First National grocery market. Jack followed, having to hurry to catch up to the fast walking Stickney.

"God, the river stinks something awful tonight," Jack said, just for something to say. Stickney grunted and continued his brisk pace. "Where we headed?"

"Main."

"Why Main Street?"

"There's no street lights on Main between the Ramble Inn and Miller Shoe. There's plenty of cars parked there. Some of them people are stupid enough to leave their doors unlocked."

They passed the trash dumpster in the back of the First National that stank of rotten produce. Past the market began an entire block of nineteenth-century brick factory buildings, all the way to the Washington Street Bridge. Construction was underway in the lower level of one of the factories to fashion a recreation center for Garrison's youth who, according to the city council, were becoming a nuisance as they hung out in groups on street corners and bothered citizens with their rude comments.

Washington Street intersected with Main Street. The boys walked north on Main in the direction of their school with its sloping asphalt playground, across the street from which was the old brick two-story building where elderly Greeks drank coffee, played cards and reminisced about the old country. Parking was allowed only on the coffee house side of the street. A hundred feet or so beyond the coffee house was the Bar Café, a beer parlor Jack's stepfather frequented (along with most of the others in Garrison). A few cars were parked outside the beer parlor. Jack had a moment of anxiety as they neared the Bar Café in case Bill Scanlon should spot him so far from the library where he told his mother he would be spending the evening.

Terry Stickney crossed the street from the Franklin School side to where the cars were parked. He stopped in front of a Hudson, looked up and down Main Street, and then peered inside the passenger side window. Jack hung back on the other side of the street, in a moment of indecision whether to join Stickney or to hightail it to the Garrison City Library where he would be safe. He was conscious of his pounding heart, and as cool as it was in the November air, he was sweating.

Stickney went into a crouch and opened the passenger side door. His upper body disappeared inside the Hudson and came back shortly. Jack could see something in Stickney's hand that he couldn't make out in the darkness.

"Come on, for Christ sake!" Stickney tried to yell and whisper at the same time. Jack hesitated, and then crossed the street. "Grab the bug deflector off that Studebaker," Stickney ordered. Jack made no move toward the Studebaker parked in front of the Hudson. "What the fuck's the matter with you?" Stickney said, exasperated. He took a vicious swipe at the hood of the Studebaker and ripped off the bug deflector.

"Sorry," Jack said in a small voice.

"You going to help me, or stand there like a hard-on?"

"Yeah, I ..." A car's headlights appeared as it turned up Main Street from Washington.

"This way," Stickney said, walking down School Street, a short street of small houses owned by Jews and occupied by mostly Greeks. The rear ends of a few cars parked in short driveways jutted out to the sidewalk. Stickney broke a reflector light off the rear bumper of a coup, and pulled off a hood ornament from a Buick parked on the street. His hands were getting full.

"Take some of this shit," he said to Jack, holding out both hands to his companion. Among the things he handed Jack was a leopard-patterned steering wheel cover that he'd taken from the Hudson.

"We need a bag of some kind," Jack said.

"Stick it under your jacket for now. We'll get a couple more things and take them to my house. Let's go."

The boys returned to Main Street and mauled four more parked cars before they came to the Ramble Inn diner (and streetlights made their work dangerous) netting another bug deflector, two side-mirrors, a steering wheel knob, and a radio antenna. This time Jack helped, his breathing and heartbeat coming fast, more from excitement now than fear. The fronts of their jackets full, they took the dark side streets back to Terry Stickney's house, and deposited their booty in the baby carriage. Stickney didn't even bother to attempt to conceal their ill-gotten goods with the crocheted baby blanket draped over the handle.

"Won't your mother say something?" Jack whispered, though he had his doubts that the catatonic Mrs. Stickney would notice if they dumped the whole lot of it in her aproned lap.

"She won't say nothing." And neither would Mr. Stickney, who sat in his armchair in the parlor listening to the radio, a glass of ale on the table beside him. He didn't acknowledge the fact that his son had a companion any more than his wife had earlier. As the boys prepared to go out again Mr. Stickney, still clad in his bus driver's outfit—short gray jacket, and gray trousers with black stripes up the side—said, in a gruff voice,

"Where you going now?"

"Out," his son replied.

"Where's your brother?"

"How the hell should I know? Come on, Jack. Let's go."

"Your mother need anything at the store?"

"Be goddamned if I know." And the boys left by the back door.

Their crime spree went on for three more nights in succession; the baby carriage was almost full of the stuff they had removed from cars parked on Garrison's unlighted streets

"How many side-mirrors, bug deflectors, and radio antennas do you think you'll need for your car, Terry?" Jack was trying to be funny, but Terry Stickney read it as sarcasm.

"Why? You maybe want some for *your* car?" Stickney wanted to make it clear that it was obvious to him that there was no car in Jack Scanlon's future. Besides, at this point the car stripping had become, for both of them, an exciting end in itself. Stickney would more than likely have no use for any of the stolen property filling up the baby carriage in the stairwell.

By mid-November they grew bored with stripping parked cars. Stickney decided they should branch out, seek something more challenging. He had observed, with his developing criminal eye, that the garage in the alley off Kirkland Avenue, where the Mission Orange Company kept their delivery truck parked, was left unlocked at night. Sunday, after it got dark, they crept up to the garage, which was at the end of the alley and therefore out of sight of Kirkland Avenue. The back of a tenement house overlooked the alley, but at that time of night the residents were most likely in their front rooms watching television or listening to the radio. No one would hear the garage door opening, Stickney reasoned.

Jack was giddy with excitement as they crouched before the garage door and began to lift it up, a little at first, to test the kind of sound it made. The back of the delivery truck was wide open. They put together a case of bottles of orange soda and of root beer in a wooden box, quietly closed the garage door, and skulked back to Stickney's house, carrying the case of stolen soda between them.

Stickney's younger brother, Larry, was in the bedroom when they arrived. He demanded three sodas in return for his "silence."

"You can have two bottles, and you got to know I'll kick the living shit out of you if you open your mouth," Stickney said, handing his brother two root beers.

"I was just fooling. You know I won't say nothing," Larry said, grinning and taking the sodas. "They're warm."

"Tough shit. Go downstairs and get an opener," Terry Stickney ordered his brother.

"You got enough shit down in that baby carriage to start your own parts store. The old man ain't said nothing about it?"

"Told him I got it out of the dump and from Goldstein's junk yard. Get your ass downstairs."

When Larry returned with a bottle opener he asked his brother if he could accompany him and Jack on their next outing.

"I don't give a shit," Terry Stickney said. He swallowed some orange soda. "Come if you want to."

Jack had wanted him to say no to his younger brother. Three was a crowd in this business, in his opinion.

"Where you going to hit next?" Larry wanted to know.

"I got to think about it. I got plenty of stuff for the car and Mission Orange's too easy."

"Why don't we break into a store or something?" Larry sounded conspiratorial, and excited.

Jack's stomach muscles twitched involuntarily at Larry's suggestion. Stripping cars and swiping soda pop was one thing, burglary was something else. He didn't know quite how to express his reservations without sounding like a chicken in the Stickney brothers' eyes.

"No, we ain't breaking into no stores. Too risky. You get caught, they send you to Manchester. Louie Purpera been there. He told me it ain't no place you want to be. No, we ain't breaking into no stores."

Although he was relieved to hear these words from Terry Stickney, Jack was left to wonder what the difference was between robbing the Mission Orange truck and breaking into a store where going to reform school was concerned. Maybe the fact that the back of the Mission Orange truck had been wide open mitigated the charge of breaking and entering. But stealing was against the law, too. He knew nothing about the law. The very sound of the words "reform school" gave him goose flesh.

By the end of the month, evenings started to get too cold for the brand of petty theft Terry Stickney and Jack Scanlon had engaged in for the last three weeks. Jack was secretly glad for the excuse. For all the excitement their illicit activities had provided him, he could not help being overcome—especially as he lay in bed nights, the adenoidal breathing of his half-brother Keith beside him keeping him awake—by feelings of shame, and doom. He knew that what he was doing was wrong not only in the eyes of the law, but in God's eyes as well. Sister Marie's influence on his soul was far reaching. He had kept up the habit of attending mass on Sundays and holy days, but had let lapse his catechism classes, classes he had attended assiduously under Sister Marie's tutelage in Vermont. She had told him that she had never been so sure of anything in her life than the fact that he would enter the priesthood. She had been so fervent in her belief that Johnny Labalm came to believe, himself, that he actually heard God's calling, especially when he performed Stations of the Cross at Our Lady of Fatima Church in Groveton.

Nowadays, Jack Scanlon merely went through the motions, not feeling any of the ardor, or the genuine mystical stirrings that had overtaken Johnny Labalm a few short years ago. He was bothered by his growing indifference to religion; he wouldn't have been able to explain it if anyone were to ask. Now that he had taken up a life of crime, sometimes his dreams featured themes of perdition, eternal hell fire. As if it weren't bad enough he had to endure the awful guilt that overtook him when he masturbated, or ate meat on Friday, now he had to bear the conscience of a full-fledged thief! Robbing the club treasury when he was seven was only the beginning. These transgressions were so abhorrent in his mind he couldn't even bring himself to admit to them in the confessional. Instead, Jack Scanlon learned the art of denial, a skill that would serve him well (and ill) for years to come.

The boys gave up their thievery in the winter months because of the cold, directing all their energy, instead, on basketball. In the meantime, Jack Scanlon's life in the three-room apartment on the third floor of the Woodman block on the corner of Center and Silver Streets was becoming more than he could bear. He was forced to share a bed in the living room with his half-brothers. Billy had not yet overcome his bed-wetting. His mother slept with Bill Scanlon in the small bedroom. The narrow kitchen lacked a refrigerator or stove. Jack's mother cooked their meals on top of a two-burner hot plate. What little milk was in their diet came out of the can. On the rare occasions they had fresh milk it had to be consumed the same day it arrived for lack of a place to keep it cold in summer. In the winter, if they kept it in the narrow kitchen window it froze.

It was in the summer of 1951, during one of Bill Scanlon's frequent extended benders, when Jack's mother, out of sheer desperation, was forced to take a job in a shoe factory to put food on the table, and to keep the landlord from putting her family out on the street. Unfortunately for Jack, it was at the very beginning of summer vacation, and it fell to him to stay home and look after his half-brothers.

His mother came home from her first day on the job looking as worn out as he had ever seen her. She wore a plain gray dress with large white buttons up the front. Even as preoccupied as he was with his own misery after passing the longest day of his life chasing his quarrelsome, whining, crying half-brothers around in the suffocating space of the apartment, his mother's fatigue didn't fail to get his attention.

"Did you take them out today?" his mother asked, sighing irritably as she plucked up articles of clothing strewn around the living room: on the sofa, on the one armchair, on the bed. "Couldn't you pick up around here, Johnny? What else have you got to do all day?"

Jack, fairly choking with anger at his mother, and resentment against Keith and Billy, whom he learned to despise after a single day of confinement in their company, said nothing. His mother's turned down mouth, her pale face, and dull hair wrapped in a red bandana, failed to move him to sympathy for her. His mother went into the kitchen to draw a kettle of water for tea. Keith and Billy followed her, whining at her for candy, candy that she didn't have to give any more than Jack had to give them when they went at him all day long.

"What have I been telling you all day? There *is* no goddamned candy! And there's not going to *be* any, so get used to it!" Jack was shaking with anger and frustration. His mother wheeled around to face him, her eyes narrowed.

"Don't use that tone with them. You hear me, Johnny?"

"Jesus!" Jack stalked to the living room door, the only door in or out of the apartment, and slammed it behind him.

"Come back here this minute, young man!" he heard his mother yell as he hurried down the stairs. "You won't get no supper," was the last thing he heard her say before he pushed out the front door to the outside of the building.

There were three cement steps to the sidewalk. He had no place to go, no money. He sat down on the top step, his heart pumping wildly. Across the street he spotted Mr. Simon, a balding little man who wore his trousers' waist up to his chest, held there by a pair of black and white suspenders. He wore the kind of rimless spectacles his grandmother used to wear; he was locking up his store. He carried a package under his arm wrapped in butcher's paper and tied with white string. He looked once toward the intersection, and then turned to walk up Silver Street. The farther west you walked up Silver Street the older and more elegant the houses became.

The barbershop next door was already closed. The drugstore stayed open till eight o'clock. He would have liked to go in the drugstore and look at the comic books on the magazine rack, but the woman behind the counter always gave him funny looks whenever he came in, as if she suspected he was a shoplifter. Besides, he seldom had enough money to buy anything, not even a ten-cent comic book.

His mother had threatened to withhold his supper. He wondered what supper would amount to tonight. For the past two days his family had dined on canned tomato soup and saltines, peanut butter and stale bread. She had brought home no groceries today, and it was more than likely that there would be none until she received her first paycheck. Jack was sick to his stomach from this realization. Not from hunger, because a day in the company of his half-brothers had taken away his appetite, but sick at the thought of having to go back to the welfare office to obtain a grocery chit. The people at the welfare office were bad enough, but not nearly as bad as the grocery clerks who looked at you as if you carried a communicable disease when you handed them the welfare document that entitled you to certain groceries. The welfare chit didn't cover cigarettes and alcohol, but somehow his mother found the money to buy cigarettes, and his stepfather had no trouble purchasing his beer and whiskey.

A taxicab pulled up to the curb. May Boulanger, the widow who lived in the apartment below the Scanlons, got out of the back seat on the street side. A girl with dark hair, wearing a sleeveless blouse and gray pleated skirt, got out on the curbside. The cab driver opened the trunk and removed two suitcases. May probed her handbag for coins, and placed them, one at a time, counting as she did with her lips moving, into the cabbie's outstretched hand. The girl picked up both suitcases and endeavored to carry them to the steps, where Jack sat. They were heavy, and she could barely get them to clear the curb. Jack's eyes were glued to the girl's ample front.

"Hi there," the girl said with a smile, "Could you possibly help me with these?" Jack sat, immobile, seeming not to comprehend the girl's request. "Please," she said, her dark eyebrows rising, her head cocking to one side.

Jack lurched to his feet as if he had been pinched. He hurried down the steps to the sidewalk and took hold of the handles of the two suitcases, without a word.

"I'll take one," the girl said, "if you can get this other one. What's your name?"

"Jack. I can get the both of them," he said, hoisting the two suitcases. They were heavier than they looked; he had to exert all his strength just to lift them off the sidewalk.

"Hello, Johnny." May Boulanger greeted him, having finished her business with the cab driver. "Let me take one of those," she said to Jack, and tried to take one of the suitcases from him.

"I can take them both."

"Say hello to Bernie, Johnny, my niece from Rochester. She'll be staying with me for a few weeks while her parents are away."

"He said his name was Jack, Aunt May," the girl said, with a gay little laugh. Jack blushed deeply, in spite of himself.

"Well, his mom and I call him Johnny. So you can call him what you want. You sure you can manage both of those, Johnny? Bernie, why don't you take one of them?" May poked around in her handbag for a moment, as if she were looking for something, and then climbed the steps and entered the building. Bernie made a move to relieve Jack of half his burden.

"I can handle them."

The girl smiled and raised a skeptical eyebrow, as if she doubted anyone as slight as this boy could carry two heavy suitcases up a flight of stairs. "Why don't you at least take them up one at a time?"

"I can take them both at once."

"Okey dokey," she said, smiling at Jack, and touching the back flip of her hair delicately with the palm of her hand. Then she followed her aunt up the stairs.

Jack Scanlon, who weighed less than eighty pounds, hauled the two heavy suitcases, one stair at a time, up to the second floor, and paused on the landing in front of May Boulanger's open door, to rest. He was sweating like a horse and out of breath. Then he grabbed the handles, and using his legs for support, muscled the bags into the apartment. May and her niece sat close together on the couch, head to head over an open magazine.

"Oh, thanks, Johnny. You're a peach," May said, looking up briefly from the magazine at Jack, her less-than-eighty-pound porter.

"Thank you ... Jack," Bernie said, with her lovely smile.

"You're welcome." Jack stood in the middle of the living room floor beside the suitcases, not knowing what to say or do next. May and her niece were back in the magazine, letting him stand there, like another piece of luggage. Jack took the opportunity to study the girl while she was preoccupied. He couldn't be sure of her age; she could have been anywhere between sixteen and eighteen. And though his eyes were naturally drawn to her breasts, he could not help but notice the fullness and redness of her lips, which brought out the startling whiteness of her skin. Because her hair was fastened back with two tortoise shell barrettes on either side of her head, her small, delicate ears were exposed. His eyes fell back to her front, and down below her waist where he could see the contours of her shapely thighs beneath the fabric of her skirt. Between the hem of her skirt and the tops of her white rolled socks, her ankles were smooth, firm, and oh so white! She had on penny loafers. She looked up abruptly, as if she meant to catch him gawking. But she smiled that lovely smile again, and this time Jack didn't blush.

"Is your mother home, Johnny?" May asked him, turning a page of the magazine without looking at him."

"Yes. She's got a job now. She's working. She just got home, about five thirty."

"A job? Well. You've got to meet Dot Scanlon," May said to her niece. "And Bill, her husband. He's quite a character. Why don't you run upstairs and ask your mother and father to come down and meet Bernie."

"He's not home. I think my mother's making supper," Jack said.

"Well, tell her to come down afterwards." To Bernie she said, "You'll love Dot. She's a lot of fun." May threw her bare arm up on the back of the couch. She was pale, with thin, reddish hair and pale freckled eyelids that Jack couldn't help looking at whenever he looked at her. Fun was not a word he associated with his mother. Grim would be a better word to describe her, in his opinion. If he'd heard her laugh a half dozen times in the three years he had lived with her he'd be surprised.

"I better be going," Jack said, making no move from his place in the middle of the living room, which, unlike his own, had several pieces of furniture, and a green rug with a low pile. May's apartment was exactly like his own, except that it looked bigger owing to the fact that there wasn't a full-sized bed in the middle of the living room. Several magazines were arranged, fan-like, on a glass topped coffee table in front of the big couch with the nubby plaid fabric. Against the short wall that separated bedroom and kitchen was a small dining room table with three straight-back chairs. May had hung crisp white curtains in the two windows overlooking Silver Street. The windows in his apartment had water-stained pull-down shades, but no curtains. May also had a gas range and a waist-high refrigerator in her kitchen. To Jack Scanlon, May Boulanger seemed well off ... for a widow. His mother had told him she was a sales lady at a dry goods store on Center Street. Jack would have preferred to remain in the company of May and her niece, but he was at a loss for a pretext to stay.

"Don't forget to tell your mother to come down and meet Bernie after supper," May said. Jack interpreted this as his cue to leave.

* * *

"Bernadette," Bernie said to Jack, as she applied red nail polish on the little toe of her left foot. Bernie had invited him into May's apartment, as he was on his way downstairs with his half-brothers to give them (and himself) relief from the oven-like heat of the apartment. Bernie had a small fan set up on the coffee table, and had left the apartment door open to let in any chance cool air that might, however unlikely, be found in the dank hallway. Her invitation had set Jack's heart to thumping. There was the problem, however, of his charges. He couldn't leave them by themselves on the sidewalk with all the traffic at the busy intersection. Between the Woodman Block and the house next door was a fenced in vacant lot overgrown with weeds. He steered Billy and Keith there, ignoring their screams of protest, closed the linked metal gate after them, and hurried back upstairs to Bernie.

"That's a nice name," Jack said, sitting cautiously on the edge of an armchair next to the couch where Bernie, lovely bare white feet on the cushion, one knee up to her ear, applied nail polish to the remaining toes on her left foot. She had on shorts and a sleeveless white blouse. Several random, flat brown moles were sprinkled on both thighs. "Why does your aunt call you Bernie?"

"Everyone calls me that. It's easier to say than Bernadette, you've got to admit." Her voice was bright, slightly high-pitched, as if she were about to break into song. "How about some raspberry Kool-Aid?"

"Sure."

"What did you do with the little ones?" Bernie asked him on her way to the kitchen. "Shall I get them some too?"

"My mother doesn't want them to have anything sweet unless she gives it to them," Jack lied. "They'd drink soda pop, Kool-Aid, whatever, all day if you let them. That and eat candy till they made themselves sick."

"I'm sure you weren't like that when you were little." Bernie returned with two glasses of raspberry Kool-Aid.

Johnny Labalm had been a soda pop glutton ever since he could remember. And not much had changed since his metamorphosis into Jack Scanlon. He had to consciously refrain from gulping down his Kool-Aid for fear of offending, or disgusting, Bernie.

The two front windows were wide open; no breeze stirred the thin muslin curtains, adding to the sensation of stifling heat though it was not yet ten o'clock in the morning. Jack turned an ear to the window side of the room, listening for the shrill voices of Keith and Billy, but all that he heard was the sound of automobile traffic. Bernie put her feet up on the coffee table and inspected her freshly painted nails, little tufts of cotton batting between her graceful toes to keep them separated.

"They'll take forever to dry on a day like this." As hot and humid as it was, Jack could detect no sign of perspiration on the girl. For his part, sweat stood out all over his face, and dark semi-circles were growing under the arms of his polo shirt. "What grade are you in, Jack?"

"I'll be in seventh. You in high school?"

"I'll be a freshman in September. I'm so excited!"

"A freshman. How old are you?"

"You don't ask a lady her age," Bernie said, with a sly smile. "I'll be fourteen next Tuesday. I can't wait for high school."

Fourteen. He wouldn't have blinked if she had said eighteen. Yet to him, even knowing that she was barely two years older than he, she was virtually a woman, out of his reach. He felt even skinnier, more sebaceous, and more immature than if she had been eighteen.

Bernie had yet to take a drink of her Kool-Aid; it sat perspiring on the glass-topped coffee table, forming a puddle of water around the base of the tumbler. Jack took a small sip. He was sweating so freely he didn't dare sit back in the upholstered armchair.

"I'll bet the work is hard. Harder than grade school."

"I'll have to get all new clothes." Bernie reached for her glass. Drops of condensed water fell on the front of her blouse, wetting it so he could see the outline of her bra. She brushed the water away with a delicate swipe of her hand, and put the glass back on the coffee table without taking a drink. Her expression changed, as if something important had just occurred to her. "You can't imagine all the things you have to think about when you start dating." Bernie paused, and looked over at Jack apologetically. "You'll be faced with this yourself before you know it," she said, like an older sister, or like his Aunt Lily. And he knew he was being condescended to, but from Bernie he didn't take offense.

He decided to play dumb. "Faced with what?"

A loud, high-pitched sound filled the room. Bernie, startled, flung her arms out to her sides and clutched at the sofa cushions with both hands. Jack went sick to his stomach. He jumped out of the chair and ran to the open window. On the street below a bus was stopped at an oblique angle at the intersection, partly in its own lane, partly in the oncoming traffic lane. Several people milled about on the street in front of the bus. Then a uniformed policeman appeared from in front of the bus, a child in his arms. Jack knew immediately that it was either Keith or Billy.

"Oh, my God, my God," he said, and ran for the door.

"What is it?" Bernie yelled after him.

"My God!" Jack leaped down the stairs and out the front door of the apartment house. Keith was sitting on the curb, looking at the activity in the street. He didn't seem in any distress. Jack ran into the street in the direction of the police car, in the back seat of which, the officer was attempting to place Billy. Billy was screaming as only Billy could scream:

"Don't take me to jail!"

Jack ran up to the policeman. "That's my brother. Is he hurt bad?"

"I don't think so, but I'm not taking any chances. I'm taking him to the hospital emergency room. Where's your mother?"

"She's working."

"Who's looking after you and your brother?"

"I am. I mean, my father's away, and ... I'm taking care of my brothers, but ..." Jack turned to point out Keith sitting on the curb to the officer, but Keith was no longer there.

"Telephone your mother or your father and tell them to get to the hospital as fast as they can. I think he's all right. He stepped out in front of the bus, but I don't think it hit him. People say he ran into the bus while it was stopped. He's plenty scared though." Billy's fright was expressed in his loud wailing. "Lucky I was coming through on a call," the policeman added, as an afterthought. "Go ahead," he said to Jack, opening the door to his black and white police cruiser. The night before, Jack had passed along May's invitation to his mother to come downstairs and meet Bernie. He remained behind in the apartment to mind Keith and Billy. It occurred to him now, as his panic began to subside, and he spotted Keith in the doorway being attended to by Bernie, that his mother might have told May where she was employed. In that case, Bernie could phone her aunt at the dry goods store and ask; she might even know herself.

* * *

Billy had not been badly hurt—a few bruises on his face and arms from pavement burn—as the bus driver had managed to bring his vehicle to a stop short of hitting him, just as the police officer had surmised. So Billy had been the one in motion when they collided, not the bus. Jack's mother was furious with him. He had no defense, of course. He didn't tell her about "corralling" them in the vacant lot. He lied and told her he had taken his eye off Billy for only an "instant" and bang, it just happened. He said nothing about visiting Bernie, either. Of course, if the truth ever came out, he'd be in even hotter water. He tried in a clumsy way to enlist Bernie in his lie, by asking her not to tell his mother that he had been visiting her instead of watching his half-brothers. Bernie felt awful enough for her part in what happened without causing him more grief. That a twelve-year-old boy was left to care all day for a four- and five-year-old was a subject that never came up. And his mother's confidence in him as a baby sitter hadn't been shaken to the point where she relieved him of this responsibility. He was back on the job the very next day. Now, he was more concerned about how the incident would play with his stepfather when he eventually returned (and to Jack's constant woe he always did). In the meantime he would be shackled to Keith and Billy between the hours of 6:30 A.M. and 5:30 P.M. five days a week. If he wanted to visit Bernie he would have to bring the boys along, and this was not something he wanted to inflict on her, as much as he was in her thrall. So his visits to Bernie were restricted to weekend mornings or early afternoons. Practically every evening during the week, and definitely every weekend, Bernie was out on a date. Jack came to despise the high school boys who pulled up to the curb in their cars and honked their horns, and he'd watch from his window as she came out of the apartment house on the run, and jump into the passenger seat, buoyant, happy, prepared for an evening of fun and freedom. He was in turmoil; of love, jealousy, and resentment. He hated Bernie for the exuberance she displayed when her boyfriends showed up in their cars, boyfriends who couldn't be bothered to climb a flight of stairs to call on her properly. Instead, they rudely summoned her with a toot of the horn. And he began to hate Bernie for allowing herself to be treated so, the same way he had grown to hate his mother for permitting herself to be under the thumb of her drunken lout of a husband. Yet, he couldn't wait until Saturday morning, when the proper hour to call on Bernie arrived. May worked a half-day on Saturday, so he had Bernie to himself for the better part of the morning. Sometimes she would greet him in her pajamas and make him a cup of cocoa, and he wondered what it would be like to be married to her.

The Saturday after Billy's encounter with the bus, Jack knocked softly on May's door and waited, holding his breath, for the sound of Bernie's voice inviting him in. He waited for what seemed like a long time. He put his ear to the door, for she often played the radio and might not have heard his knock. He didn't want to appear too eager by knocking louder. He heard no sound on the other side of the door. Sighing with disappointment, he climbed down the stairs feeling aimless with no place to go and no one to go to. Since school had ended, and he had become indentured by his mother to the day care of his wretched half-brothers, Jack had lost touch with Terry Stickney and the other kids he had become acquainted with at Franklin School. He had no idea how they passed the days of their summer vacation, but he had a feeling that none of their lot was as bad as his. The prospect of romance, however platonic, with Bernie had given him the slightest glimmer of hope for a chance to salvage a semblance of happiness from what was the bleakest of outlooks for the rest of this long summer.

Fully dispirited now by his own dark thoughts, Jack pushed through the door to the street to find Bernie on the front steps, applying lotion to her fair skin.

"Hello, Jack," Bernie said, her voice high and exuberant, as usual. She patted the cement step beside her with the flat of her hand. "Sit down and talk to me." Jack obeyed, happy to oblige, his heartbeat quickening. He had even taken pains (and it was painful indeed for him) to give himself a sponge bath when he got up this morning in anticipation of being in Bernie's proximity and not wanting to offend or disgust her.

"I just knocked on your door. I thought you were out ... on a date or something."

Bernie glanced at him and smiled. "A date? This time of day? I came down for a little air before the sun gets too high. The last thing I need is a burn." Bernie turned a bottle of sweet smelling lotion upside down in her palm, gave a little twist of the hand when she had what she needed, and started to rub it into her calf. The sun was just visible above Getchel's Sunoco station across the intersection, on Center Street. The fragrant skin lotion could not disguise the odor that issued from Bernie herself, a smell that he wouldn't have been able to put words to, but went right to his head. He had a powerful urge to put his hand on her skin, any part of it, just to find out what it felt like.

"You don't like to sit in the sun?"

"Not at all. It ruins your skin."

He liked sitting in the sun, baking, sweating, even getting burned. He liked it hot and humid too, as long he could be outside and not cooped up in the apartment.

Bernie turned toward him. "Boys don't have to worry, but if you're a girl those things are important. You've got fair skin, Jack. You shouldn't spend a lot of time in the sun yourself."

"Why? I like it."

"You don't look like you've had much of it this summer."

"I've been stuck inside most of the time with my little brothers."

"They don't look much like you, Jack. Do you have a different father, or different mother?" Bernie massaged her thighs with another portion of lotion. Jack's eyes shifted surreptiously to those thighs sprinkled with their flat brown moles, like freckles. His little pecker began to stir.

"Father."

"Do you still see him, your father?"

"He died. In the war." Jack recited his official version of the fate of his real father, the father he had no knowledge of, and didn't dare ask his mother about.

"Do you remember him?"

"No. I was about two or something. He was a pilot, in the Navy. That's all I know." Johnny Labalm's fantasy father had been everything from a fighter pilot to a submarine commander, but he was always a Navy man, like his uncles.

"I enjoyed meeting your mother. I haven't seen your stepfather."

"He's away ... working."

"What kind of music do you like?"

Nobody had ever asked him about his taste in music. He was not sure now how to characterize it. He knew definitely what he did *not* like, and that was just about anything he heard on the radio, from "How Much is that Doggy in the Window" to "Harbor Lights" and everything in between, which seemed to be all that was played, at least on the only station he could get on his mother's radio. He said as much to Bernie. She laughed.

"That's so true." She screwed the cap on the skin lotion and stood up. "Do you know how to dance?"

"Not really." He didn't mind admitting to his not being able to dance. Dancing wasn't considered manly by the boys he knew.

Across the street, customers began to move in and out of the doors of the meat market and the drugstore in a steady stream. Jack could see one of the two chairs in the barbershop through the big picture window. A little boy about Keith's age occupied it at present. A man stood beside the chair, chatting with the barber as he cut the boy's hair. Jack remembered his own first haircut. It was his grandmother who stood beside the barber on that occasion, wringing her hands, distraught at the sight of her little prince's fair locks accumulating on the black and white tiled floor around the chair. It was as if she believed they would never grow back.

"I brought my record player from home, and some records. Come on upstairs. I'll teach you to dance. The two-step's the easiest to learn. We'll start with that. You'll need to know how to dance when you start dating."

Bernie's machine was portable and plugged into the wall outlet. It came in a box that looked like luggage (luggage that he hadn't hauled up the stairs). Bernie sorted through a stack of records on the coffee table, selected one, which she held by its edge in the palms of her hands before inserting it on the turntable.

"This is great to dance to." She switched on the machine, moved the arm to the outer edge of the record, and lowered it carefully.

He recognized the Jo Stafford song; he'd heard it on the radio many times. Bernie moved to the center of the room, tugging Jack by the hand. She turned to face him, inches away, so close he could smell the lotion she had worked into her white skin, and could feel the heat from her body adding to the sultry heat of the room.

"Stand up straight. Put your feet together. Now give me your left hand." Jack obeyed. She took his right wrist and guided his hand to the back of her waist. She rested her left hand on his meager shoulder. "See the pyramids along the Nile," Jo Stafford crooned. Bernie instructed him in the two-step, and he was soon gliding around the living room rug with his dream girl in his arms. They danced at arm's length, but in skin contact, close enough to cause the blood to pound in his temples. Halfway through the song he heard heavy footsteps on the stairs outside the open door. They continued past the landing, and up to the next floor ... his floor. He knew that step. He paused.

"What's the matter, Jack? Lose the rhythm?"

"I guess so." He let go of his dance partner, and sat down in the armchair.

"Now *that's* a long face." Bernie lifted the needle off the record. She sorted through her pile and selected another one. Jack cast his eyes on the floor; he sensed Bernie was looking at him. He heard the scratchy contact of the phonograph needle on the record, and then Kay Starr's "Wheel of Fortune" filled the room.

"Was that your stepfather on the stairs, Jack?"

"I guess so." Jack almost whispered his reply, his eyes fastened on the space between his feet.

"Want to dance some more? I'll show you how to waltz if you want." Bernie's voice had taken on a quiet, almost solemn tone, as if she were accommodating his sudden change in mood. He looked up and met her large eyes, the color of chestnuts. At this moment she looked to him like Ava Gardner. But he also saw pity in her look, and he was embarrassed because the last thing he wanted was her pity, or anyone else's pity for that matter.

"People still waltz?" he asked, trying for a sardonic attitude. He forced a smile to his lips. In his mind, the waltz was a dance from another century.

"Sure. Come on, get up. I'll show you."

"This doesn't sound much like waltz music." He wasn't sure in what dance category he would place "Wheel of Fortune," but it certainly wasn't a waltz.

Bernie stopped the record. "Let's just go through the steps without music. I'll count. One-two-three, one-two-three."

Jack's mother was suddenly in the doorway, the ever-present cigarette hanging from the corner of her mouth. She had on the dress she had worn to work all week.

"Hello, Bernie. Johnny, come upstairs. I want to talk to you."

"Now?"

"Yes, *now*," his mother said. She sounded impatient, irritable.

"I'm teaching Jack to dance, Mrs. Scanlon," Bernie said brightly. "He's a fast learner."

"His father needs to talk to him," his mother replied. Jack bridled, as usual, at his mother's casual reference to Bill Scanlon as his "father." He looked at Bernie for her reaction, for she too now was aware that Bill Scanlon was not his real father. Bernie's eyes shifted from his mother to him. He thought he saw her blink. Were her blinking eyes meant to tell him that she had noticed how he resented the reference?

Whatever it was his stepfather wanted to talk to him about, it would mean something unpleasant. Maybe his mother had spilled the news about Billy's accident, and laid the blame on her oldest son. It was more likely that Bill Scanlon wanted him for an errand; that was the pattern. He would come home sick and hungover, and need Jack to fetch him something to make him "well"; probably an order of spaghetti if history could be counted on as a predictor. He made no move to go upstairs.

"Johnny, now!" His mother flicked ashes into the palm of her hand.

"I was going to Hitchcock Park to play ball. Why do I have to talk to him now?"

"Because he wants to see you right now," his mother said, exasperated with him. "I'll tell him you're on your way." His mother left the room to go upstairs without even saying goodbye to Bernie, which he thought was terribly rude, but typical of her behavior whenever her husband returned from his benders. He was embarrassed.

"I'm sorry," he said to Bernie.

"That's okay, Jack. Some other time. Come back when you can."

Bill Scanlon, stripped down to his jockey shorts, was by now passed out on the couch, his hands tucked between his knees, mouth wide open, and snoring loud enough to cause what few dishes they owned to rattle in the kitchen cupboard.

"Can I go back downstairs?" he asked his mother, with no effort to disguise his sarcasm.

"You'll have to go to Paola's first. He wants an order of spaghetti and hot sausage." Jack spotted several crumpled up bills on the floor next to the couch. Billy and Keith romped on the bed, oblivious of their father's presence. Jack wondered again whether his mother had informed her husband of Billy's run-in with the bus (from which he was fully recovered). If she had, he could expect an inquisition when Bill Scanlon recovered.

"So, there's money to feed his face, but not enough for groceries for his family." Jack trembled with rage.

"Go ahead, Johnny. Get him what he wants. I'll straighten this out later." Jack detected a sympathetic note in his mother's words. Now that she was working and earning a wage maybe she felt as though she had some leverage with her husband, maybe she didn't feel so beholden to him. But Jack had been around long enough to take the cynical view that Bill Scanlon was capable of gleefully mooching off his wife, and that she would put up with it.

"Fucking pig," Jack said under his breath, as he reached down and grabbed the bills off the floor. He heard strains of music coming from the apartment below, from Bernie's record player, or perhaps from the floor model radio in her aunt's living room. May didn't own a television, however, or else Jack would have been down there visiting her a long time ago. The Scanlon household's only contact with the outside world was his mother's little Philco radio that she kept on the bureau in her bedroom. Most of the friends he'd made in Garrison had television sets in their homes (one exception being Terry Stickney's family). He felt deprived and sorry for himself. What he felt most acutely by the lack of a television set was access to boxing matches. Out of desperation to see something of the Robinson-Lamotta fight last winter, he had contorted himself in the window of his mother's bedroom from which he had an oblique view of their neighbor's set. He had watched what he could while listening to the blow by blow on the radio. He loved boxing, and dreamed of becoming a boxer himself someday. It was the one thing he had his stepfather to thank for.

"What did you say, Johnny?"

"Nothing. You sure Paola's will be serving spaghetti this time of the morning? What if they're not?" Paola's was a good half-mile from where they lived. He was in no mood to walk all that distance for nothing. The Scanlons didn't have a telephone, but May did. "I could call from Bern ... May's," he added.

"Don't bother the poor girl any more than you already have. They'll have it, believe me."

Why should I believe you? he felt like saying to her. How many times had she promised him that she had put up with all she was going to put up with from her husband? Nothing had changed. Nothing ever would change; of that he was convinced. He left the apartment on his errand, his heart aching with hate and sorrow.

* * *

The only good Jack could see coming from his stepfather's return would be in the possible relief he might get from his babysitting duties. Bill Scanlon had blown the last job he had as a short order cook at the Monarch Diner when he took off on a bender an hour into his shift. The job had wounded his pride. Bill Scanlon fancied himself a "chef" who should be commanding a kitchen in a first-rate hotel or a three star restaurant, not turning over hamburgers and omelets in a working-class diner. Bill Scanlon's "pride" had launched more than one of his benders. The respite from his half-brothers was not to be. Bill Scanlon's excuse for not staying home to look after his sons was that he needed to hit the pavement in search of work. For all his job-hunting, his stepfather still managed to return home in the evening smelling of alcohol. For the first few days after Bill Scanlon's return Jack had been anxious, waiting for the subject of Billy's accident to come up, and the blame to be placed on him, Jack, for his negligence. He heard not a whisper from his stepfather about the incident. Billy himself had been uncharacteristically quiet about his adventure, so quiet that Jack suspected that his mother had negotiated his silence, at least in the presence of his father. In the meantime, Billy and Keith had taken up the practice of accosting strangers on the street and begging them for small change, which they immediately converted to penny candy in the corner grocery store on the Center Street side of the block. Jack watched them from the front steps; he made no effort to stop them. To do so would mean having to identify with them; for some reason he was reluctant to be associated with them. People thought they were adorable, "precocious," as they hectored passersby for money. Jack's mother was furious with him for allowing it to go on. He couldn't find a way to tell her that he didn't want people to know he was related to the little beggars. The next day, when his mother left for work, and his stepfather left for God-knew-where, Jack fashioned signs on pieces of cardboard and hung them around Keith and Billy's necks. The signs read: PLEASE DON'T GIVE ME ANY MONEY. People, of course, found the signs as "adorable" as the boys themselves, and they raked in even more coin. If Jack had been more attentive, had watched them more carefully, he could have intervened, could have put a stop to their brazen panhandling. He was too preoccupied with his own misery, however, and the only way he knew how to allay the condition was to engage in daytime fantasy and dreaming.

"Look," he told them one day, as they came out of the grocery store with all four of their grubby little hands clutching penny candy, "if you don't quit hounding people on the street for money I'm telling the old man, and you know what he'll do to you." Why he hadn't thought of this solution before he could only chalk up to indifference and, of course, his by now chronic misery. They wailed and protested, as he expected they would do, but the idea of a whipping by their drunken father had the effect he hoped for. They desisted from their panhandling behavior for two full days.

Saturday arrived, the day he had anticipated all week, the day he could visit Bernie. She was determined to continue his dance lessons; she searched her stack of records on the coffee table for something suitable from her collection to teach her pupil the jitterbug. Jack remembered (it would have been impossible to forget so rare an occasion) the time his mother and stepfather demonstrated the "lindy" in the living room of their apartment in Massachusetts. Bill Scanlon had been benignly drunk, and his mother had, grim faced, gone along with him, reluctantly at first, but when he had flung her around the room a couple of times, seemed even to enjoy it herself. Johnny Labalm had been impressed by their grace, their sense of rhythm, a sense he did not possess, and never would. He said as much to Bernie.

"Nonsense," she said, pulling him out of his chair. "Now start off the same way you do for the two-step." She maneuvered him into position, just as "Music Music Music" blared out of the speaker. But it was no good; Jack just couldn't get the hang of when to push and when to pull, which way to turn his partner, inside or out. He didn't *feel* the rhythm, not the rhythm of "Music Music Music" in any case. He didn't say so to Bernie, but he was not fond of that song. Bernie didn't press him to dance.

"You want some cold cocoa? Or would you rather have Kool-Aid? I've got a batch of lemon-lime all mixed."

"Kool-Aid." He was grateful to be off the jitterbug hook. He struggled for a way to suggest that they slow dance again, but a way to ask eluded him. Bernie looked cool and fresh in a red and white gingham blouse and white shorts. She wore no shoes; her toenails looked freshly painted, bright red. Her fingernails were the same shade of red as her toenails.

"Bruce took me to a drive-in movie last night," Bernie said, handing Jack his glass of green Kool-Aid. Bernie had opted for a glass of cocoa. Jack didn't want to hear about her date with this Bruce, didn't want to hear about any outdoor movie. "He's got a convertible. It was so nice in the open air, with all the stars in the sky to look at ..."

"What movie was playing?"

"Why ... it was ... you know, I can't remember." Bernie giggled at her inability to recall the movie she had seen only the night before, as if it were somehow funny. Jack thought otherwise. It was no doubt because she was so attentive to Bruce, and he to her, that she paid no attention to what was on the screen. It made him dislike her intensely ... for the moment. "Oh, I know. It was a gangster movie of some kind. I don't even remember the name, if I even knew it. Bruce is gone on gangster movies. He didn't listen to a word I said. Thank God the stars were all out, and the moon was so beautiful."

Jack liked gangster movies too, but he'd be damned if he'd pay more attention to one of them than he would to Bernie if he were fortunate enough to have her beside him in a convertible. Anyway, he was happy to hear that Bruce-whoever-he-was was so "gone" on gangster movies. He took a sip of Kool-Aid; Bernie sat on the couch, put her bare feet up on the coffee table, and her hands behind her head. Jack cast his eyes to the floor in case he should forget himself and stare at her breasts.

"Have you ever kissed a girl, Jack?"

"Sure." It would have been more accurate to say that girls had kissed him, somewhat against his will. He had never initiated a kiss, had never gotten up enough nerve to try, even when the urge was strong.

"Really? How many? Come on, Jack, tell the truth." She had that wheedling, teasing tone he used to hear from his Aunt Lily when she would have at him about his "love life."

"I don't know. Enough, I guess." He felt his face grow warm, and he was already sweating from the heat in the room. He turned away so that he wasn't looking directly at Bernie.

"So I guess you know how to French kiss, then."

"Sure." He had no idea what she meant by the term "French kiss."

"Come here next to me." Bernie patted the cushion beside her with her open palm. "You'll need to learn how to kiss properly for when you start dating." He couldn't believe what he was hearing. He remained in his chair, as if he were paralyzed. "Don't be afraid. I'm not going to bite you."

Like a robot, Jack rose from his chair and steered a course for a position on the couch beside Bernie.

"Sit a little closer. Now close your eyes. I'm going to kiss you first like you were my little brother. Okay?"

Jack closed his eyes and held his breath. He could feel Bernie's warmth approaching before he experienced her soft lips on his mouth. He panicked when he realized he hadn't brushed his teeth this morning.

"Now that wasn't so bad, was it?" Bernie said with a gay laugh. "Now I want you to close your eyes again, and this time open your mouth a little." Jack did as he was told, even though he felt a little silly, and vulnerable, as if he were being set up for a practical joke. Then Bernie's soft, warm lips were on his. His hands instinctively found their way to her bare arms.

"Now let's not get fresh, young man," she said, removing his hands, and giggling. "Let's try again. This time keep your hands to home. This is school, not romance. Now, watch what I do with my tongue." And her lips were on his again, and her moist tongue darted into his mouth, and flicked his own tongue. He thought the top of his head might explode. She moved away from him. He opened his eyes to find her smiling at him, and he saw the smile of an older sister, not a girlfriend. "Is that the way you remember French kissing?" He nodded his head. "If you learn to use your tongue like that the girls will be impressed. You should practice it on your girlfriends," she said, teasing again. So, she hadn't believed him when he told her he knew how to French kiss. Embarrassed, he got up and returned to his chair, picked up his drink off the floor and brought it up to his lips.

"Don't be so shy, Jack. Girls will like you, don't worry. You should shampoo your hair, though. And be sure to brush your teeth three times a day." She was beginning to sound a lot like Charlotte, and the mere thought of Charlotte Toney pained him.

Thus began the education of young Jack Scanlon in the art of appealing to the opposite sex, with the voluptuous Bernadette as his mentor. It occurred to him all of a sudden that he didn't know Bernie's last name. It couldn't be Boulanger, because May was her aunt, and Boulanger was her married name. No matter, she would teach him in the ways of seduction and love. In subsequent lessons, Bernie instructed him in the etiquette of dating, and wooing: Always listen to what your date says to you, or to the air, it didn't matter, and act interested even if you are not, which, being a boy, you probably won't be. Don't be like Bruce, and show more interest in things like gangster movies, or what's under the hood of your car than in what the girl you're dating has to say, and be sure to compliment her on her appearance. Pay particular attention to how her hair looks, and be sure to notice the clothes she is wearing and say something nice about how she looks in that skirt, or that sweater, or whatever. Jack wondered how a guy like, say, Terry Stickney would fare as a lover with his preoccupation, bordering on obsession, with cars. Maybe that would all change when he was actually old enough to choose between his cars and soft girls.

Then Bernie was gone. Jack knocked on the door one Saturday morning as had become his habit, and no one answered. Thinking she might be outside on the steps getting her air before the sun got too high in the sky, he went outside, but there was no sign of her out there either. He tried several more times that morning, and later, in the early afternoon. When May got home from work she informed him that Bernie had left the evening before, to join her parents in Montreal. She would not be back this summer. She might come for a visit next summer, but May couldn't say for sure. May didn't say whether she had left a message for him, and he didn't have the courage to ask, knowing what the answer was bound to be. Jack felt an ache grow in his chest, an ache that lasted for a week, maybe more.

* * *

While Jack and his family were living in those wretched three rooms that year, Keith was four years old. He had another thirty-five years left to live. He seemed always to long for the things he didn't, or couldn't, have. He would install himself in front of the window overlooking Silver Street when it was time for school to let out for the children in the neighborhood. He would wait for them to pass by below, on their way home. "Here they come, come, come, come, come," he would chant monotonously until the last one passed and disappeared out of sight. He would whine to Jack, or to his mother, unable to understand why he couldn't go to school with those children. When he was finally old enough to attend school, his cries were for permission to stay home from it. He had never taken kindly to school. Neither had Billy. For that matter, Jack Scanlon had no particular fondness for school either, but he enjoyed modest success there, unlike Keith and Billy.

"Are you all right, Mr. Scanlon?"

"Yeah, I'm fine, Karla."

Karla placed her warm hand on his arm. "I know." He was tempted to clamp his hand over hers, but caught himself before doing anything as unseemly as that. Karla took a step backward to appraise him. "Your color is much improved. How do you feel?"

"Much improved, much improved." He was condemned to being a

wiseass; he would be one till the day he died. Karla didn't act like she took offense. She did something with the delivery tube, then smiled and went on her way. Scanlon let his head loll on the back of the recliner and closed his eyes.

Seventeen

Summer 1953:

Jack pressed his face against Eddie Tracy's screen door for a look into his kitchen.

"You in there, Eddie?"

"Come on in." Jack let himself in. Eddie sat at the kitchen table eating toast and reading a *Captain Marvel* comic book.

"You want to hear something funny? I ..."

"How was the farm?" Eddie interrupted.

"Okay. I went horseback riding. Those babies are bigger than they look in the movies. It was like being on an elephant's back."

"So what's funny?" Eddie folded half a slice of toast and pushed it whole into his mouth. He wiped his buttery fingers on his T-shirt.

"Funny?"

"Yeah. You said 'want to hear something funny?'"

"Oh. Yeah. Well, Neil Sullivan's old man just dropped me off, and I walk in the house and it's fucking empty! Not a stick of fucking furniture, no sign of Keith or Billy, nothing. Don't you think that's 'fucking funny?'" Eddie's mother came in the kitchen just as he finished saying 'fucking funny.' Ordinarily he would have been embarrassed at using such language in front of any adult, especially a female, let alone somebody's mother, but where Marge Tracy was concerned, he felt no need to be embarrassed. On the contrary, the oaths that fell from her lips were more cause for his embarrassment. Eddie didn't seem to mind that his mother swore like a sailor, and went around the house all day wearing nothing but a corduroy bathrobe that sometimes fell open to reveal that she had nothing on underneath. Marge Tracy had enormous breasts, breasts that found their way into Jack's fantasies day and night. To entertain sexual fantasies with his current best friend's mother he considered so heinous that he couldn't even confess them to the priest. For that matter, going to confession had become a less frequent habit lately.

"They moved out yesterday," Marge said, lighting a cigarette, and using the match to light the gas burner on the stovetop. "Only took one truckload."

Jack laughed. "Did they happen to say where they were going?"

Marge shrugged her shoulders, causing the top of her bathrobe to open slightly, treating Jack to her impressive cleavage.

"Didn't say anything to me. Eddie, before you go out, run down to the store and get me a box of Tampax. Super."

"Christ, Ma, you know how I hate to buy that shit. Why can't you get it yourself?"

Jack sympathized with his friend. His mother was always asking him to go to the store to buy her damned Tampax, too.

"I suppose I ought to start looking for them," Jack said. For a couple of months his mother and stepfather had talked idly about moving, but he didn't recall them mentioning any definite plans. Bill Scanlon was known to make spur-of-the-moment decisions; and he was not one to listen to opposition to his decisions. Jack had been gone only two days, visiting Neil Sullivan on his father's farm in Maine. Now he was homeless, abandoned by his family. If only it were true. Nothing would have made him happier.

"I wonder if they moved out of town," he thought out loud. Neither Eddie nor his mother had any idea where the Scanlon family had gone, without their oldest boy.

"They didn't leave you a note or anything?" Marge asked him, leaning against the kitchen counter, her left arm across her breast, propping her right elbow with her left hand.

"I didn't see one. Jesus, this is just funny as hell. I wouldn't know where to start looking."

"You can stay here if you want," Marge said, flicking ashes into the palm of her hand. Jack often slept over at their house. Eddie had his own bedroom, but Jack had to share the bed with him. Eddie had no annoying brothers or sisters. His mother was divorced; Eddie did not know what had become of his father. Marge had a steady boyfriend, a Greek named Art Catsoulas, who owned a barbershop on Center Street next to the offices of the *Garrison Record*. Art spent most nights at Marge's house, sharing her bed. At least Eddie's mother's bedroom was downstairs, out of earshot of his own, so he (and when he stayed with him, Jack) didn't have to put up with their sex sounds. That was not the case in Jack's house, with his mother's and Bill Scanlon's bedroom next to the one he shared with his half-brothers.

"Thanks, Mrs. Tracy. Eddie, what do you say we head down to the park? There should be a game starting up by now." Eddie rose from the table, and tipped over his chair in his haste to get out of the house.

"Don't forget my Tampax," Eddie's mother said, as he was going out the door.

"Shit." Eddie returned to get money for his mother's Tampax. Jack stood on the back steps, looking at his now empty house. It had once been painted brown; the paint had long ago peeled away leaving the wood exposed to the weather. There was no central heating, and in the cold New Hampshire winter the Scanlons had to gather around the kerosene space heater in the living room for warmth. The water pipes were frozen as often as not. Jack had to lug a two-gallon kerosene can in each hand, and climb up steep St. George Street to the gas station for refills two or three times a week in winter.

Eddie parted company with Jack at the grocery store on the corner of St. George and Hitchcock Avenue to buy his mother's Tampax. Jack spotted three of Hitchcock Park's habitués sitting on the edge of the empty wading pool, watching the polluted Cocheco River as it coursed to the Atlantic Ocean.

"Scanlon," the three of them said, almost in unison. He'd crept up on them from behind hoping to surprise them, give them a little scare. They showed surprise if not alarm, as he had hoped.

"Where the fuck you been? We ain't seen you for a couple days," Pat Meserve said, dragging on his cigarette.

"Maine. Just got back this morning. Who's got the cards? Tracy'll be along in a few minutes. Let's play some cards. Might as well deal Tracy in."

Georgie O'Shea had a deck of Bicycles in his pocket; he never went anywhere without them. Georgie, Pat Meserve, and Harry "Harpo" Marks got up and headed for the picnic table next to the bathhouse. The sun was starting to show over the roof of Caledonia Electronics across the stinking Cocheco River. The river always stank from the industrial waste dumped into it by Garrison's factories. Today there was the added stench of the rotting bodies of alewives that had spawned and died over the weekend. Nobody bothered to comment anymore, they were all so used to the malodorous Cocheco River.

The Hitchcock Park boys played poker every morning except Sunday (Sunday was when the adults had their game) in summer for about two hours, or until they had enough men to start a game of baseball. They'd play ball until about four in the afternoon; then another hour of penny ante poker before they headed home for supper. They would play dealer's choice unless there were too many of them to play anything except five-card stud. By mutual agreement, no wild-card games were allowed, and it was considered bad form to check before raising.

Since Georgie had the cards, he declared himself dealer of the first hand.

"Ante up. We'll play Scanlon's game, jacks or better. Cards to the players." Georgie shuffled the cards skillfully, like a Las Vegas dealer. He slid the deck over to Pat Meserve when he finished to give Pat the option of cutting. Pat rapped his knuckles on the deck and Georgie dealt the first hand.

"I told you, deal Tracy a hand," Jack said. "I'll play it till he gets here. He's delivering Tampax to his old lady."

"Wouldn't mind delivering this to that old lady," Harpo Marks said, grabbing a handful of his crotch, and picking up his cards; he shuffled them a few times before having a look. He held them close to his face, as if he were nearsighted. Harpo was two years older than most of the boys who hung out in Hitchcock Park. He was lean, muscular, and had the best arm of any of the Hitchcock Park boys. Nobody tried to tag up and try for home from third with Harpo in centerfield.

Unlike Harpo Marks, Jack kept his feelings about Eddie's mother to himself. It bothered him to hear Harpo talk about her that way, made him a little jealous. He wondered what they said about his own mother when he wasn't around.

"I'll deal Tracy a hand when he gets here. Who's light, Meserve?" Georgie said.

"I put in!" Pat Meserve was indignant that he should be accused of failing to ante. Jack pushed a penny into the pot.

"Sorry." Jack looked at his cards and found a pair of sixes.

"Can you open, Scanlon?"

"No."

"Meserve?"

"By me."

"Harpo?"

"Ditto."

"Open," Georgie said, carelessly tossing two pennies into the pot. Everyone called. "Cards?" Jack drew three cards to his pair of sixes; Pat Meserve and Harpo each drew one card, and Georgie, the opener, dealt himself two cards, giving them the impression that he was holding three of a kind.

"Two cents without looking," Georgie said, sliding his cards, one over the other, face down, without showing any interest yet in what he had drawn. Jack squeezed his cards; the third six was the last card he looked at.

"Raise," he said, in case Georgie was bluffing his three of a kind.

"Four cents to you," Georgie said to Pat Meserve. Pat threw his hand in; Harpo did the same. Georgie made a show of slowly removing four pennies from one of the stacks in front of him and tossing them in the pot. "Back at you."

"Call, it's just you and me," Jack said. Georgie fanned out his cards on the picnic table, deeply scarred from jackknife graffiti. Jack saw three tens covering the two remaining cards. He threw his hand in face down. Georgie raked in the pot with one long-fingered hand, and pushed the cards to Harpo.

"Did you deal me in?" Eddie said, sliding in on the bench beside Jack.

"We got to see your money first," Georgie said.

"Fuck you, O'Shea." Eddie reached in his pocket and came back with a fistful of pennies and nickels.

"The game is seven-card stud," Harpo announced. "Bet two cents only if a pair's showing, and on last card." They all knew the drill, but it was a conceit of the dealer to recite it as if the information were brand new. "And a trey, and a lady, and another trey, and a ten, and a ..." Harpo paused with his own card at the level of his ear before slapping it down on top of his down cards, "a nine to the dealer. Queen bets."

"Check," Eddie said.

"Get your checks at the bank," Pat Meserve said, and bet a penny on his three of hearts. Pat had long, dirt-packed fingernails, short stiff hair that stood out on his head like porcupine quills. There was nobody who played ball for Hitchcock Park who was slower afoot than Pat Meserve. Jack could even beat him in the dash, and Jack Scanlon was no speed demon himself. If Pat Meserve was the slowest runner in the bunch, he was by far the shrewdest card player. Georgie raised a penny with his ten showing. Everybody called, and Harpo resumed dealing.

"Who's got a smoke? I'm out," Georgie said.

"You're always out." Harpo shook a cigarette out of his pack of Luckies. "I hope you win today so you can buy your own for a change."

"Spare another one of those, Harpo?" Pat Meserve said, holding out his dirty fingers.

"Here." Harpo pushed the pack to the middle of the table. "Everybody help themselves. I got cigarettes to spare, and money to burn." Everybody *did* help himself because they all believed that Harpo *did* have cigarettes to spare, and money, if not to burn, at least more to spend than any of the rest of them. His father owned a diner in Rochester, and Harpo worked the short order grill on weekends when the drunks were especially generous with their tips. By the end of the summer Harpo figured he'd have enough money saved to buy himself a used car. At present, the only guy in their crowd who owned a car was Julian Cardwell. Julian couldn't really be counted as one of them; he was twenty-one or twenty-two years old, and had a steady job at the tannery, on the night shift. He liked to play ball with them once in a while, and sometimes he'd take a bunch of them to Salisbury Beach on a Saturday night. He drove a black Packard. They got Julian to buy beer for them too. The only other person they could count on for transportation was Tex Minehan, a twenty-four-year-old queer who had his own garbage collection business, and who had a thing for younger teenage boys. He wore cowboy hats, tight-fitting blue jeans and pointy-toed cowboy boots; he drove a gray 1948 Nash and treated them regularly to ice cream and soft drinks. Like Julian Cardwell, he would buy them beer if they hounded him enough. He believed it was wrong for him to provide alcohol for minors even if he had no compunction about buggering them if they were willing. For that reason, they made sure there were at least three of them present before anyone got in the car with Tex. Sexy Texy, they called him behind his back. He was a big, strong, sinewy guy, who spent his day throwing heavy metal cans full of garbage around. He was also a trifle simple-minded, and could be brought easily to tears by any kind of mean teasing from the boys.

"Tracy tell you about tomorrow night's party?" Georgie directed his question at Jack.

"What party?" He looked at Eddie. "Raise." Jack had drawn a ten to go with the one he had in the hole, giving him two pair, tens and eights. Eddie had a pair of sevens, the only pair showing.

"Julian's making a liquor store run for us tomorrow before he goes to work," Georgie said, frowning at his cards before dropping out. "He's got to have the list and the money by tonight, so if you want in you got to come up with the scratch today."

"You talking about whiskey?" Jack said. He had never tasted whiskey even if he'd smelled enough of it, living with his stepfather the past five years. He was sure he'd never be able to swallow anything as strong as whiskey. He liked beer well enough, though it didn't take much to fill him up, and sometimes it caused him to puke.

"What do you think he'd buy at the liquor store? Pepsi? Write down what you want and give it to me by four o'clock. And don't forget your money," Georgie added. Jack looked at Eddie, who was studying his cards, trying to decide whether to raise back.

"Call," he said. So he had no better than two pair, Jack reasoned. Harpo had a seven showing so Eddie wasn't likely to have three of them. Besides the pair of sevens, he had an ace and a queen.

"What are you going to get?" he asked Eddie.

"A pint of Four Roses," Eddie said. Bill Scanlon sometimes brought home Four Roses. "I've always been a lover of flowers," he would say, and laugh like it was the most hilarious thing anybody had ever said.

"How much is it?"

"It better not be more than two bucks, 'cause that's all I can afford."

"Julian'll tell me how much it is when I show him the list. He knows all the prices." Georgie took the last puff of the cigarette he'd bummed from Harpo, and flicked it through the chain-link fence into the river. Jack didn't want to let on that he didn't know enough about hard liquor to have a preference.

"I'll go with Four Roses too, if it doesn't cost more than two bucks," he said, inserting the card Harpo dealt him between his two down cards.

"Check to the raise," Eddie said. Harpo and Pat Meserve folded, leaving only Eddie and Jack. Jack checked, as it was considered bad form to do otherwise when there were only two players left in the hand.

"Aces up." Eddie turned up the ace of diamonds from his hole cards.

Jack tossed his cards in. "I can't buy a winning hand. Where's this party supposed to be?" He directed his question at Georgie, who seemed to be the self-appointed organizer, the man in charge.

"Up on the hill." The "hill" was the one behind Caledonia Electronics. At the base of the hill the hoboes and other local down-at-the-heel drunks bivouacked, and drank Canned Heat strained though bread or dirty T-shirts. Long grass and mountain ash grew on the hill among scattered pine, maple, and oak saplings, and a few stands of young birches. At the top of the hill they had a full view of the backside of Caledonia Electronics across the river. There, they would be safe from view from the road. According to Georgie, the cops left the bums alone at their base camp, so they would have no reason to take an interest in what might be going on further up the hill. That is, unless they let themselves get out of hand, and did something stupid like start a fire.

"Julian'll stash the booze behind the rock just past the jungle. We'll play cards till it gets too dark to see, then head over. Okay?" Georgie had it all figured out.

"What if the bums find the stash?" Pat Meserve said.

"What reason would they have to look behind the boulder? They never stray far from their pit. Besides they're always too rum-dum to go exploring."

"So you say, Georgie," Pat Meserve said. "Wait'll we get there and find it gone, and the bums having a party on us."

"Too bad we couldn't get some women," Harpo said.

"We could ask Leah to come," Georgie said, chuckling. Leah Nesbitt was a fat girl with a pretty face who lived in the neighborhood. That is, she was pretty as long as she kept her mouth shut. When she smiled, all eyes would fasten on her gray teeth; one of the front ones had a big chip out of it. Georgie claimed that he'd screwed her plenty of times, and furthermore, he said she had told him that she had plans to screw all the Hitchcock Park boys.

"I'd just as soon spend the rest of my life beating off than put my dick in Leah Nesbitt," Eddie declared solemnly.

"What do you think of the new chick moved in with old lady Toussaint?" Pat Meserve said in his high voice.

"That's her granddaughter," Eddie said.

"Whatever she is, she's some kind of piece, if you ask me," Pat said.

Jack was not aware that Mrs. Toussaint, who lived catty corner across the street from Eddie Tracy, had a granddaughter visiting her. He had apparently missed a lot in the two days he had been away. He wondered why Eddie hadn't told him about the girl.

"Yeah," Eddie said, "I wouldn't have no trouble putting my dick in her. What a dish!"

"How old is she?" Jack asked.

"Our age, I'd guess," Eddie said. The card game had ceased temporarily with talk of parties and girls.

"Deal the cards, will you, Scanlon?" Harpo demanded.

Jack dealt a hand of jacks or better. If his luck didn't change soon he wouldn't be able to afford two dollars for a pint of Four Roses. And his interest was piqued by the appearance of this new girl in the neighborhood. He didn't want to let on to the others just how interested he was, however. He tried to sound nonchalant when he asked if anyone knew her name.

"I heard the old lady call her Rosemary, I think," Eddie said. "I'll open." Eddie tossed two pennies in the pot. Everybody called. Jack finally won a pot with a mere pair of queens. In the meantime, four more guys turned up. They weren't interested in playing cards, so they gave Georgie back his deck, and drifted over to the baseball diamond to start up a game of scrub. By ten thirty enough kids had showed up to play six on a side. They played till late in the afternoon.

Lying beside Eddie in his bed that night after listening to "Ghost Riders in the Sky" by Frankie Laine on Eddie's record player, Jack wondered out loud how long he could avoid reuniting with his family.

"How long do you think your mother would let me stay here?" All the clothes he had were the ones on his back, and a change of underwear he had taken to Maine with him.

"Shit, I forgot to tell you. Your mother called here today. They moved to Fern Street. My mother told me the number, but I forgot. Anyway, I forgot to tell you."

Jack sighed deeply. "Where's Fern Street?"

"Fucked if I know. Ask my mother. I guess that means you'll have to go home. You could stay with us, you want. My old lady wouldn't give a shit."

"Mine would. Or maybe she wouldn't." But Jack was only talking. His mother and stepfather had taken him hostage, but then they went and adopted him legally. He was now officially their property.

"I guess I'd better go look for them tomorrow before we play ball."

"Don't forget about tomorrow night. I never drank whiskey before. You?"

"Not really."

"What if it makes us puke? O'Shea'll never let us hear the end of it."

"Why don't you just pound the shit out of him, and be done with it?"

"He'd get his brother Donald after me."

"Donald can't touch you; he's an adult. He hit you, you could bring him to court."

"A lot of good that'll do me if I'm in the hospital."

"I think you should pound on him anyway. He's a shitass. I can't stand him."

Jack turned on his side on the lumpy mattress. He had a view out the window of the now empty house he had lived in for little more than a year. It was illuminated by a single streetlight, which made it look shabbier than it had in the morning. Except for Mrs. Toussaint's neat little white cottage, the whole neighborhood was run down. It sat, incongruously, directly across the street from the shack occupied, at present, by a family of displaced shantytowners. Nobody knew with certainty how many kids there were in the family, only that they were dirty, ill clothed, malnourished, and unruly. Mrs. Toussaint seemed not to take offense at the eyesore across the street as she tended the little flower garden that lined both sides of the brick walkway to her front door. She had window boxes of pansies, and peonies and hollyhocks planted in front of the white picket fence in front of the house. The house was built in 1693 if the legend over the door was to be believed.

"What did you say the girl's name was?" Jack asked.

"What girl?"

"Mrs. Toussaint's granddaughter."

"Rosemary, I think. Yeah, I'm pretty sure. What a piece! Hey, let's beat off again while I got a picture of her in my head."

"I'm going to sleep." Jack didn't remember falling asleep. He must have dreamed about something unpleasant, because he woke up feeling anxious and out of sorts. Then he remembered that Eddie had told him about his family's new address. He'd be obliged to look for and rejoin them.

Marge Tracy told him the next morning that Fern Street was one of those dead-end streets between Wayland Avenue and the railroad tracks, the east line of which ran to Portland, Maine, and points north and east.

"What number Fern?" Jack asked her, as she served hot oatmeal to her son and his guest.

"Shit, I forgot to write it down," she said.

Jack sighed dramatically. "I'll find it ... I guess."

On Fern Street, his ears told him which house his family had moved to. Billy's loud, plaintive crying rang out from the second story of the flat-roofed duplex with peeling paint that once had been white. Two more houses stood between that one and a deep gulley marking the dead-end part of the street. Jack hesitated before starting up the short walk to the front door, three wooden steps up from sidewalk level. A mailbox next to the front door had "Keeler" written on it in red crayon. Thinking that this must have been the former tenant or tenants, displaced by his family, Jack pushed through the door and found himself at the bottom of a stairway with a door on the right. Billy's voice was louder, and came from somewhere beyond the top of the stairs. Jack climbed the stairs as if he were on his way to the gallows.

"You got the wrong house, kid," he heard a woman's voice say. He looked up to see a woman with wide nostrils looking down at him, her forearms on a railing overlooking the stairs.

"I'm sorry. I heard my brother crying and ..."

"Your brother? If that's your brother how come you don't know how to get in your own house? I think I'm calling the cops." The woman moved away from the railing.

"I've been away. They just moved here. I didn't ..."

"Oh yeah. What's your name?"

"Jack."

"Jack what?"

"Scanlon."

She was silent for a moment, then she told him he could get to his place through the door at the top of the stairs, but made a point of reminding him that it was *her* apartment he was passing through to get there. He thanked her, but when he tried to open the door that presumably led to his new apartment, he found it blocked. He could open it only a crack, not even wide enough to see inside the room on the other side. The woman watched him.

"Guess I'm not getting in this way," he said, turning to her. She was short and stout, with short unruly dark hair, and a bad complexion. The flared nostrils he had seen from the bottom of the stairs belonged to a broad, fleshy nose. She had on a sleeveless blouse and shorts that accentuated a potbelly. She was either grotesquely malformed or pregnant.

"Around the side. That way." She pointed in the direction of the gulley.

"Thanks." Jack hurried down the stairs and out the door. He stopped outside on the sidewalk to survey his new neighborhood. It was not much of an improvement over his old one. He walked around the side of the house just as several dirty children spilled boisterously out of the adjacent house through a screen door. The pavestones leading to the entrance to his new house were broken or cracked. A short, dirt driveway separated his house from the one the urchins had emerged from.

The stairway to his house was in an enclosure. He climbed the stairs and found the door at the top open; it led into the kitchen. Cardboard boxes were scattered over the floor, crumpled newspapers spilling out of them. He could no longer hear Billy crying. No one was in the kitchen. He entered cautiously, like an intruder, as if he didn't belong here any more than he belonged in the apartment he had just blundered into. His mother appeared from a room off the kitchen, a mop in her hand, and a red kerchief tied around her head.

"You took your time getting here," she said. "I could have used some help."

"Maybe you should have left me a note." He didn't ask about his stepfather, and why he couldn't help her get settled.

"Don't be fresh. I need you to go to the store. There's one on the corner of Railroad and Wayland Avenue."

"I noticed."

"I need toilet paper and two pounds of sugar."

What, no Tampax? he felt like saying.

"Where's Billy? I heard him bawling all the way out on the street. Who's that woman next door? She was going to call the cops on me."

"Gladys Keeler. She just got married to a friend of your father." As usual, Jack bridled at the use of "father" and Bill Scanlon.

"Gee, he must be a solid citizen."

"Here," his mother said, reaching into her pocketbook on the stove. She handed him a dollar bill. He hated going to the store for toilet paper almost as much as for her Tampax. He couldn't help feeling that store clerks judged him poorly for buying that kind of stuff. Once, his stepfather sent him to the drug store to buy ointment for hemorrhoids. He insisted that Bill Scanlon write down the name of the medicine on a piece of paper, claiming that he'd forget the name of it otherwise. In truth, he wanted it on paper so he could hand it to the druggist and spare himself the embarrassment of asking for it out loud. Bill Scanlon looked at him skeptically, knowing what a good memory his stepson had, but wrote it down anyway.

"I told Eddie I'd stay overnight at his house. His mother invited me for supper." If he was going to spend the night drinking hard liquor he didn't want to take the chance of being found out by his mother.

"Haven't you stayed overnight at other people's house enough for one week?"

"Just for tonight. They're expecting me to."

"You better start paying attention to your chores around here. When are you supposed to go back to work?"

"Next week." Jack's boss, Abe Cohen, had closed down the deli for two weeks so he could spend time with the two daughters his wife had gotten custody of in their divorce settlement. He quarreled with her constantly about visitation rights. To be able to spend two full weeks with them had taken a lot of effort on his part, and he wanted to make the most of it. Besides, he was fed up with the deli business, and had been for a long time. He was happy for any excuse to get away from it. Jack didn't mind the vacation either, except for the fact that he was fast running out of spending money. The two bucks he'd shelled out for tonight's whiskey left him with a dollar seventy-five to his name. Eddie had talked about the two of them hoofing it out to the country club to see if they could make a few bucks caddying. Neither one of them knew the first thing about golf, so they gave up on the idea. Now that he was about to run out of money, Jack reconsidered. How much did you need to know about the game to lug some old man's golf clubs around the course for him? He made a note to himself to talk to Eddie about it tonight, while they leaned on each other for the courage to swallow the whiskey they'd both spent good money on.

Billy came in the room, his face tear-streaked, his protruding lower lip quivering.

"What's the trouble, sport?" Jack said. His mother gathered loose newspapers off the floor and stuffed them in the cardboard boxes.

"Keith got more than me," Billy said between sobs.

"More what? As if I didn't know."

"Jack, I need that toilet paper."

"What do you say, sport, want to come to the store with me?" Billy's eyes opened wide. Jack could imagine the wheels turning in his little brain: store-equals–candy-equals-no-sharing-with-Keith-who-always-gets-more-than-I-do-because -everybody-likes-Keith-better-than-they-like-me. That might have been true about his mother and his father, but it was not true about his stepbrother. Jack was partial to Billy. Maybe he was naturally on the side of the underdog, and Billy was an underdog in the Scanlon household if there ever was one. Poor Billy. He seemed always the object of scorn and ridicule from his mother and father, even from his younger brother. Where Keith was naturally well coordinated, even graceful, Billy was clumsy, always stumbling over and into things. His mother liked to say, unkindly, that Billy tripped over the floral patterns on the linoleum. And Keith, with his keen ear to the rebuke heaped on his brother and rival, was quick to parrot what he heard from them. If it weren't bad enough that Billy had to endure this almost constant verbal assault, he was also on the receiving end of his father's vicious slaps, especially at meal times. The fact that Bill Scanlon's eating habits were more like a swine's than a human being's didn't prevent him from pointing out to his oldest son his shortcomings at the dining table. The last time Bill Scanlon had returned home from one of his benders, sick from hangover, he had showed up at the supper table completely bare-assed and in a hateful mood. Billy's loud, open-mouthed chewing had annoyed him to the point where he backhanded the kid on the mouth, hard enough to make his teeth bleed. When Billy screamed with pain, his father answered with another vicious slap to the back of his head. Jack had more than once fantasized about killing his stepfather, but this was one time he could have brought off the act—if he wasn't so much in fear of the man as Billy was himself.

He had invited Billy to accompany him to the store so he could buy the kid candy on the sly.

"Take Keith with you too," his mother said. She was no doubt wise to what Jack was up to.

"I can't deal with both of them. Come on, Billy, let's hit the road." Jack took hold of Billy's hand on the way to the store. "How do you like the new place?" Billy skipped along on the uneven sidewalk with its broken pavement, as carefree as the kid ever got, liberated temporarily from competition with Keith for his mother's affections. It was a struggle he would never win while Keith was alive. Billy's face darkened at the question. "You'll get used to it. You'll make new friends in the neighborhood, you'll see." At the intersection, Jack looked up and down Railroad Street and Fern Street as if searching for the new friends Billy might cultivate in his new neighborhood. He saw not a living soul.

They came to the store, a white, single-story building on the corner of Railroad Street and Wayland Avenue. Jack hesitated for a moment, wondering whether he should send Billy in ahead to ask for the toilet paper, and then come in behind him to buy the sugar, and Billy's candy. He decided against it, because poor Billy would undoubtedly screw up. "Let's go," he said, pulling his half-brother gently by the hand.

He could tell instantly that the woman behind the counter disapproved of children. Whether she disliked children in general or the ones standing before her in particular, he couldn't have said, this being his first time in the place, but her aversion to them was obvious from the look of distaste on her oily face. He was frankly surprised that she deigned to accept his money for the three rolls of toilet paper and the two-pound bag of sugar he asked for. To Billy's profound disappointment, Maglaras's Corner Store didn't stock penny candy.

"What have you got for candy?" Jack asked the dour Greek woman, who looked no older than his mother. She sighed at the question, and told them all she carried were Hershey bars and Charleston Chews. She charged a dime, where every store Jack had ever shopped charged a nickel. He bought his half-brother a ten-cent Hershey's chocolate bar with no nuts.

"I'm telling you," Jack said to Billy on the walk home, "if you let Keith find out I bought you a candy bar he'll scream his ass off till Ma makes me buy him one too. So, do you think you can keep your mouth shut?" Billy nodded his head. "Sure you will."

* * *

With his personal finances so low, Jack decided it would be a bad idea to join the poker game in progress next to the bathhouse. Instead, he loitered by the swings just beyond the dirt road that marked home run territory in the Hitchcock Park ball field. There was the swing set, a jungle gym, a carousel, and horseshoe pits in the small patch of grass between the ball field and the National Guard Armory. He sat in one of the swings and tried to lose himself in pleasant thoughts, as he swung leisurely at first, before becoming caught up in the sensation of motion. He climbed higher, tilting his head at the apex of his arc for a look at the cloudless blue sky. He had never reached horizontal to the crossbar from the sitting position, and was too afraid of falling to try it standing up. Since there were no witnesses, he decided to try for horizontal now.

On the backward descent, after several oscillations, he discovered Nellie Perkins regarding him, something like a smirk on her boyish face. As far as he knew, he was the only Hitchcock Park boy who thought she was kind of pretty, a fact he never admitted to his friends. Not that Nellie Perkins gave two hoots about what Hitchcock Park boys thought about her. She was Jack's age, or perhaps a year older, and a fiercely independent tomboy. In summer she wore T-shirts like the boys; in cool weather she preferred plaid flannel shirts. Jeans, she wore in all weather, and it didn't escape Jack's notice how well she filled them out.

Nellie was the best horseshoe player in Hitchcock Park. She had hounded the boys to let her join them in their baseball games until they finally relented, grudgingly. When she outshined most of them in the field, and could hit the long ball with the best of them, they made an arbitrary decision, by mutual consent, to bar her from their games.

One time, when Jack was losing to Nellie in a game of horseshoes, he stepped behind her to retrieve one of his shoes while she was in the backswing of her throw. The horseshoe caught him in the middle of his forehead. It took all of his will to keep from crying in front of her. Nellie felt bad for her failure to see him behind her. She pulled a dirty handkerchief from her back pocket, moistened it with water from the drinking fountain, and nursed the lump on his forehead, which achieved the size of a golf ball. Nellie had a way of ministering to his injury that allayed the embarrassment he would normally have experienced at such a clumsy moment. Her hands, in particular, soothed him, rough as they were from doing tomboy things.

"Maybe we can make the bar together," Nellie said, as if she knew exactly what he was trying to do. He didn't want to admit to Nellie that he was scared to try it from the standing position.

"I'm trying to do it sitting down." As if to say that anyone could do it standing up. Where was the challenge? He dug his heels in the trough of dirt at the bottom of his forward arc, and came to a stop.

"I know." Without another word Nellie grabbed hold of the chain-linked uprights and straddled him. Her face was now inches away from his. She started them off by pulling with her arms and thrusting with her pelvis. When it was his turn to push forward in order to gain momentum, he was mortified to discover the stirrings of an erection. He clamped his jaws tightly and tried to will it away because there was no telling how Nellie would react. It wasn't out of the question that beating the living crap out of him would be one way she could react. Or if, as every boy except Jack believed, she was utterly sexless, she would be more than likely not to even notice ... or if she noticed, not to care.

They gained altitude. At the apex of Jack's forward thrust, he was looking nearly straight up into Nellie's wild green eyes instead of at the cloudless blue sky. On the descent, they discovered that they had an audience. Jack's body stiffened. Nellie *did* perceive this.

"Don't pay any attention to them," she said. "A couple more kicks and we'll be there."

"They're waiting for me. I better stop." He let the backs of his heels hit the trough at the bottom of his back swing. He didn't like the smile that appeared on Nellie's face, a smile that said, "You're no different than they are." She reached up on the swing's uprights and hoisted herself up to the standing position, her crotch in his face. She bent her knees and pumped her legs, accelerating them upward for another cycle.

"Come on, Nellie," Jack protested. "They're waiting for me. I got to go."

"I thought you wanted to shoot the bar."

"I only wanted to get even with it. We already did that ... almost."

"Well, I'm taking you over the bar now, so you better hang on!" Nellie bent her knees again and pumped hard. They sailed past horizontal. At their apex, the chain links nearest the seat crimped; as they started back down the seat snapped back with a crack. For an instant he thought the seat had come loose from the chains.

"Jesus, Nellie, are you trying to get us killed!" As they approached the bottom of their arc, Nellie let go of the uprights and leaped off the swing, right over Jack's head. The boys applauded. Jack brought the swing to a stop on the next cycle. Nellie was walking away toward the armory, her head in the air, her shoulders back. The boys catcalled after her until, back still turned, she raised her arm and gave them the finger. They hooted and laughed till she was out of sight.

"Come on, Scanlon," Georgie O'Shea said, "we got drinkin' to do."

"It's still light," Jack said.

"So what?" Eddie said. "The stuff's there. Why do we need to wait and hunt for it in the dark?" One reason that occurred to Jack for waiting until dark was that they were less likely to be seen by the cops, or worse, by the hoboes.

The seven of them made their way slowly across the baseball field, past the empty wading pool to the road that intersected with Hitchcock Avenue and followed the river, dead-ending at the big barn where the City of Garrison's vehicles were stored. An old, rusted iron bridge spanned the river, but was declared unsafe and closed for traffic. Somebody produced a tennis ball. They tossed the ball around, playing a game in which any bad throw or dropped pass meant the kid committing the error had to chug-a-lug from his bottle. Eddie Tracy was the worst of the lot at throwing and catching; by the time they arrived at the boulder where Julian Cardwell had stashed the liquor, he'd made three errors, two catching and one throwing. Pat Meserve, who was almost as inept as Eddie Tracy, also had three errors. Harpo Marks was the only one of them who was error free. Jack had one error as he was taken by surprise by a blind pass Georgie O'Shea had sent his way, while looking at Fat Bernier. Jack bobbled it two or three times, but finally lost it. Now he worried about having to chug-a-lug hard liquor, having never as much as sipped the stuff before.

The cache, in two brown paper bags, was right where Julian Cardwell said it would be, in a hollow space between a large rock and an embankment. The boys had passed quietly by the hobo "jungle," just beyond a gravel turnaround, in a sort of hollow protected by a knoll of ash saplings. They could hear their muffled voices, and see smoke rising from a campfire. Freight trains passed through Garrison every day, dropping off and picking up rail-riding hoboes. The population in the "jungle," therefore, was in a state of constant flux.

Georgie O'Shea thought if would be fun to gather some rocks, head for a piece of high ground above their campsite, and heave them down at the hoboes.

"Great idea, O'Shea," Harpo said. "I got a better one. What if we just toss your ass in there with them?"

"I seen some of them guys," Pat Meserve whispered. "They look fucking mean. I say we don't mess with them."

Harpo opened up the bags and handed out pint bottles wrapped in liquor store paper. Julian had written the names of the owners on the wrappings.

"Scanlon," Harpo said, handing Jack his bottle. "Tracy." They had both asked for Four Roses, but when Jack removed the wrapping he discovered that he had been given a pint of J.W. Dant, not Four Roses.

"What did you get, Eddie?" Eddie tore his wrapper off a bottle of Four Roses. "How come I get this stuff, and you get Four Roses?"

"Beats the bird shit out of me. I don't see what difference it makes. Whiskey's whiskey."

"It makes a difference if this shit is cheaper than Four Roses and Julian put the screws to me."

"It don't come cheaper than Four Roses," Harpo assured him. "Let's get up the hill and watch the sunset."

Harpo led the way up the hill through the waist high grass, and young saplings of pine, maple, oak, and mountain ash. They reached the top of the hill; the sun was a blood red ball perched on the western horizon, just above the gold dome of Garrison's city hall.

"Red sun at night, sailor's delight," Harpo said, unscrewing the cap off his bottle and raising it to his lips. He sipped a little before turning to the others. "All right, uncork them, and let's have a toast." Everyone did as he was told. Harpo, the self-appointed leader for the evening, raised his bottle and said, "Here's to just for the hell of it." He took a good-sized swallow from his bottle, one might even call it a "chug-a-lug," and he was the only one among the seven who hadn't dropped the ball, so to speak.

Jack brought his pint of J.W. Dant cautiously to his lips, catching the strong odor in his nostrils, which gave his stomach an involuntary turn. He pretended to drink with the others, but he kept his lips sealed shut. He licked those lips and tasted the harsh sour mash on the tip of his tongue. Once more his stomach lurched. He could only hope that the sun went down soon, and that Harpo wouldn't hold them to their chug-a-lug demerits.

The boys spread out along the side of the hill, sitting down in the tall grass to sip their whiskey and watch the sunset. Jack sat next to Eddie.

"Did you drink any of it?" He whispered because of the proximity of the others, especially Georgie O'Shea.

"Yeah, but I had to swallow my ass off to keep from puking. I don't think I can drink anymore of this shit." Eddie spoke in a low voice too, knowing that Georgie O'Shea would make a big deal of any of them who couldn't "handle his liquor."

"Me either," Jack confessed. "We should have thought to bring some ginger ale or Pepsi, or something to go with it."

"I could run down to the store and get something."

"Not now. They'll think we're pussies." Harpo, Pat Meserve, and Georgie O'Shea sat together nearby nipping from their still wrapped bottles, yukking it up. Earl "Fat" Bernier sat with his pal Leo Demers a little farther off. Leo and Fat were already in a dispute about something, their voices raised loud enough to cause Harpo to shush them. They disagreed on everything; Jack found all their concerns inane, their constant bickering tiresome.

"Hey," Eddie said to them, "are you guys married, or what?" Fat

Bernier turned and gave Eddie the finger, then took a long drink from his bottle. Jack unscrewed his cap and brought the bottle to his nose. "Oh, that's so nasty," he said, pushing it out to arm's length.

"Maybe so, but we paid for it. Might as well drink it." Eddie took a tentative sip from his Four Roses. "Try holding your breath," he said, gasping after a tiny sip. "Holy Jesus, it's like fire going down."

Fat Bernier started to gag. Leo Demers was amused. "You pussy. You can't even handle rum?" Fat, when he finished retching, gave Leo a hard punch to his upper arm. "You even hit like a pussy," Leo said, and started to laugh.

Jack took a deep breath and held it before trying another sip of whiskey. He had to swallow a few wads of saliva, like Eddie had, to keep from throwing it back up.

"You're right. Holding your breath helps ... a little." The sun had gone down behind the city hall leaving a purplish pink sky. The air was still, and humid. Mosquitoes were starting to come out. Eddie prepared himself to try another drink. So far, nobody had brought up the issue of chug-a-lug. They could hear Georgie O'Shea bragging to his companions about how he had spent one evening last week down by the riverbank, peppering the windows of Caledonia Electronics with his BB gun. Lights were on in the windows on all four stories of the factory. Jack doubted that a BB gun's pellets could do much damage at a distance of maybe four hundred feet from the bank of the river to where the factory sat, recessed from its side of the river. Yet, Georgie claimed he had drilled holes in windows on all four stories. Jack took another breath-holding sip of J.W. Dant. It seemed to go down easier this time. The whiskey's warmth spread through his belly.

"You know, for a while there, I thought you and Nellie were going at it on the swing," Eddie said. "Those guys did too. O'Shea says he thinks Nellie's really a guy. He says he'd sooner fuck a chicken."

"A chicken's probably as good as he can do. I don't understand why you guys think she's so bad looking. I think she's kind of pretty. And she's got a good body. Don't you think so?"

"Yeah, *I* do. But these guys ..."

"I don't believe Georgie O'Shea's ever had a piece of ass. He's all talk." Jack believed this statement deserved a drink for its forthrightness. He tried drinking without holding his breath. It nearly took his breath away.

"He claims he nailed Leah Nesbitt in the haunted house last week while we were playing hide-and-go-seek."

"That's not something I'd go around bragging about." Jack heard something buzzing inside his skull, like a bunch of crickets. "He claims he's screwed her plenty of times, but you can't believe anything he says." Jack took another sip of whiskey. Eddie did too.

"You feeling anything yet?"

"I think so. You?"

"Something's ringing in my ears. You see this new chick today? Mrs. Toussaint's granddaughter, what's her name?"

"Rosemary. Yeah, she was out messing around in the old lady's garden."

"What's she look like?"

"I don't know. She's a piece, I already told you."

"What's a 'piece' look like? That tells me nothing."

"I don't know how to describe girls, how they look." Eddie lay back on the grass, holding his bottle of Four Roses on his belly with both hands.

"What color's her hair, for Christ's sake?"

"Black. Black and kind of short. Almost as short as Nellie's."

"See. You can describe girls just fine if you put your mind to it."

"What's so fucking funny?" Eddie yelled at Pat, Georgie, and Harpo, who were rolling around on the ground, laughing out of control. They ignored Eddie.

"Maybe they're drunk already," Jack said in a low voice. "And O'Shea claims he can hold his liquor. What a pile of bullshit that guy is." Fat Bernier and Leo Demers were back at their argument, louder than before.

"I might have to punch him out before the night's over," Eddie said, referring to Georgie O'Shea. He swigged from his bottle and gasped for air. Dusk was giving up to darkness. The sky was suddenly black; no moon, no stars; the only light came from the windows of Caledonia Electronics across the river.

"We might have to start a fire," Eddie observed.

"Nice idea. That should make it easier for the cops to spot us."

"You can't see your fucking hand in front of your face."

"Better hang on tight to your bottle." The other boys were no more than ten feet away from where Jack and Eddie lay, stretched out in the tall grass, but they couldn't even make out their forms. They could hear them well enough. Their voices seemed to get louder the darker it got. Jack tried another sip of whiskey. It wasn't going down any easier, as he'd believed a minute ago. His stomach erupted, and he had to swallow again like crazy to keep from throwing up. The thrumming of the insects in his brain was deafening. This must be what getting drunk is like, he thought. He heard Eddie slap at a mosquito.

"Do you think we're drunk yet, Eddie?"

"I know I'm not. And I won't be because I can't get this shit down my throat."

"You better find a way. Why did we go through all the trouble to get the stuff if you're not going to drink it?"

"I suppose. So you've changed your tune. But I just know I'm going to puke."

"So what?"

"I hate to puke."

"So do I. Let's take a sip together."

Eddie sighed audibly. "Okay. On three. Ready?" Eddie counted down, and Jack assumed he drank from his Four Roses bottle. Jack sipped his J.W. Dant with his throat constricted, anything to make the passage smoother.

"Holy Jesus H. Christ, that's some awful shit!" Eddie gasped.

Jack's eyes were growing more accustomed to the dark. He could make out Eddie's recumbent form beside him, even the outlines of the others some distance from where he lay.

"Hey, Meserve," Eddie shouted. "You drunk yet?"

"Getting there," Pat Meserve yelled back, and then began to giggle foolishly.

"I'd say he was already there," Jack said.

"Where in Maine did you go?" Eddie asked him.

"Someplace near Sanford. Neil's old man's place. His folks got divorced last winter, and his old man bought this farm ..."

"Sanford? You call that Maine? That's not Maine, for Christ's sake." Eddie explained that he was from the "real" Maine. Up in the boondocks, a place called Dexter, is where he came from, and he had the accent to prove it.

"I've been to Bangor to visit my mother's uncle. The place didn't show me much. Is Dexter near Bangor?"

"Not too far." Jack was more interested in pursuing the subject of Mrs. Toussaint's granddaughter, but he didn't know how to shift the conversation in that direction without appearing too interested. This, he learned, was not something you left yourself open for with these guys.

"Come to think of it," Eddie said, "weren't we in the haunted house playing hide-and-go-seek the night O'Shea is supposed to have screwed Leah? Yeah, I'm sure of it. Wouldn't we have known it if he'd banged her?"

"I didn't hear anything that sounded like fucking," Jack said. The "haunted house" was directly across the street from the duplex Eddie lived in. It had been empty for as long as Jack had lived in the neighborhood, and judging from the accumulated neglect inside and outside the house, long before he moved there. There were eleven small rooms in the two-story house with several gables on the front of the roof; the paint was long gone, revealing the weathered clapboards. The wooden stairs leading to the front door were all broken and rotting away; all the windows were broken. The house made eerie, haunted sounds on windy nights.

Maybe inspired by overhearing Jack and Eddie talk about the haunted house, Harpo shut everybody up so he could tell a scary story. Harpo fancied himself a good storyteller, especially if the stories were about the supernatural, or the horrifically natural. Jack's mind was on other matters tonight, and he only half listened to Harpo's tale of the old man in the haunted house who liked to dine on the flesh of twelve-year-old boys. According to Harpo this old man was one of the itinerant hoboes who, for all anyone knew, could be right down there in the "jungle" below them, squeezing Sterno.

"Yeah," Fat Bernier interrupted, "Tex Minehan likes them about twelve too, but it ain't their flesh he likes to eat."

"Oh, no," Georgie O'Shea countered, "then what do you call your dick if it ain't flesh?"

"You know what I mean," Fat Bernier said.

Harpo was getting annoyed. "You think you guys could shut the fuck up while I'm telling my story?"

"Talk to the fat boy," Georgie said.

"I'm talking to the both of you. Just shut the fuck up." Harpo Marks continued his tale of the flesh eating old man in the haunted house on St. George Street, and Jack's mind invented a fantasy attended by the girl with the short black hair named Rosemary Toussaint. But the other girl with the shorter black hair intruded. He could still feel the green-eyed tomboy's legs around his middle, her weight in his lap, the thrust of her pelvis. Then Leah Nesbitt was leering at him with her mouth open, revealing those gray teeth, one of which had a big chip out of it. Her complexion was bad, and her hair was dull from lack of washing. Yet she was pretty in the way some fat girls can be pretty in the face. It was probably true, he decided, that Georgie O'Shea had screwed her. As hard up as he was for sex, Jack was pretty sure he wouldn't have been able to do it with her. O'Shea claimed she planned to screw all the boys on the Hitchcock Park baseball team. Well, she'd have to take him off her list.

"Eddie, can you see yourself screwing Leah Nesbitt?" Jack whispered, so Harpo wouldn't get mad at him for interrupting his story.

"Maybe, if it was dark enough. Like tonight."

"Are you serious?"

"Why not? It's all the same in the dark."

"How would you know?"

"O'Shea says she's starting to grow tits."

"How could anybody tell? Maybe it's just fat, not tits at all. Shit, Bernier's tits are bigger than hers."

"I heard that, you fucker," Fat Bernier said, in his high voice.

A break in the cloud cover allowed a few stars to shine through; they caught a glimpse of the half moon. "What have you got there?" Leo Demers demanded of Fat Bernier, his drinking companion.

"My sangwich."

"Well how about sharing it, you selfish fat prick."

"I need it for my bowels. I been consipated."

"You mean *constipated*, you fucking moron."

"I ain't took a shit in five days. Fat Bernier removed the wax paper from his sandwich and began to eat. Leo made a move toward him to snatch it away. Fat Bernier warded him off with one arm while shoving the sandwich into his mouth with his free hand.

"What kind of sandwich is it?" Leo said.

"Peanut butter and prune. Ma says it'll loosen me up."

"We should have brought something to eat," Eddie said. "It might have made it easier to get this shit down. I think I'm going to puke for sure this time."

"Jesus, don't do it here. I don't want to have to worry about laying in your puke."

"No shit, I think I'm really going to puke." Eddie turned away from Jack and started to retch.

"Which pussy is that, puking over there?" Georgie O'Shea said.

"You all right?" Jack asked his friend.

"Yeah. Nothing came up. I'm all right now. I think I'm drunk, though. What about you?"

"I don't know. My head feels kind of funny. Light, you know, with things buzzing inside."

"O'Shea," Eddie yelled, "how would you like for me to come over there and pound the excess shit out of you?"

"Anytime you want to try, pussy," Georgie O'Shea replied.

"I'll be right back." Eddie stood up and started to move toward the trio, a few feet away down the hill. Georgie O'Shea got to his feet to meet him. O'Shea, in Jack's opinion, was no match for Eddie Tracy with his big hands and hard fists. Georgie was soft, and stoop-shouldered, and almost as skinny as Jack was. The only kid on the hill tonight who could hold his own with Eddie was Harpo. The question was, would Harpo come to Georgie's defense?

"Ain't it a little early to start fighting?" Harpo the mediator said.

"It won't be no fight at all," Eddie said. Georgie O'Shea must have had second thoughts when Eddie took his stance in front of him, his fists clenched at his sides.

"Why don't you go back with your buddy and finish puking," he said, sitting back down on the grass beside Harpo and Pat Meserve, a little closer to Harpo.

"When I'm ready to start puking I'll come over here and do it on you," Eddie said, and his voice was menacing enough that Georgie made no reply. Leo and Fat were still in dispute over the "sangwich" that Fat refused to share.

Leo taunted him. "No wonder you're such a fat ass. All you fucking do is shove food in your mouth."

"Keep it up. I'll bust your teeth in."

"You and what army?"

Eddie sat down next to Jack.

"Way to go," Jack whispered.

"It's early. There's still plenty of time to bloody him up."

"How do you feel?"

"I'm okay now." To prove that he was okay, Eddie took a good pull on his bottle of Four Roses. Jack followed suit.

"Oh boy. I think I'm really there," Jack declared, pretty sure now that he was legitimately drunk. Something was going on in that part of his brain right behind the eyes, something that felt like warm liquid sloshing around in his skull. He felt relaxed and friendly; he wouldn't even be afraid to talk to a girl right now, if one were to appear for some reason. If, for instance, Rosemary Toussaint were to turn up on the hill, he would know exactly what to say to her at this moment, when minutes earlier he would have been utterly tongue-tied. Maybe this was the reason his stepfather was so fond of drink; alcohol made talking to people a whole lot easier, a whole lot safer. And if the uninterrupted chatter that had broken out among the boys on the hill was any indication, he was not the only one who felt this way.

"What's Art like?" Jack asked Eddie, of his mother's boyfriend, the barber.

"He's all right. He don't give me no shit, not that my mother would let him. He don't have much to say to me." Art Catsoulas was a heavy-set man with thinning hair, who always needed a shave, which Jack found odd given that the guy was a barber, presumably in favor of good grooming. Jack got his haircuts from Marcel up on Court Street. Art's place was on Center Street, across from city hall. Eddie said Art got seventy-five cents for a haircut. Marcel charged thirty-five. Jack was jealous of Art, he discovered in his newly found state of inebriation. He couldn't find a way to question Eddie about the sex that went on between his mother and Art Catsoulas, not without tipping his friend off to his own prurient interest in Marge Tracy. More clouds moved in to obliterate the moon and the few stars that had been briefly visible. Mosquitoes were more numerous, and more aggressive, but nobody paid them any attention, for which they had the whiskey to thank.

"How did you like living in Maine?"

"I liked it better than here. People were easier to get along with." Jack wondered if Eddie considered him hard to get along with. For his part, Jack felt that he got along with Eddie just fine, a whole lot better than he got along with the rest of the Hitchcock Park crowd, especially the ones he shared the hill with on this dark, alcoholic night.

"I miss Vermont too. I had a lot of good friends there. I hated New Hampshire for a long time. I'm only now getting used to drinking pasteurized milk. All we drank in Vermont was raw."

"I know what you mean."

"I couldn't understand what people meant when they talked about drinking 'tonic.' I thought tonic was something you put on your hair. Here, it's a soft drink, like Coke and Pepsi. And cigarettes have 'cock' tips instead of cork tips, and to these guys Leah Nesbitt is 'Leer.' New Hampshire accents are all fucked up."

"Ay uh."

"I can't believe what O'Shea said about Nellie. And he brags about putting the wood to Leah. Shows you what kind of taste in women he's got." Jack realized that he sounded under the influence, even to himself. And when was he ever this garrulous?

"I wouldn't trust that motherfucker around my dog," Eddie said. "Jesus, I feel like I'm on a merry-go-round."

"You're probably drunk. I know I am. Hey," Jack yelled to the others, "you guys drunk?" Nobody answered. It looked like the two groups had merged into a single one, and formed a circle.

"You're right. I am drunk," Eddie said.

"Should we go and hang with those guys?"

"I say fuck them."

"Yeah." Jack tried to get to his feet. He lost his balance and fell back down in the grass, sloshing whiskey out of his bottle onto his trousers. "Shit."

"What?"

"I spilled whiskey all over me. I'll smell like a distillery."

"I'm drunk as a fucking skunk."

"Let's talk about girls." Jack's world began to go into a spin, slowly at first, and then faster until he had to lay his head down on the grass. "I'm dizzy, Eddie. I think I'm going to puke." He belched. The taste of J.W. Dant whiskey rose up in his mouth, nauseating him. He turned on his side and swallowed saliva again. He tried to will himself not to throw up. He made another attempt to get to his feet.

"Where you going?"

"I've got to take a piss. I'm going for a walk."

"Piss where you're standing. It's too dark to go for a walk. You'll fuck yourself up. Take your piss and sit down."

"I can't. I'll get sick." He lost his balance, but managed to stay on his feet. He took a couple of steps in the direction of where the others were circled up.

"Scanlon," Harpo Marks said, "better sit down before you fall down." Jack felt Eddie's hand on his bony shoulder, then his arm around his neck, as if he were using him for support. Eddie's weight brought them both to the ground. Georgie O'Shea made a crack about how neither of them could hold their liquor. This set Eddie off, and he lunged for O'Shea and pinned his arms on the ground over Georgie's head.

"You got something to say to me, O'Shea?" Georgie yelled for Eddie to get off him. "Well, have you?" Eddie said.

"Let me up, you fucking hick," Georgie yelled. Eddie rose to his feet, pulling Georgie up with him. When Georgie was in a standing position, Eddie yanked hard at his arm sending O'Shea head first down the slope of the bank.

"You trying to kill him?" Pat Meserve shouted.

"Something like that," Eddie said. "How about you? You want some too?"

"Settle down, Tracy," Harpo said in a calm voice. "Sit down. Have a drink. He didn't mean nothing." Jack assumed he referred to Georgie, not Pat Meserve.

"I've had enough of his mouth," Eddie said. They could hear Georgie's moans coming from somewhere below them on the hill; it was too dark to see him from where they were.

"I better check on him," Harpo said, rising to his feet, as if he hadn't had a drop to drink.

"There's nothing but tall grass. He's all right," Eddie said.

"I better check anyway." Harpo started off down the hill. Eddie sat down in the space where Harpo had sat, across from Fat Bernier and Leo Demers. They were uncharacteristically quiet.

"Cat got your tongues?" Eddie said to them, a trace of sarcasm in his tone.

"You're off your fucking rocker, Tracy. You know that?" Fat Bernier said, after a few moments.

"You think so, fatso?"

"Yeah, I do."

"I guess that means I'm going to have to toss your fat ass down the hill too."

"I'd like to see you try it."

Eddie laughed and took a pull from his bottle of Four Roses.

"Jack, you think I can lift Fat over my head?" Eddie said, getting to his feet. Fat Bernier rolled over on his hands and knees and tried to get on his feet. "Here, let me give you a hand," Eddie slipped one arm between Bernier's legs, and the other under his arms and slung the heavy kid over his shoulders, fireman fashion.

"Put me down, you fucker. You're fucking crazy!"

"You want to be put down?"

"Yes!"

"Okay, but remember, you asked me to put you down." And Eddie Tracy spun around once, like a discus thrower, and flung Fat Bernier down the hill in the direction he'd thrown Georgie O'Shea a few minutes ago. They heard Fat land heavily in the tall grass and bushes just below them.

"What the fuck!" They heard Harpo's voice below. Leo jumped up and lunged at Eddie, tackling him to the ground. They wrestled around a bit; Eddie ended up on top of Leo and pinned his arms behind his head the way he had done with Georgie.

"You looking for a trip down the hill?" Eddie said to him.

"Let me up. You're fucking nuts!"

"I let you up, you going to be a good boy?"

In a little while Harpo appeared, followed by Georgie and Fat, neither of whom seemed badly hurt.

"So, you think you got it out of your system, Tracy?" Harpo said. Eddie sat on the ground with his arms wrapped around his legs, knees up to his chin. He held his whiskey bottle by the neck with two fingers.

"Depends," Eddie said.

"On what?" Harpo sat down next to Eddie. "Where's my bottle, Meserve?"

Pat Meserve handed Harpo over his bottle.

"On what those two have to say. I'd just as soon not hear anything out of their mouth, if you want my opinion."

"They got a right to talk, if they want." Harpo took a drink and wiped his mouth with the back of his hand, a gesture Jack was sure he had seen in some movie. In fact, this whole scene was a little like something he'd expect to see on a movie screen. He was amused at the little drama playing out in the dark. What he would like to see, given the choice, was for Eddie to beat the crap out of both Georgie and Fat. He was pretty sure he could handle Georgie O'Shea himself, but Fat Bernier was another matter. Bill Scanlon and his Uncle Ira had taught Jack how to box, but doing it with sixteen-ounce gloves on your hands was one thing, bare fisting was another. While Eddie was disposing of Fat Bernier down the hill, Jack had taken a couple of nips from his bottle. It must have affected his vision because he swore he could see two of everyone.

"They can talk all they want, long as they don't say nothing to piss me off," Eddie said. Georgie and Fat were subdued for the moment. Maybe being thrown down an embankment did that to you, Jack decided, smiling to himself in the dark.

A pair of car headlights appeared on the road below.

"Get down, you guys," Harpo said to Georgie and Fat who were standing. The boys went into a crouch. They watched the car's headlights move slowly down the road in the direction of the city barn. It moved a hundred feet or so and stopped. A spotlight went on and swept the side of the road adjacent to the hoboes' campsite.

"The cops, checking on the bums," Harpo whispered. "Keep quiet."

The police car (if it really was a police car as Harpo believed) swung into the turnaround, and remained there, its headlights playing into the knoll that shielded the hobo "jungle" from the road.

"You think they'll go in after them?" Pat Meserve addressed the question to Harpo in a whisper.

"I doubt it. They don't mess with the bums as long as they mind their own business."

"Maybe they're looking for the bum who eats twelve-year-olds in the haunted house," Leo said. This caused a ripple of snorts and laughs. Harpo shushed them.

"They may not mess with the bums, but they wouldn't think twice about fucking with us. They'd like nothing better, especially that prick Waterman. He's used his flashlight on more than one kid's head, I can tell you." It was common knowledge among the Hitchcock Park boys that Garrison cops got their rocks off picking on juveniles. Jack never thought of himself as a juvenile delinquent, before tonight. The label had a certain appeal for him.

"I wonder what it would be like to spend the night in jail," he whispered to Eddie, and giggled like a girl.

"Get down," somebody said. They got on their bellies. In the time they had been on the hill they had beat a good-sized area of grass down flat. Jack wondered if the cops would be able to spot this from where they were parked. His heart began to pound; he held his breath.

"Should we ditch the bottles?" Leo asked.

"Not unless they make a move to come up here. If they do, I say we split up and head for the top of the hill," Harpo said. "If anybody gets caught, mum's the word. Right?" Everyone mumbled his assent. The spotlight made a few more passes along the side of the hill, then went out abruptly. The car backed out of the turnaround and headed back toward Hitchcock Avenue where it had come from.

"They're leaving," Fat Bernier said, breaking the silence he had maintained since Eddie heaved him down the hill.

"Maybe," Harpo replied. "We better stay down till we're sure they're gone. They can be sneaky fuckers."

"I'll drink to that," Georgie said, and took a long swig from his bottle, his elbows still on the ground. Georgie and Harpo seemed to be the least affected by what they had drunk. Jack blinked several times, but he could still see two versions of everybody.

"That was close," Fat Bernier said. "My old man would kick the living shit out of me if he had to come down to the station and get me out of jail. I better think about going home."

"You can't go home, you stupid fuck," Leo said, "not in your condition. Besides, didn't you tell your folks you were staying at my house tonight?"

"Oh yeah," Fat Bernier said, as if he just remembered the pact he had made with Leo. Leo was supposed to be staying at Fat's house, Fat at Leo's. That was what Jack and Eddie had set up too. He doubted that Harpo, Pat, or Georgie had to use this ruse on their parents; none of them seemed to have much parental supervision. The plan was to drink themselves senseless, pass out, and spend the night on the hill. In the morning they would sober up and play some cards, then some baseball, the way they did every day. Not one of them considered the possibility of a hangover.

Jack had witnessed enough of his stepfather's hangovers to know that he was experiencing one of his own when he woke up at dawn the next morning, the bright sun in his smarting eyes. The region of his brain behind his eyes throbbed and pulsated; his mouth was rancid, and his stomach queasy. He had managed to get through the night without throwing up, but he remembered little of what happened after the police cruiser had left.

In the early morning light he was astonished to see just how much of the tall grass on the hill the seven of them had flattened the night before. An area maybe fifteen feet in diameter looked like a blow-down after a storm. Whiskey bottles, in various degrees of emptiness, were scattered about on the beat down grass. Just below him, a small stand of young mountain ash saplings lay bent over, their slender stems broken in half, the victims of the bodies of Georgie O'Shea and Fat Bernier no doubt, courtesy of Eddie Tracy. Eddie lay on his side beside Jack, a few feet away, in the fetal position, his hands tucked between his knees. It was the posture Jack was used to seeing his stepfather assume after returning from a prolonged bender. None of the other boys was in sight.

"Eddie, you awake?" Eddie groaned and mumbled something Jack couldn't understand. "Where is everyone? God, I am so sick." Eddie's eyes remained closed. "Wake up, Eddie." Jack's arms and neck were covered with bug bites. His internal misery was more acute than the eruptions on his skin, however. "If I don't get a drink of water I'll go stark raving crazy." The closest drinking water was the fountain near the swings in Hitchcock Park. His head throbbed more in the sitting position than it did when he was on his back. Eddie rolled over and groaned some more.

"You awake yet? I've got to have some water. Come on, let's get going."

"Oh shit," Eddie moaned. "I'm going to fucking die."

"Me too if I don't get some water. Let's go!"

"I ain't never doing this again. That's a promise, I promise."

"Me either." Jack remembered that it wasn't so long ago that he had made a promise not to let alcohol pass his lips until he reached the age of twenty-one. It was one of several surreal moments he recalled of his confirmation ceremony, the most painful being the humiliation he suffered when he tripped over his gown on his approach to the chair behind the altar rail where the bishop sat waiting to bless him and his fellow confirmation candidates. He ended up sprawled face first at the bishop's feet. The good bishop seemed not to notice Jack's oafishness, or the stifled laughs of the boys behind him. One of the boys remarked afterward that the bishop was too blitzed on confirmation wine to notice. Jack's confirmation vow to abstain from alcohol until he reached legal drinking age lasted for about forty-eight hours. But until last night, his breach of promise had involved no alcohol stronger than beer.

The dregs of Eddie's bottle of Four Roses lay next to Jack's empty bottle of J.W. Dant, just below their feet. He had no memory of drinking all of it.

"I'm never touching another drop of hard liquor as long as I live," Jack declared.

"Did I puke last night?"

"I don't think so. I can't remember much." Jack examined Eddie and saw no signs of vomit on his clothes, so if he had been sick it wasn't on himself. "What time is it, do you think?"

"Early." Eddie squinted his eyes at the sky. The sun was up. They were on high enough ground to see it over the roof of Caledonia

Electronics.

Jack got to his feet; a stab of pain shot threw the roof of his skull. "I've got to have water. I'll die if I don't get water, I know it."

"We gave this place a going over," Eddie said, looking around at the flattened grass, shaking his head.

"It's mostly your doing."

Eddie chuckled. "What happened to the rest of them?"

"Probably playing cards. Let's get out of here." They made their way down the hill slowly, Jack's head pounding every step of the way, his stomach roiling.

The picnic table by the bathhouse was empty except for two pigeons walking around on the top of it. Blue jays shrieked from the tree beside it, "Do it! Do it!"

"Do it yourself, you fuckers," Eddie shouted at the birds. They reached the water fountain to discover it was out of order.

"Oh my God," Jack said.

"Nick's Spa opens early," Eddie said. "Let's head up there."

"That's way the fuck uptown. I can't make it that far. Let's go to your house."

"My mother will know for sure we're fucked up."

Jack found it odd that Eddie's mother, who behaved at times like a libertine, was really punctilious about certain aspects of her son's behavior. She didn't approve of drinking alcohol. Her boyfriend, Art the barber, didn't drink, and Jack had never seen any evidence of alcohol in Eddie's house. So they would have to trek all the way to the upper square for a drink of water.

In front of the First National Market Jack found a five-dollar bill on the sidewalk.

"Jesus, five bucks. I'll treat you to a banana split at Nick's," he said to Eddie.

"You'd be wasting your money. I'd just chuck it up. It's what I feel like doing right now."

"Not in the street. Go behind the First National, you got to puke."

Traffic was actually light to nonexistent on Center Street on this early Saturday morning, so Eddie could have puked to his heart's content and not been noticed. The temperature must have been in the seventies already; the air was thick with humidity.

"You sure Nick's is open this early?" Jack worked at Cohen's Delicatessen, two store fronts past Nick's Spa, but he never went in to work before eleven so he had no idea how early the old Greek opened his soda fountain.

"Yeah. Art stops in for coffee every morning before he opens up."

"Shit, you think he'll be there this morning? What if he is? Won't he say something to your mother?"

"I never thought of that. Maybe we should go someplace else."

"Where? Nothing's open, and I'm going to die soon."

"What about the Ramble Inn?"

"Stoney's!" The light went on in Jack's head. He smacked himself on his aching forehead with an open palm. Stoney's Diner, from a refurbished old Boston and Maine dining car, stayed open twenty-four hours a day. It had eleven stools that were more often than not always fully occupied. "Can we make it that far? That's the question."

"It's a whole hundred yards past Fourth Street. We'll never make it," Eddie wisecracked.

"I'll make it. I could use a sliced chicken sandwich too."

"You mean a 'sangwich'?" Eddie said.

"Oh, right." Jack tried to laugh but it hurt his head too much.

Two bottles of Coke and a sliced chicken sandwich with lettuce and mayonnaise had no salutary effect on Jack's hangover. The way his stomach felt, Eddie didn't dare attempt solid food. Several times on the walk home along Wayland Avenue Jack thought he would lose the sandwich and Cokes. He made it to his new home at number 10 Fern Street without throwing up. It wasn't until he walked through his kitchen door that he lost the battle. His mother, sitting at the kitchen table drinking a cup of coffee, cautioned him that the floor was still tacky. In retrospect, it might have been the smell of floor wax that caused his stomach to finally erupt on his mother's freshly washed and waxed linoleum.

***

"There she is," Eddie whispered, nudging Jack in the side with his elbow. Jack was stopped in his tracks by the sight of her. When Eddie Tracy had referred to her as a "piece" he had not done her justice. Up to that moment, Jack Scanlon's ideal girl had been Bernie, the girl downstairs in the apartment on Silver Street. This girl, this Rosemary Toussaint, was a goddess by comparison. Her hair was short and jet black, as Eddie had said it was, but Eddie hadn't begun to describe its luster, its life. Unlike Bernie's alabaster pallor, Rosemary's complexion was like amber, or gold.

She had on a dungaree shirt and a pair of white shorts. She sat in a wicker chair on her grandmother's front porch, her legs propped up on a matching wicker hassock. When Rosemary Toussaint became aware of his gawking presence, she looked at him over the top of her book, and lowering it to her lap, smiled at him.

"Hello," she said. "What's your name?"

"Uh, Jack. I, uh, used to live here ... there, on this street." Jack turned and pointed off in the direction of Eddie's house. Eddie had continued to walk toward home, apparently not aware that Jack was engaged in conversation with the girl.

"Used to? You don't live here anymore?" Rosemary picked up a glass on the table beside her and took a delicate sip.

"No."

"Where do you live now?" Jack detected a foreign accent, perhaps French Canadian, but not as abrasive as the accents he was used to hearing from his family in Vermont, and the "canucks" living in Garrison.

"Uh, on the other side of town." Jack pointed absurdly northeastward.

"You must have moved fairly recently. I saw you walk by yesterday... with your friend."

"Yes. It's only been a few days. Eddie, that's my friend." Jack pointed at Eddie who had stopped, and who looked nonplussed by what he was witnessing. What she had said about seeing him walk by hadn't sunk into his brain yet, and he wasn't sure how to process the information. "Do you ... do you live here now?"

"Oh no. I'm just visiting Grandmamma for the rest of the summer. I live in Maine."

"Maine? Whereabouts?" Lately, it seemed that everybody was from Maine.

"Springvale. Do you know where that is?" It was only now that he recognized the name of Springvale as the town near Neil Sullivan's dad's farm, where he had visited recently.

"Sure. Nice place." He glanced at Eddie who had started to make his way back to where Jack stood. He hoped that Eddie would not take this moment to go off on one of his rants about the "real" Maine.

"There's so much more to do in Garrison," Rosemary said. The daily complaint among the Hitchcock Park boys was that there was nothing to do in Garrison, zilch.

"You think so? Like what?"

"You've got a nice library, two movie theaters, nice parks ..."

"Yeah, I guess so."

"Come on, Jack," Eddie said, "we got to go." Eddie's mother was preparing supper for the boys. Jack was in no hurry to leave Rosemary's company, however.

"I'll be right there," he said to Eddie without taking his eyes off Rosemary. "You go ahead."

"I'll wait." Jack shot him a look he hoped Eddie would read as "get lost," but Eddie held his ground.

"I guess I'd better be going," he said to the girl.

"Well, it's nice to meet you." Rosemary smiled and raised her book back to her face.

"Nice to meet you, too." He felt he should say more but for the life of him he couldn't find words that would have been appropriate. He stood there in front of Mrs. Toussaint's white picket fence with its hollyhocks and peonies for a moment racking his brain for something else to say.

"Come on, let's go," Eddie whispered. Jack looked once more at

Rosemary Toussaint, her pretty face hidden behind a hardcover book, and followed Eddie up the street.

After a supper of meatloaf, mashed potatoes, and peas, Eddie and Jack walked back to Hitchcock Park to play some twilight poker, but the usual bunch was not at the picnic table. Eddie remembered that some of the guys had talked about going to the softball game at Garrison Park to watch Caledonia Electronics clash with United Tanners. Julian Cardwell played third base for the tannery, so the guys wanted to be on hand to give him some fan support. It was the least they could do for the guy who took chances buying hard liquor for his underage friends.

"Why didn't you say something? I'd have liked to go," Jack said.

"I forgot. You should have been here anyway. Where the fuck were you today?"

"My old lady had all kinds of shit for me to do."

"Well, what's to stop us from going now?"

"It's a haul up there."

"What are you talking about? It's right in your new neighborhood. You'd be as good as home." Eddie sat down on top of the picnic table and lit a cigarette. The western sky was rose colored, as if something were burning over the horizon. The truth was that Jack didn't want to stray far from the park in case Rosemary Toussaint took it in her head to come out for a walk.

"I'd like to stay clear of my house as long as I can," Jack said, his mind's eye picturing Rosemary sipping lemonade on her grandmother's porch, the princess in the wicker chair. If only he knew what to say to her. "Where can we get some beer?'

"What, you don't want whiskey?" Eddie laughed, and dragged on his cigarette. Jack pulled the last of his ill-gotten Camels out of his pocket, cigarettes he'd stolen from Abe's deli. He wouldn't have access to any more until Wednesday when he went back to work, unless he bought them with his own money. "I meant it, Eddie. I'll never touch that stuff again as long as I live."

"Me either."

"So what about it? Where can we get our hands on some beer?"

"What about sexy Texy? He's probably parked on Center Street. Let's go have a look."

"Just the two of us?"

"I don't believe the shit everyone says about him. He's like a little kid, for Christ sake," Eddie said, flipping away his cigarette.

Jack agreed that Tex Minehan had the emotional makeup of a ten-year-old, but there was something about the man that gave him the creeps just the same. And his sheer size and strength were enough to give one pause; if he decided to go berserk over the teasing the kids heaped on him there was no telling what kind of damage he could do. In fact, kids liked to goad him into showing off his immense strength. Once he lifted the rear end of his Nash clear off the ground with three of them (one of whom was Fat Bernier) in the back seat.

"Did you puke after I left you yesterday?" Eddie asked him.

"Did I." Jack described to Eddie how he'd puked all over his mother's freshly waxed kitchen linoleum. "I blamed it on Art's Greek cooking. Hope you don't mind."

"She believed it?"

"I guess so. She didn't question me. Maybe because she was so pissed I messed up her floor. I can't believe she didn't know I'd been drinking, though. She's had enough experience with drunks and hangovers. Maybe she didn't want to believe I was following in my stepfather's footsteps." He remembered how disappointed his mother had been when she found out he was smoking cigarettes. It never occurred to him at the time that she might have quit smoking herself because she felt she was setting a bad example. To admit that he had taken up the drinking of hard liquor, along with cigarettes, would have made her believe her oldest son was on the path to damnation. The mere thought of himself doing anything in his life in imitation of his stepfather caused him to wince. For that reason alone he resolved to keep his promise to abstain from hard liquor.

"My mother wasn't home when I got back. I spent about a half an hour on my knees in front of the toilet bowl. She would have thrown a rod if she found out. I'm never going near that shit again, I can tell you," Eddie declared, raising his right hand as if he were taking an oath in a court of law.

"Yeah. We should stick to beer."

They stopped at the entrance to Hitchcock Park and sat on a slatted park bench to rest and watch the traffic in the lower square. The evening was muggy; they were both sweating from the short walk. A Ford coupe convertible was parked in front of the brass-railed fence on Washington Street. Two guys were sitting in it, one of whom Jack recognized as Terry Stickney; the other guy, the driver, he had never seen before.

"Let's go say hi to Terry," Jack said, getting off the bench.

"Who's Terry?"

"A kid I went to school with at Franklin." Since Eddie was a recent transplant from Maine, he didn't know any of the kids in town outside of the Hitchcock Park crowd. "Hey, Terry," Jack called out, "how you doing?"

"Scanlon," the laconic Terry Stickney said. He had let his blond hair grow long since school ended. He wore the collar of his short-sleeved shirt turned up in back. After their crime spree in the fall of seventh grade they hadn't hung out together much. In fact, Stickney had started to hang out with an older crowd, with guys who drove cars. The guy behind the wheel of the convertible looked about seventeen or eighteen; he had a face full of sore-looking pimples and his reddish hair was glistening with hair oil. A cigarette hung carelessly from the corner of his mouth. Jack stared at him.

"This is Dick Pickering," Terry Stickney said, finally.

"Hi," Jack said. "I'm Jack Scanlon, and that's Eddie Tracy," Jack said, turning to point out Eddie who was now perched on the top rail of the fence. The guy named Dick Pickering nodded in Jack's direction without saying anything. Mutes of a feather, Jack said to himself.

Terry Stickney looked bored, as did Dick Pickering.

"So what are you guys up to?" Jack asked. "We were looking for somebody to buy us some beer."

"No shit," Terry Stckney said, lighting a cigarette, and not looking as if he cared one way or another whether his former friend was looking for beer, or the Northwest Passage.

"Yeah. You seen Tex Minehan around?" At the mention of Tex Minehan, Terry Stickney turned to Jack with a look that didn't need words. He offered none. Jack, in a rush to explain himself and his interest in Tex Minehan to Stickney, probably came off as too anxious.

"He's a sucker for buying beer ..." Stickney said nothing; Jack squirmed.

"Let's head for South Berwick," Dick Pickering said, putting his coupe in gear and reaching for the ignition switch.

"See you later," Jack said, as the coupe backed away from the curb. Terry Stickney gave Jack half a wave of his cigarette bearing hand without looking at him. Jack felt insulted, badly treated. He climbed up on the rail beside Eddie and stared vacantly across the street at the back of the First National Market, at the garbage dumpster that Tex Minehan emptied twice a week.

"Nice guys," Eddie said, lighting up another cigarette.

"He used to be my best friend," Jack said, his voice slightly tremulous.

"Let's head up to Garrison Park. We don't need no beer."

They took the shortcut along River Road that intersected with Wayland Avenue, the end of which was located Garrison Park where night softball games were played. Eddie suggested that if Jack still wanted beer maybe they could get Julian Cardwell to buy them some after his game.

"It'll be too late." What Jack really wanted to drink beer for was to muster the courage to talk to Rosemary Toussaint if she took it in her head to go for a walk in the park, or just sit out on her grandmother's front porch in the wicker chair to get the night air.

And as if Eddie were reading his mind he said, "I didn't want to say nothing, you know, but I seen Eldon Evans sniffing around Rosemary a couple times. He was at her house yesterday; had his convertible parked out front with the top down, talking to her from the driver's seat."

"Eldon Evans. Isn't he a junior or senior in high school?"

"I think so, and I hear he's a real fucking playboy too. He's got all kinds of babes, I hear. No wonder, with that convertible. Anybody could get babes with a car like that."

"How do you know so much about Eldon Evans?'

"Georgie O'Shea, he told me all about him."

"Did she seem …" Jack wasn't sure how to frame the question that was on his mind. The news that his competition was Eldon Evans, a good-looking, popular high school guy with a late model convertible, who, if he owned such a car, must have a lot of money to spend, was enough to crush his dreams of getting anywhere with Rosemary. What chance did a skinny, wall-eyed fourteen-year-old who was just starting his freshman year in high school in September have against an Eldon Evans? None.

"I just thought I better tell you about Evans so you, you know …"

"Yeah."

The next day, in the middle of a tie ballgame between Hitchcock and Greenlaw Park, a fire department pickup truck parked on the street opposite the backstop and two men got out and headed for the teams' benches. When the batting team finished their half of the inning and they were changing field, the two men called the boys from both teams over.

"We're looking for volunteers to fight the fires that are burning in Maine. They're threatening to move into the Sanford-Springvale area and we need all the men we can get. We'll take anyone over sixteen. You got to be ready to work twelve, fifteen hours a day, and it could be dangerous. The State will pay a dollar an hour and take care of your meals. If you're interested, sign up at the station on Broadway between three and five. We could really use your help."

After the game, Jack and Eddie were walking back to Eddie's house where Jack was invited to supper again. He was, as his mother was quick to remind him, spending more time at Eddie's house since he'd moved to Fern Street than he had when he lived next door to him.

"Talk about the wrong time and the wrong place," Jack said. "First, I'm too old by a month to play in the Little League that's starting up next summer, and now I can't go fight fires because I'm too young."

"Anyway, now we know we ain't been crazy. That was smoke we been smelling. Jesus, if it's almost in Sanford it could be here in a few days. You'd think they'd want anybody they could get, sixteen or not."

Rosemary Toussaint was on her knees by one of her grandmother's walkway gardens, a trowel in her hand, and her pretty rear end in the air. She had on a pair of dungaree cutoffs. Her back was to the boys, but as if she sensed their presence behind her, she rose to her feet, gracefully, and turned around to face them.

"Hi there," she said, waving her trowel. Jack suddenly made a connection between Springvale, Maine, Rosemary, and the forest fires that threatened her hometown. Behind this realization was the name of Eldon, or Ethan, or whatever his name was, Evans and his convertible.

"Hi," Jack said.

"I'll see you at the house," Eddie said, leaving his friend to woo this girl he must have known Jack had no chance of wooing.

"Been playing baseball?"

"Yeah. We had a game ..."

"Did you win?"

"Lost by a run in the last inning."

Rosemary walked to the fence, not two feet from where he stood, on the sidewalk.

"That's too bad." This was as close as he had been to the girl since he'd laid eyes on her. She was even prettier at close range; her hair was so black it literally shined, like basalt; her bow-shaped lips looked soft and moist. Long, black, upwardly curling eyelashes; eyes as close to the color of violets as he'd ever seen; her face was perfection itself in his opinion.

"We heard about the fires near where you live. Is that why you're visiting your grandmother, to get away from the fire?"

"That wasn't the reason I came to visit Grandmama, but my parents think it's a good idea that I stay here longer than I planned, or until they get the fire under control. My parents might have to go to my uncle's in Massachusetts if it gets really bad."

"Do you have any brothers or sisters?"

"A younger brother. He's away in Canada."

"I might have to go and help fight the fires. The fire department came to the park looking for ..." Jack heard a woman's braying voice behind him, and recognized it as belonging to the hag across the street, the shantytown refugee who had so many children she didn't know what to do, like the woman in the nursery rhyme. Jack turned around to see her slouching figure in the doorway of the crooked shack she lived in with her brood. A cigarette dangled from the corner of her mouth; she squinted against the smoke. Her lank hair clung to her neck in thin strands as if it were pasted there; she had a long, leathery face like a horse, a slightly humped back, and bare, dirty feet with hammertoes.

A little bare-bottomed girl darted out of the doorway from behind her mother and started running up the street, shrieking with pleasure, or possibly pain.

"Get your ass back here, Florence, right now!" the hag yelled. "Henry, go get your sister," she said to the boy who emerged from the house after the little girl. Henry, who was about eleven or twelve, and was simple-minded and incontinent, ignored her. The neighborhood boys had nicknamed him "shitum" because he seemed always to have a load in his pants.

"Those poor people," Rosemary murmured. Poor could have several levels of meaning as it described this family, Jack decided, but he offered no opinion to Rosemary.

All he said was, "Yeah," but the depth of sympathy she expressed in those three words touched him. It was more sympathy than he, or any of his friends, felt for them. His friends, in fact, had told him that it was widely known that shantytowners were an inbred lot, which explained their poverty, their stupidity, their subhumanness. Rosemary Toussaint treated them as if they were simply down on their luck. He had a sudden, strong urge to reach over Mrs. Toussaint's white picket fence and embrace this girl. She was too good for the likes of Eldon Evans, whose intentions toward her were less than honorable. Everything he had heard from Eddie about Evans' reputation for seducing girls pointed to his low motives with Rosemary. If there was a way he could protect her from Evans, and boys like him, she might be grateful enough toward him to … to what?

"Shitum" apparently had another agenda because he turned down St. George Street in the direction of Hitchcock Park instead of taking after the little girl as his mother had asked him to do.

"Get back here and do like I tell you, you little bastard!" his mother screamed after him. He ignored her and kept walking in a stiff-legged gait, as if he had just filled his pants. The little girl was in the middle of the street, already past Jack's old house. There were seldom any cars on the street, so she was in no immediate danger, or else Jack would have sprung into action and rescued her, especially with Rosemary standing there, itching to be impressed with his gallantry, his concern for his fellow human being, although he sooner would have picked up a snake than touch that scrofulous little urchin. Her mother made no effort to go after the child either; instead she flicked her cigarette into the street and went back inside her shack, leaving the kid alone in the street.

All the time he had lived on the street he'd had the desire to look inside their shack, to witness the abomination, as it were. How could so many souls occupy such a small space? He would have been surprised to learn that there was plumbing in the house, let alone central heating. His own house had lacked central heating. How had they survived the past winter? Rosemary might have had the same random thoughts.

"How do those poor people survive in that house?"

"Have you seen the father?"

"No." Rosemary gripped the top of the fence with both hands. Jack thought fleetingly of placing his hand on hers on the pretext of giving her comfort. He did no such thing. And he decided not to characterize the father to her either in case her sympathy was so profound that she would judge him poorly if he expressed how he really felt about the drunken father of this motley group. "I asked Grandmama to call the welfare people but she says it's none of our business. She says they have a right to their dignity."

It was difficult for him to associate the word dignity with these people. Furthermore, he was no fan of the welfare department. Dignity, in his opinion, was not a concept with which the department of welfare was familiar. He tried to shift the subject, feeling he might have a chance for a little more time with her.

"Do you go to Springvale High?"

"I'll be a sophomore in September. You?"

"Me too." He instantly regretted the lie, knowing how easy it would be for her to find out, if she could be bothered. He saw no way to retract it now. He lit a cigarette perhaps believing this would validate his age, offer evidence that he was old enough to be a sophomore in high school.

"Those things aren't good for you," she said, smiling.

"I know," he said, inspecting the lit end of the cigarette between his fingers. "Coffin nails. I guess I'm hooked. I've smoked them since I was a kid." He was tempted to brag about how he got drunk on whiskey too, but for once he thought better of it with this girl. She was not like any girl he had ever met; she definitely would *not* be impressed with a boy who got drunk on whiskey. He dropped his cigarette on the ground and stepped on it. He really wanted to ask her about Eldon Evans. He should be content to savor what delight her company gave him instead of complicating matters with such questions, questions that were bound to have answers he didn't want to hear.

"Rosemary." Mrs. Toussaint appeared at the front door. She had a kitchen apron on over a gray dress, the shade of gray Jack associated with clothes his grandmother used to wear.

"Time for supper, dear. Hello, young man," she said to Jack.

"Hello, Mrs. Toussaint."

"Bye-bye," Rosemary said to him with a pretty smile.

"Bye."

Jack lay awake that night, his brain full of Rosemary Toussaint. He hadn't had a girlfriend since Ann Marie Morrissey in seventh grade. He wouldn't know how to act anymore with a real "girlfriend," if he ever knew how to act with one. Bernie's counsel on dating etiquette seemed centuries ago. And without a car a boy was doomed in the world of dating girls. The last time his Uncle Mitch had visited his family he had offered to teach Jack how to drive the next time he was in town. Mitch worked for his old high school chum delivering Oldsmobiles and Chevrolets to customers all over New England.

He tried to imagine what it would be like out on a date in a car with Rosemary, her sitting up close to him, he with his arm around her the way the high school guys rode with their girls up and down Center Street, driving aimlessly for the sheer joy of driving aimlessly. Eldon Evans in his powder blue Chevy convertible kept intruding, and Jack fell asleep in a state of agitation instead of rapture.

The next day was Jack's last day of freedom, so to speak, as Abe Cohen would return from his two weeks of visitation with his daughters to reopen the delicatessen. Jack would miss the morning poker games in Hitchcock Park, and since he didn't get off work until two o'clock, the late morning baseball game too. He wanted to make the most of his last day off so he showed up at the picnic table at eight o'clock sharp ready to play cards. He was the first to arrive. He sat at the picnic table splattered with pigeon droppings, wondering what Rosemary was doing at that very instant. He looked in the direction of her house, and the girl appeared, as if he had willed her to, heading down the street toward the corner store. She had on a blue calico blouse and white shorts. Jack turned to face the store head-on. She went inside the store without looking in his direction. She couldn't have failed to see him sitting there at that short distance—it couldn't have been more than a couple of hundred feet. Could she have been so preoccupied with her own thoughts that she hadn't noticed him? This explanation was preferable to the one that occurred to him first, namely that she had seen him but chose to make believe that she had not because she found him tiresome, and not very good looking, certainly not as good looking as Eldon Evans who also drove a spiffy convertible and ... etc. etc. He was torn between the desire to walk over to the store and to pretend a chance encounter with her, or to remain seated at the table, inert, ineffectual, and feeling wretched. If his initial explanation were correct she would find his overture boorish, forward, and unwanted. If she had truly been too preoccupied to notice him he still ran the risk of appearing too eager.

Then, Eddie appeared on the street, headed in his direction. He passed in front of the store just as Rosemary was coming out, cradling a paper bag. Tampax? Eddie waved. Just as Jack waved back, Rosemary turned in his direction and waved at him too. She walked backwards a few steps, continuing to wave at him. She said nothing to Eddie. Jack felt his heart quicken under his T-shirt.

"Man, she is a dish," Eddie said, taking a seat beside Jack. "Too bad you'll never get anywhere with her. Not with Evans all over her like a coon dog. He was there in front of the house last night for an hour."

"He was?"

"Yeah. *Over* an hour. Never got out of his car. She talked to him from behind her fence."

"She didn't get in the car with him?"

"I don't think so. I wasn't looking the whole time. I'm pretty sure she didn't leave with him. You got an extra smoke?"

Jack, on a roller coaster of elation and despair in the short time he had been in Eddie's company, was encouraged by the news that Eddie didn't think she drove off with Evans. "The guys are late today." Jack lit their cigarettes.

"They'll be here. I've only got sixty-five cents. Can you lend me any money?"

"I've got about a buck. We'll just have to win today. I go back to work tomorrow. You sure she didn't get in the car with him?"

"Car? Oh her. I'm pretty sure. She talked to him a long time though, and she laughed a lot. You don't stand a chance with her, not with him around. Face it. Why don't you go after Betty what's-her-name? She just moved in, up on Sonnett. She ain't bad looking either."

"So why don't you try her?"

"Girls don't have no use for me." Eddie was matter of fact in his self-assessment, and didn't seem particularly bothered by the knowledge.

Jack couldn't understand why his friend should feel that way, though. Eddie was not a bad looking kid, with dark hair, brown eyes, and an athletic body. Maybe he felt girls didn't like him because of the way he talked, like a hick, as Georgie O'Shea was always saying.

Georgie O'Shea and Pat Meserve showed up a few minutes later, followed by Harpo Marks, and in the space of half an hour there were ten of them at the picnic table playing five-card stud. Jack lost half of his remaining dollar by ten o'clock. He was about to call it quits anyway when several more boys appeared, enough to start up a game, seven on a side.

Jack had become absorbed in the game, so attentive that he didn't notice Eldon Evans' convertible parked on the street adjacent to third base, until he took his position there. No one was in the car. He looked around the park and spotted Evans coming out of the corner store, a bottle of Pepsi in his hand. Jack assumed he was in the neighborhood stalking Rosemary, but if that were true why was he parked down here instead of in front of Mrs. Toussaint's house? Georgie O'Shea lashed a hot grounder down the third base line. Jack was so preoccupied with Evans that he let the ball go by him on his right in what should have been an easy chance.

"Get your thumb out of your ass, Scanlon!" Harpo shouted, as he gathered the ball up and threw it back to the infield.

"Sorry," Jack said.

"Okay, heads up," Harpo yelled. "Pitch to him," he said, exhorting Pat Meserve to let Fat Bernier hit away. Pat's soft lobs, like knuckle balls, were maddeningly hard to hit. Georgie O'Shea was pitching for the other side; all he had was a sharp breaking curve ball which had no heat, and was predictable enough that, with a little patience, you could be sure he'd eventually dish one up right over the plate. In these pickup games there was no walking the batter, and the only strikeouts were the swinging kind.

Eldon Evans, holding a bottle of Pepsi carelessly by its long neck with two fingers, sauntered over to the bench and started talking to some of the guys sitting there waiting their turn at bat. Jack tried to concentrate on Fat Bernier at bat. He wasn't taking any of Pat Meserve's floaters and even his teammates were getting impatient with him.

"That was right over!" Georgie O'Shea yelled from first base. "Piss or get off the pot."

"It was over my shoulders," Fat Bernier yelled back, taking one hand off the bat to indicate where he believed the pitch had gone.

Pat Meserve stepped off the pitcher's mound, walked halfway to home plate, and served up a soft underhand pitch. Fat Bernier took a mighty cut at the ball and popped it high in the air between third base and shortstop.

"I got it," Jack called, at the same time that Eddie Tracy, who was playing short, yelled for it. They let the ball drop between them. Georgie

O'Shea, holding his position at first base, had to beat it for second to make room for the slow moving Fat Bernier who huffed and puffed his bulk down the baseline. Eddie and Jack were too busy cursing each other out for either of them to have the presence of mind to pick up the ball and try to make a play at second. Both Georgie and Fat were safe at second and first base. Larry Mercier, who was playing second base, and who had screamed at them to pick up the ball and throw it to him, was furious. So was Harpo.

"You two are fucking hopeless," he said, trotting to the infield.

"What were we supposed to do, smash into each other?" Eddie tried to defend their ineptitude, but his argument was feeble. Jack kept his mouth shut, but he knew his face was bright red. He earned a small measure of redemption when the next batter hit a sharp grounder right at him. He was able to step on third and throw out the slow moving Fat Bernier at second for a double play, which could have been a triple play except for Mercier's bad throw to first. Pat got the next batter to pop up to end the inning with no runs scored despite his and Eddie's efforts to give one away. Jack trotted in for his team's turn at bat.

"Hey, kid. You Jack Scanlon?" Eldon Evans was addressing him. He was leaning insolently against the chain-link backstop, swinging his Pepsi bottle back and forth by the neck.

"Yeah." He felt like adding, "Who wants to know?" but Evans was bigger than he was, and older, and definitely stronger. And much better looking, with his sandy hair, square jaw, and blue eyes.

Eldon Evans shook his head as if in disbelief, looking Jack up and down from head to toe. "You're shitting me," he finally said.

"I don't know what you're talking about." Jack punched the pocket of his glove with his fist.

"*You're* Rosemary's boyfriend? I don't fucking believe it. She's kidding, right?"

"Come on, Scanlon," Harpo yelled, "you're up to bat."

Jack turned away from Evans, picked up the lightest of the three Louisville Sluggers lying on the ground, and stepped up to the plate to face Georgie O'Shea's predictable curve balls. His mind, however, was all tangled up with Eldon Evans' words. He struck out with three swings at three bad pitches, one after the other. It was the first time Georgie had ever struck him out. He returned to the bench; Eldon Evans had gone, but his words rang in Jack's ears: "Rosemary's boyfriend."

"I can't believe you let O'Shea strike you out," Eddie said, swinging a bat, waiting for his turn at the plate.

"He fooled me," Jack said, his chest swelling with exultation. "It was bound to happen sooner or later."

"I'm going to hit one back in his fucking rotten teeth," Eddie said before striking out himself.

Jack's euphoria was short-lived, as it was wont to be with him. On the walk home after playing baseball the better part of the day, his mind went to work on what Eldon Evans had said to him in the park. Cold reason told him that Rosemary had declared herself his girlfriend just to get the aggressive Evans off her back. When he thought about it, Rosemary Toussaint didn't strike him as the kind of girl who would be taken in by the likes of Eldon Evans whose motives were as transparent as the insincere smile on his pretty-boy face. And she would see straight through his smooth talk where the ordinary girl would fall for it. And it was equally likely that she would never fall for Jack Scanlon either, for completely different reasons. He and Eldon Evans were as opposite as two human beings could be, as opposite as say Jack and his stepfather were. Yet he felt that he had, for want of a better way to put it, a spiritual connection with this girl with the raven hair. Any way he cut it, there were more reasons to despair than to rejoice about his future with Rosemary Toussaint. The upshot of all Jack's introspection was his determination to call on the girl tomorrow after he got off work. In fact, he resolved to call on her at her grandmother's house right after he was done playing ball.

"Hello, Mrs. Toussaint. I was wondering if I could speak to Rosemary. Would that be all right?"

"Of course it would be, young man, but I'm afraid Rosemary left this morning. Her father, my son, called last night. He's moving his family to Massachusetts with his wife's brother's family until they get those fires under control. He's afraid they'll take the house."

Jack didn't want to sound impertinent by asking the old lady why Rosemary couldn't have remained there with her. His disappointment must have been conspicuous.

"I'm sorry, dear. I can tell you're fond of her."

"Yes. When do you think she'll be back?"

"That's hard to say. Everything depends on the fires. Such a terrible thing. Rosemary mentioned that you and your friend might be going to help fight them. That would be a little dangerous for young men like you, I should think."

"It turns out you have to be sixteen, so I guess we won't be going after all. I don't see why you have to be sixteen ... I mean there must be something we could do."

"Bless you. I'm sure the authorities know best. Fighting fires is much too dangerous for youngsters, I'm sure. Can I get you a glass of lemonade? You look all in."

Mrs. Toussaint appraised him from her doorway; she had on that kitchen apron over the gray dress she seemed always to wear, as if it were her uniform. It hadn't occurred to him that it might be bad form to call on a lady as dignified as Mrs. Toussaint, sweating like a horse from his exertions on the ball field. He was suddenly conscious of his condition.

"Thank you, but I've got to get home for supper. Well, goodbye, Mrs.

Toussaint."

"I'll tell Rosemary you asked for her when she calls," the old lady called after him. He turned and thanked her again, though something told him that he would never see Rosemary Toussaint again, the way he had never seen Bernie again once she left her aunt.

* * *

Scanlon had never, in his memory, contemplated the fact that so many "ideal" women had slipped through his grasp in his lifetime. One of the first women to "stick," as it were, was anything but his ideal. Katie Durand single-handedly gave him five of the unhappiest years of his life, and a daughter to whom he remained estranged to this day, thirty-seven years after her birth. Over the years he had tried, after his fashion, to make contact with Lucy only to get the same reception he got from her mother—rejection. Until he met Judith, Scanlon had been woefully unlucky in love, if luck had a part to play in his love dramas.

He glanced at his blood bag, and saw that it was half full—or half empty. He was halfway there. Karla said his color was returning, that he looked "much improved." His rear end was numb, but the itching of his back had ceased. He supposed he *did* feel better. If he put the colonoscopy that was in his immediate future out of his mind he might even have had cause for optimism. He'd need to turn to Judith for that. She could always be counted on to show him the "bright" side, even if for herself she saw only darkness, especially where her family was concerned. Both of them came from wretched, uncaring families, even if hers was rich, and his poor.

"Can I get you some water, Mr. Scanlon?" Karla asked him, examining the blood bag and tubing. His hand ached where the IV needle was inserted.

"No thanks. We're halfway home, right?"

"You bet. How are you feeling?"

"Not bad. Did I mention how much I appreciate your staying late on my account?"

"Please don't mention it. That's what we're here for."

"Florence Nightingale and Clara Barton had nothing on you, Karla."

"Clara who? I've heard of Florence Nightingale, but Clara ..." Could a registered nurse (he assumed Karla was "registered") not have heard of the founder of the Red Cross?

"Let's say that she was a lot like you, Karla. Clara, Karla. Your names are even similar. What's your last name?"

"My maiden name's Barrett, if you can believe it."

Hearing that Karla was married deflated him for some inexplicable reason. "Why shouldn't I believe it?"

"It's just a saying. You know? Don't take it so serious."

"Do I sound serious?"

"Sort of. You kind of strike me as someone who's not too easy to convince of things."

"Is that so?"

"Don't get me wrong," Karla hastened to add, in case she had given offense. "I don't mean anything negative by it, or anything. It's just an impression. You sure I can't get you something to wet your whistle?"

Scanlon declined, and Karla hurried off before she said something to hurt his feelings, without meaning to. Of course, his feelings had always bruised easily. He knew this and disliked himself for it. In his view, it was a character flaw, one of many he had identified over the years, but had made little or no attempt to correct.

He wondered, idly, how the people he had worked with at the School for so many years would view his background, his youth. He was an imposter, in a way. He pretended to share his colleagues' values, their assumptions about what was important in life, but it was an acquired taste with him. Now, he wasn't at all sure what he really valued, what he really believed.

How many of his colleagues had been drunk on whiskey at the age of fourteen? To listen to one of his colleague's expression of incredulity upon hearing that one of his charges had been taken before the disciplinary committee for doing "shots" of vodka (fourteen in the space of a half hour) before heading out for a Saturday evening of socializing, one would have thought he believed that teenaged drinking was a recent phenomenon. He smiled to himself at the studied gentility of many of them. Some of his male colleagues could put away the juice with the best of them. To hear them tell it, they began their drinking careers in college. By the time he reached college he was already a heavy drinker. For that matter, he could have been described as a moderately heavy drinker by the time he was a senior in high school. Four years in the Navy provided the necessary credentials to enter the ranks of "serious" drinker. He knew now that his years of drinking were at the bottom of his present health problems. Up to now he had refused to face that fact. The thought of cutting out alcohol altogether made him feel faint. Could he do it? Or would he have to resort to Alcoholics Anonymous, the way his stepfather had done for years, to no avail. AA sessions were so stressful for him that Bill Scanlon used to stop by a bar after meetings and get tanked. Hello, my name is Jack Scanlon and I'm an alcoholic. He could never bring himself to utter such a groveling, sniveling confession. Scanlon forced himself to think about something else.

Eighteen

Summer 1955:

Sixteen years old. Jack Scanlon had been waiting for that birthday for what seemed like forever. He lay on his bed, sweating, listening to, for maybe the fifth time, "The Mooche," by Duke Ellington's band. True to what had become his natural state, Jack was miserable, and not only because of the oppressive heat and humidity. His sixteenth birthday had come and gone three weeks ago, and he was still a virgin. And he was convinced that this was a condition he'd have to endure forever.

A pile of dishes lay on the kitchen table and on the drain board next to the sink, waiting for his attention. This fact compounded his misery. His mother expected him to wash and dry dishes during the week, while she worked. Keith and Billy had no assigned chores, and he resented his mother for sparing them. If he failed to do the dishes his mother would throw a fit. As if he hadn't washed and dried a million and a half dishes in the four years he'd worked in Abe's delicatessen, his mother had to add more. Keith and Billy were out in the neighborhood somewhere; he cared not where. Technically, he was supposed to be looking after them; they were eight and nine years old, old enough, in his opinion, to look after themselves. For the past two years the Scanlons had lived in the four-room apartment of this duplex, on a dead-end street in east Garrison. Their apartment house was the next to the last one before the street ended; beyond it was a deep gulley where Charles Litchfield, their eccentric next door neighbor, liked to scale his 78-RPM records after he tired of listening to them. "The Mooche" played off a 45-RPM record, on the other side of which was "Skin Deep" featuring Louis Bellson, Duke's white drummer who thumped two bass drums with his busy feet. Jack Scanlon, thanks in part to his friend, Joey Costis, had become a rabid jazz fan.

"Hello. Anybody home?" He had left the kitchen door open in case some cool air decided to enter the hallway. A single flight of stairs led up from a side entrance to the kitchen. Nobody in his family used the front door because you had to pass through the hallway of their neighbors, who occupied the apartment in the front of the house. He recognized Edna Pratt's voice. He was in no mood for conversation, but she would have heard his music so he was trapped.

"I'm in bed," Jack said in a low voice, so low that he knew Edna could not have heard it. Then Edna appeared framed in the doorway of the bedroom he shared with his half-brothers.

"What kind of music is *that*?" Edna asked him, wrinkling her nose as if she smelled something disagreeable. It could just as likely have been him, as the music, which caused her to wrinkle her fleshy nose, or perhaps the smell of stale pee from Billy's mattress. Jack was sweating freely, and probably didn't smell so sweet himself. He knew that Edna's taste in music ran to country-western, which Joey Costis lumped into a category he called "hillbilly."

"Good music," Jack replied. He made no move to get off the bed to greet his visitor. He was dressed in a white, sweat-soaked T-shirt and dirty blue jeans. Edna had on a thin, bright yellow tank top and tight fitting pink shorts. She was seventeen years old, and had quit school the very day she turned sixteen. She was the oldest child in what remained of the Pratt tribe next door. There were eight or nine kids ranging from toddler to Edna; Jack had no idea of the girl/boy ratio. Like Jack, Edna had the responsibility of minding kids and doing household chores. She was seventeen but she acted older, and dated older guys, servicemen—sailors, soldiers, airmen—anybody in uniform.

Edna sat down on the edge of the bed and put her hand on his bare foot.

"I'll bet you're ticklish," she said. Jack withdrew his foot reflexively. She was right about that; he was ticklish. Just as reflexively, his pecker stood at attention. He rolled over on his side so Edna wouldn't notice. "The Mooche" finished playing, and the arm of the record player returned automatically for another play. "Can I turn that off?" Edna got up and switched off the record player. She had a shapely rear end, if a little on the beefy side for Jack's taste. Her breasts were large, the way he liked them, but her limbs were heavy, and she had bigger shoulders than his "ideal" girl should have. She had fairly lifeless dirty-blonde hair, which she wore in a ponytail pulled away from her face, revealing ears with detached lobes adorned with pendulous earrings. Her face was coarse, her complexion oily, and there was a spray of blackheads on her forehead. The last imperfection he could list had to do with her lips, which were too large, but today ... today nothing about Edna Pratt looked that bad.

She sat back down on the bed, her hand on his ankle this time, underneath his jeans, working its way up his calf. She inched closer to him on the bed, a smile that he interpreted as wicked fixed on her not-very-pretty face. He took hold of her forearm and was about to draw her down next to him when a commotion erupted in the hallway. He recognized Keith's wailing, and Billy's impatient exhortation for him to stop his wailing. Jack recoiled, and Edna rose to her feet.

"Damn!" Jack said.

"He sounds hurt," Edna said. Jack swung his legs off the bed and sat up.

"He always sounds hurt. He's such a little shit." Edna went into the kitchen; Jack got off the bed, slowly, and followed her.

"What on earth happened to you?" he heard Edna say. He came into the kitchen to find Keith with his hand held up to the side of his head, his face red and tear-streaked. He was bawling loudly, his mouth wide open. Billy came in behind him.

"He got stung by a bee," Billy said. "Stop your crying," he said to his younger brother. Keith removed his hand from the side of his head to wipe his nose.

"Holy shit!" Jack's eyes opened wide at the sight of Keith's right ear, easily five times its normal size. It looked fake, like something from a novelty shop. "Does it hurt, Keith? Keith?" Keith's answer was incomprehensible blubbering that Jack took to mean yes.

"Get a wet wash cloth," Edna said to Jack. Billy had gone to the refrigerator in search of something sweet to put in his mouth. "Have you got any meat tenderizer in the house?" Edna asked.

"Meat tenderizer? I don't know. What is it?"

Edna looked at him in mock disbelief. "It's used to make meat tender. It's good for bug bites. My mother's used it on the kids. Comes in a little bottle. Called Rudolph's or something."

What his mother kept in the cupboard was no concern of his unless it could be eaten. He was not aware of anything that fit this description in the house. Keith's crying was yielding to convulsive little sobs. The swelling of his ear wasn't lessening, however, and Jack began to worry.

"Should we call a doctor? Take him to the hospital, what?" he asked Edna, who seemed to know how to deal with such matters as these.

"Let's keep an eye on him for a while, make sure he don't have no trouble breathing or nothing. It could be he'll be all right." So they kept watch over Keith for the time being, until he quieted down, and didn't seem to have any difficulty breathing, or any other ill effects from his sting. He consented to sit in front of the television set, whimpering intermittently, but finished with his major crying. Jack would have preferred exploring Edna's mysteries on his sweaty bed, but her take-charge manner gave him an enormous sense of relief, and he was grateful for her presence. There would be other days, other opportunities, for exploration.

* * *

"I came this close to getting laid," Jack said to Joey Costis, presenting his thumb and forefinger in front of his friend's face to give him a measure of just how close he had come to overcoming the dubious virtue of Edna Pratt. Joey looked skeptical. He was of the same opinion as Jack as to the chances of their ever getting laid.

The noon rush hour was over in Cohen's Delicatessen. Abe had left Jack in charge while he went to the market to run errands. Joey Costis had come in to mooch a free soft drink. He sat on a stool at the end of the counter over the sink, near the sandwich preparation area. Jack had just finished drying the last of the lunch hour dishes. Fresh half-barrels of sour pickles and sauerkraut had just been delivered, and Jack was putting off removing the covers. The smell of sauerkraut sickened him.

Jack had taken the liberty of playing some of his own records on Abe's machine while his boss was out of the store. Abe couldn't abide Jack's taste in music. Abe's music preferences ran to light classical, stuff by Mantovani and that ilk. His favorite male vocalist was Tony Martin. He wouldn't let Jack play any of his music during lunch rush, or anytime Abe was present in the store, for that matter. In Abe's view, jazz was pure noise and nonsense, and furthermore it gave him a headache. Jack slipped a stack of 45-RPMs on the spindle—the Mulligan/Baker quartet, Dave Brubeck, and Stan Kenton. Joey was more advanced musically than Jack, and it was Joey in fact who had turned him on to "progressive" jazz one afternoon up in his room when he put on a 78-RPM record, with a Bluebird label, of Charlie Parker and Miles Davis playing "Half Nelson."

"My next door neighbor's brother from Texas just got in town, with a friend. They're musicians; they're going to spend the rest of the summer here. They're looking for a drummer and a bass man. They want to start a combo. Tom says they play progressive. I'm meeting them tonight," Joey said before sucking the last of his grape soda noisily through a straw.

"Sounds cool. Who do you know, plays bass?"

"Jim Klein's the only cat I know. Plays bass and violin in the school band. He's the only guy I can think of."

"Jim Klein is kind of a pain in the ass, if you ask me." Klein was in Jack's class in school, and he'd had to put up with the pompous jerk all last year in science class. Joey was only a year ahead of Jack in school even though he was three years older. They had known each other from their Franklin School days, but hadn't really become friends until a year ago. Joey lived at the end of Fourth Street with a woman he called his mother but who was really his grandmother. He sometimes helped out a guy he called his brother, but who was really his uncle, in his men's clothing store.

Joey executed a double paradiddle on the countertop with his bare hands. It was Joey's drumming, in fact, which first got Jack's attention. He had given a performance of the Gene Krupa solo from "Sing Sing Sing" for the students and teachers at Franklin School when he was in eighth grade. Jack wasn't the only one who had been impressed with Joey's skill as a drummer. Jack was worried that Joey's recent taking up of the clarinet was causing him to lose interest in the drums. He had endured too many of Joey's practice sessions on his new instrument, in his cramped bedroom, as he strove to become as accomplished on the clarinet as he was on drums.

Joey ceased his drumming abruptly. Jack looked up from *Downbeat* magazine, whose pages he thumbed through at random, and met Joey's staring black eyes. He had the occasional fleeting notion that Joey Costis could look stark raving crazy at times. What was he *thinking*? It never occurred to Jack to ask him.

"Can I have a dish of that sauerkraut?" he asked Jack.

"Abe could come in any minute. I'd better not."

"How's he to know I didn't pay for it?"

Jack laughed. "Abe knows all about your finances, Joey. I don't know how anybody can eat that stuff anyway."

"I like it. Come on, just a small dish. I'll eat it fast."

"Fucking no, I said. I gave you a soda; what more do you want?"

"Some sauerkraut."

"Not today."

Abe came through the door, carrying two paper grocery bags, one in each arm.

"If it isn't the little drummer boy," he said to Joey, setting the bags down on the table next to the showcase. "You didn't open the pickles, the sauerkraut?" he said to Jack. He got a screwdriver from a drawer under the counter of the grocery section to pry the covers off the barrels.

"I was just about to." Kenton's piano intro to "Artistry in Rhythm" filled the room. Jack hurried to the front of the store to take it off the turntable before Abe could offer up one of his choice remarks on Jack and Joey's taste in music. He was not angry with Jack about his failure to open up the barrels, just matter of fact.

"Jesus, you haven't been listening to that crap again." Abe shook his head and popped the cover off the sour pickle barrel.

"It's not crap," Joey protested. "It's better than that ... crap you listen to all day."

Abe popped a cigarette in his mouth, and lit up with his Ronson. He gathered smoke in his mouth with his tongue, and raised his thick eyebrows that practically ran together over his aquiline nose. He smiled privately at Jack.

"You call that noise *music*?"

"You don't know anything about music," Joey riposted, dismissing Abe with a wave of his hand. "Come on, Jack. Let's go around George's, see if there's any fish swimming."

"You finish the lunch dishes?" Abe asked Jack.

"Yeah."

"All right. Go ahead. I'll see you tomorrow."

As the boys were going out the door, Peg, the bookkeeper at Weinstock's News Store down the street, came in for her mid-afternoon coffee and macaroon. She was short, with thin shoulders, small breasts and huge hips. She had a big rear end, which Abe had taken a fancy to.

"Hello, Jack," she said, ignoring Joey.

"Peg."

On their way across the railroad station parking lot in the direction of George's poolroom, Joey asked Jack if he knew for sure whether Abe was banging Peg. He doubted it himself.

"Why?"

"For one thing, Abe's taste in music may be in his ass, but I can't see him with that broad. She doesn't look like she'd want anybody to see her with her clothes off." Jack allowed that it was true that she came off as a little prim and proper.

"Maybe she lets Abe do it to her with her clothes *on*," he surmised.

Paul Martel was currently Joey Costis's favorite "fish." He could be counted on to give up a buck or two every time he clashed with Joey. They spotted his Cushman's Bakery delivery truck parked in front of the poolroom.

"Aha!" Joey's eyes lighted up.

"I thought you were broke."

"When did I ever need money to play Martel?" Joey Costis stuck to sure things lately, after losing the ten dollars his mother/grandmother had given him to pay the electric bill and pick up groceries for her two weeks ago. He had lost it in a game of straight pool to Phil Cane, a playboy who didn't have a third of Joey's talent as a pool player. Joey had a reputation as a "choker," however, and Phil Cane had a way of working on an opponent's head. He owned Joey's head. So, these days Joey confined his pool playing activities to sure things—like Paul Martel.

"Listen, I've got to get home. What time did you say you were meeting these musician guys?"

"I don't know. After supper sometime, I guess. I'll call you." Joey pushed through the swinging door to George's upstairs pool hall and two-lane duck pin bowling alley, to reel in his "fish."

Jack chose to take the short route home, by way of the railroad tracks. He alternated between walking the rail, to short-stepping on the ties, avoiding the cinder-strewn path beside the tracks. All the way home he thought about how he would seduce Edna Pratt if she took it her head to pay him another visit. It was another steamy day, a perfect day for lovemaking. He would teach her to like jazz. Too late he realized that he had left his best records back at Abe's, the ones suitable for setting a romantic mood. He had a Lennie Tristano record at home, and a two record album of Lee Konitz and Warne Marsh, but they were both too advanced for the novice. His mother's Perry Como records wouldn't do either. He was slightly frustrated by the lack of music with which to set the mood for love as he turned down the embankment behind his house.

From the path that led from the tracks through a field overgrown with waist high weeds, he had a view of the back of the duplex the Pratts lived in, as well as his own house. Halfway down the path he spotted Edna in the back of her house, her arms wound around the neck of a sailor in uniform, his white-hat pushed to the back of his head. They were embraced in a kiss; the sailor had his right arm thrust between Edna's legs. She had on the same pink shorts she wore yesterday. He stopped walking, and stared for a moment at the couple, before he had to look away. He felt light-headed, slightly dizzy. He couldn't continue along the path without being seen by Edna and her sailor, and he didn't want to be seen, especially by her. He turned around and walked back up the hill to the railroad tracks, and continued on past his house a ways before cutting across the back yard of a house further up the street. He walked back toward his house, and hurried up the stairs before he could encounter Edna and her lover boy. Inside, he put on his Lennie Tristano record and flung himself face first on his unmade bed. A lump the size of a golf ball was lodged in his throat.

He had neglected last night's supper dishes again, and his mother lit into him when she got home from work; she threatened to keep him in the house at night for a week if he didn't start changing his ways. He sat at the kitchen table and let her words cascade over him, staring blankly at the wall, as if he were in a hypnotic state.

"What's the matter with you, Jack?" She had by now relented, and grudgingly addressed him as Jack, not Johnny. "Are you sick, or what? Answer me. Where's Keith and Billy?"

He had no idea where the boys were. The swelling of Keith's ear had gone down by morning, but neither of them was in the house when he got home, and in his present state of mind he hadn't bothered to go looking for them. He didn't answer his mother, and for once she didn't press him further on their whereabouts. She almost seemed concerned about him. She placed the back of her hand on his sweating forehead; it was eighty-five degrees or more in the apartment so why wouldn't he be sweating?

"You're acting strange. Don't you feel good?"

"I feel all right."

"Did you eat something at that place that didn't agree with you?" That *place* was Abe's delicatessen, which she found "exotic" and didn't altogether approve of, even if she had no objection to her son earning money there. In her mind his salary, however meager, might serve as a temporary buffer against what inevitably would be another bender for her husband. He had been on good behavior for nearly a year; the time was ripe for a fall. He had a construction job that kept him away from home during the week, and when he was out of sight it was likely his family was out of his mind.

"Get them dishes done, then, if you're not sick. I've got supper to make." Since she had given up cigarettes, his mother had become even more irritable, if that were possible.

"At least get Billy to help me dry."

"We wouldn't have no dishes left, you let him near them. Now do like I say."

Joey phoned at seven o'clock, just as Jack was about to give up on him and head for the poolroom.

"Meet me at George's," Joey said. "You're not going to believe how cool these guys from Texas are."

Joey Costis was correct. The guys from Texas *were* cool, as cool as anyone Jack had ever met. Maybe it was because they were older. Darren Price, the alto sax and guitar man, was twenty-two; Greg Cummings, who played piano and arranged all their songs, was twenty-five. Darren was a native of San Antonio, and Greg had settled there after taking his discharge from the Air Force. He had been stationed at Randolph the last two years of his enlistment, and had taken a fancy to the city of San Antonio.

Joey had asked the musicians if he could invite his friend along to their first rehearsal. Darren and Greg were staying with Greg's uncle, Tom Cummings, whose tiny house on Court Street was next to Marcel's Barbershop where Jack got his haircuts every two months.

Greg Cummings, naked to the waist, was tuning his uncle's piano in the small parlor when Joey introduced him to Jack. Darren Price sat in a horsehair armchair, his long leg slung negligently over one of the arms, which leaked stuffing. He was picking out chords on his electric guitar, which was not yet hooked up to the amplifier beside him.

"This is, ah, my friend Jack," Joey stammered, clutching his drumsticks in one hand, and gesturing awkwardly with the other, as if he were presenting his friend to Society. He held his practice pad under his arm. Greg Cummings turned around on the piano bench and rose up to greet Jack, hand extended. Darren Price remained seated, fingering his instrument languidly. He acknowledged Jack with a nod of his sandy-haired head, and a smile.

"Hi there, Jack," Greg said. How you doing? Welcome to Uncle Tom's Cabin. You met Uncle Tom?" Greg's upper body was deeply tanned, with a mat of thick curly brown chest hair that matched the color and curl of hair on his head. He had muscular arms with veins the size of soda straws. By contrast, Darren Price's arms were pale and freckled, with no hint of musculature. He wore a short-sleeved yellow shirt and blue jeans. On his feet, he wore Mexican huarches, and no socks. Joey and Jack had encountered Uncle Tom at the kitchen table when they came in the house. He also was bare to the waist. Uncle Tom's chest hair, as abundant as his nephew's, was pure white. He was white on top too; although what hair he had was mainly on his temples, and the back of his head. Jack learned from Greg later that Uncle Tom Cummings had been widowed eight years, and had recently retired from the Boston and Maine Railroad.

"So, Joey, is this the fella who's going to fix us up with all the pretty high school gals?" To Jack's untrained ear, Darren's accent was generically southern. He would be educated by Darren in time to listen for an authentic Texas accent, and be able to distinguish it from accents of other regions of the South.

"He couldn't fix himself up," Joey replied.

"Thanks," Jack said, feeling like backhanding his friend. Greg laughed, but Jack could tell it was not a malicious laugh.

"You must be in a hurry to go to jail," Greg said to Darren.

"We can't go all summer without women, can we now?" Darren placed his guitar carefully in its red felt-lined case, and opened up another black case beside it on the floor. It was also lined with red felt;

Darren removed a gold, Selmer alto saxophone, screwed on the neckpiece, and fitted a reed into the mouthpiece. Greg turned back to the keyboard and resumed his piano tuning. Joey sat down on a straight-backed chair, placed his practice pad on his lap and executed a series of single and double paradiddles, and flams. Darren ran the scale a few times, then started to play a tune that Jack thought he recognized, but couldn't have named.

"Doesn't Desmond play that?" he asked Darren, when he found the courage, after listening to a few more bars. Darren turned toward Jack and nodded, continuing to play.

"Yeah, 'Out of Nowhere.' Desmond's arrangement is the best," Darren said when he'd finished. "You got a good ear, Jack. You play?"

"I used to." Jack had taken four lessons on alto sax his sophomore year. Joey had talked him into it, using as his principal argument the fact that his clarinet teacher used to play with the Glen Miller band, and he was taking on new pupils. Mr. Claxton was a short, stocky man with kinky blond hair, with no sense of humor and no patience with students who didn't practice at least two hours a day, every day of the week. Therefore, he had no patience with Jack Scanlon, whose embouchure, Mr. Claxton remarked every time Jack started to play for him, was better suited to sucking on Popsicles than producing sound from a woodwind instrument. Jack put up with Mr. Claxton's insults for four lessons then quit without telling him, Glen Miller or no Glen Miller. Joey was disgusted with him. Jack's mother could not have cared less; he wondered if she even knew he was taking saxophone lessons. There had to have been a good reason why he had rented his instrument instead of purchasing it outright.

"He quit," Joey interjected. "He's got no discipline."

"Well, it sure does takes that," Darren said, and blew a few sweet notes that Jack swore sounded like Paul Desmond himself. Jack was sorry now he had let it out that he had tried his hand at playing an instrument. It would have come out sooner or later he supposed, no doubt from Joey's big mouth. His spirits had gone south, and he felt even more like an outsider with these people. And he certainly couldn't be counted on to fix these guys up with pretty high school girls. It gave him no comfort that Greg had pointed out to his companion that high school girls were "jailbait." He thought fleetingly of Edna Pratt, but he doubted that either one of them would consider her "pretty". Besides, she was no longer a high school girl.

Darren said, "How about this one, Jack. Tell me if you recognize it." Darren began to play "You Go to My Head," which Jack *did* recognize. And he could name it as well.

"I think he's ready for the blindfold test," Greg said, trying out a few random chords, satisfied that he finally had his uncle's long neglected piano back in tune, ready to go.

Jack felt himself flush up with pleasure at Greg's comment about his being ready for the "blindfold" test. He had been reading *Downbeat* that very morning and had been impressed with Clifford Brown's performance on the magazine's blindfold test, where the subject is given several pieces to listen to, comment on, and to try and identify the artist. If Jack was pretty good at identifying contemporary jazz artists from listening to their records, he was woefully ignorant about how the music itself was made. Four lessons with Claxton, and his Gestapo method of music instruction, had taught him nothing about how to read music.

Greg had warmed up enough. "Let's do 'Pennies From Heaven,'" he said to Darren. "Joey, can you get your set over here tomorrow? Uncle Tom has turned the parlor over to us. And what about the bass man you were talking about? Can you get him over here tomorrow?"

"You know Jim Klein's number?" Joey asked Jack.

"How would I know that dork's number?"

Darren laughed. Joey informed him that this "dork" was the bass player he had told them about.

"Can't you find a bass player who's not a dork?" Darren Price drawled.

"There aren't that many bass players in a town this size," Joey said.

"Dork or no dork, we need a bass man. And have you ever heard of a telephone directory?" Greg asked Joey.

"Okay. I'll call him tomorrow. Wait, I think he works for his old man. Yeah, I'll stop by his old man's store, talk to Jim in person."

Uncle Tom appeared in the doorway, a bottle of root beer in his hand, his rimless spectacles pushed up on his forehead.

"When's the concert start?"

"You might want to turn down your hearing aid, Uncle Tom, when you hear what we got to offer," his nephew said. The parlor was small and overfurnished; five people in the room made it seem even smaller. Fitting a set of drums in the room, not to mention a stand up bass, would be a challenge, in Jack's opinion.

Greg played the opening chords to "Pennies From Heaven." Darren came in smoothly; Joey didn't try to accompany them with his practice pad. Uncle Tom seemed pleased by what he heard; he had a wide smile on his face, and he conducted the music with his root beer bottle. Jack began to feel like a fifth wheel, with nothing to offer this burgeoning jazz combo.

When they finished "Pennies From Heaven" Greg asked Jack what he thought about it.

"Pretty good considering you didn't have a rhythm section. I liked the way Darren came in. Smooth, real smooth."

"We should make Jack our private critic," Greg said. Jack feared he was being condescending. He looked at Greg but all he saw on his tanned, ruddy face was an earnest expression.

"Yeah, the boy's got an ear," Darren said.

"Have you guys ever performed before, in public?" Jack asked.

"Not together. I've played at weddings and such, and Darren's played in country-western bands ... guitar, not sax. But we've never had a gig together."

Jack waited for Joey to say something disparaging about his ability to judge what was good and what was bad in music, but Joey had nothing to say one way or the other, for the time being.

"Let's do "Perdido". Jack, give us a critique afterward," Greg said, turning to the keyboard.

In truth, Jack didn't much care for their arrangement of "Perdido," but he praised their rendering fulsomely anyway, maybe with too much enthusiasm, because Greg frowned, and looked displeased.

"I rushed it," he said. "Darren, stop trying to sound like Flip Phillips. It doesn't become you."

For the rest of the evening Greg and Darren argued, sometimes hotly, over the repertoire they ought to adopt. They disagreed over tunes mainly because one or the other didn't feel it featured his solo work adequately. Joey had little to contribute, as he was more or less an interloper at this juncture, though not as much of an interloper as Jack. Jack was flattered that they even asked his opinion. In the course of the evening he grew so bold as to state what he disliked as well as what he liked. Furthermore, Greg and Darren acted as though they were interested in what he had to say.

"I think you jumped the gun a little, Darren," he said of the way Darren came in after Greg's solo on "All the Things You Are." "You obliterated Greg's last chord."

"Right," Darren said, licking his mouthpiece like a Popsicle, making Jack think about what Claxton had said about his embouchure.

"You're right, Jack," Greg said, "but his riff was pretty, you have to admit." So, "All the Things You Are" passed muster, and became part of the repertoire. Greg thought they ought to leave it up to Jack to come up with a suitable name for the group. Jack left Uncle Tom's Cabin that night walking several inches off the ground.

He lay awake in bed that night racking his brain for a name for the band; he felt alive for the first time in he didn't know how long, maybe ever. He forgot, for the time being, about his misery—his daily dishwashing chore, the long hours at Abe's delicatessen, the betrayal (he had come to look at it in this peculiar light) of Edna Pratt with the sailor, the constant irritating presence of his half-brothers, all of it. Several dozen possible names for the group occurred to him before he was finally overtaken by sleep, none of which appealed to him in the light of morning. Most of them were downright stupid; names that would have been better suited to the rock and roll bands that seemed to be the rage these days, not names that would reflect the dignity of a jazz combo. He struggled all day at work, to no avail. By the time he was ready to head over to rehearsal at Uncle Tom's Cabin he was in a near panic, not having come up with anything. If that weren't enough to put him in a low mood, Jim Klein was in the parlor, stroking his string bass with a bow.

"Well, if it isn't Garrison High's hep cat."

"Hello, Jimmy." Jack knew that Jim Klein hated being called Jimmy. Jim Klein was, in Jack's opinion, not only a dork; he was a dork's dork. He was tall and thin, with a narrow face and thick eyeglasses. He wore his shirts buttoned up to the throat, just below his big Adam's apple. He looked about twenty-eight, though he was no older than Jack. Once, in science class, Miss Chabot told him she believed he could stand to be a little less sententious. Jack had never heard this word. When he looked it up in the dictionary he smiled to himself at how perfectly it described Jim Klein, especially the last definition, "trite and moralistic." Yet, Klein wasn't really a bad sort. Jack never heard him say anything deliberately haughty or cruel to anyone whom Klein considered his intellectual inferior, including Jack himself. He just came off the way he did, naturally. Nevertheless, Jack was not pleased to find him in Uncle Tom's parlor.

"Hi, Jack. What did you come up with?" Greg asked him.

"Come up with?" He had hoped, on the walk over, for a little more time to think before they put his feet to the fire.

"Yeah. What name for the band?"

"What about the Darren Gregg Quartet. I figured if you spelled Greg with two Gs it would look like a last name ... that's what I thought."

"Right," Darren said, "G-G-R-E-G."

"No. I like it. I think it works," Greg said, playing a right hand run on the keyboard.

"Why not the Greg Darren Quartet. What's the difference?" Joey said, just to be contrary, Jack felt.

"I was looking for alphabetical order," Jack countered, quite amazed at himself for his quick thinking in coming up with the name. "I like the fact that the first name has two syllables, too. It sounds better, if you ask me," he added.

"Yeah," Joey said, "like Duke Ellington, Ray Anthony, Ralph Flannagan ..."

"You made your point," Greg said. "Anybody got a better idea?"

"I like it. Let's go with it," Darren said.

Tonight, Darren wore a short-sleeved shirt with a Western motif embroidered across the front of it—cactus plants, a mountain range in the background. He had shed his huarches, and was now barefoot. Joey had set his drums up in the corner of the room by the window. He sat behind them, a pair of brushes poised over his snare. The armchair that had occupied that corner Joey had moved to the far end of the room next to a rocker, making the parlor look even more crowded. The ceilings in Uncle Tom's Cabin were so low that Darren, who was about six-feet three, had to stoop over, and to duck his head going through doorways. Uncle Tom had ensconced himself on the horsehair sofa on the arm of which the afghan his wife had made was folded. He was shirtless; a pair of red and white striped suspenders with B & M stitched on them supported his green work pants. Tonight he had a pork pie hat on his bald dome, and to Jack he looked rather comical sitting there nursing his root beer, waiting for the music to start.

"Got any requests for us, Uncle Tom?" Darren asked the old man.

"Bet you don't know 'I Wonder Who's Kissing Her Now,'" Tom said, his pale blue eyes full of mischief. Darren licked his mouthpiece, raised his eyes to the ceiling as if he were searching for the melody, and started to play in that reedy parody of Freddie Gardiner, whom Darren considered the squarest musician on the planet, and never missed a chance to ridicule his style of play. Both Darren and Greg had strong opinions about what constituted "good" music, and they were in accord in their condemnation of the new rock and roll music that was gaining popularity by the day with America's youth.

"Say, that's pretty good, young fellow. I wouldn't have guessed you'd know an old timer like that," Tom said, applauding Darren's rendering of "I Wonder Who's Kissing Her Now." Jack remembered Aunt Lily singing it to him when he was a kid, and Darren was a good six years older than he was. Why wouldn't he have known the song too? Uncle Tom was probably just being polite. Greg was impatient to get down to the business of rehearsal.

"Okay, let's see what we can do with "Jeepers Creepers." We don't have any extra sheets, Jim. Think you can follow along?"

"Sure," Jim Klein said, drawing his bow across the strings of his instrument.

"You won't need that for this number," Darren said.

"All right. Ready?" Greg gave the downbeat, and the newly formed Darren Gregg Quartet performed its first composition together.

The room began to stink of body odor and cigarette smoke (everybody smoked except Jim Klein). Uncle Tom Cummings didn't believe in fans. The sweat flowed, but nobody seemed to mind, so intent were they on their music; Jack was oblivious of the sweat and stink himself. At about ten o'clock Jim Klein announced that he had to get home. Greg declared an end to the rehearsal.

"I think this was a good session. Can you make it tomorrow, Jim?" Jim Klein leaned his instrument against the back of an armchair, and mopped his sweaty brow with a big, checkered handkerchief.

"I can make it tomorrow night, but Friday is out. I got Temple on Friday nights."

"What about the rest of the week? Can we count on you?"

"I'm all right every night except Friday, and weekends sometimes my family goes away." Greg frowned, and shot Darren a look. Darren raised his eyebrows.

"If we get a club gig, we might need to count on you for a Saturday night. Is that going to be a problem for you?"

"Club gigs? You mean nightclubs? I didn't think there was such a thing in Garrison."

Greg asked Joey if this were true. "Maybe not in Garrison," Jack said, before Joey had a chance to answer, "but there's Portsmouth, and the beaches ..."

"You got a union card, Jim?" Darren asked him. Jim Klein said he never had the need of a union card, and neither had Joey.

"You're going to need to get cards," Darren said, "Clubs won't hire cats without them."

"What about critics?" Jack said, trying to be clever.

"Jack, what I think you ought to be doing the next few days is getting on the phone and calling around the clubs in the area," Greg said. "What do you say?"

"My old lady would throw a fit if I ran up a phone bill."

"Why don't we just stop around clubs and pitch them face to face?" Darren offered.

"All right. Where should we start?" Greg addressed the question to Jack, who had been so quick to identify where clubs were apt to be found. He had no idea how to answer. He was sixteen years old, and looked fourteen. What did he know from nightclubs? He turned to Joey for help. Joey's former mentor, a drummer named Sparky Williams, who was perpetually unemployed because he was perpetually drunk, would know all about clubs that were receptive to jazz combos. Joey said as much to Darren and Greg, and promised to look up Sparky Williams in the next day or so. So Jack was off the hook.

* * *

The next day, after lunch rush, Jack was hyperconscious of the clock, at how agonizingly slow the hour hand moved. Abe had to go to the market in Boston; he left Jack in charge of the deli. He finished washing and drying the lunch dishes, and was trying to keep his mind busy by peeling hardboiled eggs for potato salad. He put a Kenton record on Abe's machine, and listened carefully to Charlie Mariano's solo work on "Stella by Starlight," wondering if Darren Price could negotiate the higher notes Mariano seemed to play with ease. Last night at rehearsal, at one point, Darren had annoyed Greg to the point where he had stopped in the middle of a tune to say to Darren, "Enough already with the demisemiquavers." Jack learned later from Joey, who knew how to read music, that Greg referred to Darren's excessive runs of thirty-second notes. Jack had noticed himself that Darren sometimes got carried away technically, but he wouldn't have been able to articulate to anyone why he thought so. So now he wondered how Darren Price compared to big time musicians, like Charlie Mariano.

After massacring another hardboiled egg, Jack, in utter frustration, pulled a quart bottle of Kruger Ale out of the refrigerated section in front of the showcase. He fitted a paper cup into a plastic holder and poured himself some ale up to the brim. He took a sip and placed the cup in one sink, the bottle in the other. He figured Abe would not return from Boston before four o'clock.

Jack had developed a taste for beer in the past two years. He had been cured of whiskey (for the time being) after being made so ill from drinking the better part of a pint of J.W. Dant the summer he turned fourteen. Just the thought of whiskey triggered the memory of the smell of J.W. Dant, and almost caused him to retch. He liked beer and ale well enough. His stepfather kept a bottle of gin in the house. In Bill Scanlon's opinion gin was what the "casual" drinker preferred. This was his way of trying to convince his wife that his serious drinking days were behind him; from now on he would drink like a gentleman. More than once Jack had been tempted to sneak a drink of the stuff, but he'd been put off by the smell of it.

He glanced at the front door before lifting the cup to his lips. By the time Priscilla Murray appeared for her daily coffee and assorted pastry order, he had finished two cups. Priscilla shared the errand with another girl named Kitty; they worked at Weinstock's News, where the big-hipped Peg was office manager. Priscilla was a tall blonde with a high waist, long legs, and pointy breasts. She was a senior at Garrison High School, the head cheerleader for both the varsity football and basketball squads. Jack liked her; it was impossible, in his mind, not to like this affable, fun-loving girl, who was also easy on the eyes. She was also out of reach of the likes of Jack Scanlon. She dated college guys exclusively.

"Hello, sweetie." She greeted Jack the same way every time she came in the store, but he was no less thrilled for hearing it every day.

"Hello, Prissy. What have you got today, as if I didn't know?" The office staff's coffee break order varied little, to not at all, day in day out. Two cups of ale had loosened him up, made him playful.

Priscilla had her order written out on a piece of memo paper. She recited it to Jack, who had memorized it by now anyway. There was no deviation. She had been impressed with his ability to memorize their coffee orders the first time she came in, amazed at his being able to keep straight all the various combinations of black, cream and sugar, cream but no sugar, extra cream, four sugars, etc.; not to mention how he kept the pastry orders straight in his head. Jack was proud, to the point of hubris, of his memory. This skill had not gone unnoticed by Abe's customers, either.

"How's your love life, Jack?"

"My who?"

"You got a girlfriend?"

Jack Scanlon hadn't had a girlfriend since he started high school. Only guys with cars, or guys with driver's licenses whose parents owned cars they didn't mind their kids driving had girlfriends, dates. Jack had neither car nor driver's license. Furthermore, he didn't know how to drive, so borrowing a car to take a girl out on a date was out of the question. He didn't even hang out with anyone who owned a car. Joey was as bereft as he was in that department.

"No."

"Would you like one?" Jack looked up from the coffee he was pouring; Priscilla rotated back and forth on her stool. She was smiling as if to say, "I've got a secret."

"That depends."

"On what? What do you look for in a girl, Jack?"

He wanted to tell Priscilla that she would fill the bill, but he didn't have the nerve. Sometimes his diffidence infuriated him.

"I don't know. I can't think ..."

"Don't you think Kitty's cute?"

"Kitty? Sure, I guess. Why?"

"She thinks *you're* cute." Priscilla had a forefinger pressed into her cheek, her head cocked to one side. She looked expectant.

"What?"

"So, what do you think? Would you like me to fix you up with Kitty?"

Kitty was a year ahead of Jack in school. She was about his height with short, auburn hair, high cheekbones and gray eyes. She had a blemish on the right side of her face, just below her ear; it looked like somebody had bitten her, leaving teeth marks. She wore loose fitting skirts and tops that didn't reveal much about her figure. Jack had noticed that she had shapely ankles, so he assumed the rest of her was pretty good too. Kitty was very quiet; she had little to say to him when it was her turn to fetch the coffee order. So hearing Priscilla say that Kitty thought he was "cute" took him by surprise. He didn't know how to respond.

"Well, do you?" Priscilla sounded impatient.

"Do I what?"

"Want me to fix you up? With Kitty?"

"Uh ... I guess so. Why not?" One good reason "why not" was his lack of a car. And he had no idea what to do with a girl on a date. Where would he take her? To the movies? Where, after the movie? What teenage girl would want to go out on a date on foot? He thought of Bernie, and her counsel on the art of dating. It all seemed so absurd now. He had no idea where Kitty lived, or even what her last name was.

"I'll arrange everything," Priscilla said, counting out the exact change for the order. "I'll let you know by tomorrow, or next day at the latest." Priscilla gathered the bag of coffee and pastry to her impressive breast and left. Jack was in a daze. He wasn't sure what had just taken place. He reached into the sink for his cup of Kruger Ale. What had he gotten himself into?

* * *

"Christ," Jack said to Joey Costis in the parlor of Uncle Tom's Cabin that evening, "what am I going to do?"

"Take her down to the railroad trestle by my house and try to get into her pants."

"You're a lot of fucking help, Costis."

"You asked." Joey flared his brushes out of their metal handles and went to work on his snare drum.

"Where are Darren and Greg?"

"They went to buy some beer for after rehearsal."

"Beer? Great!"

"Take her to a movie or something. *Blackboard Jungle*'s playing at the Colonial. Everybody says it's great. She like movies like that?"

"How should I know? She hasn't said eight words to me since I met her. I don't even know her last name."

"So why did you agree to let what's-her-name fix you up, you fucking banana?"

"Eat shit. I'm glad Klein's not going to be here tonight. I can't stand him; he's such a dork."

"Dork or no dork, we got to have a bass man. You heard Greg."

"There's nobody else in this town can play bass?"

"If there is, I don't know about him. Klein's not that bad once you get to know him."

"I guess so. He's hard to take, though. I like his old man better than him. He comes in for a sandwich, cream cheese and olive on dark rye, once in awhile. Sometimes I feel like asking him how it feels to have such a dork for a son."

"Greg wants to get these chicks to sing with the band. Uncle Tom knows a guy in Maine he used to work with, got two daughters he says are looking for a band to sing with."

"I don't think that's such a good idea." Jack didn't think a singer, or singers, would compliment a quartet. Singers were for big bands as far as he was concerned.

"Greg thinks we'd have a better chance of getting a club gig if we had some kind of commercial appeal. Jazz don't sell drinks in club owners' minds. Singing chicks would give us a leg up, Greg says. Darren agrees."

"They'd know better than I would, I guess." What Jack really feared was a dilution of the group by the addition of more people—chicks, guys, it didn't matter. Just hearing Joey talk about it had him feeling threatened ... feeling jealous.

"What, you got something against having chicks on the scene? Afraid your new girlfriend will get jealous?"

They heard voices from the next room, among them female voices. Greg appeared through the low doorway with a girl, followed by Darren, who ducked in sideways, a girl on each arm. They had gone out for beer and returned with these attractive girls. Joey's mouth fell open, and stayed that way as he sat behind his drums.

"Say hello to the newest members of the group," Greg said, and introduced the girl he escorted into the room as Meg. The other two were named Kathleen and Karen, the sisters who were the daughters of Uncle Tom's friend from Maine. Meg looked a few years older than the sisters Kathleen and Karen, who were around seventeen or eighteen, Jack guessed. Kathleen was probably the prettier of the two, if he had to choose, with her green eyes and turned up nose, but Karen's sky-blue eyes were striking too. Meg wasn't as beautiful as the sisters, but she had something they didn't have, which Jack could only describe as sex appeal. Meg looked like the kind of girl who valued sex for its own sake. They were, all three of them, wearing tight-fitting shorts, and tank tops. Uncle Tom appeared in the doorway, and suddenly the room was so crowded that Jack experienced a moment of claustrophobia.

"You girls certainly have filled out since I last saw you," Uncle Tom observed, his eyes twinkling. "Count yourself lucky I'm not my nephew's age. You'd have your hands full." But the way Meg clung to Greg should have made it clear to the sisters that they wouldn't have their hands full with Tom's nephew either, not while Meg was around. Jack wondered how long Greg had known this Meg that she would get so cozy with him. "They're twins, though you'd never know it, looking at them," Uncle Tom said to no one in particular. Jack agreed; he was surprised to learn that they were even sisters.

"There's no point in doing anything tonight," Greg announced. "Why don't we have a few beers and get acquainted, if we're going to be working together."

The girls' favorite group was The Maguire Sisters; they knew a lot of their songs. Greg and Darren shot each other amused glances when they heard this. And they didn't express any interest in jazz, either, although Meg admitted to liking George Shearing a little. Greg and Darren didn't let on to the girls what they really thought of The Maguire Sisters in particular, that kind of commercial singing group in general. They were, after all, in search of an entrée into nightclubs, so they had to compromise their scruples a little.

Greg disappeared from the parlor, and returned in a few minutes bearing three six-packs of beer. He set them on top of the piano and began popping bottle caps with a church key, and handing bottles around.

"Here you go, Jack," Greg said, handing him a perspiring brown bottle. Jack strove for a blasé attitude toward the beer, for an instant even considered turning it down. The mere feel of the cold bottle in his hand gave him a feeling of well-being. When everyone had his bottle of beer, Darren called for a toast.

"Let's have a little toast to the beginning of a fine association. And a lucrative one," he added, and laughed, as if to inform the boys in the band that he was joking, that he would never give in to the siren call of lucre. Darren Price and Greg Cummings were musical purists, musicians' musicians. Even purists needed to eat, to make both ends meet, if only for the rest of the summer. Each of them had a separate life in San Antonio: Darren worked in a small music shop that sold and repaired instruments of all kinds; Greg would be starting his senior year at Trinity University. After Trinity he planned to apply to law school. Greg had none of Darren's illusions about making it as a professional jazz musician. He just loved to play.

"How about let's hear a sample of what y'all do," Darren said to the girls, "a cappella."

"All right. Come on, girls," Meg said, getting up from the piano bench where she had been sitting close to Greg. She gathered Kathleen and Karen in a huddle. They broke apart, after whispering briefly to each other, then, arms around each other's waist, they sang "Sincerely" a cappella. Each girl soloed for eight bars or so. Jack listened politely, glancing often at Greg and Darren for their reactions. Joey, who remained sitting behind his drums (his mouth had closed by now), mugged for Jack's benefit, and stuck his fingers in his ears. Darren and Greg looked at each other from time to time, apparently amused at the way the girls rendered "Sincerely," which surely they considered a "square" tune.

"That was super," Darren said, with more enthusiasm than Jack believed he honestly felt.

"Did you like it?" Meg looked pleased at the girls' performance; her face was radiant.

"Yeah," Greg added. "How long have you guys been singing together?"

"About a month and a half; since the twins got finished with school. Right, girls?" Meg turned to her singing partners for affirmation. They nodded in unison.

"Just like on TV," Uncle Tom chimed. "That's where I'll see you girls before long, I don't croak in the meantime."

"Why don't we do a number with you and Darren," Meg said. She didn't include Joey, and Jack wondered if she hadn't picked up on his clowning behind their backs while they were performing.

"Okay." Greg swung his legs around so that he faced the keyboard, and pumped out a few minor chords.

"Oh, let's do something cheerful," Meg said, in response to his melancholy notes.

"You name it." Darren began to assemble his horn. Joey played a drum roll, as if to let the newcomers know that he existed too, that he was part of the Darren Gregg Quartet ... more than they were, if the truth were to be told. Jack finished half his beer in a single swallow.

"What about "Our Love Is Here to Stay?" It's a nice standard. We've been working on it about a week. You know it?" Meg began to hum the melody.

"We know it," Darren interrupted, sounding a little annoyed that anyone would question their knowledge of such a well-known standard. He played a few sugary notes á la Freddie Gardiner. Greg joined in, in his characteristically smooth manner; Joey applied the brushes to his snare, and the girls, arms around each other's shoulders this time, offered their version of the song. Jack was thoroughly bored with their singing, but not with their good looks, which he concentrated on instead of the treacle coming out of their mouths. He wondered if Kitty looked half as good in shorts.

* * *

A part of him didn't believe that Priscilla Murray would follow through with her matchmaking, and there was another part of him that even wished she wouldn't.

"It's all set for Wednesday," Priscilla said when she came in on her Saturday afternoon coffee run. Jack suspected something was amiss when Priscilla appeared instead of Kitty. It should have been Kitty's turn on coffee fetching duty.

"Wednesday," Jack murmured, as if he were talking in his sleep.

"Yes. Wednesday at six-thirty. You're to meet in front of Leggett's Tea Room. I suggest you take her in for a cup of coffee or tea before the show starts, then stop in for an ice cream soda or something afterwards."

"Show? What show?"

"I wouldn't recommend the Colonial. There's an awful movie about high school hoodlums picking on their teacher or something playing this week. No, take her to the Uptown. I think there's a Rock Hudson movie starting Wednesday."

"I don't much like Rock Hudson movies," Jack said, remembering too late what Bernie had once told him about not paying attention to what was on the screen when you were on a movie date. He assumed her advice applied to indoor as well as outdoor movies. "What makes you think she wouldn't like the movie at the Colonial?" He'd personally wanted to see it since it went up on the marquee that week.

"It just sounds too ... depressing."

Jack finished pouring Priscilla's coffees; he snapped the plastic covers on the paper cups and bagged them. All of a sudden his heart started to pound. There was something more he should ask Priscilla about this date business with Kitty. His mind was vacant, empty, numb.

"Aren't you excited?"

"Yeah."

"Yeah? There are plenty of boys who would give anything to have a date with Kitty Whittaker, and all you can say is 'yeah?' I don't know about you, sweetie." Priscilla laughed. He'd begun to think she was serious until he heard the laugh. So Kitty's last name was Whittaker. That was more than he had known a minute and a half ago.

"You know where she lives? I mean, you know I don't have a car ... I ... I guess I could get a cab or something."

"That's an idea. She was going to have her brother drive her over, but a cab might be a nice touch. You're a suave one, you are." He hadn't considered the cost of hiring a taxi when he made the suggestion.

"So where *does* she live?"

"Way out on Tolend Road, almost to the Barrington town line."

"How does she get back and forth from work?"

"One of her brothers, or her father drives her. She's got three brothers with cars."

"Jesus." He could see it all; one of her brothers would take a dislike to him for dating his sister and proceed to knock the crap out of him in front of her.

"What? They're all sweeties, just like Kitty. Don't worry so much. Have a good time. See you later."

In anticipation of his Wednesday date with Kitty Whittaker, Jack paid a visit to the men's clothing store owned by Joey's brother-who-was-really-his-uncle, to buy a new pair of polished chinos and a pink shirt with button-down collar. He could have used a new pair of shoes too, but he couldn't afford them if he intended to squire his date around in a taxicab, pay her way into a movie, and treat her to ice cream and who knew what else. He did the best he could with his scuffed old shoes with what remained of a can of Kiwi oxblood shoe polish he found in the cupboard, under the kitchen sink.

Kitty hadn't come in the deli for coffee all week. Jack wondered what was going on. He was loath to ask Priscilla what the deal was, when she came in for coffee Wednesday afternoon, but he couldn't help himself.

"I haven't seen Kitty for awhile," he said cautiously. "So, is everything still, you know, on for tonight? You said six-thirty, right?

"Mr. Weinstock has her doing inventory, so I get to fetch the coffee for the next week and a half, lucky me. Yes, six-thirty in front of Leggett's. Have you decided to take my advice and go to the show at the Uptown?"

"I guess so. What Rock Hudson movie did you say was playing? I go by there every day but I forget to look."

"*Magnificent Obsession.* What difference does it make? You should pay attention to your date, not what's up on the screen."

"Yeah. I've heard that. Sorry."

"You're all out of brownies? How could that *be*?" Priscilla sounded genuinely annoyed that there were no brownies left in the pastry safe.

"How about a nice raspberry turnover? They were fresh only last week."

"Boy aren't we clever," Priscilla said, rather peevishly, in his opinion, and stalked out in a huff. He couldn't remember ever seeing Priscilla in such a state. Something told him it boded ill ... for what, he couldn't say.

Shortly after he got home from work, Jack Scanlon actually took a bath. He made it a point to clean up last night's supper dishes first, however. He had said nothing to his mother about his date with Kitty; he frankly doubted that she would care one way or the other.

He stayed in the tub a long time, going over in his mind how the evening might play out. He shampooed his hair, shaved those parts of his face that had lately started to sprout beard, and stared at his reflection in the mirror, telling himself that his wandering eye was not *that* noticeable. How noticeable could it have been to Kitty if Priscilla Murray was telling the truth about her saying he was "cute"? And she was not exactly perfection herself, with those tooth marks on the side of her face.

He doused himself with Johnson's Baby Powder, applied a liberal dollop of Brylcream to his hair, put on a pair of clean shorts and T-shirt, and picked the new polished chinos carefully off the hangar on the back of the bathroom door.

He was all dressed and ready to go, and it was only five o'clock. He had wanted to be gone before his mother got home from work, but that meant he had an hour and a half to kill, an hour and a half to get all sweaty and smelly again if he wasn't careful. His stomach was roiling, and he was afraid his breath would stink again by the time he would be meeting Kitty. He fingered the smooth new five-dollar bill in his pocket. That should be enough to carry the evening, if his calculations were correct. The only place he could think of to go where time wouldn't seem to come to a complete halt was George's poolroom. There wouldn't be any action going on that time of day, no temptation to get into a game and risk losing his date money.

Last night he had tried to act blasé with Darren and Greg about his date with Kitty, as if he went out on dates all the time. He should have known that Joey would put pay to that fiction, which of course he did.

"You banana; you never been on a date in your life," Joey declared in front of Darren and Greg as they were about to try a new arrangement of "Blue Moon" that Greg had been working on all afternoon.

"So how many dates have *you* had, greasy?" Jack riposted.

"Take my car, if you want," Darren offered.

"He don't have a license. Shit, he don't even know how to drive," Joey said. Jack could feel himself coming to a boil. At least Jim Klein and the girls hadn't arrived yet; it was bad enough that Darren and Greg should hear Joey shoot off his mouth about Jack's inadequacies.

"You don't know how to drive?" Darren sounded incredulous. He'd never heard of a sixteen-year-old male who didn't know how to drive a car. He doubted if there was anyone like that in the entire state of Texas.

"Why don't you ask shit-for-brains if he knows how to drive," Jack countered, "and he's fucking *nineteen*."

"I don't have any interest in driving," Joey said.

The only soul in George's poolroom and duckpin bowling alley was old George himself, on the nod behind the counter, the *Garrison Record* spread out in front of him on the counter top. Jack tried to walk quietly past the old man so he wouldn't disturb his nap. He picked a seventeen-ounce cue stick from the rack on the wall, and broke open the rack of balls on the "good" table near the counter, the one whose rails weren't as dead as the rails on the other three house tables. This was the table where money games were played. The collision of billiard balls against each other gave old George a start; his head jerked, and his chin lifted off his chest. He glanced over at Jack, a regular customer, and waved. Then he reached behind his ear and pulled out his hearing aid. He had on the shapeless brown cardigan sweater that he wore year around, even on sweltering summer days like today. He had to have been eighty years old, Jack thought, and he never perspired.

Jack made desultory shots, keeping an eye on the plastic electric clock that hung from a post between the poolroom section and the two-lane bowling alley. A sign hung under the clock exhorting customers to refrain from expectorating on the floor, and using profanity. There was an ample amount of expectoration underfoot, and profane language was in the air day in and day out in George's poolroom, regardless.

Before he left home, Jack had taken a long look at his stepfather's frosted, four-sided bottle of Gilbey's Gin. He had been tempted to pour himself a finger or two for courage. He could have easily replaced whatever he drank with water. He went so far as to unscrew the cap and bring the bottle to his nose. But he couldn't get past the smell of gin; it caused his stomach to rebel. He would have to face Kitty cold turkey.

The little clock on the post now read six twenty-five. Jack put his cue back on the wall, and racked the balls up so old George wouldn't have to do it.

George was reading his paper, his spectacles pushed down to the end of his nose, from which a drop of liquid was poised to fall onto his newspaper. Jack placed two dimes down on the counter.

"Can you set up pins for me Friday night, Jackie?"

"Sorry, George. I've got to work for Abe." He didn't have the heart to tell George, but his pin setting days were over. Friday night drunks had fired upon him once too often while he was still in the pit. Duckpins weren't as bad as the candlepins in the Greek's bowling alley across the street, but they could still do a job on your head. The last time he had been in the pit at the Greek's, a pin missed his head by inches. Ten cents a string was not enough, in his mind, to risk getting brained. Joey's upper arms and shoulders were black and blue from pin hits. He had finally wised up himself, and got out of the pin setting business.

Blackboard Jungle, starring Glenn Ford, was still playing at the Colonial. He would rather see that flick than any pretty boy Rock Hudson movie, but it was apparently not in his power to exert his will in the game of dating. Besides, chicks were gone over actors like Rock Hudson, for reasons he couldn't fathom.

The big clock with Roman numerals on its face, in front of the bank on the corner of Fourth and Center Streets, across the street from Leggett's Tea Room, read six twenty-five. Time had stood still. He was sweating like crazy, under the arms and in his crotch. The heat alone was enough to trigger the sweat glands, but the sweating he was doing was from sheer nervousness.

The Venetian blinds in the front window of Leggett's were drawn and closed. He looked at his reflection in the window, and was mortified to see a heavy line of blue cue chalk across the front of his new chinos at the level of his fly. He started instinctively to brush at it with his hand, which he discovered was also covered with chalk.

"Jesus, you stupid …" he said out loud. His instinct was to flee. Something held him back. He could make light of it to Kitty; tell her he was a pool hustler, and that chalk stains were an occupational hazard. She might even be impressed. It was more likely that she would think he was a jerk. Six thirty-five. He began to regain his composure, to calm down. He brushed gently at his trousers with the back of his hand. He might duck into Leggett's to the men's room, but he could risk missing his date. If her brother were to arrive with her and find no one there, he would drive off, happy to do so because he disapproved of any boy who dated his sister, etc. Instead, he paced back and forth in front of Leggett's Tea Room, turning anxiously at the passing of every car down Center Street which, since December, had become one-way, with all traffic now moving only south. He spotted Terry Stickney in his souped up '51 Ford convertible with the top down, his arm around Margaret Merchant, his steady girl, as he drove slowly down Center Street. Jack turned his back and pretended to be getting ready to enter the Tea Room. Stickney had quit school last year the day he turned sixteen; Jack had had little to do with him since they graduated together from Franklin School.

Six forty-five. He had heard stories about how girls were notorious for showing up late for their dates. It was supposed to heighten boys' anticipation, and therefore their appreciation of them. Nevertheless, the inexperienced Jack Scanlon, the sixteen-year-old small town virgin, began to fret. By six-fifty he began to doubt that he had the right day, the right time, even though he had heard (or thought he had) it straight from Priscilla Murray's mouth that afternoon. By seven o'clock, Jack had resigned himself to the fact that Kitty Whittaker was not going to appear for their date, no matter how cute she may have thought he was, if she had even said such a thing, which he was forced to question seriously. He didn't know what to do now. He felt like running, in any direction, just for the sake of running. There was a public telephone booth across the square, in front of the liquor store. On impulse, without forethought, he crossed Center Street and made his way to the phone booth. There were two Whittakers listed in the directory, both with Tolend Road addresses. He dialed the first number:

"Hello. Uh, is Kitty there? This is uh …"

"Kitty's at the racetrack. Time trials tonight. Who's this? Can I take a message?"

"Uh ... could you just tell her ... uh, tell her that Jack called? Jack from the deli. I ... uh ... guess that's it."

"Jack from the deli. All right. That's it?"

"Yes."

Racetrack? Time trials? The only place in Garrison that came to mind that could be considered a race track was the oval north of town with a rickety set of bleachers separated from the track by a wooden barrier fence. They held stock car races there on Friday nights in the summer. What would quiet, demure, Kitty Whittaker be doing at a stock car race time trial? Did she drive stock cars? Maybe one of her brothers did. But what about their date? They had not laid eyes on each other for the better part of a week, ever since Priscilla Murray had offered to manage their get-together. Could this be Priscilla's idea of a joke? To his mind, it was inconceivable. He stood, in disbelief, in front of the State Liquor Store, staring at his pathetic reflection in the big window, at his chalk-soiled polished chinos and his new button-down pink shirt. His stepfather, and drunks like him, referred to the liquor store as "Doctor Green's," where the town's drunks purchased their medicine. As his eyes took in the shelves bearing rows upon rows of liquor bottles, Jack decided he could use some medicine of his own at this moment.

* * *

Jack estimated he hadn't been in the room nine seconds before Greg asked him how his date had gone.

"All right."

"All right? That bad, huh. Where'd you take her, to the morgue?" Greg, dressed only in pair of khaki shorts, had turned around on his piano bench to appraise Jack. Darren was in the kitchen being entertained by Uncle Tom's Boston and Maine Railroad stories. Neither Joey nor Jim Klein had arrived yet; the girls weren't expected till nine o'clock.

"The movies. *Blackboard Jungle*. She didn't like it. She thought it was too depressing. I should have taken her to the Rock Hudson flick at the Uptown, Magnificent something-or-other."

The humiliation of having been stood up, apparently deliberately, had Jack in despair, and at a loss for what to do with himself. He couldn't go home, because his mother would want to know why he was home so early, and all dressed up (he hadn't told her about his date with Kitty). He couldn't join the group at Uncle Tom's Cabin for obvious reasons, and if he returned to the poolroom surely it would get back to Joey that he was there instead of where he should have been at that hour, out on his date. So, on impulse, he stopped at the ticket booth of the Colonial Theater, and paid his way into *Blackboard Jungle*, hoping no one he knew would spot him. He was unable to concentrate on the movie. All he could do was fret over the consequences of this ill-fated date. How would he ever be able to face Kitty again, or Priscilla, especially Priscilla? He racked his brain for a way to broach the subject with her. He had visions of Priscilla and Kitty having a big laugh over his naïveté, his utter gullibility. And it was simply beyond his comprehension why they would choose to play such a cruel joke on him, who had been nothing but friendly, respectful, and helpful to both of them.

Joey arrived in the company of Jim Klein, who struggled to get his bass through the narrow doorway.

"So how'd the date go, banana?" Joey asked him. "You get into her drawers?"

Jack just shook his head and gave him a look of disgust. Joey laughed his crazy laugh.

"So, how *was* your date last night?" Jim Klein asked, in his supercilious tone of voice.

"Jesus, has anybody got anything better to think about than my fucking date?" Jack sat down heavily on the middle cushion of the musty old sofa, and crossed his arms across his chest, like a petulant child.

"Oh," Joey taunted, "so now we're going to sulk."

"I got your sulk."

"Knock it off, you guys," Greg ordered, opening the sheet music on the piano. "Go fetch Darren, will you, Jack. Maybe we can get in a little serious rehearsal before the gals get here." All of them considered the rehearsing they did with the girls as frivolous, mainly a waste of their time, even if Greg insisted it was necessary if they expected to land a club gig.

Darren came in the room before Jack got off the sofa, reached for his horn, and hooked up to his neck string. "Let's do "The Song Is You." And one and two, and one, two three ..."

Greg struck the chords that introduced the number he had arranged himself. Darren came in gracefully, as usual, and Jim and Joey entered as seamlessly as if they had rehearsed the song a dozen times instead of only once. They were quiet for a few moments after the song was finished.

"Well, if we could nail them all like that, we'd have something," Greg said, removing his hands from the keyboard.

"I believe we're ready to go knocking on doors," Darren added. "What do you say, Joey? Where do you think we should start?"

Joey, drumsticks between his fingers, scratched at the back of his head, as if that could coax an idea out of it. Jack was still smarting from Joey's taunting; he thought his friend would look good with a dunce cap on his head, as he sat there behind his drums scratching at his head like a monkey.

"I don't know," he said, finally. "The beaches, I guess—York, Salisbury, whatever. Hampton's dry, so that's out. There's some clubs on Route 1, just outside Salisbury Beach we could try."

"All right. Tomorrow we head for ... what do you call it? Salisbury?

Yeah, that's the ticket," Darren said.

"What about the gals?" Greg wanted to know.

"They got their own car. They can come along if they want to, but I was mainly thinking of this as a sort of reconnaissance trip. Get the lay of the land, that sort of thing." Darren replaced his horn in its stand, and lifted his guitar out of its case. "Let's try "Tenderly" before the gals get here."

"I've got to go," Jack said at the mention of the girls. The last thing he wanted was to answer a lot of questions about his date from them. Nobody objected to his leaving. So, he left Uncle Tom's Cabin feeling lower than when he had arrived, if that was possible.

Jack lay in his sweaty bed, wide-awake, Keith's mouth-breathing the only sound in the room. His half-brothers slept in bunk beds on the other side of the small room, near enough so that he could reach out from his bed and touch theirs. There was no closet; all three of them piled their clothes on the single bureau they shared. One membrane thin wall separated their bedroom from the Keelers' apartment. Tom Keeler was a notorious Garrison drunk, a consistent spectacle, stumbling drunkenly through the streets at all hours, cursing the world and his fate, incoherently. Everybody believed he would settle down when he married Gladys Fillion, who may not have been much to look at, but who was "steady," with a reputation as a responsible person. They had a baby girl in the first year of their marriage. Tom Keeler couldn't give up his drink, not even for the sake of his wife and child. Thanks to nepotism in local government (Tom's older brother was a honcho in the department of public works) Tom was kept on the city's payroll no matter how derelict he was in the performance of his menial duties.

Tom and Gladys Keeler fought a lot, and their loud and mutually abusive arguments came through the thin wall into the boys' room with perfect fidelity. It came as no surprise to Jack that Tom Keeler got on well with his stepfather. They were birds of a feather if he ever saw such birds.

Tom Keeler was drunk tonight, of course, and by the sound of their dispute, Gladys was none too sober either. Jack tried to shut out their sounds. He envied Keith and Billy's ability to sleep through the noise. Then the baby woke up and added to the cacophony across the wall. Jack got out of bed and went to the living room and turned on the television. He had to keep the volume low so as not to wake his mother in the next room. He watched *The Tonight Show* with Steve Allen until he fell asleep on the sofa, after making up his mind to call Abe in the morning and tell him he couldn't come into work because he was sick. In the morning, however, pleading sickness as an excuse for not coming to work seemed feeble; what sixteen-year-old got sick in the middle of the summer? Abe would see right through him. Even if he could avoid an encounter with Kitty or Priscilla today, what about tomorrow, and the next day, or the day after that?

He moped into work at the usual time. As they set about preparing for the noon rush, he could see, out of the corner of his eye, Abe watching him, probably wondering what was up with his moody helper this time. As if Abe wasn't the world's moodiest person himself, sitting there on a stool at the end of the counter, sipping cold coffee with curdled cream, chain-smoking Chesterfields, and staring off into space. Maybe that was why Abe never went after him, the way adults were inclined to do, when he, Jack, was in one of his moods. He and Abe were birds of a feather themselves, like Tom Keeler and Bill Scanlon.

As the hour approached when one of the girls would come through the door, Jack grew more agitated, and morose. Abe, by now probably fed up with his mood, went home to take an hour nap. The least awful scenario would be one in which he had to face Priscilla, not Kitty. He recalled that she had said something about Kitty having to spend the week on inventory, so it was left to Priscilla to do the coffee errand for the rest of the week. He was no less at a loss for how to bring the subject up, no matter who it was that came in for coffee. He couldn't picture himself complaining to Priscilla that the date with Kitty she had worked so diligently to arrange never came off because her friend never showed; she was too busy racing stock cars, or whatever she did at "time trials." It had occurred to him during the night that maybe Priscilla had invented the ruse all by herself, and that Kitty was not even aware of it. For all he knew, Kitty could never have told Priscilla that she thought Jack was "cute."

As it neared two o'clock, the time the girls normally came in, Jack's breathing started to get shallow and rapid, his head light. He immersed both hands in dishwater, his head at counter level. He heard the door open, the tinkle of the bell above it. He felt dizzy, like he might black out.

"I couldn't sleep. Too goddamn hot," Abe said. Jack looked up from under the counter. "You're white as a sheet."

"I don't feel so good. Haven't all day. You suppose I could leave early?"

"Go on, get out of here. See you tomorrow."

Jack didn't have to be told twice. As he was going out the door he looked left surreptitiously, and sure enough, Priscilla was walking toward the deli with her long, athletic strides. He turned quickly and hurried across the street to the railroad station parking lot. He didn't care whether Priscilla had seen him or not. In fact, he hoped she had seen him, and realized what an awful thing she had done to him. He hoped Abe would tell her that he had sent Jack home because he looked "white as a sheet," and then she would know at once that she was to blame.

He was surprised to see Darren's two-tone 1953 Oldsmobile parked in front of George's poolroom.

Darren was shooting pool with Joey on the "money" table. George's seedy looking son, Louie, was behind the counter. There were no other customers.

"What are you doing out of work so early?" Joey asked him, chalking the tip of his cue, surveying the layout of balls spread out on the felt.

"Abe let me go early. There's nothing doing today, and he couldn't sleep. Hi, Darren. Giving Joey a lesson?"

"Ah'm the one getting the lesson. The boy's a regular shark. Ah should take you back home with me, Joey. You'd make us rich in no time in mah neighborhood."

"Yeah, he's good enough when there's no money on the table."

"Good enough to take your money, banana." That was true. Jack fancied himself as shooting a pretty good stick, but he was never as creative a shot maker, or position player as Joey. For some reason, Joey never choked when he played Jack for money. He had given up banging heads with Joey Costis for money.

"Want to play some rotation, for the hell of it?" Jack said, going to the cue rack.

"Why not?" Joey took aim, and sank the six-ball in the corner pocket, a long shot with plenty of green between cue ball and object ball.

"Damn, that boy is good!" Darren shook his head in admiration.

When Darren's turn came, it was apparent in the way he made his bridge—with the palm of his hand turned toward the ceiling—that he was a novice. He miscued more often than not. It seemed incongruous that such a natural musician should be so inept at a game like billiards—or anything that required manual dexterity.

"Where were you in such a hurry to go last night?" Joey asked Jack. "Meeting your new girlfriend?"

"Now don't get all tore up over one girl, Jack," Darren counseled, driving the tip of his cue into the felt, sending the cue ball flying off the table.

"Hey, be careful there, sonny," Louie shouted. "You rip that cloth, you'll pay for it."

"Sorry about that, pardner, Ah really am," Darren said, spreading the accent on thick.

"Hang up your cue till you learn how to play the game, you can't be more careful."

"Didn't Ah say Ah was sorry?" Darren said. Then, under his breath, he muttered "Asshole."

"What'd you say, cowboy?" Louie moved from behind the counter, and walked toward the table. He was short, with long, gibbon-like arms, and a lantern jaw that always needed shaving. Jack couldn't be sure how old he was—probably somewhere in his thirties, he guessed, around Abe's age. Darren didn't strike him as a fighter, a guy who would risk doing damage to his hands for pride's sake.

"Look, friend, you're right. Ah got no business tearing up your property. Ah can't play the game for beans. Ah'll stop." Darren replaced his cue stick in the rack. Louie gave him a contemptuous once-over, grunted, and returned to his stool behind the counter.

"Come on, Louie. He's not hurting anything. Give him a break," Joey said.

"Don't start with me, Greek boy. I'd as soon kick your ass down the stairs as look at you. I see you throw another cue in here and you're out for good. You understand me, hot head?"

"Yeah, yeah, yeah. Come on, let's bug this joint," Joey said, putting his own cue away. Jack followed suit, and they headed down the stairs and out into a sun that was so bright, after the dim light of the poolroom, it caused them to squint.

"You want a ride home, Jack?" Darren offered. "Joey?"

"Sure," Jack said. Joey's house was a five-minute walk from the poolroom; he declined Darren's offer of a ride.

"Is that custom made?" Jack asked, fingering the Oldsmobile's iridescent steering wheel, like mother-of-pearl, with a matching knob on the gearshift.

"That's the way it came. I got this baby second hand for a song. I'm sure it's stolen."

"You drove all the way from San Antonio?"

"Yeah, but not non-stop. We made it like kind of a sightseeing trip. Before we got here we spent four days in New York City. We hit a lot of clubs, Birdland, and all those places. Unfortunately we never got to see the man himself."

"You mean Bird? Is it true what I read in *Downbeat* about Parker digging Jimmy Dorsey? I just find that hard to believe."

"Musicians have funny tastes sometimes, tastes that'd surprise you."

"Well, hearing that Bird liked to listen to Jimmy Dorsey surprised the hell out of me. I mean, how square can you get?"

Darren laughed. As they turned onto Jack's street, he spotted Edna's pink shorts on her big rear end. She had the hand of a toddler in each of her own, half dragging, half guiding them in the direction of her house.

"Check out the caboose on that," Darren said.

"That's Edna. She prefers men in uniform."

"Introduce me. See if she takes to a civilian."

"You might want to wait till you get a look at the other side of her." By this time, Darren had pulled the Oldsmobile up to the sidewalk in front of Jack's house, just ahead of Edna and her siblings. He glanced up at the rear view mirror.

"Yikes! You're right. A beast! Introduce me anyway. Any port in a storm."

Jack was seeing his house in a new light, and he felt a twinge of shame at how really shabby it looked. And the neighborhood itself took on the aspect of a slum, with all the detritus in the yard that separated the Pratt's duplex from his own; the barking dogs, the rundown houses with peeling paint, the junky cars parked on both sides of the dead-end street. He was embarrassed to have his new friend see the conditions in which he lived. Darren Price from San Antonio, Texas, however, only had eyes for Edna Pratt. Jack got out of the car; Darren remained behind the wheel, elbow out the window. Jack intercepted Edna.

"Hi. How are you?"

"Pick up your feet," Edna said to the little girl she was towing in her right hand, a dirty, wide-nostriled redhead with a ragged little dress that barely covered her rear end.

"I got a friend wants to meet you."

"What friend?" Edna jerked at the little redhead's arm, putting her off balance. The other toddler, whose sex Jack couldn't be sure about, began to cry. "Shut your face, or you won't get no candy. What friend?"

"In the car." Jack motioned to Darren's car, which Edna apparently had been too preoccupied to notice. At the sight of the Oldsmobile, Edna perked up. She pulled her charges off the sidewalk in front of the Olds, and made her way to the driver's side.

"Afternoon, miss," Darren, the courtier, said. "Name's Darren Price." Darren reached his right hand out the window, and offered it to Edna Pratt. She held onto her siblings, and Darren withdrew his hand. "What's yours?"

"Edna."

"Pleased to make your acquaintance. Whew, Ah wouldn't have thought you Yankees would have such hot weather to bear."

"Been like this all summer. Where you from, the South?"

"Texas, miss ... Edna. San Antone."

Jack could have sworn Edna's whole body grew taught at the mere sound of the word Texas. Her shoulders straightened, her chin rose perceptibly; her big eyes seemed to open wider. Then he remembered she was a country-western music fan; she must have associated the genre with the state of Texas.

"Texas. I've always wanted to go there."

"Ah believe you'd like it, Edna. Ah really do." There was the exaggerated accent again, the one he'd used on Louie in the poolroom, with a little oil added. He sounded more like a traveling salesman than a jazz musician.

"I bet they play a lot of country-western music in San Antone, right?"

"You got that right, Edna. Matter of fact, Ah play a fair amount of country music myself, in the clubs in town."

"You're kidding. Really?"

"No, ma'am, Ah'm not. Don't have my git-tar on hand at the moment, or Ah'd give you a little song or two. But Ah'm not staying far from here, and Ah'm sure my good buddy Jack would be happy to escort you over sometime. Ah'd be happy to give you a personal performance."

"You sing too?"

"But of course."

Jack shifted his weight from one foot to the other, a spectator to this absurd conversation. He was disappointed in Darren for his barefaced artifice, and jealous of the way Edna fell for it.

"This is a nice car." Edna let go of the hand of the redhead to run her fingers over the door by Darren's elbow. In his turn, Darren ran his forefinger along the inside of Edna's arm; Jack turned away. He felt like going upstairs and leaving them to their "foreplay."

"Maybe you'd like to go for a ride in it sometime."

"Sure." The little girl, upon being released, bolted down the street in the direction of the gulley, her little arms flapping like a little flightless bird. "Come back here, you little shit," Edna shouted after her, hoisting the other kid up in her arms, and taking off down the street in pursuit.

"How was that, Jack?" Darren said with a wink.

"You're pretty smooth, Darren. You want me to run upstairs and get you a paper bag to put over her head?"

"You might have to at that; though I've had worse looking beasts, right there in the back seat." Darren jerked his thumb over his shoulder. "I'll be pushing off. See you tonight?"

"I guess so."

"*Adios*." Darren backed his car the short distance to where Fern Street intersected with Railroad, another dead-end street, and drove off while Edna chased after her shrieking sibling. Jack went upstairs to face a pile of dirty dishes.

* * *

Kitty Whittaker was back on coffee fetching rotation, Jack discovered the next day, to his horror. His whole head felt like it was coming to a boil. Abe was busy in the grocery section of the store slicing spiced beef, rolled beef, and pastrami for sandwiches, or Jack would have asked him to wait on her. As was her habit, Kitty took a stool by the door instead of coming down to the preparation area where Priscilla liked to sit and gab while Jack put up her order. He ducked his head under the counter and ran water in the sink.

"Be right with you," he managed to say, finally, his head still lost under the counter top. Kitty made no reply. In a moment, he took a deep breath, emerged from under the counter and glanced in her direction. She stared straight ahead at the beverage cooler, looking pretty cool herself, as she always did. Nothing about her demeanor struck him as out of the ordinary. It was as if nothing had changed in the way they were with each other since the last time she was in the place: no date had been arranged by Priscilla Murray, the matchmaker; no standing up of that date, no telephone message from Jack Scanlon, the guy from Abe Cohen's delicatessen. Jack walked slowly toward the front of the store, drying his hands on a towel, his face still warm though not as hot as it had been a moment ago.

"Hello," Kitty said. She opened up the slip of paper she had in her hand, and began to recite her order, the way she always did.

"Finished with the inventory?" Jack started lining up paper cups on the counter in front of the Silex coffee pot.

"Finally. I'm glad *that* only comes around twice a year."

"Yeah. I haven't seen you in quite a while."

"No."

Jack's hand shook as he poured coffee. The things he wanted to say to this girl—to shout at her—spun around in his brain but found no outlet in words from his mouth. He swallowed and put the coffee pot back on the hot plate. His back was turned to Kitty, but his breathing was so rapid he feared she would notice. Weinstock's News's coffee and pastry orders didn't deviate from one day to the next, but Jack heard himself asking Kitty if she really meant extra cream and *five* sugars.

"Right. You can guess who that's for." He knew who it was for, and he knew that it was what she had ordered. He simply had to say something, to release the pressure that had built up inside his skull.

"That's right, Priscilla likes a little coffee with her cream and sugar." He kept his back to her, and fitted the last plastic cover on a cup. He took his time getting the pastries and bagging the order, to buy time before he would have to turn around to face her. He worked hard to keep himself from blurting something out of his mouth that he would regret later.

She had the exact amount of money for the order, which she pushed toward him when he placed the bag of coffees and pastries in front of her. She offered the same enigmatic smile she always had for him. The teeth marks, or what looked to him like teeth marks, on her face looked more pronounced today, or perhaps it only seemed that way.

"Goodbye," Kitty Whittaker said, on her way out the door, the paper bag cradled in her arm.

Abe, oblivious of the extreme state his young employee was in, continued pushing the meat slicer. Jack gathered up the coins Kitty had left on the counter and rang them up in the cash register. His brain was throbbing; the sound in his ears was like a thousand whistles blowing. He would have been incapable of formulating a coherent thought if he had been required to.

"When you're finished over there, would you clean the meat slicer for me, Jack?" He barely heard Abe's request; he didn't respond. "Jack?" Abe repeated.

"What?"

"The meat slicer. If you could clean it. I'm going out for a while."

"All right." Next to cleaning out the bottom of the refrigerated showcase, which he had to do once a month, cleaning the greasy meat slicer was the most odious job in the store.

He told himself on the walk home along the railroad tracks that the most dreaded moment, the one he had feared for the past two days, had passed. He had survived it, but the matter was hardly resolved, not in his mind anyway. He knew no more today of what had gone wrong than he had yesterday. He kicked idly at cinders on the walk home, thinking that maybe it was just as well that he didn't know the whole truth of it;

what good would it do him? Heat waves rose from the railroad tracks; he was sweating like a horse.

He spotted Edna in back of her house again as he turned down the embankment. This time she was alone, hanging wash out on the clothesline. Those same pink shorts were stretched tight across her backside. He tried to walk through the tall weeds quietly, so she wouldn't notice him. He was parallel with her, thinking he was home free, when she turned around suddenly, three clothespins in her mouth. She smiled around the clothespins before taking them out of her mouth.

"Hi, Jack. You trying to hide from me?"

"No." He stopped, and dug at the ground with the toe of his shoe.

"You were going to walk right on by me without saying hi, weren't you?"

"You looked busy."

"That's a reason to not speak to me?"

"I was thinking about something else."

"Bet you were thinking about a girl."

Jack shifted his gaze from the ground to her face with its teasing smile.

"As a matter of fact, I was." Let her think what she wanted. It was partly true anyway. He wouldn't have wanted her to know the circumstances that had him thinking about Kitty Whittaker, however.

"Where's your friend from Texas? He's cute. When you going to take me over to his place?"

"I don't know. When he asks me to, I guess." So now he was cast in the role of pimp. He made a move toward his house.

"Does he really sing country-western songs?"

"He said so, didn't he?" What he really wanted to do was burst her little country-western bubble, yet he didn't want to interfere with Darren's seduction of Edna Pratt to do it. The mid-afternoon sun beat down on them from a cloudless sky. In the bright light Edna looked fairly repulsive. "I've got to go."

"Want me to come upstairs and rub your back? I'll be done here in a few minutes."

"No thanks." He saw no sign of her younger siblings. He wondered who else could be looking after them. Maybe her mother was home.

"Suit yourself." Edna turned away from him, and reached into her plastic clothesbasket. Halfway up the stairs to his apartment, Jack regretted not taking Edna up on her backrub offer. It could have been the harsh sunlight that had rendered her so ugly to look at. It would be darker in his bedroom. He wondered what Kitty's fingers would feel like on his bare back. Just the thought of Kitty Whittaker irritated him. And Priscilla had a few things to answer for herself. Who would ask the questions? If only there were someone he could talk to, confide in. Greg came to mind; Greg was older, mature, a man of the world. He was less likely to feel embarrassed or vulnerable talking to Greg. He'd die before he let on to Joey what had happened (or not happened, to put it more precisely) with Kitty, and there was something about Darren he didn't quite trust.

He walked into the kitchen to a pile of last night's supper dishes. He could hear Keith and Billy arguing over a television program in the living room. Sick at heart, Jack sighed deeply.

"What are you two doing inside on a day like this?" Jack said to his half-brothers. They ignored him, continuing their argument. He went into the bedroom, intending to lie down for a few minutes before having at the dishes.

Next thing, his mother was at him. He had fallen asleep into a dream in which Kitty and Edna had both attended, but he couldn't remember how.

"You haven't done the dishes. I work all day and have to come home to this! Why can't you help around here? That's it. You're not to go out at night for a week. You understand me?"

"I fell asleep. I meant to do them. I'll do them now."

"How do you expect me to make supper with the kitchen in this mess?"

Jack hauled himself off his bed, and went to the kitchen. He started to draw hot water into the dishpan, his heart in his chest as heavy as a slab of concrete. Sometimes he wished that his mother would go back on cigarettes; it might improve her disposition. Since she had quit herself, she seemed to harp even more on his smoking.

"Do a better job on the casserole dish than you did last time," his mother said, turning the burner on under a kettle of water. "Use some elbow grease. If you did the dishes when you were supposed to, you wouldn't have to scrub so hard."

Jack, full of gloom, worked on the dishes for the better part of an hour, while his mother prepared another supper that would produce another round of dirty dishes in the vicious, never-ending cycle that threatened to crush his spirit. He finally managed to finish drying the last of the previous evening's dishes. His mother carped at him for putting the saucepans away in the wrong order, but seemed otherwise mollified by their disappearance, and the restoration of visual order in the kitchen. She even retracted her edict that he stay in the house, evenings, for a week. She was preparing stuffed peppers, Jack's favorite dish, in the pressure cooker. He seldom ate meals at home during the week, except when something like stuffed peppers was on the menu. He ate prodigious amounts of Abe's food (except for exotic things like whitefish, sable, gefilte fish, pickled herring, and such), which was part of his salary, and he was seldom hungry at suppertime. No matter how much food he put away, Jack couldn't gain weight. He was painfully self-conscious of his physique, which, compared with most of the guys in his class at school, was insignificant. He would look for excuses not to shower with the rest of the team after basketball practice. His mother attributed his scrawny frame, his inability to put on weight, to his smoking, and the fact that he didn't take meals at home regularly.

After supper, he headed for the poolroom, thinking he might run into a fish, like Paul Moreau, and pick up a little extra change before he went to Uncle Tom's Cabin for the evening.

Paul Moreau wasn't present, but there was a three, six, nine game in progress on the "money" table. George's son, Louie, was clashing with Paul Cane and Roger Frechette. Louie had his cloth change belt around his waist, putting Jack in mind of the one his future stepfather had worn the first time he met him at the carnival where he worked.

"You want in, Scanlon?" Louie asked him.

"What's the action?"

"Quarters."

"What the hell." Jack selected a seventeen-ounce cue stick off the rack, rolled it on the table to test for warp, and got in the game. He figured he could afford to lose a buck or two, but no more. Paul Cane, the guy who had relieved Joey of the ten bucks his mother/grandmother had entrusted to him, broke open the rack and sank the two -ball. He had no clear shot on the one, and had to use three rails to try and make contact. He left Louie with an easy combination for the six ball, a pay ball, and the first blood began to flow. Jack found himself stitched his first three turns, and was getting frustrated as he saw five pay balls go down in the first rack alone. He was out a buck and a quarter, just like that. Two racks later he was down two seventy-five, and was about to hang up his cue. Then he got an open shot, and ran the two to the nine. Now he was down only fifty cents. His fortunes began to turn for the better. He became so absorbed in the game that he lost track of time. He went over to the window for the talc and noticed that it was dark outside. The clock read 8:30. He went to the toilet to check his cash; he was up three dollars. Now was as good a time as any to bow out. Besides, they'd be expecting him at Uncle Tom's.

"I've got to call it quits," he announced to his competitors, hanging his cue in the rack.

"So, you're one of them hit and run drivers, eh," Louie said. "See if I invite you into a game again."

"I've got to be somewhere. I'm up a lousy couple of bucks. What are you talking about, 'hit and run'?"

"Go on. Get lost," Louie said, gathering up balls in the diamond shaped rack. Jack looked at the others for commiseration, but they held their tongues, acted as if he didn't exist. Suddenly he was a pariah, a bad sport, the kind of guy who quit when he's ahead; somebody to avoid in the future.

* * *

Jack glimpsed Uncle Tom through the kitchen window. He was

sitting, bare-chested, at the kitchen table, turning over playing cards in one of his endless games of solitaire.

"Sorry I'm late," Jack said. Uncle Tom looked up at Jack over the top of his spectacles.

"Late for what?"

"Rehearsal."

"They didn't rehearse tonight. Greg took his lady friend to the movies, and Darren went off somewhere, don't know where." Uncle Tom thumbed three cards off the top of the deck and turned over the nine of spades. There was no place to put the nine of spades, so he peeled off three more cards.

"What about Joey and Jim? The girls?"

"Don't know. Haven't seen 'em tonight. Want a glass of cider?"

"No thanks. I guess I'll be going," Jack said, then as an afterthought, "When did they decide not to rehearse? I didn't know anything about it."

"Be damned if I know. Greg never said anything, just that he was taking Meg to the show."

"I must have forgotten. Well, see you later, Tom." Jack bid the old man goodbye, and went back outside. It was an overcast night, no moon, and not a star in the sky. It felt like rain. It hadn't rained in weeks. The air was muggy and still, the sound of insects deafening. He had been so anxious to get into the house, for fear of missing something (what?) because he was so late, that he hadn't even noticed that Darren's car was missing from where it was usually parked, in front of the house. As if his absence at rehearsal would be missed; the fact that nobody had bothered to let him know that rehearsal was off tonight should have told him how much his presence mattered. Of course, somebody could have called his house. He had left for the poolroom right after supper. But Uncle Tom would have known if Greg or Darren had tried to call him; the telephone hung on the wall in the kitchen, right next to the old-fashioned refrigerator. He began to fret, to worry that they were deliberately trying to push him out of the group. Why didn't Joey show up at the poolroom tonight, if he wasn't rehearsing? He had no other place to go. Because Darren had taken him somewhere with him, Jack reasoned as he walked along the middle of the dark street, feeling desolate and unhappy.

As he turned onto his street, Jack thought he heard singing coming from the direction of his house. He drew closer and he could definitely hear singing, with a guitar accompaniment. He was only a few feet from his walkway before he noticed the outline of two figures on Edna Pratt's steps. The music had ceased. He hurried along his walkway, assuming one of the shapes he saw in the darkness was Edna, the other, one of her suitors from some branch of the armed forces, a singing sailor perhaps.

"Hey, Jack." Jack stopped, recognizing Darren's voice.

"Darren?"

"In the flesh. Come on over and sit a spell. Ah'm teaching Edna here some country tunes she never heard before, being a Yankee and all." Jack spotted the shape of Darren's car at the broken curb in front of Edna's house. There was no third shadowy figure on the steps, no Joey Costis. He walked toward the steps. Darren occupied the top step, his guitar across his lap, and Edna was on the bottom step, at his feet, her arms clasped around her bare knees. He couldn't tell in the dark, but he would have bet anything she had on the same pink shorts he had seen her in most of the summer.

"I didn't know you owned that kind of an axe," Jack said, when he saw the guitar he was holding was not the one he hooked up to his amp. Darren laughed and strummed a few chords. "I just came from Uncle Tom's. He told me you didn't rehearse tonight."

"No. Greg decided he'd rather go to the movies with Meg. He was hot to see *Mister Roberts*. He's a big Cagney fan." Jack wondered if Darren had noticed how much of Greg's time was being taken up by Meg. She seemed to be always around. He decided not to mention it to Darren at this moment.

"Did Joey show?"

"Don't say hi," Edna interjected.

"Hello, Edna."

"You ever hear this one, Edna?" Darren said, and broke into a twangy lyric: "Ah'm mah own grampa," he sang. Jack cringed.

"No. It's cute. Go ahead and sing it."

"Not now, my dear. Ah doubt Jack would like it."

"You're right. He likes strange music. I can't understand what he sees in the stuff he listens to. I couldn't even describe it."

"It's what I *hear*, not what I see," Jack said, his voice icy in the warm night air.

"Sing, 'Your Cheatin' Heart.' I love that song," Edna said, ignoring Jack.

Darren obliged without hesitation. To Jack, it was a blatant parody of a country-western singer's interpretation. If Edna had an ounce of perceptiveness she should have been offended. On the contrary, she seemed enthralled with Darren's rendering, as if she were listening to something honest and authentic.

"Can we go for a ride now?" Edna asked Darren when he finished.

"Why of course. You'll excuse us, won't you, Jack?"

You don't need my permission to take the slut for a ride, he felt like saying.

"Good night, Jack," Edna said. He thought he detected a taunt in her voice. "Sweet dreams."

"Yeah."

"Goodnight, old buddy," Darren said, rising and brushing off the seat of his pants with one hand, his other gripping his instrument by the neck. "Where would you like to go, missy? Downtown to look at all the bright lights?"

"I know a better place." Edna tried for a teasing voice. Jack was disgusted with her feeble attempt to be coy.

Jack ran upstairs without another word. His mother was asleep, as were Keith and Billy; Darren's crooning and strumming of country-western songs had not awakened them, apparently. Jack was conscious of the Gilbey's Gin bottle on the kitchen counter. Bill Scanlon was due to come home for the weekend day after tomorrow. The bottle was two-thirds full. He got a water glass down from the cupboard, and poured two fingers of gin. He replaced what he had removed from the bottle with tap water. He brought the glass to his nose; his stomach reacted immediately. Knowing that he would never be able to drink the stuff down straight, Jack went to the refrigerator in search of something with which to dilute it. He found half a bottle of ginger ale that had gone flat. He poured it into the gin until he filled the glass, and then took a cautious sip. The ginger ale diluted it enough so he could get it down in small sips.

Jack took his drink into the living room and turned on the television. He sipped gin and ginger ale, and looked at the flip-flopping screen without really seeing the images. What he was looking at was in his mind's eye, and it wasn't pleasant viewing. He finished off what was in his glass and went back in the kitchen for a refill, wondering how much dilution of his stepfather's gin he could get away with before Bill Scanlon got wise, put two and two together, and took his stepson to task. At this point, Jack didn't really care. He fell asleep on the sofa. He awoke later to discover that he'd spilled drink on his chest; the smell of gin was strong in his nostrils. He dragged himself to bed, and slept till eleven o'clock, which made him late for work for the first time in the four years he'd worked for Abe Cohen.

* * *

Scanlon's head ached, but not enough to justify complaining to the nurse, to Karla. He had, in his life, been blessedly headache free, unless one counted the normal vicissitudes that gave rise to what people metaphorically called "headaches." His meditation on his first encounter with gin reminded him of the source of most of the actual physical headaches he had suffered in his drinking life, and would no doubt continue to suffer in what remained of it. That is, unless he changed his ways. But why bother now, under the circumstances?

It almost amused him now to recollect that summer of 1955 when girls like Kitty Whittaker, Priscilla Murray, and even Edna Pratt had flayed his tender ego. Nineteen- fifty-five. Einstein had died that year; Thomas Mann, too. Not to mention Charlie Parker. It was not a good year for geniuses in their field. That summer, Darren had taken him to Storyville, in Boston's Copley Square Hotel, to witness his first live jazz performance. That night the newly formed Gerry Mulligan Quintet was playing. Mulligan had Bob Brookmeyer on valve trombone and Jon Eardley on trumpet. Young Jack Scanlon had been disappointed when Mulligan split up with Chet Baker, but he forgot all about his disappointment the moment he was seated at the small table to the right of the bandstand, so close to the musicians that he could eavesdrop on their conversation between numbers. He had passed off Greg's Texas driver's license as his own, and was as amazed that the waitress let him pass for twenty-five, unchallenged. And even if the discrepancy between his youthful appearance and the date of birth on Greg's license hadn't aroused her suspicion, surely she should have been tipped off when he ordered a Tom Collins, the drink of choice of the underage set. By now he had acquired a taste for gin, thanks to his stepfather's unattended Gilbey's. Darren assured him that the management didn't care about how old you were as long as you could come up with the price of the drink. At the time, there was no cover charge, and no minimum at Storyville.

The Darren Gregg Quartet never realized its ambition that summer to secure a nightclub gig. They should have known from the start that they had come on the scene too late in the season. They managed, as individuals, to sit in with established groups in a few Salisbury and York Beach clubs that featured jazz combos, but they never played a club date together as a group. Meg had become such a clinging vine that Greg started to feel closed in by her almost constant presence. It was not in his nature to be rude or surly, but Meg forced him to resort to harsh words and cold indifference just to get her off his back. It didn't work. The more he spurned her, the more she clung, and the more lugubrious and morose she became so that in time even the twins avoided her. Darren alternated in his pursuit of the twins, never getting very far with either one of them, certainly not as far as he got with Edna Pratt, "the beast in the back seat," as he liked to refer to her.

And what about young Jack Scanlon? As far as old Jack Scanlon recollected from forty-four years out, he never got a satisfactory explanation for having been stood up by Kitty Whittaker, or what part Priscilla Murray played in the whole, pathetic, humiliating affair. The whole episode had, like his memory of it, simply evaporated without resolution. He had learned a long time ago how to sidestep some of life's unpleasant offerings. As for the incident with Priscilla and Kitty, he was at a loss for a reason why he had not pressed either girl for an explanation. Except, knowing how he was then, and perhaps how he was even now, the risk to his ego would have been too great, his embarrassment too acute. He must have simply gone on in his relations with them as if nothing had happened. For the life of him, Scanlon could not remember. He was sure of one thing; he had not made it up.

Having acquired a taste for gin that summer, he nipped away at Bill Scanlon's Gilbey's, cautiously in the beginning, more boldly later on, until one day his stepfather, feeling no pain, said to him, "Why don't you get your own gin, you like it so much?" Not sure whether to take his stepfather's words as tacit approval to drink in the house, to keep his own stock on hand, or as a way to entrap him, Jack made believe he hadn't heard him, and let it drop. Bill Scanlon said no more, and Jack desisted from nipping from the man's bottle after that.

September, and the start of school arrived too soon to suit him. Jack began his junior year in high school; Greg and Darren packed their gear into Darren's '53 Oldsmobile and headed back to San Antonio, but not before stopping by the high school to have Jack and Joey called out of class, to say goodbye. They promised to write, to keep in touch. Greg made them promise to pay him and Darren a visit in San Antonio when they finished high school. They exchanged one or two letters and holiday greetings for a couple of years, then they heard nothing more from their friends from Texas.

Scanlon sighed, and tried for a more comfortable position in the recliner; he glanced up at the blood bag. It was still two-thirds full. He hadn't expected that the transfusion would go in a hurry, like getting the oil changed in his automobile, but this was maddeningly slow. What if the tube was clogged? What if they had messed up on the anti-coagulant? Darren would be sixty-seven years old by now, Greg pushing seventy! If they were still alive. "Gone with the Wind" was one of Darren's favorite numbers. He tried to reproduce Desmond's interpretation. Desmond was his favorite alto sax man; he liked Desmond even more than Bird. Gone with the wind was the way of Scanlon's friendships throughout his life. They burned brightly for awhile, then became "smoke rings," and were "gone with the wind." How many relationships in his life had been thus, he couldn't have counted. It was miraculous, in a way, that he had lasted so long with Judith. It was his fault, he was convinced, that the many incipient friendships he had made over the years had failed to endure. He suspected that there was a basic flaw in his character. What had brought it about? He had often asked the question, but never as deliberately or intensely as he had since being rigged to this IV contraption, with his mortality on the line. He was also aware that he was quite capable of indulging in melodrama.

"Just who are you, Scanlon?" he said out loud, and was startled to hear his voice echo through the empty corridor. He heard quick footsteps behind him.

"Are you all right, Mr. Scanlon?"

"Yeah, I'm fine, Karla."

Nineteen

Spring 1957:

The knowledge that he would be graduating from high school in less than a week had Jack Scanlon savoring the June sun's warmth more than he usually would have. He had removed his shirt to expose his too white skin to the sun's UV radiation which, Abe Cohen was quick to point out to him, could do him harm. A few yards away, Andrew Philip Dow was in his swim trunks, already tawny from spending days in the sun, unmindful of UV radiation (even if he was fairer, with his blond hair, than Jack). He shared a beach blanket with Betsy Fuguet and Gloria Hill, also in bathing suits. The blanket the girls had brought, and were happy to share it with Andrew Philip, who was practicing his lines from *King Lear* on them. Jack didn't know the girls except by name; furthermore, they had not invited him to share their blanket. For that matter neither had they invited Andrew Philip; he had brazenly invited himself.

Jack lay on his back on the warm sand, his eyes closed, the sun hot in the blue, cloudless sky above. The swimming area was not officially open for the season yet; in fact, swimming was forbidden in that part of the Glidden River, roped off for that purpose, until lifeguards came on duty. The No Swimming signs on wooden stakes had no power to deter anyone from swimming in the river, however. Andrew Philip had worked as a lifeguard here last summer. It was only pure luck that a kid had not drowned during his watch. Andrew Philip Dow was more alert to young-girl-bearing blankets scattered on the beach than he was to young swimmers in distress out on the river.

Jack listened to the giggles of Gloria Hill, a chesty junior, and Betsy Fuguet, an equally voluptuous sophomore. As soon as Dow had spotted the girls spreading out their blanket on the sand he had begun to sing the Fats Domino tune, with variation: "I found my thrill on Gloria Hill." Andrew Philip Dow, unlike Jack and most of his friends, didn't have to fantasize about bedding down girls like Gloria Hill. He could get just about any girl he wanted, and he wanted them all—all the attractive ones anyway.

"I prithee, daughter, do not make me mad.
I will not trouble thee, my child, farewell.
We'll no more meet, no more see one another.
But yet thou art my flesh, my blood, my daughter ..."

Betsy and Gloria giggled like silly pre-adolescents. Andrew Philip had given Jack his copy of Crofts Classics *King Lear* to keep in his pocket while he tried out the lines he'd memorized, on the girls. Andrew Philip had convinced himself, and he wanted everybody else to believe, that he was destined to become a stage actor, a Shakespearean stage actor. He could memorize lines well enough, and recite them convincingly, even if Jack knew that he scarcely understood what he had committed so well to memory. Andrew Philip was a poor student. Otherwise Jack would not have had to spend the last week of school not only catching up on his own work (he was not the most diligent student himself) but also having to rewrite Dow's English essays in order that his friend might graduate. If Jack was no great shakes as a scholar he was infinitely more able than his would-be thespian friend.

"I will endure.
In such a night as this! O Regan, Goneril!
Your old kind father, whose frank heart gave all!
O, that way madness lies; let me shun that!
No more of that."

Betsy and Gloria were now giggling out of control at Andrew Philip's theatrics. Dow unscrewed the cap of a pint bottle of vodka and raised it to his lips. Then, hesitating before drinking from it, offered the bottle to the girls. They looked at each other, shook their heads in the negative as if they had rehearsed the move, and resumed their giggling. Andrew Philip winked at them, shrugged his shoulders and took a good swallow from the bottle.

Jack raised himself up on his elbows and squinted at the three of them on the blanket. Andrew Philip looked his way and said, in his Lawrence Olivier voice, "Excuse me, ladies, while I see to young Edmund." He rose gracefully from the blanket and walked over to where Jack lay in the sand.

"Would you be desiring a drink, lad?"

"Yes, I would." Dow handed Jack the bottle.

"Why don't you join me and the lasses then?" Andrew Philip was now working on his brogue. Jack removed the cap, constricted his throat and took a cautious sip, glancing sideways at the girls. They were engaged in conversation, their faces close enough together that at his angle they appeared to be kissing.

"I don't know them," Jack said, catching his breath from the harsh vodka.

"Then it's time you got acquainted, man." Dow dropped to his knees in the sand beside Jack, and fell back to a cross-legged sitting position. Jack wouldn't mind getting acquainted with Betsy Fuguet whose skin was so white it seemed to give off its own light, and made her jet black hair seem even blacker, like anthracite. And in his opinion her breasts were shapelier than Gloria Hill's even if they were not as large. But even if he was two years ahead of her in school, she was as aloof, as out of reach to guys like Jack, as if she had been a college instead of a high school sophomore.

"Which shall I sample first?" Andrew Philip wondered aloud. "You know something, Jackie, you should refrain from putting that hair oil on your head. You have a fine mane, lad. Why taint it with such vile potions?" Jack didn't bother to correct Dow on the correct use of the word "potion." He turned away from Dow so he wouldn't see the color rising in his face. "Why, man? Andrew Philip requires an answer."

"It sticks out every which way if I don't," Jack mumbled.

"Then let it stick out, man." Andrew Philip's wavy blond hair was never unruly. He kept it long, in a DA style, and spent an inordinate amount of time running a comb through it. If he was not muscular in the usual sense, he was solidly built, in stark contrast to Jack's almost skeletal frame. Jack slipped his shirt back on over his meager shoulders. "Now come and be sociable with the lasses while I make up my mind." Jack took another pull at the vodka, and handed the bottle back to Dow.

"Say hello to noble Edmund, my fair ones," Dow said, dropping down on the blanket next to Betsy Fuguet. Jack's jealous heart lurched. He wanted Andrew Philip to choose Gloria even if he knew his chances with Betsy were next to zero.

"His name's not Edmund," Gloria Hill said, not looking at Jack.

"Not Edmund?" Andrew Philip replied with mock astonishment. "Then what name hath he?"

"I don't know," Gloria answered, still not looking in Jack's direction, "but it's not Edmund."

Jack had thumbed through Dow's copy of *King Lear* and had noted in the *Dramatis Personae* that Edmund was listed as the "bastard son to Gloucester." Why Andrew Philip had chosen to introduce him to the girls as Edmund instead of Edgar had him wondering if Dow had somehow gained knowledge of his uncertain paternity. How could he know?

"Well suppose we just call him Jack," Dow said, resting his hand on Betsy's lovely calf. Then he rested his head on her bare thighs; Betsy, as if by instinct, began to stroke his hair with her hand the way she would fondle a pet. Gloria Hill turned over on her stomach and opened a paperback book. Jack sat wretchedly on the very edge of the blanket.

Now at its zenith, the sun beat down on the open sand unopposed by even a single cloud. Jack began to sweat; he was loath to remove his shirt again in such proximity to the girls; as if they would notice. Betsy was occupied with Andrew Philip's hair, Gloria Hill with her paperback novel. They maintained this tableau for what seemed to Jack an hour but what in reality was no doubt no more than ten minutes; the only sound the murmuring voices of Betsy and Dow, and the occasional deep sigh from the jealous throat of Gloria Hill.

Finally, Andrew Philip rose to his feet and pulled Betsy up by the hand. He tossed the vodka bottle to Jack.

"Leave a little for me, lad," he said.

"Where are you going?" Gloria wanted to know, her voice tremulous.

"For a forest promenade," Dow said, leading Betsy by the hand in the direction of the path that led through dense woods to a small pond called Cold Springs where kids went to skinny dip.

"Don't be too long, Betsy," Gloria called after them. "I have to be home by one." She watched them till they disappeared into the woods. She looked as wretched as Jack felt. He might as well have been invisible for all the attention she paid him. When he could take the silence no longer, he asked her what she was reading.

"Oh, why don't you just go away," she replied, and Jack realized that she was crying. He did as he was told, and went away. He didn't "leave a little" vodka for Andrew Philip Dow, either.

* * *

Nate Silverman sat at the counter, on the last stool, drumming on the countertop with his fingers for dramatic effect.

"I had to write a paper," Jack said, by way of explaining to his boss why he was an hour and a half late for work. Nate stared at him, his lips parted revealing a gap between his two front teeth; he tried to look reproachful, but Nate Silverman simply lacked *gravitas*. Jack wasn't sure yet whether he despised Nate or half liked him. One thing he knew—he didn't respect him. All those years Abe Cohen had threatened to sell the place, get out of the deli business, indeed, out of any kind of business in which he had to deal directly with the public, Jack had written off as Abe's innate need to complain about his lot. But apparently he had been serious. Jack was devastated when Abe sprang it upon him that he had sold his place to Murray Isaacs. That was two months ago.

Nate Silverman was Murray's brother-in-law, married to Murray's sister Vivian. Murray hoped that by giving Nate the responsibility of managing a business he might actually learn to be responsible, if not respectable. Murray had no particular fondness for Nate; he put him in charge of the deli mainly as a favor to his sister, hoping it might spare her a little grief because in her brief marriage to Nate Silverman there had been an abundance of grief. Nate gambled and chased women even if he did not drink alcohol. How he had ever managed to hook up with Vivian Isaacs was more than Jack could comprehend.

"You couldn't have called?" Nate finally said, palms up, shoulders raised to his earlobes.

"I lost track of time. If I didn't finish that paper I might not have graduated." Jack could lie to Nate without the least compunction.

"What's more important, your work here or a lousy high school diploma?"

"Since you put it that way, I guess I don't have a legitimate excuse."

Nate slid off the stool, hitched up his pants and picked up the receiver off the public telephone on the back wall. He checked the coin return slot before reaching in his pocket for a coin of his own. He couldn't connect with his party, so he hung up and waited for his coin return. The phone ate it up. Nate slammed his open palm into the phone box.

"Fucking goniffs!"

"How many times has that happened, Nate? You're surprised?"

"It's not the principle, it's the fucking money!" He gave the phone box another smack. "I was going to the track with Arsey, and now, thanks to you for being late, I missed him."

Jack felt like telling him to stop whining. Nate was a big guy, over six feet tall, with a high waist and big shoulders. But he was soft, physically, easily made to cry uncle, Jack guessed. And he was a whiner. Jack decided that he disliked Nate more than he liked him. Part of him was glad he had made Nate miss his date with Arsey, the Lebanese proprietor of the Army-Navy store down the street. Arsey was as black as any Negro Jack had ever seen but his features were Middle-Eastern, not Negroid. In the afternoons when business was slow in the Army-Navy store, as it was after lunch rush in the deli, Arsey would come over and play gin with Nate for a nickel a point. It was a matter of which of the two was the wiliest cheater that decided who won or lost in each session.

"I'm sorry, you know, about making you miss Arsey and ..."

"Forget it. I'll catch up with him." Nate looked at his wristwatch instead of the big electric clock on the wall above the phone. "If my wife calls, you know what to say."

Jack reminded him that Murray had planned to come in for supper with Vivian after he closed the store (Murray owned a jewelry store on Center Street).

Nate smacked his forehead with an open palm. "Shit, I completely forgot." Jack saw the wheels turning inside Nate's head, his lips open and close several times as if he were mouthing his thoughts the way he probably moved his lips when he read print. He smiled suddenly when the light went on in his devious brain.

"Tell them I had to go to Haverhill," (Nate pronounced Haverhill as if it were two words) "to pick up the Russian rye on account of Solly's kid is being bar-mitzvahed and he can't make the delivery tomorrow."

"You expect Murray to believe that?"

"Doesn't matter what Murray believes, so long as my wife believes it." Jack didn't like lying for Nate, but being an hour and a half late for work himself, and lying about his reason for it, didn't put him in a moral bargaining position. And he didn't relish having to deal with Vivian and her brother either. Vivian gave him the heebie jeebies. She had apparently gotten carried away with plucking her eyebrows, trying for a thin line over her dull eyes, only to end up removing all of them. Her eyebrows now consisted of pure pencil line. For some reason this made her yellow skin take on an even sallower hue. Jack shared Nate's opinion that Vivian was a "royal pain in the ass." It was no wonder Nate was always on the prowl for something "strange." At present, he was in pursuit of the new waitress he'd just hired. She was a pretty, air-headed nineteen-year-old brunette whose large breasts were, in Nate's view, what qualified her for the job. Even Jack, enamored of her himself, found himself forgiving of her incompetence as a waitress. Her name was Joy, and she was nice to Jack in the way an older girl is nice to a little boy—the way Bernie had been nice to him a few years ago when he was really a kid. He resented Joy for being taken in by Nate's overtures, by being too stupid to see that all he wanted to do was get into her pants. He was afraid to admit that maybe Joy welcomed Nate's come-ons. In any case, he was absurdly jealous.

Nate left the deli to catch up with his pal Arsey at Rockingham racetrack, leaving Jack to face his wife and brother-in-law. They came in a little after seven o'clock.

"So, where's Nathan?" Murray Isaacs asked Jack, sliding onto a stool. Vivian examined the display case, her back to the counter. Jack braced himself, for he knew exactly what she was about to say, as if it were he who was responsible for the display and not her husband, the proprietor of "Nate's Delicatessen."

"The sable doesn't look fresh," Vivian said, looking sideways at the display case as she moved toward the stools, her face looking as though she smelled something disagreeable.

Jack had tried, unsuccessfully, to imagine what their courtship—Nate and Vivian's—had been like. What had possessed him to marry the woman? And in the short time he had known the man, Nate had wondered the same thing himself. It had to have been the money in her family, and Nate came, according to him, from a poor family himself. Jack didn't believe that there were any really poor Jews in America; he took Nate's claimed poverty to be relative.

Jack turned his back on them and rolled his eyes. When he turned around, Vivian was perched next to her brother, her elbow on the counter, her chin in her hand. Her dull eyes were on the menu board on the wall above the coffee maker.

"What are you going to eat?" she asked Murray. Murray studied the menu as well. He need not have. Jack knew with certainty what Murray would order; Vivian he was not so sure about since she seldom came into the deli to eat. Her dull brown hair was cut short, and adhered to her skull the way hair does when it has just come out of the water.

"I think I'll have the whitefish with ..." A side order of borscht and sour cream, Jack said to himself. "maybe a little side of borscht and sour cream. What are you going to eat, Vivian?"

"The whitefish doesn't look fresh," Vivian observed. So none of the fish looked fresh to Vivian Silverman, the fishmonger. If she couldn't deign to ask him, Jack wasn't about to volunteer the fact that the fish had come in fresh that very morning. The stuff would have to be fresher than fresh to tempt Jack Scanlon to bite into it. He would have none of the "delicacies" of the local Jewish palate, including borscht, with or without sour cream, chopped chicken livers, chopped herring, gefilte fish, liverwurst, potato pancakes, cheese blintzes … you name it. He restricted his diet to beef by-products and potato salad.

Murray stuck to his guns and ordered the whitefish, and Vivian agreed, reluctantly, to a small dish of creamed herring with some dark rye bread. It was the weekly loaf of Russian black rye that her husband was supposed to be fetching from Haverhill, Massachusetts, that went best with creamed herring, Jack had been told. But that didn't arrive till tomorrow, normally, and would be gone in a day and a half. He would have given anything to see the look on Vivian's face when Solly brought the twenty-pound loaf, still hot enough to give off steam, into the store tomorrow on schedule. But he was dreaming; Vivian never came in the place on Saturdays. Still, he wished there was some way he could give her a comeuppance.

Jack set about serving his only customers, longing for the moment when they'd be gone. Nate had none of Abe Cohen's mawkish tastes in music. In fact, Nate had no musical taste at all. Jack had never met a human being who was so utterly indifferent to music. Until he met Nate, he believed everyone liked some kind of music, no matter how dreadful it was to his own ear. The absence of music in the place, even the treacle of Mantovani, or The Melachrino Strings, produced the effect of profound melancholy on Jack. Now the nasal abrasions of Vivian's mundane conversation with her brother over whitefish and creamed herring made the lack of music even more acute. He eyed the nine remaining quarts of beer in the cooler and felt the urge to pluck one of them out, open it and quaff it right in front of Murray (the real owner of the place) and his gorgon of a sister. Nate (at Murray's suggestion) had decided to discontinue the sale of beer because it brought unsavory customers into the deli, and Murray claimed that some of the more orthodox customers had complained.

In spite of himself, Jack actually liked Murray Isaacs. He had always been kind and respectful to Jack. How such a gentle soul, with his tweed sports jacket, bow tie, and slicked-back hair graying at the temples, could share genetic connections with a harridan like Vivian was beyond Jack's understanding.

"The whitefish doesn't look fresh," Vivian repeated to her brother, picking at the carcass on Murray's plate with her fork.

"Believe me, Vivian, it's fresh enough. Jack, can I have another cup of coffee, please?" Jack brought the Silex coffee pot to Murray's cup and refilled it. Vivian studied Murray's whitefish, her forehead wrinkled in a frown. She had managed to force down all the creamed herring on her plate, even after complaining to Murray about its lack of "freshness."

Clearly annoyed that she had made a special trip to the deli only to find her husband absent from the premises, Vivian exhorted her brother to finish his (not so fresh) whitefish so that they could be on their way.

"At least let me finish my coffee, and maybe a piece of coconut cream pie …" Vivian sighed, and began drumming on the countertop with her long fingernails so that Murray, who loved coconut cream pie almost as much as apple strudel, acceded to his sister's wishes and passed up his dessert. How would she react, Jack wondered, if he planted that virgin cream pie square in her homely face? Secretly, Murray would probably consider it an extravagant waste of good pie; what would Nate do? Fire him, no doubt, not because he would take it as an insult to his wife, but because his wife would insist on it. Besides, it wasn't in his nature to do anything quite so audacious as to throw a pie in the face of a lady, even a lady as odious as Vivian Silverman. In any case, Jack didn't see a long future for himself in Nate's Delicatessen. He was getting restless by the day, and the feeling that something momentous was about to happen in his life grew stronger the closer he got to graduation.

No sooner had Murray and his sister disappeared from the sidewalk in front of the deli than Andrew Philip Dow pushed through the door, as if he had been lying in wait until the couple left.

"So, why the disappearing act?" Andrew Philip said, sliding onto a stool and casting an eye toward the beer cooler. "And with *my* bottle." He smiled to signal Jack that he was not serious about the vodka.

"I didn't expect you back anytime soon, and I had to get to work."

"I would have thought you'd make a move on Gloria. That was one reason I took Betsy off the scene."

"Sure." He looked Dow in the face for signs of mockery, for surely he knew that Jack was incapable of making a "move" on anybody, let alone one so sought after as Gloria Hill. He didn't tell Dow that Gloria had ordered him off her blanket and out of her sight, however.

"So what did you say to piss her off?" Dow asked. He slipped off the stool and reached in the cooler for a quart bottle of Miller High Life. "What do you say to a taste?"

"Why not? Piss who ... whom off?"

Dow handed Jack the quart of beer. "Gloria Hill, man. Who are we talking about? When I came back with Betsy she wouldn't speak to either of us. I figured you said something to piss her off." Jack used the bottle opener attached to the bottom of the counter to open the beer. He glanced once at the front door before taking a swallow. He handed the bottle to Dow. For all his skill at memorizing Shakespearean soliloquies and regurgitating them in his Laurence Olivier voice, Andrew Philip Dow could be pretty obtuse about people and the things that motivated them.

"All I did was ask her what she was reading. Did it occur to you she might have been jealous of you and Betsy?" Jack reached in his back pocket and came back with two folded yellow-lined sheets of notebook paper. "Your book report."

"Thank you, my good man," Dow said, eagerly unfolding the sheets. He wrinkled his forehead. "You didn't type it? I'm joking."

"You maybe ought to copy it over in your own handwriting before you hand it in to Ma Murdoch. And it wouldn't be a bad idea if you actually read the book, in case she decides to give you a surprise oral. You know how she worships *Arrowsmith*."

"You don't really thing Murdoch has all her students' handwriting figured out, do you?"

"Do it for my sake."

Andrew Philip turned the pages over in his hands. "So many words. It will take me forever."

"Try composing them if you think copying words takes forever."

"You are a prince among men. All is forgiven for drinking my mead."

"No, you're the one who's the prince." Part of him wanted to hear what had happened between Dow and Betsy Fuguet at Cold Springs that afternoon, but he didn't dare ask. There was damage that could be done to his ego, not to mention the fantasies he harbored involving Betsy, if he gave Dow the opportunity to boast of his conquest. Then he heard himself, in a small voice, asking how it had gone with her that afternoon.

"Very disappointing, my friend, one might even say discouraging," Dow said, before taking a gurgling swallow of beer. Jack felt his heart quicken.

"Oh. How so?"

"I would have bet my castle that I was about to deflower a virgin. Alas, the lass—you get it? Alas, the lass?"

"I get it."

"The lovely thing has a vagina the size of an Olympic swimming pool. It was like throwing a necktie into an empty closet, it was ..."

"I get your point."

"Why don't you fix us some cups so we can toast properly."

Jack assembled two paper liners in plastic holders and poured beer into each. He handed a cup to Dow.

"Too much head for my taste," Dow said, blowing the foam off the top of his cup.

"Forgive the crap out of me." Jack raised his cup in anticipation of the toast Dow threatened to make.

"To the prince of Garrison High, class of 1957," Dow said before drinking from his cup.

"To the Prince of Darkness," Jack said, and drank from his own cup, one eye on the door. At this point, having all but made up his mind that his deli days were numbered, Jack didn't care who came through the door.

"Did you do Fortier's paper?" Dow asked him.

"Yeah, but if he wants it he's going to have to come and get it. I don't do deliveries."

"He'll be at the Cavalier Club tonight."

"I told you, I'm not taking it to him. Let him come to me." Jack resented Bruce Fortier on several levels, not the least of which was the fact that Fortier had been accepted at the university while Jack had been rejected. Fortier, having cheated his way through four years of high school, had the audacity to ask Jack to write his final book report for Ma Murdoch after learning from Dow that Jack was writing his for him. Miss Murdoch was probably the only teacher on the entire faculty who saw through Fortier, and unless he received a passing grade on his final book report, he could fail English for the year. And if his diploma wasn't in jeopardy (the way Andrew Philip's was) a course failure on his transcript wouldn't look good to the people at the university. So Bruce Fortier had cheated his way into the upper two-fifths of his graduating class, while Jack, who no doubt owned the all-time absentee record for Garrison High, had missed the cut, as it were, by a hair's breadth. Consequently, he was required to take a university entrance exam. When he received his letter of rejection it was like a blow to the solar plexus. How could he have failed to pass the entrance exam? Only then did he begin to regret his four years of truancy, his utter neglect of his studies. He had told no one, not even Andrew Philip Dow, of the letter.

"Come on, man. We were going to the Cavalier Club anyway. Fortier won't think you're making a special trip for him."

"He won't if I don't bring it."

The little bell above the door tinkled furiously as Kyle Stoddard and Neil Sullivan burst into the room.

"Drink, drink, drink," Kyle Stoddard sang operatically. Neil Sullivan plucked a quart bottle of Budweiser out of the cooler with his big mitt and flipped it to Kyle Stoddard who snatched it deftly from the air. Jack supposed he should lock the door behind them, if for no other reason than to protect Nate's customers against his friends' antics. It was an hour before closing time. To hell with Nate's customers, Jack thought, especially the well-dressed ladies shopping for Jewish delicacies in the showcase, and their constant questions about the "freshness" of everything. Let them come.

Jack assembled two more drinking cups for his newly arrived guests. Nobody offered to pay for Nate's beer, and Jack wasn't about to make a federal case out of it, not with these guys. Neil Sullivan, all six-feet five inches of him, had come behind the counter and was at the sandwich prep bar helping himself to corned beef and hard salami.

"Don't get carried away, Neil," Jack said. "Nate's got that stuff accounted for to the fraction of an ounce."

"So what?" Neil stuffed his mouth with sandwich meat.

"Because the prick will accuse me of stealing, that's so what."

"You're not stealing. *I'm* stealing. What's he going to say when he finds all his beer gone?"

"We might consider paying for it," Jack argued.

"Fuck that," Kyle Stoddard said, pulling another quart from the cooler. "Uncork that will you, Jackie my boy. Let's drink a toast."

"To what?" Jack said, opening another quart.

"To guns for the A-rabs and sneakers for the Jews!"

"Wait," Neil Sullivan said. "For all Americans, a nigger in every woodpile!"

"Where have you guys been?" Jack had the feeling the two of them had already gotten a head start.

They were down to the last two quarts, and only fifteen minutes remained before Jack could lock up for the night when the little bell over the door tinkled, quietly, meekly; Mister Bostwick poked his balding head inside, his eyes wary; behind him, at his elbow, was his old mother. They were Friday night regulars, though never this late. Their purchase was always the same: four beef knockwurst for their Saturday night dinner. Jack guessed that Mr. Bostwick was over forty years old, with a high-pitched mama's-boy voice; the old lady was ancient, and slightly daffy.

"Good evening, Mr. Bostwick," Jack said, his words slippery on his beer-thick tongue.

Mr. Bostwick, not accustomed to hearing Jack use this tone, and no doubt the spectacle of the giant Neil Sullivan chugging from a quart bottle of beer (they had given up on the amenities of drinking out of paper cups) caused Mr. Bostwick to withdraw his head from the room and close the door quietly behind him and his mother.

"You're scaring Nate's customers away," Jack said to Neil.

Andrew Philip suggested they call their sometimes friend, Paul Embry, who owned a car, to come get them and take them to the Cavalier Club since Nate's beer was about to run out.

"Embry would jump at the chance of having you two back in his car." Kyle Stoddard addressed Jack as well as Andrew Philip. Jack bridled at being coupled with Dow, even though it was probably true that Paul Embry would sooner have a boa constrictor for a passenger in his car than Andrew Philip Dow after that night back in May at the Meadowbrook Drive-In Theater. But he doubted that Embry would include him in his list of undesirables.

Jack had sat in the front seat with Embry; Andrew Philip and George Stacy were in the back seat. They were, except for Paul Embry who didn't drink, sharing a bottle of vodka and chasing it with beer. Then, when they had got sufficiently drunk, Andrew Philip and George Stacy took it in their heads to collect speakers off the posts of the unoccupied parking spaces near Embry's convertible. Embry panicked as they began to fling speakers with their severed cords in the back seat of his car. Jack panicked a little himself, even as drunk as he was, and feeling concerned about Paul Embry, endeavored to remove them as fast as Dow and George Stacy deposited them in the back seat. He couldn't keep up. Dow and Stacy seemed crazed, under the influence of more than alcohol—the Devil perhaps. Finally, Paul Embry unhooked his own speaker from the driver's side window and sought out a new place to park, away from the "scene of the crime." And they might have gotten away with it if Andrew Philip had not had the bad judgment to urinate in front of a car bearing a young man and his girlfriend, who took offense at the spectacle of Andrew Philip Dow flaunting his genitals. The gallant boyfriend leaped out of his car to confront Dow and soon found himself on the ground with a bloody nose. Then the police were on the scene, and the next thing Jack knew he was in the Portsmouth police station with his companions waiting for his stepfather, Bill Scanlon, to come get him out of jail. For that little adventure, in which he had been an innocent bystander by his (and Paul Embry's) lights, but not in the eyes of the Law, he was given a year's probation, as were his three cohorts, even poor Paul Embry who was more innocent than Jack himself.

"Too bad Embry can't come to California with us," Neil Sullivan said. "Be better than hitchhiking."

"I thought you were gung-ho to hitch," Kyle Stoddard said. "Besides, Embry's mommy and daddy would never let him go all the way to California with the likes of us. Anyway, he's starting college in the fall, like Jack."

"Not like this Jack," Jack said, after a moment of thinking of a way to disabuse his friends of the idea that he would be attending the university in the fall without revealing the true reason.

"What are you talking about? You been telling us all along you can't go with us because of college. You change your mind?" Stoddard said, taking the bottle out of Jack's hand.

"I'd like to, but there's the small matter of our probation." The terms of their probation included a provision that forbade them to leave Garrison unless it was to accompany their family or to join one of the armed services.

"You see that stopping Andrew Philip? Right, Dow?" Neil Sullivan said. Andrew Philip was on the phone, trying to reach Paul Embry.

"There's no answer," Dow said.

"Let it ring." Neil Sullivan held the last brown bottle of beer up to the light to inspect the dregs. "I don't feel up to a five-mile walk to the Cavalier Club."

"What makes you think Embry would want to take us to the Cavalier Club? To watch us drink?" Jack offered.

"Embry thinks it's cool to hang out with us," Dow said, his ear still on the receiver. Jack knew better, but he didn't say so. Dow finally hung up the phone.

"Let's go around Monty's," Neil Sullivan suggested.

"I can't get served there," Kyle Stoddard said.

"Monty's is out for me too," Jack said. "My old man hangs out there sometimes." What beer joint in Garrison did his stepfather *not* frequent? Perhaps only the Railroad Café, haunt of Garrison's truly down-and-out, where one could purchase flat, six-ounce beers for a nickel. The bartender was too old and feeble to bother checking I.D.

"I know where we can go," Jack announced.

"After we get good and shitfaced," Kyle said, "what do you say we pay a visit to the Padre. I'll bet he's anxious to see how our souls are progressing under his instruction." Kyle Stoddard was the first among them to renounce Catholicism, and the rest of them had followed suit like lambs. For his part, Jack was happy to cast off the yoke of religion and the guilt it had brought to bear on his life. He had even lost his fear of eternal damnation. Yet he was in no hurry to rub Father Mosher's nose in his faith. The priest had been decent to him, had even offered to write an unsolicited letter of recommendation for him to St. Michael's College in Vermont. Then, Sully had it going around that Mosher took a fancy to his altar boys, and suggested that his sudden interest in Jack's and his friends' spiritual welfare was a cover for his real motives.

"I'm not shitting you. He likes to diddle boys," Neil Sullivan declared, a quart bottle still in his big mitt.

"Jack would know," Andrew Philip taunted. "The Padre took a shine to Jackie boy the second he laid eyes on him. Isn't that right, Jacko?"

"You tell me. You're the one who served him as an altar boy. Eighth grade, wasn't it? I remember how you used to claim he was such a wine hog at high mass."

Dow laughed heartily, so confident in his virility, his heterosexuality, that one would have to be delusional to believe that he could fall victim to a pedophile. Jack had been really trying to deflect Andrew Philip's keen perception of Father Mosher's interest in him. In fact it was true, and Jack was pleased by the attention the priest had paid him. He saw nothing prurient in Father Mosher's interest in him, however. And he was sensitive to such matters, having never forgotten the incident with the man in the hand-painted tie, who remained faceless in his memory.

As for Kyle Stoddard, it was not his intention to taunt the priest about his sexual predilections. No, Kyle's intentions were more malicious than that; he wanted to make Father Mosher feel that he had failed in his mission to save the boys from spiritual oblivion. Jack had often suspected Kyle Stoddard of having a perverse streak, and now he feared that he might be shown the nature of it if they did as he suggested and paid Father Mosher a drunken visit.

* * *

Jack came into work at the deli a little after 8:00 AM Saturday, hung over from Friday night beer drinking there at the deli, and later at the Railroad Café. He found waiting not only Nate, stone-faced, but Murray Isaacs, and of all people, Vivian. This tribunal sat on the last three stools at the counter, turned ninety degrees in his direction. The condition of the deli must have been as Jack and his friends had left it, though Jack would have been hard put to remember leaving it last night. Had he even locked the door behind him?

Nine empty quart beer bottles were lined up single file on the counter top. Jack's queasy stomach took a sideways turn. Nobody said a word for a long while; they merely stared at him like some despicable species of creature—like a slug, or a child molester. It required all his will (which didn't amount to a great deal) to refrain from laughing out loud. Instead, smiling, and trusting that his smile conveyed the proper superciliousness, he said: "Am I late for the party?"

Vivian literally gasped and swiveled around on her stool to face the wall behind the counter.

"Don't be a wiseguy, Jack," Nate said with as much solemnity as he had ever heard from the man.

"Why?" Murray asked, rhetorically, raising both hands above his head as if he were being robbed at gunpoint.

"You know how it is," Jack replied. "Boys will be boys." He moved behind the counter and grabbed his apron off its hook. Something told him he wouldn't need his apron today, or ever.

"I cashed up," Nate said. "You and your friends didn't pay for the beer or the food."

Jack knew better than to argue with Nate about short receipts in the cash register; he monitored sales maybe twenty times a day. He had surely checked the day's take yesterday before he left for the track.

"What friends?"

"I got a call from Mr. Bostwick first thing this morning ..."

"Oh, *those* friends."

"I could have you prosecuted for drinking alcohol, you know, not to mention for stealing," Nate said, getting off the stool, and hitching his pants up to his high waist.

Jack, practically giddy with this newly discovered sense of liberation, and in spite of his throbbing hangover, replied quickly,

"And what would you say to the prosecutor about allowing a minor to sell alcohol in your establishment?"

Nate turned to his brother-in-law. "Didn't I tell you he was a wiseguy?" Murray seemed to be put off balance by Jack's assertion that Nate permitted his underage employee to sell beer. He dropped his chin on his chest, and seemed to be inspecting something on his shirtfront.

"Tell him, Nathan," Vivian said, impatience in her voice.

"I'm going to, so just ..." Nate's words were cut off by the appearance of Solly from the Jewish bakery in Haverhill who had just pushed through the door bearing the twenty-pound loaf of black Russian rye bread, the Russian rye bread that Nate had ostensibly gone to fetch himself last night. Jack was amused by the confluence of the huge loaf of bread, Solly (whose son was supposed to be bar mitzvahed today) Nate's wife and brother-in-law. Nate was an adroit enough liar to explain away the fact that Solly was delivering the bread on schedule, as he usually did, but Jack would enjoy watching him "squirm" a little beforehand.

"So how was your son's bar mitzvah?" Jack said to Solly. Solly looked at Jack without comprehension. "Well?"

"I'm not married," Solly replied.

"So, what's one thing got to do with another?" Jack, feeling as playful as he ever had in his life, used this phrase, which was one of Nate's favorites. He glanced in Nate's direction.

"I thought I told you to stop being a wiseguy," Nate said quickly. "Come out back a minute. I need to have a word with you."

"That's all right, Nate. You can talk in front of these folks. Let me guess. You won't be requiring my services anymore."

"Something like that. You brought this on yourself, you know."

"Don't forget the money!" Vivian fairly shouted.

"You owe four-fifty for the beer. How much of my food did your friends eat? Don't lie to me. I know there's corned beef missing, salami ..."

"Work it out, Nate, and deduct it from my pay," Jack said, hanging his apron on the hook. Saturday was payday; Nate, like Abe Cohen before him, paid him off in cash, peeling the bills off the roll he kept in his trousers pocket. Jack earned seven dollars and fifty cents a week. Nate reached in his pocket for his wad, flared it open and handed Jack two singles.

"I'm sorry it had to be this way, Jack, really I am, but you brought this on yourself."

"I know. Don't worry about it."

"You don't have to apologize to him," Vivian interjected. Murray looked embarrassed by it all, and Solly, looking even more confused, hurried out to his truck to bring in the rest of the bread order. Nate looked at his wife; his mouth opened, but if he intended to say something to her he must have thought better of it.

Jack turned the pair of dollar bills over in his hands trying to decide whether he should give them back to Nate in a show of contempt for his money. But then he realized that two dollars bought two six-packs of non-premium beer, so he pocketed the bills. Nate, awkwardly, stuck out his hand for Jack to shake. Jack turned away from him and looked down the aisle to the sandwich prep area; a sudden, and unexpected, surge of emotion filled his chest. He had worked in this place nearly six years, since sixth grade. To leave like this, so ignominiously, seemed wrong. He turned and walked briskly toward the door so none of *them* would see the tears starting to fill his eyes.

* * *

"Have a seat, Jack." Sean Casey motioned to an armchair with embroidered seat and backrest in front of his big mahogany desk. "How have you been?"

"All right, I guess." Casey had to know that he was anything but "all right" after last Friday night's business. Casey was his probation officer, and also county solicitor. Jack had been reporting to him weekly since

May, when the Portsmouth judge had sentenced him to a year's probation for his part in the drive-in theater fiasco.

"Would you like to tell me what happened Friday night?"

"What's to tell?" Casey would have the police version of what happened Friday night out at the Glidden River recreational park, so asking Jack to recite his version of it seemed disingenuous. These so-called "officers of the court" always took the word of the police over that of the juvenile delinquent.

"All right, let me ask you, how much did you have to drink?" Casey held a sheet of paper in front of his face. Probably the police report, Jack surmised.

"I don't know, a couple of beers." Jack shifted around in his chair, his "hot seat." He'd drunk a lot more than "a couple of beers" but what good would it do to admit it?

"Under the circumstances don't you think that was, shall we say, stupid?" Casey dropped the paper on the desk, leaned back in his swivel chair, and made a church steeple with his long fingers. Jack, even though he wasn't looking directly at Casey, could almost feel his eyes boring into him from behind those big, black-framed glasses.

"It was graduation night. We were just celebrating." Celebrating something so once-in-a-lifetime as your high school graduation was a blameless act in Jack's opinion. But his probation officer had used the qualifier "under the circumstances," and Jack could find no way to argue against Casey's charge of stupidity.

"You broke the law, Jack, celebration or no celebration. You violated the terms of your probation. Do you understand what the consequences could be?" He had a good idea what the consequences could be, now that he was eighteen. The police had released him to his mother and stepfather's custody without informing him (or them) with what, if anything, they were charging him. His most potent fear was that he would be required to do thirty days in the "county farm."

Jack had an oblique view of a framed photograph on Sean Casey's desk of a woman and two young children—little girls they looked like from his angle. He had been relieved to learn that Sean Casey would be his probation officer, and embarrassed at the same time. Casey was a frequent lunch customer at Abe's (now Nate's) Delicatessen. He had grown to like the man; he seemed down to earth, a straight shooter.

"So it was stupid. The police didn't charge me with anything, and I haven't heard from them since it happened." Jack looked at Casey, the unasked question on his face.

"You're not being charged. But you're skating on very thin ice in case you don't know it."

"I know it."

"Nate tells me he had to let you go."

"What did he say?"

"He said something about how you and your friends drank all the beer he had in stock, and ate some food—and neglected to pay for it. He felt bad about having to let you go, but ..."

"I brought it on myself. I know. He got his money, out of my pay."

"Jack, that's hardly the point. You're too smart to let yourself get out of hand like this. I thought you were planning to attend the university this fall. What happened?"

"I flunked the entrance exam," Jack said, before allowing himself time to invent feeble excuses.

"I see. Well, won't you get another chance for spring semester? In the meantime, maybe you should review the areas where you felt you were weak."

"I didn't think I did that badly. That's how out to lunch I am." He had never been this candid with any adult, except Abe Cohen.

"You've got to make up your mind to stay out of trouble, or else all this talk of retaking entrance exams is for nothing. You understand?" Sean Casey picked up a glass paperweight with a liquid center in which snowflake-like particles floated. He looked intently at it, as if it were a crystal ball in which he could foretell young Jack Scanlon's future. "You know what your father wants you to do?"

"Stepfather."

"He wants you to enlist in the Navy. Has he talked to you about it?"

Jack laughed.

"What's funny?" Casey put the paperweight back down on his desk, and leaned back in his swivel chair again.

"My stepfather was a Navy man."

"That's funny?"

"It's funny when you consider that he got an undesirable discharge. You'd think he'd rather I joined the French Foreign Legion."

"What do you think about the idea?"

"The French Foreign Legion? I wouldn't rule it out. There's no future in Garrison." Jack told Casey about his friends' plans to strike out for California. He knew Casey wasn't Andrew Philip's probation officer, but he refrained from naming him, in case their lot compared notes on their charges.

"I hope you're not thinking about doing something stupid like going with them."

"Don't worry." Jack, restless, got up from his chair and stood by the window overlooking Fourth Street. The Colonial Theater was directly across the street from the block in which Sean Casey had his offices, on the second floor. On the floor below was a meat market, an Army/Navy store (owned by Nate's pal Arsey) and the Honeybee Café, a beer joint catering to Garrison's hard-core boozers, of which Bill Scanlon was a charter member. The *Ten Commandments* starring Charleton Heston was into its third week at the Colonial. Jack idly watched passersby on the street below.

Spiro Gravas, in his cook's whites, his virtual "uniform," came out of

Leggett's Tea Room on the corner of Fourth and Center Streets, where he was currently employed as head cook. According to Spiro's buddy, Abe Cohen, Spiro had worked just about all the restaurants in the seacoast area. Like Bill Scanlon, Spiro was susceptible to periodic benders, benders that cost him jobs, but his reputation as a first-rate cook kept restaurant owners hiring him; he was worth the risk. Spiro was in his late thirties. He looked like a man in his fifties. He had a paper bag cradled in his arm; a cigarette hung from his lips. He paused at the crosswalk to wait for the light to change. Jack knew where he was headed. His girlfriend, Clara, worked the counter at Lord's Snack Bar on the corner of the block. Spiro had tried to get Leggett's to hire her on as a waitress, but the management wanted no part of their relationship. It wouldn't look good for business to have their chief cook shacked up with a nineteen-year-old at the Emerson Hotel in a room paid for by the week.

Abe used to send Jack down the street to Leggett's to get things that he had run out of in the deli. Spiro would always oblige. Jack grew to like Spiro a lot; he was a wizard with a cleaver. Jack would watch, transfixed, as Spiro shredded a head of cabbage in less than a minute without taking his eyes off Jack as he talked to him. He must not always have been as adroit with a knife because his left index finger was only half as long as his right.

Around town Clara had a reputation as a slut, yet Jack had a different opinion of her, having had occasion to talk to her over a Coke at Lord's once in awhile. To him, as truly slutty as she looked with her heavily made up face, and hair dyed a shade of maroon, she was warmth itself, and in her own way, quite innocent; slut or not. He couldn't quite get his mind around the fact that she was shacked up with an old man like Spiro, but there were a lot of things he didn't understand about people.

He ached to get out of Garrison; he sorely wished to join his friends on their trek to California.

"Are you going to tell me what happened Friday night?" Casey was a stickler for details. It must be a common trait among lawyers, Jack thought.

"Weren't you just reading about it? What more can I tell you?" Jack referred to the sheet of paper Casey had been perusing when he first posed the question. Casey looked puzzled. Then the light must have gone on for him.

"This?" He held up the paper. "This has nothing to do with you. All I know about Friday night is what your ... stepfather told me, which wasn't much."

"That's because there's not a lot to tell. We were just, you know, like I told you, a graduation celebration. Every high school graduating class in the history of the world has done it. We started off in Ogunquit Beach, and ended up in Glidden Park. The next thing I remember, we saw lights coming down the dirt road in back of the park, and somebody said it was the cops. Everybody scattered. I hid underneath some bushes. I must have fallen asleep or something because I remember thinking it was so quiet, and dark. Not even a moon out. I figured the cops must have gone away, if they really were cops. So I crawled out from the bushes and then there was a flashlight in my face, and ..."

"How many beers did you say you had?" Casey interrupted, his voice expressing skepticism at the "couple of beers" Jack had admitted to earlier.

"Okay, maybe more than a couple. Anyway, next thing I know I'm in the police cruiser on my way to the station."

"Anybody else get caught?"

"Just me."

"Luck of the Irish." Jack was mostly French, he believed, but he didn't feel up to getting into that with his probation officer. "Who's this Neil Sullivan character?"

"How'd you hear about him?"

"I told you. I got the bare bones from your stepfather. He mentioned something about how some lunatic named Neil Sullivan showed up at the station, obviously under the influence, demanding your release. So who is this guy?"

Jack was confused by Casey's reference to the Neil Sullivan incident, not because it didn't happen pretty much the way Casey outlined it, but because he could not have heard it from Bill Scanlon. His mother and stepfather had not arrived on the scene until after Sully had made his appearance, and had already been put behind bars for creating a disturbance, for being inebriated and underage, etc. etc. Therefore, Casey could not have gotten the story from his stepfather, Jack reasoned. He thought better of saying anything else, but Casey pressed him.

"He's a friend."

"He must be a very good friend to put himself in jeopardy for you. Of course he must not have been acting rationally. The way your stepfather put it, he was pretty gone himself."

Sully had turned up at school the next day when seniors were signing each other's yearbooks and the yearbooks of their underclassmen friends. He told them the story of how the cops let him sleep off his load in an unlocked cell, and let him go in his older brother's custody that morning with a warning. He had no recollection of the night before, or of his antics at the police station on his friend Jack Scanlon's behalf. Jack was disappointed to hear that Sully had not acted solely out of loyalty and friendship to him, had not acted "rationally."

"You say my stepfather told you about Sully?"

"He heard about it from the desk sergeant, so he couldn't be sure about the details."

"Oh."

Solicitor Casey leaned back in his chair and scrutinized Jack. Jack kept his eyes on his lap, but he could tell he was being scrutinized.

"What do you want to do with your life, Jack?"

Jack looked up at Casey, whose pale gray eyes behind those large framed glasses looked sympathetic. His face was not unkind. Jack had no idea how old he could be. His hair was light brown, slightly gray at the temples; he wore it short with no hairdressing.

"Do you mean what do I want to be when I grow up?" Jack tried to smile.

Casey's smile was genuine. "Something like that."

"A fireman."

Casey laughed. "A noble profession. How long have you had this desire to fight fires?"

"Since I was little."

"Do you plan to get married, have a family?"

Jack glanced at Casey's family portrait before answering. "I doubt it." It was true that marriage and domesticity were the very last things Jack Scanlon ever thought about except with loathing. He added quickly, in case the solicitor had taken offense, "There's nothing wrong with the institution, I suppose. It's not for me, though."

"You might change your mind."

"I doubt it." It was clear to Jack that Casey was trying to build an argument for his staying out of trouble by convincing him that it could affect his future.

"You going to stay out of trouble?"

"I'm going to try."

* * *

Scanlon heard voices behind him. Then Doctor James Dunham, with his funny new mustache that didn't go with his face, was standing beside him, examining the blood bag.

"How are you doing?" the doctor asked his patient, taking Scanlon's wrist in his hand to feel for a pulse, perhaps by force of doctor habit. Scanlon hesitated a moment as he segued from his reminiscence with solicitor Casey to the real presence of his "primary care physician," as his ilk was called these days. He was frankly surprised to see him outside the examining room cubicle at the clinic across the street. House calls, as it were, had not been in vogue for a long time.

"As well as can be expected … for a terminal case."

Doctor Dunham laughed. Dunham, Scanlon had observed in the year or so he had been his doctor, seemed to be one of the most humorless men he had ever met. Perhaps for this reason, he was encouraged by the man's laugh, which for him could be described as mirthful.

"You're no more terminal than the rest of us."

"How comforting."

"I came over to see how you were doing and to tell you I've made two appointments for you to see Dr. Burrough's, first for an endoscopy, then for a complete colonoscopy. You'll have to go off your blood thinner starting tonight." Scanlon's mind was busy with "Burroughs" and the association with William Burroughs, author of *Naked Lunch,* and the connection with the loony doctor—what was his name? Benway? Then, what Dr. Dunham had said to him about going off Coumadin sank in.

"Off Coumadin? Isn't that like inviting the little clot-meisters to take up residence in my brain's arteries?"

"Exactly. That's why we have to take precautions." He pulled a small piece of paper out of his jacket pocket and handed it to Scanlon. "This is a prescription for Lovenox. It's a low molecular weight anti-coagulant that clears the system faster than Warfarin. You'll have to inject yourself twice a day, starting tomorrow, till the day before your procedures."

"Did I hear you say inject yourself?"

"Either that or come into the clinic and have the nurse do it for you. I recommend you do it yourself. I'll have the nurse show you how before you're discharged."

For the past five and a half hours or so he had been receiving blood. What Dunham said to him now made him feel as though he had lost it all. He felt light-headed.

"Can't you prescribe this "low molecular weight" stuff in an oral form?"

"Afraid not." Dr. Dunham let go of Scanlon's wrist. "When the results of the tests are in we'll sit down and discuss them. You look better than you did the other day, by the way."

"Thanks." And Dr. Dunham vanished behind Scanlon's recliner.

One would have thought that by now Scanlon would be inured to the unpleasantness of being probed with needles and catheters, plumbed by ultra-sound, CAT-scanned, shocked electrically in an attempt to get his heart back in rhythm, and all the rest. The thought of having to inject *himself* with a needle twice a day for ... how many days? ... was unsettling. Furthermore, Dunham had failed to tell him on what days next week he was scheduled for these ... GI tract probes.

"What have you got there?" Scanlon asked Karla, eyeing the objects she carried in both hands.

"Doctor Dunham asked me to give you a lesson in how to give yourself Lovenox injections." She produced an oval shaped pincushion-like object made of a rubbery material, and a hypodermic needle. "This is your tummy," she said, holding up the rubbery thing, and I don't have to tell you what this is." She held up the hypodermic needle for him to look at.

"Is that the actual size of the thing I'll be using?"

"Yes. That's why it's important you do it the right way, or else it could really hurt ... a lot." Karla proceeded to demonstrate the proper technique for an abdominal injection. The trick was to execute a bold stroke, rather than pushing the needle into your flesh slowly. She gave her wrist a deft flick and plunged the needle into the "pincushion." Scanlon cringed. "Think you can do that?"

"I can probably do it to that thing, but …"

"I'll leave these here with you to practice with. It's not so bad, once you get used to it. Remember, don't depress the plunger till the needle's in your tummy all the way."

"My tummy? What part of my tummy?"

"It's best to use the area below your belly button. Are you an inny or an outy?" Karla smiled playfully.

"That's a very personal question, Karla." Scanlon refrained from asking her if he could expect it to hurt much, for fear of coming off like a sissy. What would be the risk of another stroke if her were to forego the injections?

Karla swirled away to tend to other duties, leaving him with his "toys." He stabbed at the "tummy" a few times in the manner Karla had demonstrated, his innards recoiling. Twice a day. That no doubt meant morning and evening. In the evening he could fortify himself with a couple of stiff ones, but even he couldn't see himself drinking first thing in the morning, not even for this.

His mind went back to 1957. Sean Casey had tried to help him figure out what to do with his future. He had asked Jack if he was going to stay out of trouble, and Jack had told him he would try. But if he had not deliberately gone looking for trouble, neither did he do anything that made trouble hard to find.

His friends, Andrew Philip Dow, Kyle Stoddard, Neil Sullivan, and Joey Costis decided to spend the rest of the summer in Garrison before lighting out for California after Labor Day. Jack, the words of his probation officer still fresh in his mind, could not bring himself to agree to go along with them. Of course, he couldn't admit to them his reasons for hedging. Instead, he told them he was still trying to make up his mind about going into the service. Not that his mother would put up with his violating his probation. His stepfather had been harping on his enlisting in the Navy since Jack's last brush with the law. Also, at the time, Bill Scanlon had bumped into an old drinking buddy from his Vermont days, an older guy named Earl Langlois. Unlike Bill Scanlon, Earl Langlois had got himself on the wagon ten years ago and stayed there. While he was on the booze, Earl had been an itinerant cook, the way Bill Scanlon, among other things, had been. It seemed that Earl had opened a restaurant in a little town just over the state line in Maine. There was space for rent next door to the restaurant, and Earl was thinking of turning it into a take-out place—hamburgers and hot dogs off the grill, French fries, chicken, fried clams, and the like. He needed someone to run the place, and maybe for old time's sake, he offered Bill Scanlon the chance to manage the place with an option to buy him out if he made a go of it.

Bill Scanlon may have been an alcoholic but he was no work-a-holic. That's where his recently out-of-work and on-probation-and-walking-on-thin-ice stepson came in. Jack suddenly found himself behind the counter of the fried food take-out joint working nights by himself while Bill Scanlon crawled the bars and beer joints of Garrison. In no time he grew to hate the work; after a week on the job the smell of fried food permeated his clothes, his pores, his very soul. He had taken to walking the mile and a half to the Cavalier Club, across the bridge on the New Hampshire side of the river, after closing the restaurant. There, he drank with his friends till closing time; then he'd go with whoever had a car, to ride around through the early morning hours, drinking and raising hell. In this manner, young Jack Scanlon passed the month of July and half of August. Then, one sultry night in August, while Jack was in the back seat of Jimmy Flynn's Hudson Hornet drinking beer and yukking it up with his companions, the cops, having come from out of nowhere, were shining their rude flashlights in at them.

Next day, back in Sean Casey's office, his probation officer gave him this ultimatum: Join the U. S. Navy now, or plan on spending time in the hoosegow. Thus began Jack Scanlon's Navy career.

Twenty

April 1958:

Jack Scanlon boarded a DC-6 at Boston's Logan Airport bound, non-stop, for Los Angeles. It was only his second time on an airplane, and he was both excited and anxious at the prospect of being thousands of feet aloft over the planet for the time it would take to cover the three-thousand or so miles to his destination. He had a week before he needed to report to his new duty station, a heavy cruiser homeported in Long Beach. He had arranged to spend some time with his Aunt Jeanette and her husband Bernie and their kids in Pacoima, out in the San Fernando Valley. They lived not far from his Uncle Will whose home was in Van Nuys. Uncle Will, he had been told, had a new wife; his first wife, Eunice, had recently died in a mental hospital where she had been confined for many years. Jack was also looking forward to hooking up with his high school chum Kyle Stoddard, the one remaining member of the "Four Horsemen of the Apocalypse" who had struck out for California the September after graduation.

Clutching the arms of his cramped seat, his face pressed against the port side window, Jack strained his eyes at the cloud saturated darkness as the DC-6's engines groaned in the plane's descent. Then the starboard wing dipped, and his heart lurched; he was sure they were going to roll ... and not on purpose. But then the aircraft leveled off. Jack allowed himself to exhale, even as the whine of the engines had him wondering if the plane might be in trouble. The port wing dipped abruptly, and they were suddenly out of the clouds. Below him, on the ground, in every direction of his field of view, lights burned. The voice of the pilot crackled over the address system announcing that they would touch down at Los Angeles International in about twenty minutes. Transfixed by the lights below him, Jack was forced to wonder how he would ever find his way about on the ground. Aunt Jeanette's husband, Bernie, was supposed to meet him at the airport, but Bernie wouldn't be there for him indefinitely; eventually he would have to learn to navigate on his own.

Someone had once told him that in greater Los Angeles automobiles outnumbered people by two to one. As the plane bumped along its glide path toward the runway, Jack could see first hand how this could be true as car lot after car lot appeared beneath him.

The DC-6 touched down hard; it actually bounced off the runway, and instead of coursing down the length of it, airbrakes slowing it down, the plane lifted off and was once more airborne. The address system crackled again as the plane banked to starboard and gained altitude. The captain actually laughed and told the passengers that they would have to circle the airport and have another go at it as soon as air traffic control gave them the green light. Jack looked around surreptitiously at his fellow passengers. No one looked concerned. A baby several rows back started to cry again, but it had been crying on and off the whole trip. A stewardess sat near the first-class compartment facing aft, her face impassive. Jack found her impassivity reassuring.

The aircraft landed successfully on the next pass. When the plane taxied down the runway and came to a stop, Jack discovered, as he fumbled with his seatbelt buckle, that his hands were trembling.

He spotted Bernie in the crowded terminal standing under a ceiling clock. He was dressed in khaki slacks and a blue short-sleeved shirt with white daisies. Jack hadn't laid eyes on Bernie since 1952, but there was no mistaking his bloodhound face with the perpetual five o'clock shadow. He still wore his hair in a crew cut even if his hairline had receded some since 1952. Bernie apparently recognized his wife's nephew, too, because he started to walk toward Jack.

"Good to see you, Bernie." Jack extended his hand. "It's been awhile, hasn't it."

"Yes it has, Johnny." Bernie shook Jack's hand and reached for his AWOL bag.

"I go by Jack nowadays."

"Hmm. Seems I recall your mother mentioned that in her letter. I'll probably forget and call you Johnny once in a while."

"That's all right."

Bernie led him to the baggage claim area where, after about fifteen minutes, Jack spotted his sea bag, shouldered it, and followed Bernie through the crowd out to the parking lot. Bernie had always been a man of few words, and as they walked silently to his car, Jack felt somewhat relieved not to have to engage in conversation. The parking lot was immense. They walked for a long time before they arrived at Bernie's '55 Ford station wagon. Jack stowed his bag in the back seat and looked up at the sky, which held none of the clouds they had flown through less than an hour ago—only a multitude of bright stars. The air was warm and soft, just the way he imagined California air to be. He had heard all the stories about the smog, but there was no evidence of smog on this pleasant April evening.

Bernie somehow found his way out of the labyrinthine parking lot onto a freeway where the traffic was heavy. In a while, he turned off the freeway onto a well-lighted boulevard with palm trees, and clean white office buildings, apartment houses, restaurants, and storefronts. Scanlon tried to take it all in, as Bernie drove in silence. It was exactly the way he pictured it, just the way it looked in the movies. His longtime dream had come true at last! He experienced a surge of well-being. He could have ridden all night, happily, in Bernie's ugly station wagon.

"We're now officially in the San Fernando Valley," Bernie announced. Soon, they were on Pacoima's main drag; Bernie turned off the main street and executed several acute right and left turns before he came to his own nondescript bungalow on a narrow street with similar closely packed ranch-style dwellings.

Jack's Aunt Jeanette sat in a rocker in the living room in front of a floor model TV, with a lapful of embroidery. She got up and turned off the TV when he and her husband entered the room.

"My, my," she said, "hasn't it been a long time since we've seen you, Johnny. Look how you've grown." To Jack, his aunt looked no different than she had the last time he saw her, six years ago. All the women on Jack's mother's side of the family took after their father in looks, and they were all very short—his mother was four feet ten inches, and Jeanette was no more than five feet tall herself. What set Aunt Jeanette apart from the other girls (she was the oldest) were her hairy arms, as hairy as any man's arms he had ever seen.

"Well, you haven't changed, Jeanette, and neither has Bernie. How are the kids?" For a moment he panicked because he couldn't remember the names of their two children.

"Bernard starts first grade in the fall; Elizabeth goes into kindergarten. They've grown like weeds. Let me get you a piece of pie and a cold glass of milk, Johnny ... excuse me ... Jack." Jeanette laughed and left the room to fetch him his snack. Bernie announced that he would be getting ready for bed since he had to get up at five in the morning. He felt a little guilty for making Bernie stay up past his bedtime, for making the man drive all that way to the airport when Jack should have been able to find his way to their place on his own. He was almost nineteen, had been in the Navy for eight months; he should be more independent.

Bernie, as Jack remembered him, was a relentless creature of habit, whether it was going to bed at night, and arising in the morning at a certain hour, or taking his meals at precisely the same hour every day, weekends included. Because of Bernie's punctilious ways, members of his wife's family kidded him endlessly. Jack's mother hadn't mentioned what kind of work Bernie did these days. The last time he had visited Bernie and Jeanette in Maine, Bernie had a janitor's job in an all boys' prep school. He was almost stereotypical in his taciturn, down-Maine demeanor. Bernie had contracted malaria while serving in France during the Second World War. He suffered frequent relapses, even these many years later.

"I appreciate your taking the time to come and get me, Bernie. It probably sounds corny, but Los Angeles is just the way I imagined it would be; the warm air, the palm trees, the lights ..."

"The traffic."

"Yeah. I've heard stories about the freeways. It didn't seem so bad tonight."

"Try 'em during the morning and evening commute. I'll be turnin' in now. Be seein' you, Johnny."

"Good night, Bernie. Thanks again."

Jeanette brought her nephew a large slice of blackberry pie and a cold glass of milk. It was the first food he'd had since he'd been somewhere between Boston and Los Angeles and had been served the airlines' tasteless fare of chicken breast.

"You haven't lost your pie baking touch, Jeanette."

"Well, I don't bake like I used to, to be sure. The kids do like their pie."

He wondered if she had baked blackberry pie especially for him. The summer he spent a month at their place in Maine, she had baked many blackberry pies simply because Johnny Labalm said they were his favorite.

"This brings back good memories of Maine."

His aunt's face changed. She looked almost wistful.

"We loved living in Hebron. But the school just didn't pay enough to keep us there. I miss the peace and quiet, the nice neighbors." His aunt removed her embroidery from the hoop and smoothed it out on the arm of the sofa.

"How do you like California? The weather's certainly an improvement over Maine."

His aunt sighed, and seemed to be making an effort to choose her words carefully before she replied. "The first year was pretty awful," she said with a nervous laugh. "We were ready to chuck everything and go back home. But you know how stubborn Bernie can be. And proud. He'd have sooner died than go back to Maine. He wouldn't have been able to face his people. It would have been like admitting failure, to him."

"Yeah, Bernie was always his own man." He finished off his pie and washed it down with a swallow of milk. He wondered if his aunt had anything to drink in the house—some beer, or something harder. He couldn't think of a graceful way to ask. Then he remembered, with chagrin, that Bernie was a teetotaler, and Aunt Jeanette had never taken a drink in her life.

"How's Uncle Will getting along?" Jack had not seen his uncle in many years, since his Johnny Labalm days. He had fond memories of the diminutive Will Labalm who stood no more than five feet five inches tall. It had been Will, the oldest of his grandmother's eight children, who had caught Johnny Labalm's fancy when he was a pre-schooler. Will had a gift for storytelling, especially stories about the supernatural, populated with ghosts and other out-of-this-world creatures. Will's son Roddy was Johnny's age, and Jack had memories of times when they would be together in his grandmother's house and Will, after a particularly vivid bedtime ghost story, and after the boys had retired to a second floor room, would clomp up the stairs making monster sounds, and enter their room to screams of delight inspired by a kind of benign fear. Will's daughter, Pauline, was two years younger than Roddy and Johnny. After Pauline's birth, Will's wife, Eunice, suffered an emotional breakdown and had to be hospitalized fairly regularly.

Will, a journalist, moved his family to California in 1947 for health reasons of his own. The harsh New England winters exacerbated his arthritic condition.

"He's not at all the way you remember him, Johnny ... Jack. You should prepare yourself. He's bent over so bad ..." Jeanette paused to take in some air and to grimace. "He's a hunchback; he can barely walk. Melinda has to look after him like an invalid, which I guess he is, really."

"Melinda? Is that his wife's name?"

"Yes. You knew about Eunice, of course."

"My mother told me. It was sad." Eunice, Will's first wife, had not made the adjustment to life in California well. She was diagnosed with schizophrenia and committed to an institution in Norwalk where she died five years ago. Will didn't find California's climate tonic either, and his arthritic condition worsened to the point where he could no longer work and care for Roddy and Pauline. He had to give them up to an orphanage, which he promised them would be a temporary condition. But it wasn't a temporary condition, and Pauline still resided in the orphanage even though, according to Aunt Jeanette, Melinda was perfectly capable of looking after her husband's daughter, who was now sixteen, as well as her husband. Roddy, having turned eighteen, promptly joined the Army about the same time that Jack had enlisted in the Navy.

"Is he able to work now?"

"Not steady. He gets freelance things from an agricultural magazine from time to time. Melinda's well off; they don't have financial worries, which is more than I can say for some ..."

His aunt's suggestion that she and Bernie could have money "worries" gave Jack a moment of uneasiness, as if his visit might be a financial burden on them.

"Do you think I could see him tomorrow?" he asked his aunt, adroitly sidestepping his inner qualms.

"Don't see why not. I called and told them you were arriving tonight, so it won't come as a surprise to them or anything. Your uncle's anxious to see you."

"Me too." Jack was eager to see his uncle, but fearful as well. Fearful of what he would find, if his aunt's assessment of his condition were accurate. "I was hoping to get to see a friend of mine who's living out here too, before I report to my ship."

"Does he live out here in the Valley?"

"The last address I have for him was on some street off of Sunset Boulevard and Alvarado Street. The letter's in my sea bag. I forget the name of the street. Do you know that part of the city?"

"Heavens no. I can barely find my way around the Valley. Melinda knows Los Angeles like the back of her hand. She'll know. In the meantime you could give him a call and get directions."

"He didn't give me a phone number."

"Maybe information can help you."

"Yeah, I'll try in the morning."

"Well, Johnny, it's getting late and you must be tired from your traveling. Come, I'll show you to your room."

Jack was not the least bit tired for all the traveling he had done. He was eager to get out into the city, to find Kyle ... to have some fun. He was relieved when the room his aunt took him to did not include her two children; he didn't feel up to bunking with a couple of young kids.

***

The next morning, as his aunt drove him to his uncle's house in Van Nuys, Jack tried to imagine his Uncle Will the way Jeanette had described him, by way of "preparing" himself for their meeting. His first inkling that Jeanette's relations with her brother, and perhaps with Melinda, his new wife, were cool was when she dropped him off in front of their tiny flat-roofed house on a street of similar small flat-roofed houses.

"You're not coming in?"

"I've got errands to run, and Melinda isn't comfortable around children." Little Bernard and Elizabeth sat quietly in the back seat of the station wagon. Jeanette had gotten up early to take her husband to work so she could have the car. "Melinda will drive you back to our house for supper."

For all his "preparation" in anticipation of how his uncle would look, Jack had to make a conscious effort to hide the repulsion he felt upon seeing him. As his uncle made his way into the front room with a kind of sideways shuffle, bent over double, just as Jeanette had described him, he looked sixty or older. He was forty-three years old. He had a couple of days growth of beard on his gaunt face, and he combed his thin gray hair straight back. He looked up at his nephew, his head cocked involuntarily to the right, and smiled. His uncle's eyes were clear and gave off a mischievous light, the way Jack remembered his eyes.

"It's great to see you, Johnny boy, though I wouldn't have recognized you if I passed you on the street." Uncle Will offered his nephew a hand of deformed knuckles. He couldn't bend his fingers. Jack grasped this gnarled fist, feeling sick to his stomach.

"Uncle Will ... It's been a long time. What, eleven, twelve years?" He could not bring himself to say "good to see you." A large woman with pure white hair came in the room, hand extended.

"Hello, Johnny. I'm Melinda. Welcome."

Jack took her large dry hand, and for once refrained from reminding his uncle and his new wife that he was called Jack these days. Jeanette had told him the night before that Melinda was "well off," that they had no financial worries. But even Jack, who was not especially observant, could see no evidence of the comforts he associated with this phrase in the austere room with its severe wooden-armed sofa and two uncomfortable-looking matching chairs. There was a magazine-strewn coffee table in front of the sofa, a table model TV set with a small screen against one wall, a long narrow table with small, framed photographs of various children and adults Jack had never seen before—obviously not from his uncle's side of the family. A large oval shaped braided rug lay in the middle of the black floor, which consisted not of wood, but of some kind of vinyl material.

"Can we interest you in something to drink, Johnny?" His uncle pivoted on one foot and regarded him with his peculiar sideways look, undoubtedly because he lacked the ability to move his neck. It was not yet noon, so Jack thought better of asking for anything alcoholic, as much as he could have used an alcoholic drink. He was, after all, grown up, on his own, or at least not under parental care unless the U.S. Navy could be considered *in loco parentis*. "How about a bottle of beer?" his uncle offered, his eyes twinkling. "I'm told sailors like their beer."

"I guess I wouldn't say no to a beer," Jack said, and hastened to add, "if you'll join me."

"Why don't we all have one?" Melinda said. "This is a special occasion, after all; a cause for a little celebration."

Melinda left the room to fetch their drinks. The "one" beer they were to have turned into two, and then the beer ran out and Melinda produced a bottle of vodka. They had at the vodka until the time grew near when Melinda was supposed to drive him back to his aunt's house for supper. Melinda, no doubt perceiving Jeanette's coolness toward her, and therefore capable of judging her unfavorably if she delivered her nephew drunk to her supper table, suggested that she call Jeanette and ask if she wouldn't mind if Johnny stayed for supper at their place, and even spent the night. And Jack noticed that Melinda was feeling no pain herself, and might not be willing to get behind the wheel of her car in that condition. Melinda made the call to Jeanette; she had a peculiar contemptuous look on her face after she hung up.

She had promised Jeanette that she would drive her nephew back to Pacoima the next morning. To her husband she said, "If this doesn't convince her that we're libertines nothing will."

Melinda ordered Mexican take-out (Jack's first, but by no means his last, encounter with Mexican cuisine), and had some Mexican Tecate beer delivered. They stayed up till two-thirty in the morning talking and getting acquainted.

Will's hands were too deformed to allow him to hold a glass of beer in one hand. Consequently, he had to hold his glass between his two fists and raise it to his lips like a baby. Melinda had to thread a fork between his crooked fingers so he could feed himself; he used the fork to cut his food because he was too proud to ask Melinda to do it for him, Melinda told Jack, when Will took a bathroom break. Jack imagined that Melinda spent a good deal of time cutting his food for him when no one else was around, pride or no pride.

Jack asked Melinda if she were familiar with that part of the city around Alvarado Street and Sunset Boulevard, where his friend Kyle Stoddard said he lived. She became animated at the mention of Sunset Boulevard and went on about how some of the happiest days of her life were spent in Hollywood, especially her days at Hollywood High School. She knew the area intimately, and could take him anywhere he wanted to go, blindfolded. Jack was encouraged, but when Melinda asked him for an address, he drew a blank. Kyle's last letter, which bore his address, was buried deep in his sea bag back at his aunt's house.

"I remember it had a low number, maybe two digits. Coming from the airport with Bernie last night, I noticed all the buildings had four or five numbers."

"There are a maze of short streets off Sunset," Melinda said. "Get me an address and I'll take you right to his door."

"I wouldn't want to put you out."

"Will would enjoy a change of scene, wouldn't you, dear?"

"It would be nice. A way to reaffirm one's existence," his uncle said. Jack liked the way his Uncle Will talked.

* * *

Martel Street was lined not with palms but with maple trees, and could have passed for a street in an East Coast town, even like one in Jack's hometown. Melinda pulled her huge Buick up to the curb in front of number ten, a two-story structure with clapboard siding, not what he would have envisioned as a "California" building (in his mind all California architecture involved stucco). It was set back from the sidewalk by a short flight of cement steps.

"I won't be long," Jack said to Melinda. His uncle, diminutive in the big back seat, told him to take his time, no one was in any hurry. Filled with excitement, Jack took the cement steps two at a time. Two black mailboxes were attached to the outside wall next to the front door. He read the names Stoddard and Kemp on the one labeled, second floor. He was met by a disagreeable odor in the vestibule, one he could not identify.

The door at the top of the landing was ajar enough for him to see a sliver of carpet on the floor behind it. If he had not seen the name *Kemp* on the mailbox alongside Kyle's name he would have pushed through the door, and walked in on his old friend. It was what he had hoped to be able to do, on the ride over. Kyle liked surprises. But since he apparently shared the apartment with someone named Kemp, he thought better of pushing through the door unannounced. He rapped softly on the door.

"Yeah, it's open," a voice, not Kyle's, said. Jack pushed open the door to find on the carpeted floor a young guy, maybe two or three years older than himself, dressed in only boxer shorts; he was muscular and deeply tanned, with a head of curly brown hair. He sat Indian fashion, polishing a brown wing-tipped dress shoe. There was an open can of shoe polish beside him, the lid half full of water. It was the way Jack had learned to "spit shine" his shoes since joining the Navy.

"I'm looking for Kyle. I'm a friend of his from back east."

"He's out," the guy said, not looking up from his earnest shoe polishing. Jack's eyes took in the room. There wasn't much to look at: a big sofa with an empty walnut coffee table in front of it, one armchair, a large heavy rocker, a floor lamp. There were no other tables, no other furniture except for a floor model TV set in the near corner by the door that seemed to lack a picture tube because he could see the wallpaper behind it through the front of the set. An open doorway leading into a small kitchen was cut through the back wall. To Scanlon's right, a door opened into another room.

"Do you expect him back anytime soon?"

"Hard to say. Depends." The guy didn't look at him. Jack would like to have asked on what Kyle's time of return depended, but he felt he had suffered enough rebuff already.

"Would you mind telling him Jack Scanlon stopped by?"

"Yeah, sure."

"What's your phone number?"

"We don't have a phone." With his hand inside the shoe, the guy held it in front of him and tilted it for inspection.

"That's a nice job. I've got a pair I could turn you loose on." The guy looked up and grinned.

"You in the service?"

"Navy."

The guy rocked forward and gracefully rose to his feet without using his hands. His left hand still wore his polished shoe; he offered his right to Scanlon.

"I'm Tash. You said what? Jack Lincoln?" Tash was nearly a head taller than Jack, and with his sturdy build Jack expected a strong grip. Instead, Tash offered him a soft weak one.

"Scanlon. Kyle and I went to high school together. I haven't heard from him in a while. He's not expecting me. I wanted to surprise him."

"Does that mean you don't want me to tell him you were here, now?"

"That's an idea. Just tell him a guy was around looking for him. You don't have to say who it was. Ask him to call this number." Jack recited his aunt's number in Pacoima. "I'll be there for a few more days."

Tash Kemp repeated the phone number, but didn't make any attempt to write it down.

"What, is Kyle at work?"

"I doubt it, this time of day." Tash picked up his other shoe off the floor, and walked off through the door to the other room. Jack stood just inside the front door for a while, until he knew that Tash would not be back.

"I've got to be going," he said to the empty room. He listened for a moment, expecting a reply from the other room, but none was forthcoming. Feeling odd, and slightly annoyed, he went down the stairs and out to the big Buick.

* * *

"You knew it was me right away?"

"Why wouldn't I? Tash said a guy named Jack Scanlon had come around looking for me. What's to know?"

"Shit, I asked him not to tell you it was me. That's one strange dude, by the way."

"And an asshole too, but he pays his share of the rent."

"I'm out in the Valley. How do I get to your place?"

"Easy. Get on the hound to L.A. Walk up to the corner of Sixth and Hill and wait for the Hollywood bus. Take that to the corner of Alvarado and Sunset. You'll get off in front of Fortunado's Deli. Cross the intersection to the other side of Sunset and walk about two blocks ... are you writing this down? ... about two blocks until you come to a sandwich take-out joint on the corner. Take the left at the corner, then bang a right on Martel two blocks later. You think you can find number 10 again, you with your keen sense of direction?"

"I'll find it." He had written down Kyle's directions, and he repeated them back to make sure he had gotten them right.

"Stay clear of Pershing Square. It's right across from the bus stop on Hill."

"Why?"

"I'll explain later. When can I expect you?"

"I can't make it today. What about tomorrow? I'll try to get there before noon. Is that all right, or will you be working?"

"I'll be here."

If Kyle's strange roommate was good for his half of the rent, Jack wondered how Kyle managed to come up with his share. He was not a man of independent means, and something told him that Kyle didn't hold a steady job. He would explain everything tomorrow, including his caution about Pershing Square, Jack imagined. He would have preferred to see his friend today, but he didn't want to risk offending his aunt who had made plans to show him around the San Fernando Valley today, and prepare him a nice supper this evening.

* * *

"I would have bet the store you'd get your sorry ass lost. It's good to see you, you dork," Kyle Stoddard said to Jack, pumping his hand.

"Yeah. I even took your advice and stayed out of Pershing Square. Thanks for the warning. Those old geezers sitting on park benches staring at their shoes had me scared shitless."

Kyle stood in front of the kitchen range with its three gas burners, and forked spaghetti into his mouth out of an aluminum kettle. He asked Jack if he wanted some. Jack looked in the pot. "I'd have to be a hell of a lot hungrier than I am at the moment to eat that."

Kyle shrugged his shoulders and wound strands of spaghetti around the tines of his fork. "It's only a few days old. Think of it as *mature*."

"Pershing Square looked like a slice of paradise. Beautiful palm trees, fountains, statues ... what's the deal?"

"I'll take you there some night. Then you can tell me if you think it's a slice of paradise."

"Your roomie at work?"

"No. He's still asleep. He works nights."

Jack opened the refrigerator hoping to find some beer. The inside was utterly and starkly empty. "Kyle, you really let your hair grow." Kyle's wavy blond mane grew half way over his ears, and the back spilled over his collar.

"Chicks out here like guys with long hair." Kyle dropped his fork in the pot of spaghetti. "C'mon. Let's get some beer."

"You got I.D.? All I got is the air force one I used back home."

"Don't worry about I.D. Let's go."

"What's that stink?" Jack asked in the hallway.

"Old lady downstairs. She's German; cooks a lot of cabbage and shit. I'm used to it. She's a crazy old broad. Wait till you see her garden."

They walked to Fortunado's Deli on the corner of Alvarado and Sunset where Jack had got off the bus.

"Here's the routine," Kyle said outside the store. "There's never anybody in the place this time of day, so this should be a cinch."

"What should be a cinch?"

"Listen, the dude who owns the place is a little soft." Kyle pointed a finger at his head. So what you do is walk to the back of the store to the meat counter and look over the cold cuts. Ask the dude to come down and help you. Don't make him slice anything because you don't want to buy anything, right. Just ask him shit, like is the corned beef lean, or how much is the horse cock, whatever. All you have to do is keep him busy for a minute or two. The beer cooler is just inside the front door. When I spot him heading down back to wait on you I'll duck in, grab a couple six-packs and beat it. Tell him you forgot your money or some such shit, and that you'll be right back. Then you split. Dig?"

"I don't know, Kyle. If we get caught, there would be hell to pay for me. The Navy would hang my ass from the yardarm."

"I've done this plenty of times. There's no sweat. Besides, I'm the one heisting the brew."

"I hope you know what the fuck you're doing, Kyle."

"Go ahead. Believe me, the guy's softer than a grape. A wall-eye, just like you."

"Fuck you." Jack entered the deli, his heart racing, to decoy for his friend.

On their way back to the apartment, with Kyle toting a six-pack of Lucky Lager in each hand, Jack worried out loud that the cops might spot them.

"I've never seen a cop in this neighborhood as long as I've lived here, which is going on two months," Kyle said. "I think they're on the take from the pot pushers on Alvarado."

Tash, dressed only in his skivvies, was at his shoes again when Kyle and Jack returned to the apartment.

"How was last night?" Kyle asked his roommate.

"Thirty bucks."

Kyle whistled. "Not bad, not bad at all. How many?"

"I got lucky with this middle-aged rich dude. Gave me twenty to tie him up in his garage and jump on his ass while his wife watched. I scored a couple of five dollar jobs and called it a night."

Jack wasn't exactly sure what he was hearing, but to his ear it sounded unwholesome. Kyle rummaged through a kitchen drawer in search of a can opener for their beer.

"I'm meeting a dude at Coffee Dan's at eight," Tash continued. "He mentioned he had a friend need's a date. You interested?"

"I got company. Here it is." Kyle produced the can opener and popped open two beers.

"What about you, Tash? A brew?" Jack asked.

"No."

"What's Tash short for?"

"Tashtego," Kyle said, "As in *Moby-Dick.* His real name's Walter, but no self-respecting fruit hustler would admit to a name like Walter."

"All I remember about *Moby-Dick* was Ishmael, Queequeg, and Ahab. And the whale, of course," Jack said.

"Tashtego was an Indian dude from someplace called Gay Head," Tash said, and giggled like a girl. Inexplicably, a chill ran along Jack's spine.

"Gay Head's an actual place, Walter," Kyle said in a condescending tone. "The western end of Martha's Vineyard. Ever hear of Martha's Vineyard, Walter?"

"No." Tash dipped his polishing rag in water, and continued to work his shoe.

"I thought you said you read *Moby-Dick,*" Kyle said to Tash.

"I never said I read it."

"Then how did you know about Tashtego, and that he came from Gay Head?"

"This fruit told me. He's the one give me the name. He called me a *noble savage.* Tash giggled again. Jack chugged his beer and hastened to open another one for himself and Kyle.

"Where's the head?" Kyle pointed to the door off the living room, the one Tash had disappeared behind the day Jack had come looking for Kyle. The door led to the bedroom, the only bedroom, and two unmade beds that, judging from the twisted condition of the filthy sheets, looked like they had been used for sex. The floor was strewn with dirty clothes, as was the one bureau. There was no nightstand, no lamps in the room. A curtain hung in the doorway to the bathroom; there was no door. The tub, sink, and toilet bowl were black with dirt, filthy enough to give him second thoughts about relieving himself in there. Evidently Tashtego's fastidiousness didn't extend to his housekeeping. Jack knew that Kyle had always been a dedicated slob.

Jack did his business quickly and came out of the bathroom to find Tash preening naked in front of a mirror hanging from the inside of a closet door.

"Sorry," Jack said, hurrying out of the room. Tash seemed unaware of his presence, flexing his biceps at his reflection as if he were utterly alone.

"That guy gives me the creeps," Jack whispered to his friend in the living room.

"Didn't I tell you he was an asshole? We got to be nice to him, though. Nice to him long enough to get him to the store for some more beer. He's got legitimate I.D. We'll have to lay a couple bucks on him. You got any bread, Jack?"

"A little. I can put up with him being an asshole, but he still gives me the creeps. You sleep in the same room with that guy?"

"I'm still hungry. You hungry, Jack?"

"I told you, not hungry enough to want to eat the stuff you got in that pot."

"Okay. We'll go down to the take-out place, get some sandwiches. They got pretty good pastrami. Not like Abe's, but you know what they say?" Kyle never revealed what it was "they" say.

"Inga Leuthold" was printed on adhesive tape on the other mailbox next to the front door. This would be the woman whose cooking smells filled the hallway. Kyle had made reference to her garden, and Jack had half a mind to ask Kyle to show it to him. Kyle, however, was not prepared to detour.

"Keep on your toes, Jack. Just follow my lead. Don't second guess me," Kyle said as they approached the take-out restaurant, a squat one-story building with a flat roof and a walk-up window on one side, a drive-through on the other.

"Let me have ten pastrami sandwiches on bulkie rolls with hot mustard," Kyle said to the girl who came to take their order. "And extra pickles."

"Anything to drink?"

"No, but I'll take your phone number, sweet thing." The waitress sighed, and shoved a pencil in her hair bun.

"What are we going to do with ten pastramis? What's that going to cost me?"

"Don't sweat it."

When the girl came to the window with a large white paper bag full of pastrami sandwiches, she no sooner had the window pulled up than Kyle reached in and snatched the bag from her, and bolted up the street. Jack instinctively ran after him. When they made the turn onto Martel Street, he was out of breath, and Kyle was laughing so hard tears had come to his eyes.

Back in the apartment, they wolfed down three sandwiches each, along with two cans of beer.

"I'd rather eat shit," Tash said when Kyle offered him a sandwich.

"Good," Kyle said, wiping mustard from the corner of his mouth, "all the more for us."

Kyle was correct when he said that the pastrami wasn't as good as Abe Cohen's, Jack decided, but he ate voraciously just the same.

"Walter, how about picking up a case of beer for us before you head out," Kyle said to Tash who, fully dressed now in light slacks and striped polo shirt, lay on the couch thumbing through a surfing magazine. Jack noticed he had on a pair of huarches over his socks instead of his highly spit-polished wing tips.

"I'm not about to run your errands, Kyle."

"We'll pay you."

"How much?"

"Two bucks."

"Okay, but I'm not lugging it back here for you."

"All you have to do is hand it off. We'll do the heavy lifting," Kyle said, winking at Jack.

"I've got to catch the bus anyway; what the hell."

"What time you got? It must be close to watering time for Frau Leuthold. C'mon, Jack. This you've got to see." Kyle pronounced the woman's name "Looth hold." "Don't try and run out on me, Walter. We've got a deal, right?"

"Get lost," Tash said, engrossed in his surfing magazine.

Mrs. Leuthold wore an apron, stitched with red and yellow tulips, over a blue dress. She had on heavy black shoes with sturdy heels. She looked fiftyish, with iron gray hair and a stout figure. She aimed a stream of water from a galvanized steel watering can at the bright colored flowers of various types: pansies, gladiolas, tulips, (like the ones embroidered on her apron) and daffodils that were planted in a bed that ran the length of one side of the house, front to back.

"Ah, Mrs. Loothold. I thought I'd find you watering your pretty flowers," Kyle said, shoving an elbow into Jack's side.

"Loit-hold, Loit-hold, you *dummkopf,*" the woman said with a guttural laugh, "but you may call me Inga. And whose is the fine looking gentleman with ..." and Inga peered intensely into Jack's face, "the odd eyeball?"

"I'd like you to meet Jack, Mrs. Luthhold. His friends call him Jack the Ripper."

"Such a schmart aleck and a *dummkopf.*"

"Nice to meet you, Mrs. Leuthold. Inga." He pronounced her last name the way she had pronounced it. "Your flowers are very ... colorful."

"Sank you," she replied, intent on her watering. Jack Scanlon was no expert on horticulture, but even he could see that these flowers were not the real thing, but wax replicas.

"You would perhaps like to see my new zink, eh, *leipshen*?" She looked directly at Jack, her eyes suddenly opening wide. He glanced at Kyle for an explanation.

"Inga had a new kitchen sink installed last week, didn't you, Frau Loothhold?"

"Loit-hold, you ..."

"Jack would love to have a look at your fucking zink, but some other time, darling. We have heavy drinking to attend to."

"I have peppermint schnapps. I would share. Would you not like to see my new zink, Mr. Ripper?"

"I would, Mrs. Leuthold, but as your neighbor has said, we got serious business to transact."

"You don't like peppermint schnapps?"

"I'd rather drink your urine," Kyle said. "And you know what you can do with your zink? Let's go, Jack."

"Goodbye, Mrs. Leuthold." Jack bid the strange woman farewell. Mrs. Leuthold had gone back to her watering, muttering under her breath in German.

After Tash, or Walter, handed over the beer to Kyle and Jack, and boarded the bus for Hollywood and his assignation with a "strange fruit" at Coffee Dan's, they returned to the apartment to drink and catch up on what had gone on in their lives in the seven months since they'd last seen each other.

In the course of an evening of beer drinking, Jack came slowly to the realization that he didn't much like his erstwhile friend Kyle Stoddard. And it wasn't just because of the way he had treated Frau Leuthold, although his treatment of the woman Jack considered reprehensible. It brought back the memory of what had happened nearly a year ago, in the office of St. Jerome's parish priest Father Mosher.

"You look deep in profound thought, young man," Kyle said, with that insolent smile on his lips. "Metaphysics?"

"Actually I was thinking about that night last year, the week before graduation. Remember, the night we paid Father Mosher a visit?"

"Sure. That was fun. We got the little faggot good, didn't we?"

"As I remember it, it was you who got him good. I was just a spectator."

"I gave him what he deserved. Pious, sanctimonious faggot—the worst kind."

"Did you really know for sure that he was molesting altar boys, or were you going just on what you heard?"

Kyle took a swallow of beer, belched, and scratched at his crotch. "If you remember correctly, I never went after him for that. That was something he could deny till he was blue in the fucking face. No, I went after his so-called faith, so I could expose him for the hypocrite he was, the hypocrite all of them are." Kyle had begun to sound agitated. Jack knew that what he said about that night was true. He had been amazed at how knowledgeable Kyle had sounded, how well read he must have been. He hadn't understood much of what he hurled at the priest, however.

"You amazed me at how much you knew about ... what's it called? Theology, whatever."

"Remember Sully?" Kyle laughed. "What a psycho. I wish I could have snapped a picture of Mosher's face when he looked out the window." Kyle referred to the sight of Neil Sullivan urinating in the reflecting pool on the rectory lawn, a pool overlooked by the illuminated statue of the Virgin Mother. Kyle had drawn Father Mosher's attention to Sully in the act. Neil had excused himself, superciliously, to go outside to be with "that questionable virgin."

"Yes." Jack had thought it abominable at the time. If he could have figured a way to leave them that night he would have. "How do you know so much about arguments for the "existence of God" and all that crap?"

"I read, young fellow."

"I thought priests had to go through all those arguments in seminary so that when they bumped up against assholes like you and me they could have us for lunch. Father Mosher never even tried to argue with you."

"Precisely. You want to know why?"

"Yes, I'd like to know why."

"Because there *is* no argument for the existence of God, at least not one based on logic. And frauds like Mosher and the rest of them know it."

"What about the Thomists, or whatever they're called? Don't they have the "first principle" thing on their side? I remember you threw that in his face as if you knew what you were talking about. *Do* you know what you're talking about, Kyle?"

Kyle answered with a snort. "How much Thomas Aquinas have you read, Jack? My guess is nothing. A bunch of tedious regressions ending with ... guess what."

"God, I guess."

"Right. How fucking lame is that? Mosher knew better than to try and lay that on me. Nobody, except maybe an eight-year-old, can really believe that there's a supernatural being somewhere out there whose ego is so fragile that he feels offended when little kids play with their dummy, or eat meat on Friday; and who gives a sweet shit which of two nations blowing each other's brains out on the battlefield wins. And they make fun of the Greeks for believing that Zeus, and Hera, and that crowd, meddled in the affairs of mortals!" Kyle got up to fetch two more beers. Jack had the feeling he was in over his head. When Kyle returned with their beers he tried to shift the subject.

"How exactly do you hustle these fruits? Tell me you don't do what I think you do."

"That depends on what it is you think we do." Kyle smiled. "You'll see for yourself soon enough what kind of people are running around out here. They're coming out of the fucking woodwork, and they have the law on their side. You can't touch them. Why do you think Neil and Andrew Philip went home? They couldn't deal with the fairies. You want my opinion, I think they were afraid of them. Well, I'm not afraid of any queer, I can tell you that."

Jack's attention was on two framed photographs he hadn't noticed before, on the wall by the door, profiles, one of Andrew Philip Dow, the other of Kyle. They looked like a professional had done them. Jack asked Kyle about them.

"Dow hired a professional photographer to put together a portfolio for him he could shop around to Hollywood agents. I went with Dow to the session and this photographer, who turns out to be a fruit, of course, wants to do one of me ... *gratis*."

"What about Joey Costis?"

"I don't know what happened to Costis. He was acting so weird, even weirder than he usually acts. The last I heard about him was from Sully, before he left. He said Joey got to sit in with Curtis Counce at a club downtown, and he fucked up again, like he always does. Dropped his fucking sticks in the middle of a four bar break. Haven't seen him in a couple of months. I assumed he headed back to Garrison."

"What does Tash *do* with these people?"

"You sound like you just left the farm, Jack. What the fuck do you think he does with them? Do you think he gets paid for his sparkling conversation? It's lucrative too. I haven't had to do a day's work since I found out just how lucrative it was."

"So, you're into it too. Jesus, Kyle."

"Don't worry, old man. Hustling queers doesn't mean you have to be a fag yourself, necessarily. You think female prostitutes enjoy their work? It's the same way with fruit hustlers. It's a job. Understand?"

He didn't understand. Neither was he in the mood to pursue the subject further.

They sat and nursed their beers in silence for an uncomfortably long time. Finally Kyle said, "You know Bobby St. Hilaire, right? Dude from

North Berwick."

"I've heard of him. A lady's man, I hear."

"He's out here, or at least he was, stationed at Camp Pendleton."

"A jarhead."

"Yeah. And you're right about Bobby being a lady's man. That would be the understatement of the year. He's so smooth he can have a broad confiding in him about her ovaries after knowing him for ten minutes."

"I'm happy for him, but what's that got to do with anything?" The "anything" Jack referred to was the subject that had brought on the recent silence between them.

"Let me tell you. Bobby and one of his buddies were shacking up with these two airline stewardesses in North Hollywood. When the girls had weekend flights, and Chico—that's his buddy from Chula Vista—and Bobby were in town they'd go out in Chico's car and cruise Sunset and Hollywood Boulevards looking for young fruits. They liked to pick on the young ones, the teenagers. They'd act like they were interested in the kids' favors, lure them in the car then take them up to the Hollywood Hills or Mulholland Drive, beat the living shit out of them, leave them there, and beat it. This is how they got their rocks off when the girls were working. Bobby must have shipped out because I haven't seen him in about three weeks."

"Sounds like a lot of fun. They ever ask you to go along?"

"They invited me, but you know me, I'm a lover not a fighter. I got no love for fruits, but I draw the line at beating on them just for kicks."

"Unless they pay you to do it."

Kyle laughed. "Then it's business, you dig?"

"Interesting but …"

"Let me finish. There's a twist to this tale." Kyle began to chuckle, as if something funny had occurred to him suddenly. He held up his hand as if he were instructing himself to cease chuckling and get on with his story. "Sorry, it's just so funny."

"What? *What* is it that's so damned funny?"

"I didn't have the heart to tell Bobby. I see these Camp Pendleton jarheads all the time in Coffee Dan's. They dress in civvies but they stick out like sore thumbs with their stupid haircuts, and their spit-shined Marine shoes. You can't go a day in there without seeing them swapping spit with each other in some back booth. If Bobby knew some of his gung ho buddies were fruits he'd throw a rod. *Semper* fucking *fi*." Kyle fell to laughing again.

"Is that supposed to be news? Queers in the Corps? You think I don't know that?" In truth, Jack knew it now, but the news had come to him only recently, and had come as a bit of a shock. Last winter, in Newport, while he was waiting for classes to start in supply school, he had been assigned to the personnel office on base to perform menial clerical duties (because he could type maybe twenty-five words a minute). One of the office clerks was a flamboyant seaman by the name of Hoover. The expression "flaming queen" was not part of his vocabulary at the time, but he knew now that it aptly described Hoover. They happened to share the same barracks as well.

One cold Sunday night, Jack was hitchhiking back to the base from Garrison, after a weekend home, and a car driven by a burly middle-aged man picked him up on Route 128 in Massachusetts. By the time they reached the Route 138 turnoff to Fall River, the guy had made his intentions known. Jack politely declined the man's suggestion that he drive him all the way to his destination if certain conditions were met, and bailed out at Route 138, badly shaken up because the man was large and had he been insistent, Jack wasn't sure he would have been able to handle him.

In his naiveté, Jack confided to Hoover his hitchhiking experience, characterizing it as unwholesome and repugnant. Hoover merely laughed and told Jack he should have leaned back, let it happen, and enjoyed himself. That's when the light went on for young Jack Scanlon. Homosexuals could be found as easily in uniform as in civilian clothes.

Jack got up to fetch another beer. Kyle drained his can and asked for another. When Jack returned from the kitchen he was aware that Kyle was scrutinizing him, an amused expression on his face.

"What?" Jack said, lowering his eyes.

"So, what do you think?"

"About what?"

"About fruits in the Corps."

"What am I supposed to think? Didn't you hear me? This isn't news to me."

"But *Marines*! I just think it's hilarious."

"St. Hilarious."

Kyle mocked a pained expression. "Jacko! That was unworthy of you."

"Sorry."

"Good thing Bobby shipped out. It would have been only a matter of time before he ran across one of his own on the boulevard." Kyle produced a thunderous belch. "Unquote."

"You think he'd flip out? I can't believe he doesn't know. I thought he was a sharp guy."

"Even sharp guys have their blind spots."

"Yeah." He wondered if Kyle ever considered his own blind spot?

"You know," Jack said, regarding the photographs of Kyle and Andrew Philip Dow on the wall, "Andrew Philip looks a little like Tab Hunter in profile." Kyle was in the process of drinking from his beer can, and Jack's observation caused him to spew beer out of his mouth."What the fuck's wrong with you?" Kyle was laughing out of control.

"At the risk of disillusioning you further, young man," Kyle said, when he'd regained control of himself. He went on to report that Tab

Hunter was a well-known fruit around Hollywood; that he played the "femme" role in his relationship with a young weight lifter who worked out at Vic Tanny's gym, and they could be seen practically every night cruising up and down Hollywood Boulevard cheek to cheek in Hunter's red Thunderbird convertible.

"Tell me, how're the chicks out here?"

"Hah. You have to practically beat them off with a stick. And they put out at the drop of a condom. You'll see." Kyle finished off his beer and burped again, loudly. "I could use another sandwich. You?"

"I'm all right. Are you seeing anybody in particular or playing the field?"

He learned that Kyle was playing around with two sisters who lived in the Hollywood Hills. Betsy, the older sister, was the one he was officially dating, but he had made overtures to Tanya, the younger, and according to Kyle, the better looking one. Now he had to keep up the pretense of going with Betsy while at the same time pursuing Tanya. Betsy was the jealous type, and she had a violent temper. If it got back to her that Kyle was two-timing her with her little sister there was no telling how she might react. Betsy had a number of good-looking girlfriends, and Kyle promised to fix Jack up with one of them. He was eager to meet a California girl, especially if they were as pliant as Kyle claimed they were, but he was committed to spending the remainder of his leave with his Aunt Jeanette and her family, and his Uncle Will and Melinda. Next week he would report to his ship in Long Beach, and the only chance he would have to visit Kyle and his offering of female companionship would be on the weekends that he didn't have duty.

The days he spent in the company of his Aunt Jeanette, her laconic husband Bernie, and their two dull children were unbearably long. Aunt Jeanette was as chatty as Bernie was silent. Little Bernard, who was to start first grade in the fall, took a fancy to Jack and demanded his attention for every minute the boy was awake. Elizabeth, Bernard's little sister, on the other hand, was passive like her father, and was content to play with her dolls by herself, cooing over them in the living room. Bernard would hoist himself onto Jack's lap, squirm like a little reptile, poke his fingers in Jack's face, and pull his hair and ears. When he tired of Jack's lap he would go to his toy box and drag out every toy he owned, place them at his cousin's feet, and demand that Jack inspect them all. Then he would expect Jack to play with him and his toys. Jeanette, apparently oblivious of her nephew's aversion to the boy, blathered on endlessly about her domestic life.

His only relief from this torture was when he could take legitimate leave of them to visit Uncle Will and Melinda who had no annoying children in their house. He had by now gotten somewhat used to his uncle's affliction. He enjoyed talking to Will and his talented wife. Melinda took him to visit her ex-husband, with whom she was on amicable terms. His name was Samuel, and he was a highly respected sound engineer in the film industry. He lived with his current wife in North Hollywood, in a beautiful Spanish style house with stucco walls and ceilings, and large dark oak doors. On the walls were many photographs of famous movie stars, like William Holden, Deborah Kerr, Elizabeth Taylor, Van Heflin, and Montgomery Clift. The living room was sparsely furnished with ultra-modern (and to Jack's mind, uncomfortable) pieces. Samuel was eager to demonstrate his new high fidelity equipment. Jack was duly impressed with the quality of the sound coming into the room from hidden speakers.

In his uncle's house, among the magazines displayed on their coffee table, was a fair amount of literature about Rosecrucianism. Jack learned that his uncle and Melinda were devout followers of the cult. But when he asked for details about the movement, they were mysteriously evasive on the subject. One evening, as they were preparing to leave for a meeting of the sect, they spoke to each other in hushed, secretive voices. Jack began to wonder if there was something illegal, or even subversive about the group. While they were at their meeting, he thumbed through the pages of a few of the pamphlets, feeling like a voyeur. He was left with a vague feeling of unease about what he had read, as if he had witnessed something ... loony. That his uncle and Melinda, whom he considered quite intelligent, would be taken in by such mystical and occult doctrines was unsettling to him. From what he had read of the coffee table literature he decided that Rosecrucianism was rubbish.

On Wednesday, Jack got into his dress blues, followed his uncle's directions for getting to Long Beach, first by Greyhound bus to Los Angeles, and from there to Long Beach by way of the "Red Car." The Metropolitan Transit System's Red Car line consisted of rickety old cars that looked to him like they had been manufactured at the turn of the century. On the train ride from L.A. to Long Beach, he was struck by the conditions of the Negro neighborhoods in places like Watts, Compton, and South Gate. He looked out the grimy window of the coach at the backsides of rundown tenements, or squat single dwelling shacks, at Negroes of all ages sitting idly on the steps staring vacantly off in the distance, seemingly unaware of the train, their dark faces expressionless. By the time he reached Long Beach, Jack was filled with a melancholy he was all too used to feeling.

This feeling was short-lived, however, as he stood in awe on the pier where his new duty station, all six hundred seventy-five feet, seventeen thousand five-hundred tons of the USS *Columbus CA74,* was tied up, with its magnificent eight-inch fifty-caliber gun turrets fore and aft. Scanlon shouldered his sea bag and made his way up the after brow. He made his first mistake, pausing on the threshold of the quarterdeck, turning smartly to aft and saluting the ensign, which, too late, he remembered didn't fly after sunset. The O.D., a young lieutenant JG, smiled as Jack recited his reporting-for-duty spiel, and refrained from pointing out his gaffe. He ordered the seaman on quarterdeck watch to show Jack below decks to his S-1 division compartment.

At quarters the next morning, Jack met his new division mates, which included Myers, a first-class petty officer in charge of his office, Chief Matthews, Lieutenant Awalt, the S-1 division officer; and finally the supply officer himself, Lieutenant Commander Mason. Jack found the men in his division quite friendly and welcoming, and he was delighted to learn that he would not have any watch-standing duties, and that all his weekends, starting at thirteen-hundred hours on Friday, would be free.

Only officers could leave the ship and return aboard in civilian clothes. Jack left the ship on Friday in uniform; he carried his civvies and his "douche kit" in his AWOL bag. He got on the shuttle bus at the end of the pier that took him to the Red Car stop. He had no way of contacting Kyle, as Kyle had no telephone. Kyle had told him that he and Tash were not in the habit of locking the apartment door, so in the event that neither of them was there when he arrived, he should just go on in and hang out until Kyle returned. Even the prospect of having to sleep on the uncomfortable living room couch could not dampen Jack's excitement about the weekend and the possibility of meeting girls … girls who were not shy about sharing their sexual favors. It was his own shyness in these matters that caused him to worry. Then, there was always alcohol to help him with his inhibitions.

Loud music blared from a radio sitting on the open bedroom windowsill facing the street. The door to the apartment was open, and the first person Jack spotted as he entered the room was Inga Leuthold, sitting on the couch, one leg crossed over the other, sipping schnapps from a water tumbler, her bottle within easy reach on the coffee table. Sitting in the armchair next to Inga was a girl in her late teens with auburn hair with blonde streaks. She wore a champagne colored dress, and had no stockings on over her shapely, well-tanned calves. She smiled at Jack when he came in the room. Over Inga's shoulder, Jack could see Kyle with a girl in the kitchen. Kyle had his arms around her waist, his face buried in her neck. Her back was against the stove.

"Mister Jack the Ripper!" Inga exclaimed, raising her glass.

The girl laughed. "Is that really your name?"

"Yes."

"How queer."

"Actually I'm Jack … Scanlon, a friend of Kyle."

"Hi. I'm Patty. I came with Betsy. She said Kyle had someone he wanted me to meet. Nice to meet you."

"And that would be Betsy," Jack said, motioning toward the kitchen, "fighting off Kyle?"

Patty turned to glance over her shoulder. "Yes, that's her. She can take care of herself."

"Hey, old man," Kyle said, coming from the kitchen with Betsy, a chunky, mannish blonde with hair not much longer than Kyle's. Jack was a little surprised that his friend would be interested in her; she didn't strike him as Kyle's "type." Then a short girl, who couldn't have been more than fifteen years old, stepped into the living room followed by a thin, lanky boy with hollow cheeks and long straight hair. The girl was short and voluptuous. She had on a clinging dress that accentuated her shapely breasts and rear end. This would be Tanya, though she bore no sisterly resemblance to Betsy.

"Brew's in the fridge," Kyle said. "Help yourself."

Patty had said that Betsy had brought her here today to meet Jack, but Kyle could not have known that he would show up today. He was puzzled, but at the same time pleased because Patty was looking at him with what he thought was keen interest. The music coming from the bedroom made conversation difficult to hear.

"I'd like to change," Jack said, holding up his bag.

"Who's to stop you?" Kyle said, producing a can of beer from behind his back. "Want Tanya's help?"

Jack glanced in Tanya's direction. Her attention was on the thin boy; she seemed not to have heard Kyle, which was likely given the noise level in the room. Jack headed for the bathroom to change, hoping that he wouldn't find a naked Tash behind the bedroom door. The radio that was blasting music sat on the windowsill, but there was no sign of Tash. Kyle had not bothered to formerly introduce Tanya or the young guy who had been in the bedroom with her—or Betsy for that matter.

Both beds were in the same condition they had been in the other day. Jack turned the volume on the radio down and went behind the curtain into the filthy bathroom to change into civilian clothes. He checked out his cleanly shaved face in the mirror and fretted that Patty would notice his aberrant eye as quickly as Inga Leuthold had the other day. Everyone he had known in his life had gotten used to his eye, and he had never felt that it was a real handicap. It wasn't worth getting neurotic about now.

When he finished dressing, Jack came out of the bathroom to find Patty lying on the bed nearest the bathroom. She lay on her side, supporting herself on one elbow, her chin in her hand. A lock of hair had fallen across her eye. It was more agreeable than finding Tash standing bare-assed in front of a mirror, he decided.

"Hi. You look like Veronica Lake with your hair like that."

"I do?"

"Sort of." Jack sat down on the bed next to her and pushed the hair away from her eye with the back of his hand. Patty took his hand in both of hers and pulled him toward her. He kissed her, and lay down beside her. He was about to insert his knee between her legs when Kyle came through the door.

"Don't mind me," Kyle said, "but the lizard needs bleeding." But hearing his friend's stream in the toilet extinguished Jack's passion.

"I could use a beer," he told Patty and got to a sitting position. "How about you?"

"Sure." Patty smiled. "It's still early," she added.

"Why don't you go on out. I need to have a word with Kyle."

Patty smiled in a way that informed him that she was aware that he was buying time so that he would not have to appear in front of people in the other room in an "aroused" state.

"Go ahead," Jack said. "I won't be long."

"We'll come back later." She gave Jack a peck on the cheek, and slid off the bed.

Kyle finished and came out to find Jack on the bed.

"Jesus, you weren't kidding."

Kyle laughed. "Patty get you all riled up? Well, just slap it down and come on out and get busy drinking. She's not going anywhere. That is, unless I piss Betsy off, which I'm very capable of doing."

"Has Betsy got some kind of control over her?"

"You might say that. Betsy's got the wheels and the driver's license. Why do you think I have anything to do with her?" Kyle went over to the radio and turned the volume back up. "Just in case someone has their ear to the door," he whispered.

"You seemed pretty amorous there in the kitchen." Jack got up from the bed.

"Don't get me wrong. I don't mind banging her, but she can be a royal pain in the ass. And she's too fucking moody for my taste. It's like she's constantly on the rag. I'm biding my time until I get to nail Tanya. What do you think of her, huh, Jack?"

"Reminds me a little of Brigitte Bardot."

"And God created Tanya! You all right now? Let's get out there."

"*...dumm wie Bohnenstroh sein,*" Inga said to Kyle who had deliberately mispronounced her name just to get a rise out of her.

"That didn't sound complimentary," Jack said to Kyle in the kitchen. Kyle pulled two Lucky Lagers out of the refrigerator and handed one to Jack.

"Roughly translated, she thinks I'm a stupid shit. I love to needle the bitch." Kyle took a long drink of beer.

Patty sat next to Inga on the couch, engaging the old woman in conversation; Tanya sat in the armchair next to the couch, pouting. Conspicuously absent were Betsy and the boy who had emerged from the bedroom with Tanya. Kyle made a move toward Tanya; Jack hung back in the kitchen doorway. Patty turned to look at him. She winked; he winked back.

"Jack thinks you look like Brigitte Bardot," Kyle said to Tanya. He sat on the arm of the chair, next to her and let his hand rest on her shoulder.

"Who?" Tanya frowned.

"Breejeet Bardoe, the French movie star. Jesus, Tanya, even an air brain like you must have heard of her."

"All the girls remind Jack of movie stars," Patty said, smiling playfully at him.

Jack flushed. Had he been so transparently disingenuous? And he was forced to wonder how Kyle expected to get anywhere with Tanya with that approach. Tanya had returned to her pouting; Kyle began to stroke her arm, but she seemed oblivious of his tender gesture.

"Where did Betsy go with Rat Face?" Kyle asked the room.

"To buy some more beer," Patty replied.

"You should drink the schnapps," Inga offered. "American bier, it is like water."

"Mind if I turn that down?" Jack asked Kyle. An annoying (to Jack's ear) currently popular novelty song about one-eyed, one-horned, purple people eaters was filling the room.

"I like that song," Tanya said, her pouty lips pursed.

"Yeah. Tanya likes her music deep," Kyle said, moving behind the eviscerated TV console. He crouched behind the set, put his face where the screen should have been, and mugged for the room.

Betsy and "Rat Face" returned with a fresh case of beer.

"Hamms?" Kyle said to Betsy. "We prefer Lucky Lager in this household."

"Take it or leave it," Betsy retorted. "Cory, I want a glass with mine," she said to "Rat Face."

"So I'll take it." Kyle put his arm around Betsy's waist, worked his hand up inside her blouse and palmed her breast. Betsy did not resist; she seemed not even to notice. Jack busied his mind thinking of ways he could get Patty back in the bedroom. Cory went to the kitchen to pour beer in a glass for Betsy. He handed Tanya her beer in the can. Inga Leuthold held a glass of schnapps on her knee.

"Betsy, how about we show Jack around town tonight? Take him to Figueroa Street, Pershing Square. I want him to see the *real* Pershing Square, the one after dark."

"I've got rehearsal tonight, Kyle. You know that. And you know how Jet is if we miss rehearsal."

Kyle laughed. "How did you guys get under that moron's spell? He's not going anywhere in the music business. Anybody with eyes can see that ... and hear it."

"You're just jealous," Betsy said, starting to file her nails.

"This clown calls himself Jet Power," Kyle said to Jack. "He's got these guys believing he's on the verge of becoming a rock and roll star. What's the jerk got you doing for him tonight?"

"You wouldn't understand," Betsy said, sighing and shaking her mannish head. She held her hand out in front of her and inspected her nails.

"Betsy and Myra are the chorus, you know?" Tanya chimed in. Cory had disappeared into the bedroom to listen to a song he liked, but couldn't hear to his satisfaction in the living room since Jack had turned down the volume.

"We'll hop a bus," Kyle said to Jack. "You should get acquainted with your new town."

"I was hoping to get a look at Hollywood. You know, Hollywood and Vine, the Capitol Records building, and all that."

"I can do a better job than he can," Patty offered. "I happen to live there. I can introduce you to Rick Nelson."

"Ricky Nelson! You hear that, Jack?" Kyle laughed derisively. "Jack's been dying to meet him, haven't you Jack? Or was it Ozzie and Harriet you were dying to meet?"

"I've thought about little else since I got here." Jack regretted instantly saying it, as a little dark cloud moved across Patty's face. Kyle's sarcasm was infectious, and always had been for him. "How do you come to know him?" he asked Patty, trying for some damage control.

"I go to Hollywood High."

"Oh." Jack didn't pursue the question her answer raised in his mind for fear of alienating her further. "I see."

"We've got to go," Betsy announced. "We'll come around tomorrow if you want." Jack looked at Patty, the unasked question all over his face.

"See you tomorrow," Patty said, rising off the couch, and smiling at Jack. Tanya got out of her chair, and went in the bedroom to retrieve Cory. Jack was disappointed they were leaving so early, and was slightly annoyed at Kyle for making what little time they had spent together unpleasant. But there was always tomorrow.

"Give my warm regards to Jet," Kyle said, as they were going out the door. Inga had expressed her disapproval of Kyle out loud to him, telling him off in German for his rudeness, which no doubt accounted for the premature end to what to her was a splendid party.

"Get the hell out of my apartment, you old douche bag," Kyle yelled. Inga stalked out in a huff, muttering to herself in that guttural tongue that grated on Jack's nerves.

* * *

Betsy dropped Patty off at the apartment late the next morning, but neither she nor Tanya—nor Cory—came in. Patty explained that rehearsal had not gone well the night before, and this Jet Power character expected them to rehearse all afternoon. Hearing this, Kyle hurried downstairs to bum a ride to Hollywood with his so-called girlfriend. Tash had not returned from whatever nocturnal errands he had been on last night. So Jack found himself alone in the apartment with Patty, who today had on a pale yellow dress and ballet style shoes. His observation that her hair had put him in mind of Veronica Lake evidently had an effect on Patty because today her streaked hair spilled over the whole right side of her face.

Jack had slept fitfully on the hard couch, uncertain as to whether Tash would return. Without a word, Patty took hold of his hand and leaned into him. They kissed, and Patty started to move him toward the couch.

"Not there," he whispered. He pulled her gently in the direction of the bedroom, and the two beds whose sheets, Jack guessed, hadn't been changed in weeks, maybe months. It wasn't quite as sublime as Kyle said it would be, but if Patty didn't consent to going "all the way" she brought him as far as any girl had ever brought him. And who knew if he wouldn't have gotten to pay dirt if Tash hadn't made his abrupt appearance? Walter was tired from all his work on the boulevard and wanted to go directly to bed. Jack and Patty cleared out of the bedroom.

Patty wanted to know all about him, and the first question she put to him was how old he was. It was an innocent enough question, but Jack hedged with his answer. He had known girls who had strict rules about the ages of guys they made out with. One girl he knew in Garrison would make out in the back seat of a car with anyone, no matter what he looked or smelled like, if he had reached the age of eighteen. It could have been Brandon de Wilde and she wouldn't let him near her if he hadn't yet celebrated his eighteenth birthday. She had been known to ask guys for identification. Something told Jack—because it was the first question she asked him—that Patty had an age standard, too.

"How old are *you*?" he countered.

"Seventeen. I'm graduating in June."

"I'm nineteen." He would turn nineteen in June, but since it was already April, he was closer to nineteen than he was to eighteen so he wasn't that much of a liar.

"What kind of boat are you on?"

"Ship. A very big ship. You know what a heavy cruiser looks like?"

"Can I look in your wallet? I love looking in guys' wallets."

She had him. One look at his I.D. card would put pay to his little lie. He tried to steer her off the subject of his wallet by encircling her waist and drawing her to him. She complied and they kissed a while, but she had not forgotten what she had asked him.

Gloomily, he turned over his wallet to her. He never kept money in his wallet, only photographs and his I.D. cards—one, his "drinking" card, actually an Air Force document without a photograph, the other his legitimate Navy card with the picture of himself that made him cringe. It had been taken in boot camp after his hair had been shorn. He looked all ears, and his walleye showed up prominently.

"Are these your nephews or something?" Patty held snapshots of his half-brothers Keith and Billy.

"Brothers."

"They don't look anything like you."

"We have different fathers." Scanlon was uncomfortable with this admission.

"Where's your mother's and father's pictures?" Patty had the entire contents of his wallet stacked on her lap, as she examined each piece one by one.

"I don't have any."

She came to his I.D. cards. "This one says you're in the Air Force, and that you're, let's see, twenty-four. But this one with your picture on it says you're in the Navy, and that you're … eighteen." Patty frowned. He began to perspire under his arms.

"Well, as the chief at my last duty station used to tell us, young sailors need two I.Ds: one to live by and one to drink by."

"Could you keep your voices down?" Tash yelled from the bedroom. "I'm trying to get some Zs."

"Why don't you close the door?" Jack said, and held his breath in case Tash decided to get out of bed and make something of it. In a moment he did get out of bed, but only to slam the door shut.

"So, the one you "live" by says you're eighteen. I thought you said you were nineteen," Patty the interrogator pressed on.

"Personnel screwed up my birthday. They typed 1939 instead of 1938. I haven't bothered to have it changed."

"What about when you really turn twenty-one? You won't be able to prove it." Her earnest questioning had the effect of taking the edge off his ardor. He got off the couch and headed to the kitchen to get a beer.

"I'll probably get around to having it taken care of by then. Get you a beer?"

"Sure. Are you really nineteen?"

"Yes. Why does it matter to you? Why is it such a big deal?" He handed Patty a can of Hamms, Betsy's choice of beer, without offering to pour it in a glass. Patty was content to drink from the can.

"I like guys older than me." Patty swallowed some beer. Some of it dribbled down her chin.

"Well, eighteen would be older than you. Do you like Tash? He's older."

"He's conceited. He's always looking at himself in the mirror; either that or polishing his shoes so he can see himself in the shine."

"He must do other things."

"Would you like me to be your girl?" The guileless, unabashed way she put the question surprised and delighted him. He couldn't find the words to respond to her. His mouth opened, but no words came out. Patty's eyelids flickered and she looked down at her lap. "You don't like me. I'm too nosey."

"No, no. That's not true. Yeah, I'd like it very much … really." Patty looked up, her face brightening.

"You're not wearing a class ring. You *did* graduate from high school."

"Yes, of course."

"Well, could you give me something I could, you know, show people so they'd know we were going steady?" Jack was not practiced in the rituals of courtship. In high school he had never formally dated a girl.

One reason had to do with the fact that he had neither car nor driver's license. Another reason, probably the most cogent one, was that he was almost pathologically shy around girls.

"I had a class ring, but I lost it a couple of months ago." He had lost his class ring to a Boston pool hustler on Washington Street. "I can't think of anything else I can give you. I can't very well give you my dog tags."

At the mention of dog tags, Patty became animated. "Why not? You could say you lost them and have them give you new ones."

"You don't *lose* your dog tags." He wasn't eager to go through the red tape of petitioning for a new set of dog tags. "I suppose I could try." Then he'd have to admit to his new superiors that he wasn't responsible enough to hang on to the ones he was issued.

He left Kyle's apartment at a little after midnight on Sunday, after a weekend of hot petting with his new steady girlfriend, to return to his ship in Long Beach. After waiting at the bus stop for fifteen minutes without seeing any buses on the boulevard in either direction, he looked up at the sign and saw that buses stopped running after midnight on Sundays. He was in uniform and felt confident that he could hitch a ride to the MTS and still make the 1:30 a.m. Red Car. There was plenty of traffic on Sunset, even at that hour. Jack stuck out his thumb at the first car. It pulled over to the curb, and he jogged to the passenger side and opened the door.

"Get in," a young man whose face was in partial shadow said. "I *adore* seafood."

"That's all right." Jack slammed the car door and stepped up on the sidewalk. The seafood lover sped off.

He encountered the same thing with the next two cars that stopped for him. One of the drivers, a very fat young man, actually had his business in his hand when Jack opened the door; the other driver promised to take him all the way to Long Beach if he would "make it worth my while."

He began to worry that he would miss his train and have to cool his heels for two hours in the creepy MTS station on Los Angeles Street. The driver of the next car that stopped for him was clearly of the same persuasion as the previous ones, but not as aggressive, so Jack threw caution to the wind and got in with him. He sat rigidly in his seat, his AWOL bag on his lap, keeping the curly haired young driver in view peripherally. He was relieved when the guy pulled over to the curb on the corner of Los Angeles and Main Street. Just as he opened the door and started to get out of the car, the driver reached for his crotch. He caught the guy by his thin wrist before he could make contact.

"Nice try, faggot. Thanks for the ride." Jack slammed the door shut hard, as the car squealed off down Main Street. Kyle had described Main Street as the "bad" part of town.

So these were the kind of people Tash and Kyle trucked with, he thought, and the mere thought troubled him.

When Jack returned to his ship, the officer-of-the-deck ordered him to report to his division officer right after reveille in the morning. He lacked the temerity to inquire of the O.D. what it was his division officer wished to see him about; consequently, he lay in his bunk unable to fall asleep for wondering what possible kind of trouble he could have gotten himself into.

"You wanted to see me, sir?" Lieutenant Awalt, who had a reputation for absentmindedness, blinked his pale eyelids and gave Jack an uncomprehending look. Then, the light apparently went on for him.

"Yes, Scanlon. At ease. Sit down."

He took a seat in the metal chair beside the division officer's desk.

"We were worried about you, Scanlon. If you hadn't come back when you did we would have been obliged to report you A.O.L."

"A.O.L.? I was on liberty; I was on a weekend, sir."

"That's what Chief Matthews figured, but we couldn't find your chit. Chief figured you must not have known you had to fill one out for weekends, you being new. In the future, be sure you fill out the proper chit before you take weekends. We won't bring you to Captain's Mast this time, but in the future be careful. That will be all."

"Aye aye, sir. Thank you."

Jack's interview with his division officer left him feeling embarrassed and stupid. First he salutes the ensign after sunset, now he goes A.O.L. without even knowing it. What a stupid boot his new shipmates must think he was.

On Tuesday the ship left port to go on two weeks of maneuvers, and to visit the ports of San Diego and San Francisco for overnight stays. One of the exercises involved bombardment of the southwest shore of San Clemente Island with the ship's eight-inch fifties. Below decks, at his damage control battle station, wearing headphones, Jack wasn't prepared for the fearsome noise of the big guns' recoil. The bombardment seemed to go on for hours. A second-class machinist mate assigned to the same station noticed his fright.

"You'll get used to it, sailor. When I served on battlewagons during Korea, those sixteen-inchers going off were enough to make a man shit his pants."

Something was coming in over Jack's headphones, but all he could make out were the words, "damage control central." The rest was gibberish to his ear. It seemed that he was one of only a handful of men on the ship who didn't speak with a southern accent, and he was having trouble understanding many of his shipmates when they spoke, (even after Darren Price's instruction on how to identify various accents of the South). He asked the caller to repeat. He had to ask two more times before he understood that it was now permitted to secure from general quarters.

* * *

The ship anchored in San Diego harbor for one day and night to take on machine parts. Jack had liberty that day. He had been looking forward to going to Tijuana with a couple of new guys like himself, where, according to the veterans on board ship, a man could get just about anything he wanted in the way of sexual adventure. It was as if they were describing someplace "east of Suez." All one had to do was be on guard against the hustlers, pickpockets, and money changers, and of course those vectors of clap, syphilis, and chancroid—the bar girls.

In a manner of speaking, Jack lost his virginity that night in a Tijuana strip joint and cathouse. That is, he believed that he had, until he overheard talk in the supply office about the wily Tijuana B-girls:

"They can spot a cherry boy the minute he steps through the door," Crawford, a third-class storekeeper said. "By the time they get him to the back room he's too hot to trot to figure out that when the senorita's on her back he's sticking his dick in her fist not her twat. That's why they keep those back rooms so dark."

Listening to the talk, Jack felt a blush grow on his face as he matched Crawford's description with his own experience in the dimly lighted back room of the bar. Whether or not it had happened as Crawford had described it, he had come away from that airless back room feeling not the exultation he hoped he would feel, but wan and unclean. The experience had spoiled the rest of the evening for him. He could only hope now that if and when he managed to overcome Patty's scruples (if she had any) that he wouldn't feel the way he had in Tijuana.

* * *

Patty had given him her phone number, and he called her as soon as his ship returned to Long Beach. They agreed to meet at Kyle's place on Friday. She promised to show him around Hollywood. He asked her if she could let Kyle know that he would be coming that weekend.

The uniform-of-the-day had changed from blues to whites by the time they returned to Long Beach. Jack stood on the pier waiting for the shuttle bus, feeling sharp in his freshly starched white jumper and trousers. He was eager to get to Kyle's so he opted to get a cab to Long Beach instead of waiting around a half hour for the shuttle. He bought a carton of chocolate milk from the mobile canteen and opened it up in the back seat of the cab. On the way to Long Beach, the cabbie had to stop abruptly at a traffic light just as Jack was poised to take a drink from the milk carton. Chocolate milk spilled down the front of his jumper and onto his lap.

"Fuck," he said out loud. The Mexican cabbie turned half way around. Jack was torn between telling the cabbie to return to the ship so he could change, or to proceed to Long Beach with him in his soiled uniform. He was bound to draw stares from people. "Fuck," he repeated.

"What's the matter, *esé*?" The cabbie asked him.

"Nothing. A little accident."

On the Red Car to Los Angeles, and on the walk to the corner of Sixth and Hill Street, and finally on the bus ride to Alvarado and Sunset, he avoided eye contact with fellow passengers and pedestrians. He'd change into civvies when he got to the apartment, and get his whites to the Laundromat.

"What the fuck did you do to yourself?" Kyle said, laughing.

"Don't ask." He headed straight for the bedroom to change. He went to the closet to fetch his clothes. "Kyle," he said after moving all the hangars from one side of the closet to the other, and back again. "Where the fuck are my threads?"

"How about where you left them? I'll get you a brew."

"They're not here. What happened to them?"

"How should I know?" Kyle came into the bedroom bearing a can of beer for Jack. Neither Kyle nor Tash were his size, so it wasn't likely either of them had taken his clothes.

"Who's been here since I've been gone?"

"Nobody. Just Tash and me and the girls. Wait. Rat Face was here last week. I remember he was still in the apartment when I left. Yeah, I'll bet it was Rat Face took your clothes. He's a slimy little fucker."

"A lot of good that does me now." Jack removed his neckerchief and pulled off his jumper and trousers.

"Let me have those. I'll take them down to the Laundromat for you. I've got some stuff to do myself. Let me have a half a buck."

Jack handed over his chocolate milk stained uniform to Kyle who stuffed it in a pillowcase along with some of his underwear.

"Where can I get hold of this Cory asshole so I can get my duds back before I pound the bird shit out of him?"

"I don't know. Ask Patty. Betsy's dropping her off before she and Tanya go to their fucking rehearsal with Jet, the bunghole, Power. They'll be back to party when they finish. Patty said she was showing you around Hollywood tonight."

"Yeah, if I can find something to wear. You coming along?"

"No. I got to work Coffee Dan's tonight. I need the bread … bad. Why don't we meet back here say around ten thirty, eleven." Kyle took off for the Laundromat with his pillowcase.

Jack sat on the living room couch in his skivvies thumbing through Kyle's dog-eared copy of *Look Homeward, Angel*. Patty came through the door without knocking. She carried a brown paper bag. Jack pulled the bottom of his T-shirt down over the opening of his fly.

"You're kind of casual today," Patty said, sitting down beside him and putting her warm hand on his bare thigh. He told her about his chocolate milk accident.

"Kyle's at the Laundromat now. He thinks Cory stole my clothes from the closet."

"He's wrong about that." Patty opened the paper bag beside her and pulled out his neatly folded shirt and trousers. "I took them home, cleaned and pressed them for you. I didn't think to tell anybody. Sorry."

"Thanks. That was very nice of you." Patty withdrew her hand from his leg. She got up from the couch and headed for the kitchen.

"Why don't you put them on," she said.

"There's no hurry. Why don't you come back here and finish what you started?"

"What do you mean?" Patty stood in the kitchen doorway, smiling coyly.

"You know very well what I mean. Don't be a tease, Patty."

"Put your clothes on. Somebody could walk in."

"All right, but I don't like being teased." He stood up and pulled on his chinos, and started to button his shirt when Patty was behind him encircling his waist with her arms. He took her hand and moved it down to his crotch.

"Not here," Patty said. "In the other room."

On the bed, Jack ran his hand up inside her skirt along her thigh. She offered no resistance. He got inside her with his finger; she moaned and wound her arms around his neck. Then she let go of him, removed his hand from under her skirt and turned over on her side with her back to him.

"What's the matter, Patty?" He could see her shoulder blades moving under her thin blouse, as if she were crying. He put his hands on her shoulders and tried to turn her toward him. She resisted. He didn't know what was going on; he had no idea what to do next. "Are you crying?" he asked her.

"You think I'm cheap," she said, finally, and started to sob.

"Jesus, Patty, I don't think that at all. What gave you that idea? I thought ..." What he thought was that she was as willing to play as he was, but he didn't quite know how to phrase it.

"I know what you think. You think I'm a slut. I've been too easy for you. It's all my fault." Patty turned her head and looked over her shoulder at him, her face streaked with tears.

"I got the crap out of your uniform," Kyle said, coming into the bedroom. "Oops. Love in bloom. Sorry. Hey, where'd you find your duds?" Patty got off the bed and hurried into the other room. "What's with her?"

"Beats the shit out of me."

"So your clothes were in the closet all along?"

"No. She took them. Gave them a press job. She thinks I think she's a slut."

"Well, isn't she?"

"You'd know better than I would." Jack got into the sitting position on the edge of the bed.

"I don't know anything for sure. Anybody hangs around Betsy; I just figured, you know, birds of a feather. For all I know she could be a virgin."

"You never had a go at her?"

"Too flat in the chest. I like my chicks with big bazooms."

Patty returned with two cans of beer. She handed one to Jack, one to Kyle.

"Thanks," Jack said. She avoided looking him in the eye.

"I got to get on the road," Kyle said. "Don't forget, we'll meet back here around eleven. Betsy and Tanya should be done with Jet boy by then, right, Patty?"

"I have to be home by twelve," Patty said.

"So be late," Kyle said on his way out the door.

"I'm sorry about ... you know ... in the other room," Jack said, when Kyle was gone.

"Don't be sorry, Jack." Patty sat down on the couch beside him and tucked her legs underneath her. "I just need a little time. You know I love you."

He was not sure he had heard her right. He wasn't prepared to hear a declaration of love from a girl he hardly knew. He felt a blush forming on his face. He turned away from Patty.

"Do you love me too, Jack?" She put her arms around his shoulders.

"I, uh ... I don't know. We only just met. I thought something like that took time."

"Have you ever heard of love at first sight?"

"Yeah, sure." He was by now painfully aware that Patty was waiting for him to tell her that he too had fallen in love with her "at first sight." He would not have known how to utter such words even if he meant them, which he most certainly did not.

"Say it, Jack. Say you love me." Patty rested her head on his back.

"I ..." He remained mute. Then he felt her trembling, and sobbing quietly. He rose from the couch.

"I need a beer. Can I get you one?"

"If I let you do it, will you say you love me?"

Jack turned around and looked at Patty's tear-stained face, half covered with a veil of her streaked hair. He came back and sat down beside her and took her in his arms.

"Why don't we go sight-seeing, and talk about it later." He was not unaware of the huskiness of his voice, and was pleased because it struck him as appropriately dramatic to the moment.

* * *

Betsy, Tanya, Kyle and Tash were in the apartment when Jack and Patty returned at eleven. Patty took Betsy aside and whispered something to her. Tash had his nose back in his surfing magazine. Jack saw no sign of Cory, who he had believed stole his clothes and whom he had been ready to pound on. Betsy and Kyle had been making out on the couch when he and Patty came into the room. Tanya seemed engrossed in a movie magazine.

"I'm going to take Patty home," Betsy announced.

"Jack, why don't you go along; escort your girl home, like a chivalrous lad?" Kyle said, winking at Jack and nodding almost imperceptibly in Tanya's direction.

"Sure. Do you mind?" he asked Betsy.

Betsy just shrugged her mannish shoulders. "Come on, Tanya."

"Ah, let her stay here and keep me and Tash company," Kyle said, with an ambiguous smile. Tash, in Jack's opinion, was as indifferent to Tanya's presence or absence as he was to any one else's, so absorbed was he in himself.

Betsy had a long look for Kyle.

"What?" he said, smiling, his palms turned toward the ceiling. Tanya's attention remained fixed on the magazine, as if she were deaf to the conversation in which she was the subject.

"We'll be back in forty-five minutes," Betsy said, finally.

"Here you go." Kyle handed Jack a fresh can of beer. "One for the road."

"What about us?" Betsy said. Kyle shook his head. He went to the refrigerator and pulled out two more beers for Patty and Betsy. Jack wondered how far Kyle thought he could get with Tanya in forty-five minutes.

On the ride back to Kyle's apartment, he was at a loss for anything to say to Betsy. She had talked to Patty non-stop on the drive to her house, which was in some neighborhood off the Hollywood Freeway. Jack had kissed Patty goodnight at the end of her driveway, which led to a gated pathway lined on both sides with flowerbeds to a house with a red-tiled roof that looked to him like the dwelling of someone well off. So busy had Patty kept him telling her about his own life that he knew virtually nothing of her background.

After all the chatter between Betsy and Patty, the silence between Betsy and Jack, now that they were alone, was oppressive. Betsy finally said, as she turned onto Sunset Boulevard,

"Kyle's in for a big surprise if he thinks he can get to first base with Tanya."

"Tanya? What makes you think he has any interest in her?"

Betsy turned to look at him. "Are you trying to be funny?"

"No, I'm not trying to be funny."

Betsy made a snorting sound that he interpreted as contempt. "Tanya's Jet's girl, and if you don't think that eats at Kyle's guts you don't know your friend as well as you think you do."

"How do you know that?" He felt his face grow warm, like a child caught in a lie.

"Because I got eyes, is how I know that. And Tanya's my sister, in case anybody's forgotten. Kyle thinks he's so smooth."

"Why do you go out with him if that's the way you feel?"

"He amuses me. I don't think he will for long."

"Why tell me this? Aren't you worried I might say something to Kyle?"

"Say anything you want to Kyle."

They drove the rest of the way in silence. Patty had not touched any of her beer. Jack finished it off as they pulled up to the curb in front of Kyle's apartment. The beer Kyle had given him before they left he'd killed before they reached Patty's house.

Betsy and Tanya left at two o'clock in the morning; Tash had gone to bed an hour before that. Jack and Kyle sat around drinking beer; neither of them was tired.

"How'd it go with Tanya?"

"She's a weird chick, but she'll come around. What did you think of Patty's pad? Not bad, huh?"

He told Kyle what Betsy had said about Tanya being Jet's girl. He didn't repeat what she had said about Kyle.

"It doesn't matter to me whose girl she is as long as I get into her pants."

"Betsy predicts you won't get to first base with her."

"So she's wise?" Kyle laughed. "At least she spared us one of her conniption fits. Tanya must have blabbed."

"She wouldn't have to. You're pretty obvious."

"I guess so. Who gives a shit?"

"You make any bread off your little friends tonight?"

"Five lousy bucks. I waited for two hours in Coffee Dan's for the creep Walter set me up with, and he never showed. While I'm waiting, this fucking guy, turns out to be a schoolteacher, was giving me the eye the whole time. I had to settle for him. Pissed me off. Walter told me the other creep was good for twenty."

Jack didn't press for details. He wondered if Betsy had an opinion about Kyle's activities. There was a single knock on the door. Inga Leuthold came in the room without waiting to be invited. She had the schnapps bottle by the neck in one hand, her water tumbler in the other.

"I cannot sleep with all your noise. I may join you?"

"Pull up a chair, Inga," Kyle said. "We were counting on our noise to get you up here. We enjoy your company so much."

"Schmart alek." Inga sat on the couch next to Jack. "You must see my zink, *leipshen*. It is *vunderbar*!"

"Not the fucking zink again, Inga!" Kyle said. "Tell me, Inga, do you piss in your zink or is it always too full of dirty dishes?"

"Where is your pretty *fraulein*?" Inga directed her question at Jack.

"She had to be home by midnight. Like Cinderella."

Inga leaned toward Jack and said in a conspiratorial voice, "You make whoopee with *fraulein* Cinderella?"

"That's really none of your business, Frau Leuthold."

"Inga makes whoopee with her schnapps bottle after the lights go out, don't you, Inga?" Kyle said. "Hey, I got an idea. Inga, Tash is asleep. Why don't you go in and crawl in bed with him? He's got the hots for you. He told me so. Go ahead, Inga. Make some whoopee with Walter."

"I do not think that one much like the girl, eh, *leipshen*." Inga winked at Kyle.

"Believe me, Inga, Kyle digs you. Go on, you'll find out."

"I do not sink so." Inga poured more schnapps in her glass.

Jack laughed with more gusto than her remark demanded, glancing at Kyle to see if he picked up on the double meaning. Kyle was preoccupied with his navel.

"I think I would like to try a taste of your schnapps, Mrs. Leuthold," Jack said. But Frau Leuthold had taken umbrage at Scanlon's laugh, and rose from her seat and was making for the door, muttering under her breath in her usual fashion.

"Shit," Kyle said as Inga Leuthold clomped down the stairs in her heavy shoes, "I'd have given a lot to see Walter's face when the old bag crawled in with him."

"Inga doesn't seem to think Tash likes girls."

"So what? Inga's no girl, by anybody's definition. That would have been something to behold." Kyle chuckled and wagged his head.

They continued drinking till the beer ran out. Kyle disappeared into the bedroom without a word, and Jack fell instantly asleep on the hard couch, fully clothed.

The sun was bright in the room next day when Jack awoke to the touch of Patty's hand on his face.

"What time is it?" His mouth was rancid from all the beer he had drunk, and all the cigarettes he had smoked the night before.

"Around noon. Gee, you guys drank a lot of beer." Patty giggled as she surveyed the room with all the empty beer bottles on the coffee table, the floor beside the couch and the armchair, on top of the TV set.

"Yeah, it got drunk out last night." He rubbed sleep out of his eyes with his fists, then slid his hand underneath Patty's skirt.

"Fresh," she said, pulling his hand away, giggling again, which this morning he found unattractive.

"Is Kyle up?" Jack rose to a sitting position and reached for his cigarette pack on the coffee table. Patty beat him to it and shook out two cigarettes. She put both of them in her mouth and lit them up with his Zippo. She handed one to Jack.

"Betsy's trying to wake him up." Patty blew cigarette smoke toward the ceiling.

"Jesus, my head is bad." He rested his elbows on his thighs and put both hands to his head. "And we're out of beer."

He had to use the bathroom. He knocked once on the bedroom door and went in. Tash was not in his bed. Betsy lay on top of Kyle in his bed; the sheet was pulled up over them to their necks.

"Good morning, old man," Kyle said, flipping the sheet away to reveal Betsy's ample white ass. She reached behind her and recovered the sheet.

"Bastard," she said.

Jack was too inhibited to go to the toilet with Betsy within earshot. He brushed his teeth, letting the water run in the filthy sink. The Navy had got him in the habit of shaving every morning, even on weekends. To draw a sink full of hot water in the festering bowl gave him pause, however. If he was constrained from using the toilet by Betsy's presence, she had no such compunction in her intimacy with Kyle. Her moans he could hear over the running water.

Betsy and Kyle's antics in bedroom inspired Scanlon to try again with Patty. He buried his face in her neck and reached under her skirt again. This time she let him.

"Ouch. You'll give me whisker burn."

"Guess what they're doing in there?" he whispered, his voice husky with lust.

"I don't know. Playing cards?" There was that inane giggle again. He pulled away from her and lit up another cigarette. He didn't offer Patty one. She took one out of the pack and waited for him to light it. He lit his own and flipped the cover shut. She took the lighter from his hand and lit her own, saying nothing. Kyle came in the room, a towel wrapped around his middle.

"Betsy's going to replenish us before she goes to rehearsal," he said, picking up Jack's cigarettes. He snapped his fingers for Patty to give him a light. "What do you say, Patty?"

"Hello, Kyle."

"You being nice to my buddy?" Kyle said, leaning down to take the flame Patty offered.

"Nicer than he's being to me."

Kyle raised his eyebrows. "Jack's got a ton of things on his mind: our national security, the Red Menace, the Jews and A-rabs going at it. Don't judge him harshly, peppermint Patty."

Betsy came in the room probing inside a carry bag. She had on blue jeans and untucked, loose fitting blouse.

"Let's go, Patty. We don't want to be late."

Jack looked at Patty. "Since when did you join the group?"

"I'm helping with the sound system. My dad's with Universal. He showed me stuff."

Jack was reminded of Melinda's ex-husband, the soundman. He experienced a brief stab of guilt when he considered how he had been avoiding contact with his relatives since taking up with Kyle and his friends.

"Will I see you tonight?" he asked Patty.

"Are you sure you want to?"

He wanted to, but somehow to admit as much in Kyle and Betsy's presence made it difficult to say so. "Hell, I'm not sure about anything."

Kyle said, "Don't forget our brew."

"Shit. Get some clothes on and come with us to the store. You're going to have to haul it back here yourself. I'm not going to be late and get yelled at again."

"Jack, why don't you go along and pick up the beer. I'll throw some clothes on and meet you on your way back."

* * *

"Salud," Kyle said, back in the living room, a fresh case of Lucky Lager safely stowed in the refrigerator.

"To temperance," Jack said, raising his can. "Ah, do your stuff. Make me well again."

"All right, old man. Out with it. Did you get into Patty's skivvies, or what?"

"She's on the rag." Jack turned on the couch so that he was not looking directly at Kyle.

"I know some chicks like it when they're pumping."

"You ever make it with Patty?" Kyle had denied it before when he had asked him. Something made him ask again. Patty had proclaimed her virginity to him and Jack wasn't sure how he would react if Kyle answered in the affirmative.

Kyle looked at him and frowned. "You asked me that already. I told you, she's too flat-chested for me. As I told you before, I think she's still a virgin."

"That's what I thought too. She's probably lying about being on the rag."

Despite his recent encounter with the Tijuana whore, Jack was not convinced of his own authenticity as a "non-virgin." It was on Patty that he now depended for validation.

"That fucking Jet Power dude is probably banging all of them. How they can go for a creep like that?" Kyle shook his head in disbelief.

"You've met this guy?"

"Once. He's got to be seen to be believed. He thinks he's fucking Elvis the pelvis. He's got his hair style, and he goes around in this red, one-button roll jacket with black velvet lapels, black pegged pants, suede shoes, the whole bit. He even tries to talk like Elvis. That ought to tell you something—anyone would want to ape that asshole."

"Chicks love Elvis Presley. I can't figure it. Maybe this Jet guy is hipper than you give him credit for, Kyle."

"Yeah. Probably getting more ass than a toilet seat."

"I don't get the appeal of this rock-and-roll crap," Jack said.

"Me neither. Hey, I bet Patty didn't show you around any of the jazz clubs on Hollywood Boulevard when she had you on tour."

"No. She took me to Hollywood and Vine, the Capital Records building ..."

"All right. Tonight I'm taking you to Irene Vermilion's Jazz Cellar. Bud Shank's a regular there. He's got Chuck Flores on drums; you remember, the kid broke in with Woody Herman's band when he was about fourteen? Flores, not Herman. There's never anybody there; we'll have the joint practically to ourselves. Then we can walk a couple of blocks and catch Lennie Niehaus and Zoot Simms. This club on Hollywood Boulevard thinks it's the West Coast version of the Metropole. Remember the night we caught Bean at the Metropole?"

"Of course." Kyle and Scanlon had skipped out on their senior class trip to Washington, D.C., stayed behind in New York, and stayed up for two days going to jazz concerts and nightclubs. The night they saw Coleman Hawkins at the Metropole, Judy Holiday, escorted by two young men in suits, had come in the club. She was so drunk the young guys had all they could do to keep her on her feet. "I wasn't born yesterday," Jack added, to show Kyle that he too could be clever. "What about the girls?"

"They got no interest in jazz."

"But aren't they planning to come around and hang out with us?"

"Let 'em wait. Do 'em good."

"So, you're not busy with clients tonight?"

Kyle stopped fingering his navel, and looked up at Jack. "You're not still on that tune, are you? Didn't I tell you, it's just business? Snap out of it, Jack, for Christ's sake!"

"It's just when I think about you letting them ... touch you and whatever ... well, I guess I just don't understand."

"I guess I don't know how to explain it to you then."

"Don't you have to be, you know ... up for it too if you're going to, you know, give them ... what they want?"

"What the fuck are you trying to say, Jack?"

"I'm trying to understand."

"You're saying I'm a fruit. That's what you're saying, isn't it?"

"Jesus no, Kyle ... I don't know what I'm saying, all right? Let's just drop the subject. All right?"

"You saw me in action with Betsy. You still think I'm a fucking fruit? Well?"

"I said let's drop the subject, and no I don't think you're a fruit. All right?"

Jack had heard about people who liked both sexes, people who "swung both ways." He wasn't about to go there with Kyle, in his agitated state.

"What would you know about it anyway? You've probably never

made it with a chick yourself. What about it, Jack? It's the truth, isn't it?"

"Fuck you. You want another beer?"

"Of course I want another beer."

* * *

On the bus ride to Hollywood, a young woman with her infant child sat across the aisle from Jack and Kyle. She had the baby on her lap, cooing to it. Kyle, sitting in the aisle seat, jabbed his elbow in Jack's side to get his attention. He addressed the woman:

"That's some baby you got there. How old is it?"

"Four months," the woman said, smiling. "This is Jason."

"Ah," Kyle said, "a boy. Who does it take after?"

"Oh, he's definitely got his father's looks."

"Really," Kyle said, nudging Jack again. "What was his father, an anteater?"

Jack glanced in the woman's direction in time to see her smile disappear. She clutched her baby to her breast and turned toward the window. Jack turned toward his own window and tried to concentrate on the storefronts along Hollywood Boulevard.

Try as he might, Jack could get no further with Patty, and by the first of August, when his ship was ready to deploy for a six-month cruise to the Western Pacific, he had given up any hope of success with her. He continued to visit Kyle on weekends, but Kyle's time seemed to be increasingly taken up with his Coffee Dan's clients, so he spent most of his weekends in Patty's company. Each weekend she seemed to grow more querulous, more resistant to his blandishments for intimacy. He grew weary of her. By August, when he was scheduled to sail, he was more than ready to get away from her, from Kyle, and all the other Martel Street characters. Patty made him promise to write to her at least once a week, but his heart was not in it. He was excited about the forthcoming cruise, eager to visit exotic ports of call in the Far East, places he'd heard about all his life—Hong Kong, Manila, Tokyo—and places he'd never heard of, places with exotic names like Keelung, Subic Bay, Chi Chi Jima, Cebu City. It was in Subic Bay in the Philippines, in fact, that he received Patty's "Dear John" letter. It seemed like more than coincidence that he received a letter from Kyle in the same mail call. If Patty's letter was vague in its reasons for breaking off their relationship (she was young, she needed to see other guys, etc.) Kyle's was more specific. He reported that Patty had been "banging" this Jet Power guy steady, even when she was seeing Jack on weekends. Then Jet Power dumped her and she attempted suicide by inflicting superficial razor cuts on her wrists. Kyle found it all amusing. What Jack found most disturbing in Patty's letter was the postscript she included: "You were never affectionate." He answered neither of their letters, and when his ship returned to Long Beach in March, he went to see his relatives in the

San Fernando Valley. He never saw or heard from Kyle Stoddard again.

* * *

For years Scanlon had had recurring dreams about returning to the Navy, to sea duty; and of course dreams of missed exams in college, and even dreams in which as an adult he was back in high school, enrolled in classes that he never attended and which he consequently failed. In the past couple of years these themes had vanished from his dreams. What he was left with of late were bizarre, amorphous dreams bordering on nightmares, which lacked coherent thematic content, at least none that he could identify. It was hardly worth going to sleep anymore. Dreams of a return to the service, and to sea duty, had given him immense pleasure. He didn't need a Freudian to inform him that such dreams spoke of a deep wish for freedom, a freedom he imagined he might have had as a young sailor, but in truth did not exist, unless one equated the state of being carefree with freedom. In any case, he no longer dreamed of being carefree. Whatever good memories he had of Navy life he would have to conjure in the waking state:

Twenty-one

Yokosuka, Japan 1958:

"EM club, cabbie-san," Bonano said to the unsmiling taxicab driver whose face in the rear view mirror looked malevolent to Jack Scanlon, which is no more than he would have expected from a Japanese national. He, Jack Scanlon, would have borne a grudge against any military representative of a country that had tried to vaporize him. He had asked his shipmates who had visited Japan before how much resentment from the natives he could expect. Everyone said that there was no evidence of it in Yokosuka. Nagoya was another story. Conklin, a third-class corpsman Jack had become friendly with, had told him stories of the saturation bombing raids the allies had perpetrated on Nagoya, the way Dresden, in Germany, had been obliterated. Conklin's supervisor, Satterfield, a dental technician first-class, claimed it had "served the fuckers right."

They showed their I.D. to the jarhead at the main gate; the cabbie turned right on what Bonano explained was Yokosuka's main drag, which consisted of shops, restaurants that catered to the natives, tea rooms, and locker clubs where G.I.s kept their civvies. In the street behind the storefronts, which ran parallel to the main drag, was "black market alley" where the city's bars were most highly concentrated. The EM club was a short ways from the main gate. The cabbie pulled up to the curb. Frenchie had remarked, trying to be funny, that they drove on the wrong side of the road in Japan, and most of the other countries they'd be visiting on this trip, just like in Europe.

"You got any yen?" Bonano asked Frenchie.

"A couple hundred."

"Then pay the man. We'll settle up with you when we change our money."

Frenchie grumbled, worried that he would get screwed for the cab fare, but paid off the driver just the same. Bonano told Jack and Thompson that the driver would have been just as happy with MPC, but he didn't want to get into a money conversion beef with the dude.

"I'm getting me a chiliburger before I change my money," Bonano said, rubbing his hands together. He had talked for days, before pulling into port, about the quality of the Yokosuka EM club's chiliburgers. One would have thought he was describing the cuisine at Antoine's. Jack had no desire for a chili, or any other kind of burger; he was eager to get to town. He had been hearing for a long time how Yokosuka was the best liberty port in the Far East, better even than Hong Kong, and he was itching to see for himself.

Jack converted ten dollars of MPC into thirty-six hundred yen and cooled his heels while Bonano and Frenchie indulged themselves in chiliburgers and 3.2% beer. The EM club was a three-story building on Yokosuka's main street. Drinks in the various club bars were cheap, and Bonano claimed the Japanese waitresses didn't challenge even the youngest-looking sailor for identification. But Jack and his division mate, Van Thompson, were hot to get to town.

"We going to fuck around all day eating, or what?" Van asked, rhetorically. He argued that unlike Bonano, who was a third-class petty officer and therefore entitled to an overnight, the rest of them were on Cinderella liberty. "We're wasting precious time," he added.

"Patience, young man," Frenchie said. Despite being in the service as long as Bonano, he was still only a seaman. He had made third-class a year ago, and promptly lost his crow at Captain's Mast a month later for getting drunk and being A.O.L. for forty-eight hours. The *Columbus*'s Old Man was strict; he had no use for men who offered alcohol as an excuse for breaking rules. Frenchie was intent on getting his rate back on the next examination. Jack, too, hoped to make third class, as did his fellow strikers in S-1 division, including Van Thompson.

"Ah, that's fine dining," Bonano declared, dabbing at the corners of his big mouth with a paper napkin, with exaggerated delicacy. "Now let us proceed to the bright lights and exotic beauties of the night."

Bonano stopped at the EM club liquor store and purchased two fifths of whiskey (two bottles per customer was the limit) before the four of them set off on foot for Yokosuka's nightlife.

The entrance to "black market alley" reminded Jack of an amusement or theme park. The carnival atmosphere was immediately apparent, and Jack's heart started to pump stronger as the bar girls, with their formal ballroom gowns, pitched their wares from the doorways of their establishments. "Hey, USS *Columbus*, come in Lily Bar, have good time."

"They look like kewpie dolls," Van Thompson whispered to Jack. "How come the Chinks can't say their Rs and the Japs can't say their Ls? They're both gooks, ain't they?"

Bonano, apparently recognizing a girl who pitched them from the Lily Bar, stopped to exchange a few words with her, his arm around her waist. Thompson was ready to take her up on her offer.

"Come on," Frenchie said. "Only a boot would get sucked in to the first bar he came to."

"What about hit man? He seems to know her."

"He doesn't know her from Eve. He's just being Bonano. Come on, Bonano, these guys are getting restless."

Bonano gave the girl's rear end a tweak and joined the others. The pavement was black and wet, as if it had just rained; the air smelled of something foreign, exotic, like a mixture of gunpowder and raw fish. There were no sidewalks in the alley; doors to the bars opened up right on the street. If one were to have enough to drink in one of them he would risk being run down by one of the many vehicles that were careening through the alley in both directions, heedless of pedestrians. Electrified paper lanterns strung between the buildings flanking the alley hung from above, their multi-colored hues reflecting off the wet pavement.

"USS *Columbus*! Come Texas Bar. Show you good time, best in Yokosuka," and so forth.

"How come so many of the bars are named after southern states?" Van Thompson wondered aloud.

"You ever hear of the Crossroads Bar?" Jack asked Frenchie.

"The Crossroads? Sure. Nothing but spades hang out there, spades who think they're cool. The girls aren't bad but they prefer chocolate to vanilla. Where'd you hear about the Crossroads?"

"Layton."

"Layton. Talk about spades who think they're cool."

Jack didn't say so, but he did think that Layton, a second-class storekeeper, was cool. He had introduced Jack to the music of Lambert, Hendricks, and Ross, and Ahmed Jamal. Everything about Layton was cool: the way he talked, the way he walked, even the way he moved papers around on his desk in the supply office where they both worked, was cool.

Van Thompson asked Bonano, who was a self-proclaimed expert on Yokosuka, if not the underworld culture of all of Southeast Asia, why it was called black market alley. Jack had noticed the conspicuous absence of moneychangers on the street, so different from other ports he had visited on the cruise so far, like Keelung, and Subic Bay, where the hustlers swarmed you the minute you set foot ashore.

"You should have heard Mr. Peepers last night," Frenchie said. Because Harvey Goulet looked like Wally Cox, the actor, guys in the division called him "Mr. Peepers." Harvey didn't appreciate the nickname, but his displeasure didn't stop the men from calling him it to his face. Jack had talked to Goulet a few times down in the after storeroom that he ran by himself, and treated like a fiefdom. He had been struck by how simple and guileless, yet sweet, the guy was.

"I asked him," Frenchie continued, "Peepers, you going to change your money legal or on the black market? So Peepers says, get this, 'You don't have to go to the black market. There are people right on the street who will change it for you.'"

Bonano offered them another "Peeperism." "If you had half a brain you'd dance on it." Jack felt something tug at the sleeve of his jumper. He turned to find a petite Japanese girl in a tight fitting peach colored chiffon dress, flashing a gold-toothed smile at him.

"Hey, good-looking sailor. Come in Rose Bar, buy me drink. You won't be sorry," the girl said. The others didn't notice that Jack had been intercepted, and proceeded down the alley. Jack removed her hand gently from his sleeve and tried to explain to the girl that he had to go with his friends, even if he was tempted to take her up on the offer. "Come on, cute sailor, buy Kimi-san drink. Won't be sorry."

"Scanlon, let's go," Thompson yelled.

"I'll come back later," Jack said to the girl, but she had already spotted another "cute sailor," and turned to him with her pitch. "I'm coming," he called back to Thompson.

Thompson asked Frenchie what he thought their chances of getting laid were tonight.

"Not with the bar girls unless you got an overnight. You can always go to a cathouse; there's no shortage of those in Yokosuka, but the bar girls want to take you home with them after the bar closes. It's not like in Okinawa. We got Cinderella liberty, so you can forget about banging the bar girls."

"What are Yokosula whorehouses like?" Thompson sounded as if he were asking about the real estate market.

"I don't frequent whorehouses," Frenchie said. "Remember, I'm a married man with two kids." At this he laughed. Everyone knew what a whoremonger he was. "Ask the hit man, you want to know about whorehouses."

Jack spotted the well-lighted sign of the Tennessee Bar on his right, a few feet in front of them. This was their preordained destination according to John Bonano. There were no girls stationed at the entrance, unusual enough from what he had seen of the bars in the alley so far, but the door was shut as well, which was unique in itself.

"Aha!" Bonano exclaimed, rubbing his hands together the way he did after he had finished off his chiliburger.

"How come the door's closed," Van Thompson asked. Jack had come to the conclusion, after knowing him these few weeks, that Van Thompson was not the world's keenest observer, so the fact that he had noticed the closed door of the Tennessee Bar as an anomaly was practically significant.

"The management has higher standards than the rest of these joints," Frenchie explained. "It's a classy place. Why do you think me and Bonano come here?" Jack let Frenchie's remark go by without comment. He glanced over at Thompson in time to see the grin on his face. Perhaps he had underestimated Thompson's sense of irony as well. Bonano pushed open the door to the bar. They walked, single file, into a narrow, dimly lighted room. A bar with perhaps a dozen stools was on the right; the left side consisted of several booths. A beaded curtain hung in the back of the room, behind which, Bonano had explained, was another small room with private booths for "special" customers. It was obvious to Jack from his tone that Bonano considered himself one of the special customers. Several B-girls sat on stools, their backs to the bar so that they could inspect the clientele. Sailors accompanied by bar girls occupied several booths.

An older Japanese woman, short, stocky, and wearing a Chinese dress slit up the sides, like the Hong Kong B-girls, came from behind the beaded curtain. Bonano pushed his white hat to the back of his head and opened his arms in greeting. It seemed to Jack that Bonano exaggerated his joy at seeing the old "mama-san" in order to impress his new companions, to demonstrate that he was "known" in exotic places like the Tennessee Bar. The mama-san put on a show of affection of her own that was at least as disingenuous as Bonano's. They embraced in the middle of the room and exchanged words while the rest of them stood around, eye flirting with the girls at the bar. The girl Jack had singled out to flirt with tried winking at him, but couldn't manage it with only one eye. If she hadn't been so cute she would have looked ridiculous. After the mama-san and Bonano finished with their contrived bonhomie, the woman, clinging to Bonano's arm as if he were her escort, approached the others. She gestured to the girls on their stools at the bar, matched them up and assigned them to booths. Jack and Thompson were paired with two girls, one of whom Jack had been flirting with and who couldn't master the art of the wink. The mama-san matched her with Thompson. Jack would have preferred her to the one he was "assigned." The mama-san seated them in a booth in the front section of the bar; Frenchie and Bonano she took behind the beaded curtain where the "private" booths were, with their companions.

Jack's girl sat close enough to him that their thighs were touching. "What your name, good-rooking?" Thompson giggled at the r-l inversion.

"Jack. What's your name, beautiful?" He shot Thompson a disapproving look for laughing at the girl.

"My name Connie." Connie smiled. Jack was not surprised to see a couple of gold-capped teeth in her smile. Thompson's companion called herself Mariko. Jack wondered idly why Connie should choose a Western name, while Mariko retained her native one. He considered asking her, Connie, but decided against it in case she might consider it rude of him to ask. "You buy me drink?" Bonano had checked the two bottles of whiskey he'd purchased at the EM club with the bartender, a little guy with a white short-sleeved shirt and red bow tie. Bonano explained that they were obliged to pay for setups only, as long as the whiskey held out.

"What are you drinking, doll?" Jack made a mental note to himself not to get carried away with condescension. Thompson was having a dialogue with Mariko. To Jack she seemed more animated, more vivacious than Connie, his girl. He began at once to scheme for a way to swap girls with Van Thompson.

Connie interrupted Mariko and Van's conversation, in Japanese. Mariko replied in kind. They talked back and forth, rapidly, and seemingly in earnest. In his brief experience with the denizens of Far East bars, Jack had become suspicious of their motives. They were no doubt conniving to get the maximum out of their "clients" while committing the minimum of their hostess charms.

"Hey, how about talking English," Thompson said, with a good-natured laugh, which caused Jack to squirm, nevertheless, as he considered the remark gauche, though not unexpected from the likes of Thompson.

"Be careful," Jack said, careful himself not to offend Thompson, "remember this is people-to-people." He winked at Van Thompson after invoking Eisenhower's foreign good-will policy that had been hammered into their heads by the officers since they left Long Beach. The girls giggled, hiding their mouths behind their hands.

"Sorry," Mariko said, her voice almost apologetic. She offered an impish grin, showing a few gold-capped teeth of her own. Jack saw her face in the dimly lighted bar from a new angle; she looked older than his Connie—maybe in her late twenties, even early thirties. To Jack, this was ancient. He looked sideways at Connie, surreptitiously. He thought he could discern where her makeup ended, or began, behind her ear. A mask, behind which who knew what lay?

The bartender delivered glasses of ice for Jack and Van Thompson, accompanied by two shot glasses of whiskey. The girls were served two glasses of a foamy pinkish concoction. No one had given the bartender drink orders.

"What's that stuff?" Thompson asked of the girls' drinks.

"Sloe-gin fizz," Mariko replied.

"Is there any alcohol in it?" Thompson wanted to know, having been in enough Far East ports to have learned that bar girls were seldom served alcoholic drinks.

"Of course." Connie drawled the words out. "We get stinko just like sailor." Both Mariko and Connie got a kick out of this and laughed like little children.

The four of them sipped their drinks and exchanged banalities for a while. Then the girls excused themselves to go to the "binjo," which was the Japanese name for the powder room.

"I can't see spending the whole day here," Jack said. "There must be livelier places than this in Yokosuka. The music is just like the shit they play all night aboard ship." Indeed, the music coming from the Tennessee Bar's speakers was a Johnny Cash tune, the artist of choice of the USS *Columbus*'s on-board radio station. "How high's the water, ma. Three-feet high and rising," crooned the man in black. "I don't know how much of that shit I can take," Jack said. He was thinking of the Crossroads Bar where, according to Layton, jazz was played exclusively. He mentioned the Crossroads to Thompson.

"You heard Frenchie. There's nothing but spades hang out there. Probably waiting for white boys like us so they can cut our throats with their razoos."

"Don't be ridiculous. So let's try someplace else, you're afraid of colored people. This place is nowhere."

"What about our bottle?"

"What about it? We can come back. And it's not likely Frenchie and Bonano are going anywhere. They can look after it. Come on; let's get out of here. We're not going to get laid, so what's the point?"

"What about the girls?"

"What about them?"

"We don't want to hurt their feelings, do we?"

"Thompson, tell me you're joking."

"No shit. What'll they think?"

"Who cares what they think? Thompson ..." The girls returned, asking for fresh drinks.

"We have to go out for a while," Jack said.

"Will you wait for us to get back?" Thompson asked, like a naïf.

"I doe know ..." Connie started to say, which Jack interpreted as "Time is money, sailor. We should wait for you clowns if two new suckers come through the door?"

"We won't be long," Thompson added.

"Okey dokey. We wait half-hour," Mariko said, making eye contact with Connie.

"Half-hour," Connie said, with a hint of ultimatum in her tone.

"Great. Let's go, Thompson."

Outside, a banzai cab driver almost ran down Thompson. "Holy shit!"

"Why don't you go back inside, Thompson. I know you don't want to leave."

"What are you going to do, Scanlon? You don't know this place any better than I do. Why not come back inside with me?"

"I'm going to catch a cab and try to find the Crossroads. I need to hear some civilized music."

"You don't want to hang out with a lot of niggers, do you?"

"I don't mind colored people." Jack didn't like the phrase "colored people" much more than he liked hearing "nigger." He even hesitated to call the race Negro. He recalled that even Charlotte Toney had referred to herself as colored. What his problem was he couldn't say. He knew that he didn't want to go back inside the Tennessee Bar— not right away. He talked Thompson into going back in the bar by himself; he hailed a cab and asked the driver to take him to the Crossroads Bar.

The inside of the Crossroads Bar was as dimly lit as the Tennessee Bar, and made to seem even darker by the dusky complexions of the clientele. His first impulse was to do an about-face and return to Connie, Mariko, and Thompson at the Tennessee Bar. He was on the verge of doing just that when he heard his name called.

"Scanlon! Hey, slick, where you think you goin'?" He turned around to look for the speaker. He saw an arm raised at a booth at the back of the room. Attached to the arm was Layton, dressed in civvies and sitting with three other Negroes, none of whom Jack recognized.

They were all dressed, like Layton, in civilian clothes. The throb of a heavy bass line filled the room, followed by the sound of a vibraphone that Jack recognized as belonging to Milt Jackson (Bags as he was known among jazz musicians and their aficionados). Jack walked cautiously to where Layton was seated with his three companions.

"What do you say, Layton?" The men with Layton were unsmiling; Jack would have described them as hostile if anyone were to ask.

"This my man Scanlon. He cool," Layton said to the men seated in the booth with him. Jack thought he saw their expressions change, to soften a little.

"I know it's the MJQ, but I don't recognize the number," Jack said.

"Ooee," Layton exclaimed, stamping his feet on the floor and bobbing his head. "What I tell you? He cool, or what?"

Jack had never heard Layton carry on like that in the supply office. On board ship his manner of speech was always pointedly refined, a studied, almost pedantic way of speaking.

"Sit down, Scanlon. Let me buy you a drink. Slide over, Benjamin," Layton said to the man beside him who looked up at Scanlon with his watery eyes. He did as he was told, but Scanlon had the strong sense that he was not pleased to yield his seat to this "white boy." Several bar girls were sitting together in a booth near the front door. The handful of men in the bar were unaccompanied by bar girls. Frenchie had said that Crossroads girls preferred "chocolate" to "vanilla." Layton ordered a whiskey for Jack from his own bottle, and explained that what they were hearing was a cut from a new MJQ album called *Fontessa*.

"It's haunting," Jack said.

"Haunting?" the guy across the table from Scanlon said, his mouth twitching.

"You guys from the *Columbus*?" Jack said, quickly.

"These dudes be in S-4 division," Layton said to fill the void left by Jack's question. "They keep house for the Man." Now, Jack thought he recognized the guy Layton had called Benjamin, but he looked different in civilian clothes than he did in his white steward's jacket. Steward's Mates were either Negro or Filipino, at least on the USS *Columbus*. Layton may have meant it to sound ironic, meant it to express contempt for the "Man," to say that they kept house for him, but it came off as demeaning, to Scanlon's ear. Layton was proud, which inspired some men in the division, men such as Frenchie, to characterize him as uppity, the "NIC," nigger-in-charge. Frenchie was nice to the point of obsequious to their faces. As soon as they turned their back on him he'd mock them by pulling his white-hat down tight over his head (the way the Negro sailors liked to wear them) and insert his tongue under his lower lip to simulate "nigger lips." Even Kyle Stoddard, Jack's former best friend, made no secret about his views on race and ethnicity; he hated Jews with as much gusto as he despised Negroes, or "niggeroids," as he liked to call them. Jack began to feel uneasy in the company of

Layton and his friends. He may have imagined it, but it seemed to him that conversation in the bar had become subdued since his arrival.

Benjamin quaffed the last of his drink and announced he was leaving.

"Goin' to the Black Orchid. Get me some laig." Layton and the other guy responded with deep-throated chuckles. Jack had heard enough Negro talk to know what Benjamin meant by "leg." It had taken him a little longer to realize that "cock" meant the same thing in their argot. Layton slapped palms with Benjamin, shared "skin" with the man before he slid out of the booth and went on his way. Layton's other friends soon followed suit, and Jack found himself alone in the booth with him.

"I hope your friends aren't leaving on my account?"

"No, no. They're not big jazz fans like you and me. They're anxious to see their regular chicks over at the Black Orchid, and see to their homeboys. It's not you."

"That's really fine stuff," Jack observed of the MJQ's music.

"You can tell these cats had classical training." Two bar girls appeared at their table, seemingly from thin air. Jack had not been aware of their approach.

"Jim-san," one of them said to Layton, "buy me drink, you stingy man, before you get too stinko." The other girl giggled and made eyes at Jack, despite his being "vanilla."

"Now move your pretty little *derriere* to the bar, Tommiko. My man and me got serious things to talk about. I'll call for you when I'm ready."

Jack knew that Layton had a wife and two kids stateside. So did Frenchie. There weren't many, if any, of the married guys in his division who were constant. He'd heard plenty of stories, too, about the antics of Navy wives while their men were away on a long cruise. He couldn't understand why they bothered to get married. He couldn't even imagine himself in such a predicament, either as a sailor or civilian.

Tommiko took her girlfriend by the hand, and they retreated to the bar. The girl with Tommiko smiled at Jack over her shoulder.

"Too bad you don't have overnight privileges, Scanlon. You'd enjoy that one's company." Layton referred to the girl with Tommiko. He had no doubt sampled more than one of the Crossroads girls.

"It's the best incentive I can think of to make third-class in December."

"You got that right." Layton chuckled in his guttural, Negroid way. The girl with Tommiko waved at their table from the bar, her fingers pointing to herself as though beckoning to him to join her. "So what are you doing on the beach by yourself? I thought you were steaming with Thompson."

"I did. Then we got tangled up with Frenchie and Bonano, and they sort of dragged us into this bar where the music is … well, like what you hear on the ship's radio. Thompson fell in love, and I had my fill of Johnny Cash, so …"

"I hear you. Nakamura," Layton yelled to the bartender, "put on that Art Pepper album when this one's finished. Arigato."

Jack told Layton about seeing Miles Davis and John Coltrane in Boston in '56.

"He had Red Garland with him, right?"

"Yeah. He actually took time to talk to my friends and me. We were the only customers in the house for a Sunday matinee. Miles couldn't have cared if the house was empty, and for all the attention he paid to us it could have been ... empty. Shit, he even turned his back on the audience, and stuck his fingers in his ears when Trane was soloing." Layton's head was bobbing up and down as Jack spoke, and he smiled knowingly.

"That's Miles all right. All whites are motherfuckers to Miles."

"Coltrane was in his own world, wrapped up in whatever music was playing inside his head. I got the feeling your friends, Benjamin and those guys, were of the same opinion as Miles where white people are concerned."

"Comes from waiting on the Man. They're good dudes at heart."

Two Negroes in civilian clothes came in the bar. They looked familiar; they approached the booth he shared with Layton.

"What's happenin', home?" Layton said to the one dressed in a well-tailored Italian silk suit, probably purchased in Hong Kong. "You lookin' clean today, home." The guy's companion was also dressed in a suit, although not as stylish, or as well cut as Layton's "homeboy." Jack might have been invisible for all the attention the two of them paid him.

"Gimme your loose yens, Layton. I catch you back the ship." Now Jack recognized him as a second-class stew-burner from S-2 division who hung out with Layton sometimes. He studied the other guy who had nothing to say, but who was busy looking over the girls in the front booth. Layton reached in his jacket pocket and tossed some coins and a 100-yen note on the table.

"That's all I got on me, home. You best get yo ass to the slush you out of bread already."

"I ain't goin' fo' no ten foeteen."

Forty percent interest, pay day to pay day, was the best deal one could get at any of the ship's slush funds, and there was no shortage of Shylocks on the USS *Columbus*. The last strains of "Willow Weep For Me" melted away and were seamlessly replaced by Art Pepper's alto saxophone virtuosity.

"This my man Scanlon," Layton said to the two of them by way of an introduction, one which they failed to acknowledge with as much as a glance or a nod in Jack's direction. "You know Keeble," Layton said of the Italian silk suit guy, "and that ape be Grady."

Keeble deftly swept the money Layton had left on the table into his big pink-palmed hand and deposited in his trousers pocket.

"We be goin' round the Black Orchid, drink some Akadama wine.

Come on over ... after you finish wiff yo man."

"Later, home."

"I recognize Keeble but I don't think I've ever seen the other one, what's-his-name, Grady?"

"First division deck ape. They all look alike." Layton raised his glass delicately to his lips, pinky out. Jack assumed Layton was trying for irony by declaring that all deck apes, like the white man's conception of blacks, looked alike. "Would you like me to arrange some female companionship for you? I've got to get over to the EM club and change some money." Layton finished his drink and prepared to leave.

"I'd better get back to Thompson before he gets led astray." The truth was he had no desire to be left "unescorted" in the Crossroads. He left the bar with Layton who showed him how to get back to the Tennessee Bar on foot.

Jack had apparently exceeded his half-hour grace period because Connie was in a booth by the front door snuggled up to a beefy second-class gunner's mate. She glanced at him with a coy smile when he came in. Jack was relieved to see her with another customer; he had designs on Mariko, Thompson's girl. They were together in the same booth; Thompson was stretched out, with his shoeless feet on the seat across from where he sat, Mariko cradled in his arm, a sloe gin fizz on the table in front of her. Thompson was feeling no pain. His baby face was flushed, his pale eyes behind his spectacles glassy.

"It's about time," he said. "I thought maybe them spearchuckers had did you in."

"I'm still in one piece."

"Hello, Scanlon," Mariko said, "Connie no can wait ..."

"I understand." The sailor in the booth behind them was singing along to the Johnny Cash tune blaring from the speakers. "I keep a close watch on this heart of mine," the guy wailed.

"Better to keep a close watch on your wallet, sailor," Jack said, but not loud enough that the crooner could hear him. Johnny Cash fans were quick to anger and more likely than jazz music enthusiasts to translate that anger into punches. "The joint's jumping," he observed. He turned to look over the house and saw that every booth was occupied, and there were no girls left unattended at the bar.

Bonano came through the beaded curtain from the back room, an empty glass in his hand. He went to the bar and had words with the little man in the red bow tie. He stopped at their booth with his refill.

"Where'd you disappear to?" he asked Jack.

"Didn't you tell him?" Jack said to Thompson.

"I told him," Thompson said into Mariko's neck.

"I didn't believe him. You didn't go hangin' around with them niggers on purpose. Say it ain't so."

"It ain't so. I told Layton I'd stop in on him. He was with a couple of his buddies, stewards and stew-burners. We had a drink, listened to some *good* music. I don't think I got anything on me." Jack pretended to inspect his hands and his uniform. Bonano pushed into the booth beside Mariko who sat on the outside.

"Hello, doll. You treatin' my friend good?" Bonano's hand disappeared beneath the table.

"You better believe it," Mariko replied with a gold-toothed smile. Bonano's hairy hand reappeared above the table guided by Mariko's delicate one. She let his heavy hand fall on the tabletop.

"How are you guys doing?" Jack asked Bonano.

"I'm all set with Shafumi for tonight. Frenchie's talking cathouse. He's on his ass and hornier than a bear." Frenchie had a reputation for not having a great capacity for alcohol.

"He'd better watch his step if he wants his crow back. He can't afford another trip to sick bay," Jack said. Bonano agreed. When Frenchie got drinking, all his brains flowed to the head of his dick, Bonano observed.

"He's over twenty-one." Bonano added that he had better things to do than play brother's keeper today. "Anyway, Conklin will look after him on the QT, he gets another dose." Conklin was the third-class corpsman who had turned Jack on to Ben Hecht, and was known to treat clap cases on the sly if the victim was a friend of his, or was in danger of losing a pay grade. Bonano left to rejoin his Shafumi and Frenchie in the back room. Thompson got up to go to the head, leaving Jack alone with Mariko.

"I talk Connie," Mariko said, "maybe get her come back see you."

"Don't bother. I'd rather see you."

"Oh." Mariko narrowed her eyes mischievously. "Butterfly boy."

"That's me, a regular Monarch." Mariko looked puzzled. "A kind of butterfly. What if I came tomorrow by myself? Could I persuade you to let me buy you a drink?" Jack knew that Thompson had the duty tomorrow, clearing the way for him with Mariko.

"Tomorrow day off."

"Can I meet you somewhere?" He assumed there were no real "days off" for girls in her business, and that she might even jump at the chance to "freelance."

"What time you liberty?"

"Thirteen hundred."

"Okay. I meet you main gate. You take me EM club?"

"Sure." Thompson was back. Jack felt a little twinge of guilt (but only a little one) for getting slick with this girl behind his back. Then he realized the absurdity of the deception and laughed out loud.

"What's funny, Scanlon?"

"What isn't funny?" Thompson turned to Mariko and rested his head on her shoulder.

"He's always saying off-the-wall shit like that," he said into Mariko's neck.

***

Mariko, wearing a clinging beige knit outfit that revealed her bowlegs more prominently than the ball gown she wore on the job, was waiting for him outside the main gate just as she said she would. He was struck by how tiny she looked out there on the street compared to the confines of the dark bar.

"You're a little squirt, aren't you," he said, with a short laugh.

"Small girl, big heart," Mariko replied in her scratchy voice and a bright-eyed smile. "We go EM club?"

"Sure, if that's what you want." Jack remembered what he had read in Ben Hecht's book about small women having large vaginas.

"You buy me carton cigarettes?" She had trouble with the pronunciation of "Pall Mall," but Jack knew what she meant. "Japanese cigarette no good." He'd choked on one Bonano had given him on the ship so he knew what Mariko was talking about.

"How about something to eat? I hear they have great steaks in the downstairs restaurant." To his surprise, Mariko was not interested in steaks, or any other form of American food. Cigarettes and a few cosmetics were the things she was interested in. When he offered to at least buy her some drinks she declined again, claiming to have given up drinking alcohol.

"What about those sloe-gins you were tossing back with Thompson?"

"No alcohol. Mama-san don't like girls get stinko." She slipped her small hand unselfconsciously into Jack's and led him across the busy street to the EM club side. They walked along the sidewalk, crowded with pedestrians in a hurry, mostly natives, with a sprinkling of G.I.s, many of whom were stationed at Yokosuka's big naval base, the rest off the ships tied up at pier one, the carrier *Coral Sea,* and Jack's ship, the USS *Columbus.*

After Jack had made the purchases Mariko requested at the EM club Navy Exchange, she led him by the hand up an alley and several flights of wooden steps to a cinder path that ran parallel to black market alley below them. The path followed railroad tracks, above which were, on a higher piece of ground, densely packed houses with low, sloping roofs. They eventually came to a railroad station platform.

"Train come soon," Mariko said.

"Train? Where are we going?"

"Go home. My house. What you want, nay?"

"Sure." While he had been shopping for Mariko at the EM club store, Jack had been busy thinking of a way to ask her to take him home with her. He had managed to talk Lt. Awalt into giving him a special overnight pass on the pretext of traveling to Tokyo for "cultural" broadening. He was somewhat disappointed that Mariko had made it so easy, had preempted his wooing skills. But he had only to look around him at the G.I.s in the EM club accompanied by bar girls to be reminded that this was a "professional" date, and there was no need for such courtship skills. It was just that Mariko didn't act like the stereotypical tart. Offering to take him home with her seemed like a perfectly natural, hospitable thing to do, no more than what she would be expected to do for a man who had spent good money on her for cigarettes and cosmetics. Or perhaps there would be a surcharge. It mattered not to Jack Scanlon whose ardor was on the rise even as he hurtled through space on the fast moving train, packed to standing room only with Japanese passengers. They got off at the fourth stop and walked a ways along a narrow street with houses packed closely together, all one-story dwellings; on the corners of the intersecting streets were small "saki" stores, or barber shops, or public baths, and telephone booths. He found himself mouth-breathing in defense against the powerful smell of raw sewage.

Mariko led him down one narrow street after another until he felt completely disoriented, the way he felt when trying to negotiate a corn maze back home. Finally she paused in front of a slatted wooden fence with a latched door. She pushed through the door to a passage wide enough to allow only one person at a time, between two dwellings. The muddy path was covered with wooden boards. She pulled open a sliding door to gain entrance to the living room of her house, sparsely furnished with an armchair and a tatami. Against the wall facing the sliding door was a religious temple, a kind of tabernacle of black lacquered wood, the kind he associated with Chinese restaurants back home. A large string of prayer beads, like a Catholic rosary, hung from the temple. Another sliding paper door separated the living and prayer room from the bedroom, beyond which, and separated by yet another sliding paper door, was a narrow space where was located Mariko's sink, with a single cold-water tap, and an icebox on top of which sat a single burner hot plate. Maybe two steps from the bed, a sliding door separated the toilet, or "binjo" as it was called in Japan, from the bedroom.

"I make you cup green tea," Mariko said, placing her bag of cigarettes and cosmetics at the foot of the low bed.

"Haven't you got anything to drink? Like beer or liquor, or what have you?"

"Sorry."

"Ah, yes. You don't drink. What about the little store on the corner?" Jack pointed over his shoulder. "I saw bottles of Asahi on display outside." He didn't mind Japanese beer if there was nothing else to drink. He would have bought a case of 3.2 beer at the EM club but was afraid of embarrassing himself in front of Mariko by not being able to prove he was twenty years old. He had told the girls in the Tennessee Bar the day before that he was twenty. It had become a habit with him to add a year to his age when girls asked.

"I go get you beer. How many you want? You sure no want green tea? Good."

"I'm not a fan of tea of any color. How about a couple of those big bottles of Asahi," Jack said, pulling some yen out of his breast pocket, a bad place to carry money, he'd been told, when walking around in Southeast Asian ports. Mariko took the money.

"I be right back. Make self comforble."

Scanlon eyed the big bed and glanced at Mariko with a grin. "By the way, I've got an overnight." He caressed Mariko's arm just before she left by the sliding kitchen door to run his beer errand.

Mariko turned out to be nimble in bed, if not as uninhibited as he would have expected, or wished for, of a girl in her profession; in fact, her behavior bordered on prudishness.

"No, Jack-san. Don't put hand there." Or, "Wait, I put out right (light)." Or "Don't go down there! Dirty!" Or "I no do that. Not that kind girl!"

"I guess that leaves us with the missionary posture," Jack said, somewhat exasperated at this girl's lack of sexual adventure.

"I not streetwalker," Mariko declared, taking pride in the fact that she was no common whore. She might have been described as puritanical, even by Jack Scanlon's New England standards.

"I'm sorry, Mariko. I didn't mean to suggest that you were," he said, lighting her cigarette in the darkened bedroom. Part of him was charmed by her old-fashioned, strait-laced attitude toward sex and carnality. It was as if she were not really a whore at all, but just a girl who had fallen for him. And so far she had asked for no remuneration, only the cigarettes and cosmetics, which had not set him back more than three dollars.

"You different kind guy, Jack-san. Not like most sailor."

"Thanks ... I guess."

"I mean as compremen." (Compliment).

"I'm teasing. Are you working tomorrow?"

"Yes. Have only one day off. Thompson come see me tomorrow. What you think that?"

"Now *you're* teasing. Ask Connie to entertain him."

"I thought Connie your girl." Mariko kept up the teasing. He had made it plain yesterday that he was not interested in Connie; otherwise he would not have been engaging in pillow talk with Mariko tonight. "Thompson like me. Say he gonna buy me takusan present."

"So if Thompson got an overnight and brought you a big present you'd take him home with you, like you did me?"

"You better believe it." Mariko slid down beside him and planted a hickey on his chest. "I working girl. Have to take care self."

"Why don't you find yourself a steady boyfriend, a sugar daddy? There must be plenty of base sailors—or jarheads—to choose from."

"I used to have chief. One, two year. But he old, and all time stinko. How old you say you are, Jack-san, twenty?"

"Yes."

"I twenty-nine. Too old for you."

"But I'm at the peak of my sexual potency. Doesn't that count for something?" Mariko neither understood his vocabulary nor his feeble attempt at wit. "Besides, I'll probably never see you again. We're not scheduled to come back to Yoko before we head back to the states."

"You got one more week. We can see each other. You get overnight again?"

"Not likely."

Mariko made herself fit more securely against his chest, a gesture that beguiled him, for the moment, into thinking she might actually regret the fact that she would never see him again. He tried to sneak his hand between her legs but Mariko was not having any of it.

"No put fingers there." She felt for his cock. "Little friend wakey." And he made love, in the conventional way again, to the little bow-legged prude whom he believed he would never see again after next week.

* * *

The next Thursday, their last day in port, Jack and Thompson rented bicycles with Mariko and Connie and pedaled to the northern outskirts of Yokosuka, along a seaside road. The girls had negotiated a special day off with the Tennessee Bar's mama-san so they could entertain the boys in what was to be their final day in Yokosuka. Since neither Jack nor Thompson could wangle an overnight, they could expect the day they spent with the girls would exclude sex, at least until nightfall (Mariko, for one, would never consent to sex in the daylight hours). Thompson had no knowledge of the night Jack had spent in Mariko's bed. The very next day, in fact, Jack and Thompson had gone directly to the Tennessee Bar where Thompson took up with Mariko where he had left off, and Connie rejoined Jack. Every chance they got, Mariko and Jack exchanged looks and "inside" giggles. Later, Jack marveled at how ludicrous this deception had been, given whom they were dealing with. But prostitutes or not, neither Connie nor Mariko had brought up the subject of payment for their companionship for the entire day and part of the night. And they had sacrificed some income as B-girls by obtaining the day off.

Connie had invited them all to her small rooms in a little house that faced the outer breakwater of Yokosuka harbor for green tea and Japanese sweets. It was, as Thompson remarked, "like being out on a regular date with some girls from school."

Thompson made a face after biting into a piece of soft candy with a gelatinous interior. The girls noticed. Connie frowned.

"You no like Japanese candy?"

"I don't much like any kind of candy," Thompson said, putting the uneaten candy aside. Jack knew this to be a lie as Thompson spent more money on gedunk candy than he spent on cigarettes. Japanese cuisine of any kind was repulsive to Jack's parochial tastes, no less than it was to Thompson. Not daring to refuse the candy for fear of offending Connie, Jack swallowed it, and washed it down with large quantities of green tea, which, to his surprise, he found agreeable.

In Keelung, Jack had been the guest of some Chinese Nationalist Army officers in charge of entertaining their American naval guests, at an eighteen course Chinese dinner that included bird's nest, shark's fin, and tomatoes stuffed with fish eyes among other equally abominable (in Jack's eyes) dishes. Jack had forced that food down his throat with rice wine, not green tea. Rice wine had the advantage of giving him a pleasant buzz, which was more than he could claim for the tea. After a while, sitting cross-legged on a tatami in Connie's cramped room, Jack began to crave a drink.

"You got anything to drink besides tea?"

"No. You want to go bar? One not far from here down road," Connie said. In the light of day, Jack could not help noticing that Connie's broad face was also quite coarse, especially without the benefit of makeup. Mariko, on the other hand, despite the fact that she was an ancient twenty-nine years old, had clear skin, and even with those bow legs, a better figure than her friend who was a trifle thick in the hips.

They biked about a mile down the road to a bar named The Carousel. It was far enough from downtown Yokosuka that Jack wasn't surprised to see that no sailors or Marines were inside. And no B-girls. There was a long bar with a large mirror occupying the entire wall behind it. There were a few tables scattered randomly around the room; no booths. Why The Carousel? Jack wondered. The four of them took seats at a table and Connie called out drink orders to the two bartenders, and went to the bar herself to fetch them, like a waitress. There were a handful of Japanese men seated at the bar, who turned on their stools to stare at them. Suddenly the sound of a piano filled the room.

"Hey, that's Erroll Garner," Jack said. He told Thompson how he had beat it out of a four-hour barracks watch when he was stationed at Newport just to see Erroll Garner in concert on the base.

"You get away with it?"

"Yeah. Got back just in time to play taps. Nobody was the wiser."

"You play bugle?"

"No. We had a recording. I'm no Robert E. Lee Prewitt." Thompson didn't understand the allusion to *From Here to Eternity* and wasn't curious enough to ask.

"You could have got a summary for that stunt."

"I know. It was worth it. Listen to that guy! The "elf," they call him."

Thompson was hard-core country and western in his musical tastes, and Erroll Garner's piano wizardry didn't impress him. Jazz gave Thompson a headache the way country-western set Jack's head athrob.

The girls were unimpressed as well. Jack was slightly annoyed that he had no one with whom to share his appreciation of the music. Under the table Mariko was working her toes up Jack's pant leg. He sat across the table from her; otherwise he would have endeavored to get his hand up her skirt. But then he remembered how she didn't like people's fingers in her "business."

The girls ordered Chinese dumplings and ate them noisily and voraciously, as if they had just come off a hunger strike. Jack found the eating habits of Asians disgusting; the way they shoveled chow in their maws as if every meal would be their last.

Connie tried to interest Jack in a dumpling. He used late chow on board ship before coming ashore as an excuse to refuse. The girls couldn't understand why one should refuse food just because one had eaten recently. Get all you can whenever you can was their way of looking at it. Mariko had no success with Thompson either. Thompson was honest (or obtuse) enough not to use the same excuse as Jack, but went on record with his aversion to Japanese cuisine.

"Dumpling not Japanese," Mariko explained. "Chinese. Very good and tasty." Thompson reminded her that she had no use for American food, so they were even on that score. Jack had a moment of panic at Thompson's knowledge of Mariko's distaste for American food. How would he have known this unless Mariko had informed him of her date with Jack? Yet Thompson showed no sign of knowing anything about the day and night he had spent with his "girl." They didn't push the Chinese dumplings too hard, no doubt familiar with the parochial tastes of American sailors.

"I know sailor who like squid, octopus and all Japanese food," Connie declared, almost defiantly. She had tried to get him to try a piece of dried octopus in the Tennessee Bar when he was oiled enough to throw caution to the wind and try the stuff. It looked harmless enough, in his inebriated state. The vile taste remained in his mouth all night, refusing to be washed away with whiskey and beer.

"No wonder their breath smells like they been eating dead animals," Thompson had observed.

Jack found himself preoccupied with discovering a way he could bring off a switch with Thompson so he could end up with Mariko at her house for a farewell soiree. The exec had declared a moratorium on overnights for all hands on the ship's last night in port not wanting any of the men to miss movement, as they were getting underway at 0800 the next morning. Jack doubted that he would have been able to get one anyway. He had only until midnight to arrange an assignation with Mariko. The clock behind the bar said three-fifteen. Mariko's footwork under his pant leg he interpreted as a signal for him to get busy. He wracked his brain to no avail, and it was Mariko, finally, who took action. She began to jabber to Connie in Japanese. Jack and Thompson exchanged desultory conversation until Connie announced that she had to catch a train to Nagoya to visit her ailing mother. Thompson asked her why she hadn't said something about having to do this before. Connie resumed chattering to Mariko in Japanese, sidestepping Thompson's question. Then she told them that Mariko had agreed to accompany her on the train. Mariko, who was incapable of the one-eyed wink, gave a surreptitious one to Jack when Thompson's head was turned.

"What time you got to catch this train?" Thompson asked. He sounded dubious.

"Six clock," Connie said. Thompson whispered something in Mariko's ear that Jack guessed was a request to take him home with her so that he could do what Jack intended to do with her ... again. Connie's part in the deception surprised him. He had begun to think she was fond of him, and therefore might even be a little jealous, or at least unwilling to give him up to her friend. And she wasn't even getting Thompson in the bargain. As for Thompson, it was left up to Jack to invent a way to ditch his buddy.

"Why don't you come with me to the Crossroads," he suggested to Thompson, knowing that Thompson would rather go back to the ship early than go there.

"What? To sit around with a bunch of niggers? You out of your fucking head?"

"Come on, the blues won't hurt you."

"I ain't afraid of them. I just don't want to drink in a bar full of spades. Why don't we go to the EM club? Why do you have to go now if you're train don't leave till six?" he asked Connie.

"Got to pack and get ready," she said without hesitating.

"I say we go to the Tennessee Bar," Thompson said. "I still got a little left in my fifth. What do you say, Scanlon?"

"You no butterfly with Tennessee Bar girl," Mariko said, snuggling up to Thompson. "I jealous."

"I think I'm going to the Crossroads. I'd like to hear some decent music."

"Well, you'll have to go by yourself. When you're done there you can find me in the downstairs bar of the EM club."

Mariko had slipped him a piece of paper on which she had written her address in Japanese for him to give to a cab driver. He would never have been able to find her place again on his own.

* * *

Thompson was playing solitaire in the supply office when Jack got back to the ship, just before midnight.

"I waited for you for two hours. I ran into Frenchie and Bonano. We went to the Tennessee Bar. They asked the mama-san about Connie's mother in, where was it, Nagoya? She told them Connie's mother been dead since before the end of the Korean War. What the fuck was she up to?"

Thompson was agitated, slapping his cards down hard on the desktop.

"I guess she was trying to ditch me," Jack said, sitting at his desk, with his back to Thompson. "She always gave me the impression she'd rather be with anyone but me."

"Hmm. But why would Mariko go along with her?"

"I don't know, Thompson. How the fuck would I know? Why don't you write to her and ask?"

"Yeah, sure. Layton just left. He told me he been in the Crossroads all night and didn't see you."

From the moment he stepped through the door into the supply office, Jack had felt his lies closing in on him. He was a perjured witness in a court of law with Thompson, the prosecuting attorney, homing in on him. "I chickened out. If I'd known Layton was there ... I didn't want to ..."

"Sure."

He was reasonably certain Thompson couldn't have figured out that he had spent the evening in Mariko's bed, but all the hurt feelings and resentment he was expressing at his apparent perfidy made Jack feel awful, like he had betrayed his best friend. He felt compelled to lie some more, even if Thompson was by no means his "best friend."

"Layton had put me on to this other joint that played jazz. It doesn't cater exclusively to Negroes."

"Yeah. What's the name of this place?"

"Shit, I can't remember the name of it. Why don't you ask Layton tomorrow." Jack counted on Thompson not calling his bluff with Layton.

"It don't make a fuck to me."

"I'm sorry, Thompson, I ..."

"What you got to be sorry about?" Thompson gathered up his playing cards and said he was hitting the rack. He left Jack in the office without saying another word. The ship's next port of call was Subic Bay, in the Philippines. Thompson didn't seek him out when it was time to go on liberty.

* * *

All of Scanlon's colleagues at the School who had served in WWII had retired. That left him as the only member of the faculty at present who had served in the military. He had kept up the story of his Vietnam experience here as he had done at Fairfield High School in Vermont when he taught there in 1968-69. Four days in Saigon did not a Vietnam veteran make, any more now than it did in the '60s. Nowadays nobody even seemed interested that he had done a stint in the U. S. Navy. No draft, no interest in military service for the kind of students he dealt with; most of them anyway. Some kids he had taught or advised had joined after college; a few had even seen action in Desert Storm. He could count them on the fingers of one hand.

It was on the return voyage to Long Beach in February of 1959 that the personnel office put out a memo seeking volunteers to serve aboard the Seventh Fleet flagship, a heavy cruiser like the *Columbus*, that was due to deploy from Long Beach in April, and would be homeported in Yokosuka indefinitely. What better way to spend the last two and a half years of his hitch, Jack told himself, thinking of Mariko and that last night of passion in her low bed.

Twenty-Two

Scanlon decided to put an end to his worry over self-injection, and instead to seek ways to avoid being bored stiff for the hour or so that remained of his transfusion. He had asked Karla if anyone had called, or stopped by to see him. The only call he had received was the one from Judith, and Mo Weber had been his only visitor, and that was hours ago. Now he felt he may have been hasty in turning Weber away. He felt, all at once, overtaken by loneliness, out of touch with humanity. Whom would he wish to see? Lately, even the kids, who had over the years the power to buoy his spirits, who had been his first and last lines of defense against what he considered his boorish colleagues, failed to lift him up. He could not think of one student now who he would be glad to see. And the only one of his colleagues of the past ten years who could cheer him up had retired two years ago. Then Dr. Dunham's words came back to him:

"You're no more terminal than the rest of us." How could he be so sure? If he knew something, something medically relevant about Scanlon's condition, shouldn't he have shared that information? He couldn't even remember to inform his patient of the day, or days, of his GI tract examinations. Wasn't it professors who were supposed to be absentminded, not physicians? A few hours ago he had convinced himself that he had colon cancer. As odious as the subject was, Scanlon resolved to research it on the Internet if he was ever so lucky as to find himself disentangled from these tubes and needles. Why wasn't he screaming? Why didn't the mere thought of the Oblivion, of Nothingness, cause him to sweat and hyperventilate? Once, when he served on the School's admissions committee, he had read the application of a fourteen-year-old girl that had affected him profoundly. In her personal essay she solemnly vowed never to take life for granted, never to reach the state that she saw manifest in her parents, and other adults of her parents' generation, who went through life—watching television, working their jobs like automatons—as if they expected to live forever. He had been stunned upon reading such sentiments, especially from someone so young. He saw the essential truth in it, too. He realized that he had gone through most of his life with that very attitude. There was that five years of misery, when he was married to Katie; at the time he was *sure* he would live forever—to do penance, penance for what he knew not.

He hadn't given Katie Durand much thought in the last twenty years, and the last time he heard from his daughter Lucy was when she sent him a generic announcement of her marriage to some man with a Greek name, in Oregon. He had not laid eyes on his daughter since his wife spirited her away, out of his life, New Year's Day 1968. Lucy was a

Gemini, like her father. God help her! An old ache in his chest returned, like the ache he used to have chronically those first few years of his estrangement from his daughter. What if he were to die without ever seeing her again? As far as Lucy was concerned, he was as good as dead now. For that he had Katie Durand to thank.

* * *

Late August 1961:

Jack Scanlon, feeling the ravages of all night drinking in Tijuana with his pal George Stacy, crumpled up and tossed in the wastebasket the third sheet of paper in his attempt to write a letter of explanation to Mariko. How could he make her understand why he had not come to say goodbye his last night in Yokosuka? He didn't know, himself. Instead of seeing her, he had made the rounds of as many bars as he could in black market alley, something he had not done in the two years he had been Mariko's steady boyfriend. Mariko had been patient but persistent in her determination to break down his will, to get him to marry her and take her back to the states; it was the cherished wish of many if not all Yokosuka's B-girls. He had never really been tempted, had never been able to conceptualize returning home with a Japanese "war bride." Neither did he have the courage to say a final farewell to the girl. So he had crawled the bars in the alley, wretchedly unhappy, not because he was going home, but because he was naturally averse to change. Now, he couldn't find the words to convey these feelings.

He picked up George Stacy's copy of Boswell's *Life of Johnson*, which George was using in one of his classes at San Diego State, and was on this line from Dr. Johnson to his biographer: "If you have been prudent, do not now be rash," when Katie Durand, one of George Stacy's sister's high school chums, was in the room. Jack was alone in the Stacys' house—George had a morning class, both his parents were at work, and Sylvia was no doubt out somewhere on the boulevard with her friends. What puzzled Jack was why Katie Durand was not with her; they were so thick, so inseparable.

"Sylvia went out about an hour ago," Jack said, averting his eyes so as not to appear to be gawking at the scantily clad Katie Durand, dressed in the shortest of shorts and a halter-top that revealed the tops of her freckled breasts.

"I know," she said, circling the love seat where Jack, dressed in polished chinos and T-shirt, reclined. He let Boswell's ample volume rest open on his lap. Katie Durand traced her finger along the back of the love seat. On her second revolution, Scanlon pulled her down onto his lap. Boswell fell to the floor with a thunk. Katie wriggled out of those tight fitting shorts, while Scanlon went to work on her top, which was not work at all. It was over in no time, really, and then Katie Durand was squirming off his lap and prancing to the bathroom, those meager short shorts, and panties in her hand.

"Gotta go," she said, planting a sisterly kiss on the top of his head before disappearing out the kitchen door.

Jack said nothing to his friend George Stacy about his morning encounter with Katie Durand. George would not approve of his fooling around with his kid sister's friends; it would be, in George's mind, tantamount to seducing his little sister. It wasn't likely that George would believe that it was Katie Durand who had done the seducing, with her sexy outfit and blue eye shadow. Besides, Jack was due to fly home to New Hampshire in the morning. Nothing would be gained by upsetting his friend with news like that.

At 9:37 A.M. the next morning, his mind full of Katie Durand's pliant little body (along with the ominous sounding words STATUTORY RAPE), Jack boarded a plane for Boston. From there he would take a train home to Garrison, New Hampshire, from where he had been absent for better than two and a half years.

* * *

Jack's family had moved to the second story of a double-decker on the north end of Center Street, since he had been away in the Far East. He had not revealed to his mother exactly when she could expect him home, leaving open the possibility that some interesting opportunity might present itself during his brief stay in California.

He was not surprised to find the door unlocked, and nobody home. No one locked their door in Garrison. He unshouldered his sea bag on the threadbare carpet (a carpet he was unfamiliar with) covering the living room floor, and tentatively explored the apartment. Not much exploration was required in the four rooms—two bedrooms, the living room and kitchen—which were only slightly more commodious than the ones he'd lived in with his family on Fern Street.

He returned to the living room and sat down on Bill Scanlon's "get well" sofa, and lit a cigarette. Was his stepfather on a bender? The last letter he had received from his mother said that his stepfather had been laid off from his latest job; Jack could not remember where his mother had said that was. In the time Jack had been away, Bill Scanlon had held and lost more jobs than most men have in a lifetime. He heard footsteps on the stairs; the door leading into the living room opened, and his half-brother Billy was suddenly framed in the doorway. His mouth fell open when he saw Jack. Then he smiled his familiar smile, and Jack's heart took an extra beat. His chest filled with something. Love?

"Holy shit! It's you!"

Jack rose from the sofa and embraced his half-brother. "You've shot up. How the hell are you, Billy?"

"Good. Ma never said when you were coming home."

"She didn't know. Let me have a look at you." Jack stepped back to size up this kid he hadn't laid eyes on for so long. He had been barely twelve years old when Jack left, Keith not quite eleven. "How tall are you now?"

"Almost as tall as you," Billy said, standing beside Jack, grinning at him sideways. Then he eyed Jack's sea bag, no doubt wondering what exotic gift his world-traveler half-brother had brought back for him. Jack had brought no gifts home with him, for anyone. It was not in his nature to buy gifts for people, especially not his family.

"Ma tells me you're the king of the jitterbug. You've won dance contests and shit like that?"

"Want to see my trophies?"

Trophies for dancing! Billy, who had always been the object of his family's ridicule for his flawless clumsiness; who his own mother had accused of being so badly coordinated that he couldn't negotiate the floral patterns on the kitchen linoleum. How he had shown them all; Jack was immensely pleased.

"Sure. Later. So, where is everybody?" Jack sat back down on the sofa. Disappointment flickered in Billy's eyes. He wanted to show his big brother his trophies, *now*.

"Keith's at early practice. He's out for freshman football. Ma's working, and the old man's ... who knows?"

"He's not working?"

"Got laid off a couple months ago."

"I heard. Is he here?"

"Yeah, he's here." Talk of his father had a conspicuous down effect on Billy; it always had. His mouth turned down at the corners, subduing his smile.

"Has he got anything to drink in the house? I could use something."

"There might be some gin in the cupboard."

"Gin. He still drinks that shit?" Jack had never acquired a taste for it. It was about the only distilled spirit he had not acquired a taste for. "Well, any port in a storm." Jack got up and headed for the kitchen, followed by Billy. "You say Keith's out for football? How big is he now?" Keith was always somewhat of a squirt, a feisty squirt, but a little squirt all the same.

"He's the smallest kid out. He's tough, though. He don't take no shit from the bigger guys."

Jack opened the cupboard doors in search of his stepfather's gin. All the old familiar plates, bowls, cups, saucers, even drinking glasses, all looking the same as he remembered them when he was last home. He could find no gin.

"He must've drank it all," Billy said, sitting down at the kitchen table covered with oil cloth and on which sat a small radio, a sugar bowl, salt and pepper shakers. "Booze don't last long in this house with him here." Jack detected bitterness in Billy's voice. Why shouldn't he be bitter after all the years of abuse? He was glad to hear the bitterness; it represented some spark of, if not rebellion, at least resistance.

"How's Ma? She complained in her last letter about how hard she had to work."

"She looks tired all the time. She *does* work hard." As if he heard sarcasm in Jack's remark about his mother's claim of having to work so hard, he was fast to her defense.

"So you guys are still sleeping in bunk beds, I see." He had noticed his old thin-mattressed bed there as well, so he need wonder no more if he would be required to sleep on the living room sofa. "I assume you're done with bed wetting." Conspicuously absent in the boys' room was the smell of stale pee.

"Yeah." Billy grinned. Jack was startled to see how he was beginning to resemble his father, the way Jack himself, he guessed, must resemble his own father, because he bore none of his mother's looks. Billy turned on the little radio.

"Would you mind a lot not playing that, Billy? I've got myself a traveling headache." Billy switched off the radio at once. One of the first great shocks to his system upon returning to the United States was the alien noise blaring out of barracks radios from San Francisco stations. The hyperactive narration from disc jockeys, the frenetic music, announcers speaking in high-pitched, agitated voices as if they were describing a national emergency instead of some local, mundane event. One day back and he couldn't bear to listen to a radio; and television was no better. The other shock was more pleasant. Walking along Market Street, San Francisco, he was overwhelmed by the sight of so much leg beneath the hem of women's skirts and dresses. America had changed in his absence, and he wasn't sure he was ready for it.

"Let's have a look at those dance trophies," Jack said, lighting a cigarette.

"Can you spare one of those?" Jack shook another cigarette out his pack for Billy.

* * *

Jack's mother got home from work at 4:30. She seemed genuinely surprised, and pleased, to see him.

"You're thin as a boy."

"Not as thin as when I went in," Jack reminded her. Billy was right; she looked tired, worn out. At present, she worked as a maid at Sisters of Mercy Hospital. He couldn't quite understand how this work could be any more exhausting than what she used to do in the shoe factory, which she had done for over ten years.

"I'll put some water on for coffee."

"Don't do it on my account, Ma. I drink a cup in the morning, is all."

"I usually have a cup after work, before I make supper." Billy had gone out after showing Jack his dance trophies, and Jack had begun to unpack his things. For reasons he couldn't have explained if asked, he stowed his uniforms in the bureau drawer reserved for his use. Maybe there was still a chance that he would be called back to service. He hadn't been discharged a week when he heard rumors that the Navy had extended the enlistments of guys at Treasure Island who were in the same barracks as he was, awaiting discharge. Apparently Vietnam was on the minds of the military honchos.

"So what's been happening around here since I last heard from you?" Jack took out his cigarettes, and offered the pack to his mother, forgetting that she had given up the habit.

"Not very much. I'm glad I gave those things up, the way they cost today."

Her talk of money Jack saw as an opening to ask about his own money.

His mother's face sagged. She lowered her eyes and fingered the saucer her son was using as an ashtray. "It's all gone, Jack. I'm so sorry. I was desperate. You know how he is." Even if he could have predicted her answer, the news still had the effect of stunning him. He sat for a long while, staring at the wall above the kitchen sink, unable to speak. "I'll make it up to you, somehow."

"I was going to use that money for college," he said in a phlegmy voice. He had known that his mother had used some of his allotment money to make ends meet when her husband was off on one of his toots, but *all* of it! He hoped that there might be enough to pay for at least a year or two.

"I know, Jack. It's been hard. If it wasn't for your money I don't know what would have become of us."

"I think I'll go out for awhile." Jack rose from his chair.

"Do you want some supper? I was just going to make spaghetti. If I'd a known you were coming home I'd a made something you like, stuffed peppers or ..."

"No. I'm not hungry. I think I'll just go downtown, see who's around."

"Joey came by a couple days ago looking for you."

"Joey Costis? Are you sure?" His mother looked hurt that he would question her in such a fashion, even though he meant it to be rhetorical.

"Of course I'm sure. He looked strange. Then, he always looked a little weird to me."

It was a little over a week ago, when he arrived in San Diego, that George Stacy had informed him that Joey had cracked up on the Mexican side of the Tijuana border. He had been to the jai alai games with some guys he'd hooked up with from L.A. and as they were waiting in line to get passed by the border guards, Joey "flipped his lid," in George's words. Joey swore that aliens were waiting for him on the American side of the border to spirit him away in their space ship. The upshot was that the authorities seized him and had him committed to the loony bin in Norwalk. George said that Joey had not had an easy time adjusting to Southern California life. Jack asked George if he'd heard anything from Kyle Stoddard. He had not. Later, when they were both properly drunk, they decided to hitchhike to Norwalk and make a call on their old friend in the loony bin. They learned that Joey's brother-who-was-really-his-uncle had come to take him home a couple of days before.

"I wonder if he's back with his mother—his grandmother, whatever," Jack said, more to himself than to his mother.

"He didn't say. He looked kind of crazy if you ask me." Jack didn't tell her what he had heard about Joey's crack-up. And now, all of a sudden, the last person in the world he wanted to see was a "crazy" Joey Costis, whom he always suspected was crazy from the first day he met him.

He felt resentment welling up in his breast, (and it was more against his mother than his stepfather), for squandering the money he had counted on to launch his future. Now, he supposed he would have to look for work. After a two-week spree in San Francisco and San Diego, he had about six hundred dollars left of his mustering out pay.

"I'm going out," he announced to his mother.

"I'm sorry, Jack."

Three months later, he got a phone call from George Stacy with news that Katie Durand was pregnant and had named him, Jack Scanlon, as the father of the intruder who had taken up residence in her womb.

"What am I going to do?" he had said, rhetorically.

"What do you mean *do*? You don't have to do a damned thing! I'm just telling you this so ... you'll know. Don't go *doing* a fucking thing. She won't make a fuss. I can give you the names of a dozen guys who've banged her. It's not your concern. I just thought you'd want to know, you know? I can't fucking believe you did this. When did it happen?"

But Jack knew that do something he must. Something of the Puritan had taken root in him somewhere along the line, his stepfather's libertine example notwithstanding. He had barely enough money left to book a flight for San Diego.

* * *

Karla was by his side again. He looked up in time to see her lifting the empty blood bag off its stand.

"Bet you thought you'd never see the end of it, did you? She smiled down at him with the affable condescension that he didn't mind at all.

"There were moments."

Karla's forehead wrinkled in a little frown as she scrutinized him. "You really do look a whole lot better."

"Thank you, Karla. Thank you for everything, for staying over ..."

"Please, Mr. Scanlon. Don't even mention it. As soon as I disconnect you, you can be on your way." And Karla proceeded to do just that. Then he was free of the needle, delivery tube, and blood bag. All he had to do was extract himself from the recliner where he'd been confined for … how long?

"What time is it, Karla?"

"A little after eight. It's still light outside. I love daylight savings time." He had been taking on new blood for over seven and a half hours.

Scanlon lingered outside the automatic doors of Day Surgery, and looked out over the vast parking lot. The Emergency Room entrance was next door; an ambulance, red lights flashing, was backed up to the door. Two blue-uniformed EMT were pulling a stretcher out of the back of the vehicle. Scanlon smiled to himself. It was dusk; streetlights were lit. The air was heavy with the smell of lilac mixed with automobile exhaust, and it was warm and soft as only late May air can be. He breathed it in deeply, and realized that he had eaten nothing since morning, and then only coffee and an English muffin. But he was feeling so … full of blood!

He walked to his car and paused, his door on the handle, to look out at the street below the hospital campus. Cars passed in a steady stream in both directions. Could it be true that he was "no more terminal than the next guy?" He put his hand in his pocket and felt the Lovenox prescription Dr. Dunham had given him. He should drive around to the hospital pharmacy and have it filled. Next week would tell the story. Was it possible that he would be given a reprieve (or, as one of his friends had once declared after receiving his own negative biopsy report, "condemned to more life") after all? And if it were true, would he change his ways?

A blue van pulled into a parking space across from where his car was parked. A black woman in a bright yellow dress got out and slid open the door on the passenger side to let out three small children, impeccably dressed, each carrying a stuffed toy in his arms. For some reason this tableau put Scanlon in mind of a piece he had read (probably in *National Geographic*) when he was a kid about a pygmy hunting party somewhere in Central Africa that had taken down an elephant with their primitive spears. A series of pictures showed the pygmies disappearing inside the eviscerated carcass without having to stoop, in later frames reappearing, bearing the beast's steaming entrails in their arms, wide smiles on their faces. The images had stayed with Johnny Labalm for a long time. Perhaps that was what it was all about, Scanlon thought; life is just an inside joke, seen from the outside.

With that thought, he got into his car and started the engine. He got into gear and headed for home, his mind on a strong, well-earned drink; he forgot about filling his prescription.